Praise for *Auraria* by

"Fact and fancy are intertwined cleverly and seamlessly in a top-notch, thoroughly American fantasy."

Publishers Weekly (starred review)

"Envision Lewis Carroll on a romp through the mountains of Georgia, discovering a land of shimmery mystery and spirits, humble monsters, quirky characters, singing trees and vengeful fish. This whole world has sprung from Tim Westover's brain yet remains firmly and lovingly the real thing, the actual Georgia landscape echoing with folk traditions of the southern Appalachians. The best part is that Tim Westover can really write. I'd give an Aurarian pot of gold to do what he's done with language in the service of imagination."

Josephine Humphreys, Hemingway/PEN Award Winner, author of *Dreams of Sleep* and *Rich in Love*

"Mr. Westover brings my beloved Georgia to life, complete with spells, haints, and moon maidens. Not since Wendell Berry has an author woven such a beautifully intricate southern community."

Ann Hite, author of *Ghost On Black Mountain*

"The legends, myths and history of the North Georgia mountains (along with some very inventive additions) are woven into a wonderfully entertaining story."

Victoria Logue, author of *Touring the Back Roads of North and South Georgia*

The Winter Sisters

A Novel

Tim Westover

QW Publishers

THE WINTER SISTERS

QW Publishers
Grayson, GA USA
www.QWPublishers.com

ISBN: 978-0-9849748-9-4

First edition published in 2019 by Q W Publishers

TO HONEYBEE

"It was, of course, a grand and impressive thing to do, to mistrust the obvious, and to pin one's faith in things which could not be seen."

—Galen, *On the Natural Faculties*

Prologue

1811

The fat orange moon, reflected in the silver bowl, seems so small. Effie, the youngest of the three sisters, cups her hands to lift the moon out, but the water slips through her fingers. The ripples break the moon's reflection into streaks of light.

The sisters work on the bare granite of a clearing, a bald on the mountainside, under a sky rich with stars. People of a superstitious persuasion say the devil once trod on the balds. They say that's why nothing will grow there and any remnants of trees look lightning blasted and scorched. But the balds have plenty of life. They're slick with moss and lichens, and the tenacious stems of asafetida and yellow lady's slipper and jack-in-the-pulpit have taken root in crevices.

"Leave it alone, little one," says Rebecca, the eldest. "The water has to be still."

Rebecca's face is yellow from the light of the candle she holds in front of her, and her brown hair falls straight past her shoulders. The bowl is their mother's, etched with an Old World design none of the sisters understand. Effie had fetched the water from the river, venturing into the rushing current up to her hips. The candle comes from their mother's trousseau. Rebecca found it hidden in a linen shroud, wrapped together with an ebony-bladed knife and a length of copper wire. They hadn't opened the trousseau until their mother had been gone for three years. Three is a powerful number. Three years, three sisters. They haven't found a use for the knife or the wire, but their mother taught them how to pour molten wax into cold water and tell their fortunes from the shapes.

"It's only a game," says Sarah, the middle sister. "Why does it matter if she touches the water? It's not going to hurt her, is it?"

"It has to be pure," says Rebecca.

9

"Mother never troubled with the full moon or with river water."

"And that's why she only saw pigeons and salmon and silly things."

"I liked the silly things," says Effie.

"Are you going to marry a fish?" Rebecca's voice betrays her impatience. Effie is ten years younger than Rebecca. She is too immature to understand the importance of ceremony.

Rebecca empties her hand into the water. Crushed sassafras leaves and calendula petals float toward the edges of the bowl. All this is in Mother's books. Rebecca can't read the Latin or the Old German, but she recognizes the drawings of the herbs, and she remembers enough of Mother's craft to serve in her absence.

Sarah scratches her nose. "You sure this is how you make moonshine?"

"We're not making moonshine," says Rebecca. She wants a solemn mood, appropriate to the ritual. The candle flame flickers in the draughts of her breath.

"Be better if we were. We could sell it at the crossroads. Maybe buy a gun," says Sarah.

"Mother didn't need a gun," says Rebecca.

"Bullets, too. Sell moonshine for lead shot."

Effie crouches in front of the chestnut stump in which the bowl is cradled and looks at her reflection in the water. The moon sits atop her head like a jewel in a crown. She reaches out a finger, and her face disappears at its touch.

"Effie, stop it." Rebecca's voice rasps. "Just sit there and do nothing."

Effie withdraws, wrapping her arms around her knees. Her plain white dress gathers moss stains.

Wax drips from the candle onto Rebecca's finger. She hisses, but the pain fades quickly. The next drop, falling onto the same piece of skin, rolls away.

Sarah makes a show of cleaning dirt from her fingernails with a kitchen knife as Rebecca tips the candle. The wax touches the water and sputters.

"Why is the candle red?" asks Sarah. "Is it made from blood?"

"Don't be silly," says Rebecca. "Be quiet and watch."

The globules of wax have already finished their work and have congealed at the bottom of the bowl.

"Looks like a passel of nothing," says Sarah. "Waste of time."

"It isn't nothing." Rebecca reaches into the water and takes out the largest piece. "What do you see?"

"A damn piece of wax."

"Hush your mouth." Rebecca studies the thin piece of wax between her fingers. One side is jagged, the other straight. "Looks like a saw. Think they're going to build a sawmill down at the crossroads once other people move up here?"

"There's plenty of trees," says Sarah. "Of course they're going to build a sawmill. The air will fill up with sawdust so thick you can't breathe. Doesn't take a prophecy to tell us that."

"Could be a kind of knife," says Rebecca. "Any kind of blade."

"A man of blood," says Effie, trying to take it.

"Don't touch it," says Rebecca, frustrated.

"She's not going to hurt herself on a piece of wax," says Sarah. "I'd watch out for real knives." She ruffles Effie's hair.

"So I'm going to marry a man with a blade," says Rebecca. "A man of blood, says Effie."

"Why are you so fixed on marrying?" asks Sarah. "Hasn't done anyone I know a bit of good."

"Who do you know that's married? A Cherokee?" says Rebecca. "Now, are you going to choose a piece of wax or not?"

"Hell no. Waste of time."

"Where did you learn such a filthy mouth?"

"Effie taught me," says Sarah.

Effie looks up at the mention of her name but says nothing.

"Are you going to get a piece?" Rebecca asks Effie.

Effie puts her fingertips into the water. A piece of wax floats into her grasp. She pulls it out. It has an improbable shape—a flat disk, formed when the wax settled at the bottom, has joined to a long, thin piece.

"A banjo," she says, turning it over in her palm. "Nothing else it could be."

Affliction

"Although the art of healing is the most noble of all the arts, yet because of the ignorance both of its professors and of their rash critics, it has at this time fallen into the least repute of them all."

—Hippocrates

April 2, 1822
Dear Doctor Waycross,

Your February letter arrived here yesterday. The mail is slow to these parts. I don't know about what all you wrote, scientific methods and the latest cures, but the truth is, we need a doctor here. Goodness knows folks up here couldn't afford to pay you what you might be getting in the city, but I figure that if you're writing to us, way out here, that you must need a job. The healers we used to have—well, there was some bad business that I'm sure you'll hear about. So we've got no one now in town to look to the snotty noses and blood poisoning.

This is a little town. Maybe with your help and some luck, it'll be a bigger town. I'll tell you that there's plenty of forest. Plenty of pigeons, if you like pigeons. A wagon show rolls through every few weeks—that's our best entertainment. We grow vegetables bigger than any you've ever seen. Some of the sweet potatoes that come out of the ground are bigger than a man's head, and once I saw a watermelon as big as a hog. Why not come see that, Doctor, and stay for the doctoring?

If that doesn't convince you, our pastor is on a tear about these rabid dogs. He says that's key, to put in the letter about the rabid dogs. And the panther. Come quick as you can, says the pastor. Rabies, he says. Hydrophobia. Come at all, is what I say. I need a doctor. He doesn't even need to be a good one.

Richardson, Mayor
Lawrenceville, Georgia

I

HOT DAMN AND PASS THE PEPPER SAUCE

The coachman hadn't wanted to make the journey to Lawrenceville in the first place. It had taken all my money to persuade him. Perhaps from nervousness, he hadn't hushed his mouth for the entire journey through the forest, babbling about all the dangers.

Bandits, of course, although not many because there were not many travelers foolish enough to come all this way. Animals: skunk bears, mountain lions, polecats, and a plat-eye, whatever that was. Hunters with guns and hair triggers. Slippery creeks to ford, where a hapless traveler was likely to fall and break his leg. Weird groves with oranges and lemons in the middle of winter. How these latter were really dangerous escaped me, but I found that asking any questions only provoked another garrulous rant.

The people of Lawrenceville were no better, said the coachman. They've got witches—used to have them living right on the town square in a little house. Ghosts too, a few of them, and now this panther terrorizing the forest might be a ghost, too. It certainly seemed to be everywhere at once. Every townsperson had seen it or heard it or smelled it.

He wouldn't tell me anything about Mayor Richardson or the pastor, and most infuriatingly, he knew nothing about the mad dogs.

"Maybe it's got to do with that panther," he said.

"The hydrophobia?"

"I don't even know what that is, Doctor."

"It means rabies. Fear of water is a symptom, so we sometimes call the disease hydrophobia."

"A city-folk word. Is that why you got your doctor's diploma, so you could say 'hydrophobia' instead of 'mad dog?'"

We crossed a little rise, and suddenly I could see the town of Lawrenceville emerge from the wild forest pressing on it from all sides. In two minutes, we were in the town square.

"Well, here we are, Doctor. Safe and sound."

I climbed down from the coach, every joint protesting the vigor of the rough travel. I would have to bleed myself later to restore my shaken humors to their right places. The coachman unloaded my boxes and crates, which immediately began sinking into the mud. I thanked him for the safe passage, in which we'd encountered not a single one of the dangers he'd predicted, and told him I had no more money to give. He touched his hat crisply and mounted up his coach again.

"You just be careful, Doctor," he said. The clattering wagon disappeared in a splatter of grime.

Lawrenceville was empty. I was alone in the town square, save for the hogs. A great herd of them rooted around the muddy field, pushing their snouts against the walls of a clapboard courthouse. Having lived all my life in Savannah, I had hoped for a life in a place more civilized than this. If I traveled any farther north, I'd enter the wild mountains of Cherokee territory. That, perhaps, would have been a forest worth fearing, filled with savages and wild animals rather than rumors and bad dreams.

My journey had been long and harrowing. Passenger coaches carried me over worn routes from Savannah to Louisville, the old state capital. Pine trees separated fields of rice and corn and cotton. Slaves and freemen, all under the same overseers, worked the land. I rode another scheduled service to Milledgeville, the lately appointed capital, where well-dressed people hurried from restaurants to factories and supervised the sales of corn and cotton. The voyage onward was more difficult. No regular coach service proceeded farther north. I persuaded the mail carrier, on the strength of my charitable profession, to take me as far as Eatonton.

The next morning, my luck held out. An attachment of Georgia's militia was heading to the new state of Alabama, which the Federals had recently created. Their clean uniforms and stiff boots told me it was their first campaign. The captain permitted me to join them as far as Jug Tavern, a town just a day away from Lawrenceville. I balanced my baggage on top of the ammunition wagon and trudged along with the infantry for three days, sharing their goober peas. When I reached Jug Tavern, I'd been two weeks on the road and was anxious to complete my travels, but there my good fortune finally expired. I'd missed the mail wagon, and no traders were heading through anytime soon. My sole option was to engage a private coach from the only fellow brave enough to make the trip, which depleted the bulk of my funds. I could not have walked the last twenty-five miles, given all the equipment I was bringing, and I had no need for money upon arrival, embraced by a grateful town.

I wondered why the coachman was so fearful. The town was an unremarkable frontier outpost. Now that I was in Lawrenceville, all I could see—besides the swine—were shoddy rows of stores forming the west and south sides of the square. To the north were a few houses that looked more respectable. A church slumped in the northeast corner. All stood empty of human life. I was befuddled. Perhaps the farmers in Lawrenceville stayed home and sent their hogs to town for shopping and gossip.

Then I heard a shout accompanied by strained chords of music and applause. "Glory, hallelujah!" Ah, the welcoming committee. But when the noise persisted with no sign of greeters, I took the risk of leaving my baggage and followed the sound to its source.

I found myself in a narrow space enclosed on one side by muck-filled stalls and on the other by the back walls of Lawrenceville's shops. A riotous crowd encircled a stage made of a few boards thrown on top of a mule-drawn wagon. A canvas backdrop was meant to evoke a doctor's study. The painting showed shelves of leather-bound books, anatomical samples floating in jars, a leering skull, and a bust of Hippocrates. The canvas was wrinkled and spotted with rot.

I turned to the fellow nearest me. "What is this place called?"

"Honest Alley," he replied.

I could not hear anything else he said because the denizens of Lawrenceville were applauding a wiry huckster on the stage.

"Glory, hallelujah! Hot damn and pass the pepper sauce!"

Boys climbed atop each other for the best view. Daughters begged for seats on their fathers' shoulders. Sun-crisped farmers clambered up the clapboard stores to get above their neighbors, and a pair of Negroes, along with a Cherokee trader dressed in a white man's clothes, struggled for a place from which they could see. I noticed a woman with a kerchief drawn across most of her face. What physical ailment was she hiding beneath that red cloth? Consumption? Warts? An infected sore? She saw me looking at her and moved her kerchief, which concealed nothing unusual, so that she could stick out her tongue at me. Affronted and disconcerted, I turned my face back to the presentation.

"Ladies and gentlemen!" The entertainer crashed his right hand down on the strings so hard that his banjo contorted into the loudest chord I'd ever heard. "You don't want a remedy that only promises a single cure, not when there are so many troubles in the world. Well, for all that's got you hot and bothered, there's Grove's Tasteless Chill Tonic!"

I snorted, but no one marked me.

"Take a spoonful, morning, noon, and night, to ward off dyspepsia, lumbago, scrofula, catarrh, flatulence, worms, and brain congestion. For starters!" At the mention of each disease, he jabbed his finger toward a different member of the crowd, diagnosing us all in one swoop.

I should have expected no better from rustics on the frontier. Such quacks knew nothing of suffering, only of entertainment and easy cures. For the best years of my life, all through my official training as a doctor, I'd suffered for knowledge and for science. I paid my tuition by working as an apothecary's apprentice, learning the mixtures that purged, blistered, and flushed away our infirmities. After I bought the volumes of Hippocrates and Galen and acquired the necessary chemical apparatus and assorted lancets, I rarely had much money left for food. I did not mind the deprivations, for they left me lean and hungry for my true purpose. I disassembled hogs to study their viscera. I apprenticed with the bone saw and the cauterizing iron, practicing on spoiled poultry. I memorized the contents of the doctor's pharmacy—mercury, calomel, sugar of lead, blistering oils—and distilled my own supply according to the proven recipes.

This medicine showman, though, with no such experience to his name, sang out to his credulous crowd:

"Grove's Tasteless Chill Tonic will add years to your life, and Grove's Tasteless Chill Tonic will make those years worth living."

> *Weary of the hard-knock life?*
> *All the sickness, storm, and strife?*
> *Well, bang the drums and toot the fife!*
> *And best of all, you'll please the wife!*
> *Get some Grove's Tasteless Chill Tonic.*

He lifted his fingers from the banjo strings and gestured to the crowd. "Good sirs, are you worn and wearied and plain tuckered out?"

"Yes!" the men replied.

"Can't shovel it, chop it, or reap it like you used to?"

"Yes!"

"Grove's Tasteless Chill Tonic!"

The quack played a series of major chords. I couldn't stand it any longer. I threaded my way through the rapturous crowd, aiming for the stage. The woman with the red kerchief stepped into my path, and I had to move her aside with my hand so that I could continue forward.

"Good ladies, are your fingers worked down to raw bone?"

"Yes!" the ladies shouted, right on cue.

"Soap burned your skin, ironing singed your eyebrows, broom straw caught 'tween your toes? Are you beat like your laundry, whipped like your eggs, flat like your bread?"

"Yes!"

"Grove's Tasteless Chill Tonic!" The entertainer tossed a bottle up, giving it a twirl so that it flew end over end, higher than the rooftops. He spun around and caught it behind his back, and in the same motion, he turned back to the crowd and beamed. He'd meant for the trick to seem effortless, but I was nearly to the stage by then and noticed that his pinky finger was rigid, arthritic.

"Good husbands, can't do your manly duty? Zip gone out of the tip? Zing gone from the thing? Power faded from your tower? Grove's Tasteless Chill Tonic!"

Some people blushed, but others roared with laughter, emboldened by the scandalous turn.

"What's the cure? Say it with me!"

"GROVE'S TASTELESS CHILL TONIC!" roared the crowd in harmony.

I hauled myself onstage. "Now, see here! I mean—"

The crowd murmured at the intrusion, and my righteous indignation sputtered. I am no orator. I can bleed people, rinse their bowels, and restore their health and life and joy—but I cannot win their affections. I stammered, and I stumbled. Words would not come to me. The longer I wavered, the quieter the crowd became, and the entertainer seemed content to let me fail in front of the hundreds of eyes of my new charges.

"Just say it!" said the woman with the red kerchief. "Say whatever it is you want to say, and then get the hell off the stage!"

Her curse was enough to shake me from my stupor. I puffed myself up as best I could. "What's your name, sir?" I asked, jamming my hands into my waistcoat pockets as I'd seen important men do. "Not Grove, is it?"

"No, sir, not Grove," said the entertainer. "If only I were! Grove is seven feet tall, with shoulders as broad as a steamer chest."

The crowd oohed.

"He's eighty-four years old and doesn't look a day over thirty."

The crowd cheered.

"No, sir, I'm not Grove. What's my name? You don't know it, but they surely do."

"Salmon Thumb!" roared the crowd.

"Why, that's right, it's Salmon Thumb! How can you forget a name like that? But that's the one I got in my cradle, and that's the one I'll take to the grave." Then he lit into a little melody, and the crowded applauded.

I raised my voice above the song and noise. "Well, Mr. Thumb—"

"Dr. Salmon Thumb, if you please, sir."

"Clobber that blowhard, Dr. Thumb!" chimed a voice from the alley.

"Mister Thumb. I am no blowhard. I am a real doctor, Dr. Aubrey Waycross, and I blow with the wind of truth." This raised a chuckle from the audience. "I accuse you, sir, of falsehood. Of hollow promises and easy cures. I accuse you of misleading the good folk of Lawrenceville and distracting them from healers who can benefit them."

"Hear, hear!" said a man from the crowd. "Go up to Hope Hollow if you've got the rheumatism! The Winter sisters set me right!"

"Witches! Haints and devilry!" someone countered with derision.

Then another farmer in the crowd held up a small, sweat-stained bag. "Naw, good medicine! I've carried this bag of fennel, what the Winter sisters gave me, for three days, and I haven't sneezed since."

"Wait," I said, turning to the crowd and holding up my hands. "That's not what I meant. I meant a real doctor, a physician—"

"Right, the Winter sisters! Preacher ran 'em out of town a while back, but they're the best doctors the world's ever seen." The fennel-carrying farmer turned from the stage and addressed what was now his audience. "Are you gonna forget about them because of a medicine show?"

"What are they gonna do about the panther, hmm? What are they gonna do about the rabies?"

Rabies! My ears perked at the very word that had brought me from Savannah to Lawrenceville, from the bright center of

Georgia life to its darkest corner. Before I could interject, though, the shouts of the crowd took over.

"What's a medicine show gonna do about the rabies?"

"Medicine show ain't no harm," said someone else in the crowd.

"I need that tonic to sleep!"

"I need it to wake up again in the morning!"

"Ain't nothing for the rabies except praying!"

"Ain't nothing 'cept for a bullet!"

"Come on, Dr. Thumb, give us some more banjo!"

Thumb started another tune:

> *"You ain't even got to listen*
> *To what this guy's been pissin'.*
> *He says he's a physician,*
> *But I'll bet he is wishin'*
> *He had Grove's Tasteless Chill Tonic!*
> *I'll give you all an honest tip:*
> *If it's a bleedin' you're to skip,*
> *To soothe that aching hip,*
> *Just take a little sip*
> *Of old Grove's Tasteless Chill Tonic!"*

A cheer of jubilation erupted, and buyers surged forward. Coins flew. Bottles of the tonic sailed back. The rabies and the Winter sisters were forgotten in the exploding of popping corks. Old and young believed they were drinking to their health, but I knew they were ruining it.

"Want some, Doctor?" Thumb beamed at me, showing perfect white teeth—a radiant smile for a haggard backwoods huckster, which made me wonder how he kept them so pearly. "For you, it's free."

"Not a sip," I said. "Not even if you paid me a thousand dollars."

"It's good for what ails you." Thumb pulled the cork from a bottle of Grove's Tasteless Chill Tonic and took a short pull. "It's no hard feelings, Dr. Waycross." Thumb held out his hand as though he meant for me to shake it. "Really, Doc, it's no hard feelings."

"Still, Mr. Thumb, I won't shake your hand."

Sweat had collected on his hatband. His skin looked oily. I turned my back on him and walked toward the rear of the stage.

"I'm not a bad fellow, Doc," he called after me.

"I think, sir, that you are."

The crowd paid no attention as I slunk to the edges of Honest Alley. I walked past the muzzles of horses, who let their nature fall onto the muddy streets. Mules and donkeys brayed at me. Dirty urchins and rheumy-eyed matrons jostled me. The malodorous breathing of man and beast made me sneeze. I hastened to vacate the noxious street, but a hand landed on my shoulder.

"A moment, Doctor!"

The man was both too young and too fat to be respectable. Given his wide straw hat and tattered trousers, I took him for a farmer.

"Can I help you, sir?" I said, exhaustion filling my voice.

"No, I'm quite healthy. A little whiskey fixes most troubles, and a great deal of whiskey fixes the rest." He patted his rotund belly.

"Then, if you've no urgent business, I will ask your leave." I was weary from the road and weary from the foolish display in which I'd become embroiled. "Unless you can take me to the mayor. You wouldn't happen to know the man, would you?"

"That's me," said the fat youngster, doffing his hat, and he was barefoot.

Imagine, no shoes in a place with drifts of manure three inches deep!

"I mean, the mayor himself. Mayor Richardson."

"Yep, that's me. Elected executive officer of the incorporated town of Lawrenceville, Georgia." Mayor Richardson stuck out his hand.

"I beg your pardon," I said, astounded. I shook his hand although goodness knows what pestilence clung to it. "You're not what I expected."

Mayor Richardson laughed. "Well, Doctor, one's got to be a real fool to get elected mayor. Doesn't pay anything. You don't even get a pair of shoes! But a town's got to have one, like a town's got to have a doctor and a body's got to have an asshole."

I hid my chagrin at my mistake by straightening my collar. "Again, I beg your pardon, sir. I'm sure you have the health of your constituents in mind. You called for a trained physician to look after them, and here I am. You said it was hydrophobia. Rabies."

The place, a town at the edge of civilization, was not tempting. But any hesitation had vanished with one word: hydrophobia. I'd seen one life claimed by it, a life very dear to me, and if I could spare another mother, another little brother from seeing the horrors of that disease, if I could cast out the false hopes peddled by hucksters and replace them with the honesty of real medicine, then I would count my life useful.

The mayor put a meaty arm round my shoulder. He spoke kindly though his grin faded. "See, the truth is... I had to find a doctor. I wrote several with the honest truth, and no one wanted the job way out here, what with what's out in the woods. So I said to the pastor, 'What should I write?' and he said, 'Write to this Waycross fellow and say rabies.'"

"Your pastor knew my name? He meant for you to summon me especially?" I did not make a habit of associating with pastors. I couldn't imagine any that would have recognized me.

"He saw your letter and said that you'd come straightaway if I said rabies. Ain't nobody got it. But folks are scared, real scared."

"How many infected? How many dead?"

"Well, not a one, yet. But that's just a matter of time, ain't it? Pastor says creatures out in the woods are sick with it. A few dogs have shown the signs. We shot them. Had to do it, sad as it was. But what's worse, there's this panther..."

"Do you mean you summoned me across this vast state, at the cost of all my money, and there is no hydrophobia? Just some foamy-at-the-mouth mountain lion."

"Ain't no mountain lion. Folks wouldn't be afraid of a mountain lion."

"I take it you've seen the creature?"

"Naw, but why do you have to see it to believe it?"

"Because that's science, sir!" I placed my foot down, and the mud and ichor of the alley splattered all over my trouser legs. There was no chance a panther was in the woods of northern Georgia. The climate, the geography, and the fauna were all wrong. I would have been less surprised to see an albino kangaroo, but I shouldn't have been rankled by mistakes in zoology. It was the mayor's lie that should have bothered me—his false pretenses to snare a respectable doctor in his hog-cursed, mud-soaked, huckster-plagued little hamlet.

"Pastor Boatwright says we'll have sick people soon. But that's 'tween you and him. And the panther."

I fumed in disappointment that I was not arriving in the midst of an epidemic. That would have afforded ample opportunity for study and good works, for me to offer consolation and succor, but then remorse took me. I felt guilty that I had wished rabies on anyone. No one should suffer for my edification or absolution.

"The plague of hucksters is more deadly, I think, than this rumor of a panther."

"It's the legislature that needs a doctor," continued Richardson. "The muck-mucks in Milledgeville want any town aiming to be the county seat to have a respectable physician. But I don't expect that you'll find many takers for your bleeding and puking, Doctor. Lopping off arms and calling that a cure... If anybody will come to see you, it's because they're too afraid of the panther in the woods to go up to see the Winter sisters."

I moved my mouth, but no sound came out. Richardson gave me a squeeze, and I found myself squashed against his flesh.

"Now, Doc, don't look so glum. We'll get a huntsman, not a doctor, who'll kill this panther, and folks can go back to their regular healings. Meantime, the farmers might let you take a look at the livestock. Mules with cracked hooves, cows with sore teats.

You can bleed a dog same as a person, right? Snell's got a place out back where you can set up a little office in case anybody does come by. There's a hayloft, too, where you can sleep."

I had a mind to shake the dust of this cursed place off my feet and catch the next stagecoach for somewhere—anywhere—else, but I'd spent the last of my money to get myself to Lawrenceville. I didn't have a nickel for supper, and if I had the money to leave, where would I go? No other town had called for me. Lawrenceville would have to suffice until I could make other plans.

"Where's this hayloft?" I asked.

Mayor Richardson pointed toward a store at the northwest corner of the square. As I tromped through the mud of the alley, staining my boots and trouser cuffs, I thought: A hayloft will be drier than sleeping under the stars.

I gathered my possessions from the square. The hogs had left well enough alone, and Salmon Thumb's show had distracted any thieves. I made my way to a storefront with a hand-lettered sign that read Snell's Merchandise.

The shopkeeper was waiting on a female customer, measuring out bolts of calico cloth to her exacting specifications. She wore an old-style bonnet, which conveyed modesty and virtue and made her look perfectly ridiculous, like a portrait of a Puritan.

As I waited, I studied the shelves. They were stacked with burlap sacks, paper cartons, glass vials, sugar, coffee, beans, ink, tooth soap, tobacco, cigars, mirrors, lead shot, almonds, coconuts, and vinegar. Advertising lithographs smiled from several places around the store. Each plump-cheeked beauty with shining curls had eyes glimmering with desire for the product named in red capitals above her hair: Silverwhite Shoe Polish, True Brass Candlewax, Edgar's Own Argentine Soap, and Pharaoh's Flour. There were no advertisements for Grove's Tasteless Chill Tonic, but I saw a long row of bottles placed at eye level.

"Anything else, Miss Samples?" said the shopkeeper, unable to hide his exasperation.

"No, Mr. Snell," she snapped. "I suppose that will do. Though you really should order better stock. For a Sunday dress, it isn't very suitable."

Miss Samples collected her purchases despite her objections, and when she turned toward the door, she noticed me for the first time.

"What do you mean, sneaking up on a woman like that?" she barked.

"Nothing, ma'am," I sputtered. "I was only waiting for my turn."

"You're not from here, are you?" The scent of her suspicion was as thick as that of onions on her breath. "Come in for Thumb's song and dance?"

"No, ma'am, just arrived. I'm the doctor, or I was supposed to be—"

Snell clapped his hands. "Ah, the doctor! Yes, the doctor. Well, you've been expected. Welcome, welcome."

I was glad of the kind words, the first I'd gotten in town, and he read the relief in my face.

Miss Samples did not seem mollified by Snell's welcome. "The Great Physician is all that we need," she said.

As if I did not have enough rivals in Salmon Thumb and the Winter sisters, I was apparently also in competition against the Lord.

Miss Samples curtsied perfunctorily as she left, and Snell came over to shake my hand. "I took the liberty," he said, "of ordering some ingredients that would be of use to you." He pulled out a trunk, which contained glass bottles. Each had its own label: witch hazel, willow, foxglove, and sassafras.

"What are these, sir? I am a doctor, not a gardener."

Snell frowned. "I only thought it would be things you'd need. How about turpentine? Lots of turpentine."

"I have no need of it."

"Well, you are a queer sort of doctor."

I began to have suspicions. "Are these the sorts of ingredients you sell to the Winter sisters?"

"They usually fetch up their own, but I wasn't sure about you. No sassafras and no turpentine. What do you do, then?"

"Real medicine," I said. "If you'll wait a moment, I will show you a diploma."

Snell held up his hand. "Naw, I believe you, Doctor. Real city medicine, I guess."

"The body of a city man is no different from that of a country man."

"Here, let me show you where you'll be sleeping, City Doctor." Snell opened a door no bigger than a pantry's, revealing a room that, while spacious enough, was not unoccupied. The south wall of the room was slid open like a barn door, and a brace of hogs was roaming the threshold. Sacks of corn ringed the chamber, and hams hung from the ceiling rafters. A ladder in the corner led up to a hayloft. The tongues of barnyard animals had polished the pine floor to a smooth shine. The chinking had fallen out between the boards, admitting both light and pestilent miasmas.

"It is, Mr. Snell, more... rustic... than I had wished."

"Were you expecting a marble mansion?"

In my embarrassment, I said nothing. Snell took this for haughtiness.

"If you can't make the best of it, Dr. Waycross, we'll let the hogs take it back. They're not so choosy as doctors."

Sarah Winter hadn't come into town for the medicine show, and she certainly hadn't come to see the spectacle of a new doctor making a fool of himself on stage, humorous though it had been. She'd come to Lawrenceville because the sisters needed a few things from Snell's store.

Rebecca still wasn't much for coming to town—even after six months, there were too many hard memories—and Sarah would always rather Effie stay safely tucked away at Hope Hollow. So she made the journey alone, hiding her face behind a red kerchief. It would not really stop the curiosity of anyone, but it would mark that she didn't want to be seen. People would leave her alone, and that suited her all right.

Sarah saw the doctor—Waycross, wasn't it?—go ahead of her into Snell's store. If he introduced himself to her, the poor fellow would find himself arguing his principles against an even more mischievous opponent than Thumb, and it would draw attention that Sarah didn't want. She was only there for coffee, after all, and what few things they couldn't make or grow up in Hope Hollow.

Sarah kept an eye on the general store, walking past every few minutes to see if Waycross had finished his business there so she could do hers. While she waited, she saw that not much in Lawrenceville had changed since her last visit, nor since they'd lived here, before the fire and the pastor. Sarah saw all the same faces that had been there the night Boatwright had fanned the terror of the mill fire into a hot and angry mob. One face she didn't see, of course: Everett's. He was in the graveyard, cooling with the clay.

Still, the same sad little shops and church were there, as worn and weather-beaten as the farmers and sawyers and other settlers despite not being as old. The spring was still crowded with more hogs than people, and the little house Everett had built for Rebecca was still a pile of black cinders.

The spindly willow tree in the yard had survived the mob and the fire. Three poppets hung from its branches—three sisters, made from twigs and twine. No one had cut down those effigies in the months since, not even Snell or Richardson or any other person who came up to Hope Hollow for a cure, and it made Sarah burn with anger. The sisters were not friendless in Lawrenceville, but no one had the courage to cut the effigies down.

Sarah, her mother, and her sisters had been in Hope Hollow longer than the town of Lawrenceville had existed. Before the militia pacified the Cherokees, old Indians—men and women, their faces hewn as if from rock—had come calling regularly. Taciturn natives wanted to trade ginseng, willow bark, and sassafras for half-pint bottles of turpentine, and desperate ones fell at the Winters' door, pleading in a foreign tongue for foreign cures. Sometimes Sarah's mother gave them hyssop tea, or she covered their open wounds in honey, or she wrapped their fevered foreheads with cold rags. That was straight medicine, and Rebecca, being older, attended at her mother's side and fetched the herbs and kept the tea on the boil. Sarah was left to look after Effie.

Each new year, though, brought a new crop of chimneys and a new crop of white farmers who pushed the Indians northward. Sarah's mother did not like the white settlers. When there was a rap at the front door, Sarah's mother would look out through the chinking between the logs to see who it was, and if it was a white woman huddled beneath a bonnet or a hard-scrabble sawyer with a mangled hand, she'd let Rebecca see to their needs instead.

"Where's your mother?" they'd ask, and Rebecca would say, "Sick."

Perhaps she was sick, rotten with an illness inside that even she couldn't cure, but that was probably a lie, for how could there be a sickness that couldn't be cured?

Then one night—the moon a crescent, cicadas crying—a circle of Cherokees drew up around the Winters' house, and they made sounds that were not quite singing. Sarah's mother brought her girls out, and the Cherokees surrounded them. They drew a circle on the ground with charcoal that circumscribed the girls. They braided lavender and sage and dove feathers into the girls' hair. As long as the three sisters stayed together, their protection would never be broken.

Sarah's mother was not in the circle, but she drank from a wooden cup, and she vomited onto the earth, and the women turned over the soil so that the sick was buried, and the fresh ends of earthworms glimmered in the moonlight.

Sarah had never seen a more delightful or ridiculous or powerful thing. There was no magic: no enemy would be afraid to step over a charcoal line, and no bandit would be frightened away by the smell of lavender, but force and grace were writ on the faces of everyone assembled. Everyone there believed in the charm.

The most fervent believer was her own mother. After the ceremony, she'd be gone for weeks at a time, and the oppressive authority that Rebecca adopted in their mother's absence made the time seem even longer. Effie was still little. When their mother would come in from the woods, her skin browned, her cheeks hollow, her eyes yellowed, Sarah came to understand that she wanted to die alone. She didn't want her children to bury her.

"Sarah, Sarah—remember that you're bound with your sisters. If you keep together, you'll be protected. Your enemies will fear what three of you can do, more than what any one of you can do alone. Your talents and your faults will remedy each other."

And it had worked, hadn't it? She and Rebecca and Effie hadn't been hanged, except in effigy. They hadn't been burned—only Everett had. And they hadn't been harmed, save for the harm they did to each other.

Sarah left the straw effigies to hang. Would it be another six months or a year before someone cut them down? Or would Nature have to rot away the string?

Finally, Sarah passed by the barn behind Snell's store and saw Waycross busying himself inside. That meant she could get to the store without mixing up in conversation, and she could buy her coffee and be done with that place for another few weeks, until they needed coffee again.

A tinkling bell announced her entrance.

Snell at once looked up. "Miss Sarah, I need your help. It's my arm."

Sarah Winter dropped the red kerchief from in front of her face. "My disguise isn't fooling anyone, is it?"

"Boatwright and Lizbeth Samples and Mrs. Maltbie and their friends won't see you. They don't want to see you. Those of us that need you, though, we'll see you fine."

Sarah considered that for a moment, and then she folded the kerchief and put it into her pocket. "Let me do my shopping first, Mr. Snell, and then you tell me about your arm."

Snell nodded. "What can I get for you?"

"I'd been aiming for coffee and some blue silk thread. Rebecca can't make her coffee tree bloom, no matter how much pigeon shit she heaps on it, and the silk—well, silk comes from bugs, and none of us fancy bugs that much. But after that display in Honest Alley, I'm thinking that a bottle of Grove's Tasteless Chill Tonic would do me more good than any coffee you could scrounge up here."

Snell reached up toward the shelf where he'd placed a few bottles of the tonic that he'd bought from Thumb. He winced as he reached.

"Did you try Grove's for your arm?" said Sarah.

"It's sprained real bad." Snell rubbed the muscle below his shoulder. "I was lifting a ham. Grove's isn't going to do that a bit of good."

"And you didn't want to ask the doctor that was just here? The one you put out into the barn by your hams?"

Snell grunted. "Doesn't seem like much of a doctor. Didn't even want any turpentine."

"It was a hell of a sight to see him try to out-talk Thumb," continued Sarah. She plucked down a brilliant-blue jar labeled Hamilton's Great Fastener, the Nev-R-Un-Stick Glue, and tossed it from hand to hand. "Like seeing a mule and a chicken get into a kicking contest."

"He's just back there in the barn. He'll hear you."

"I don't give a right damn if he hears me." Sarah put the jar of glue on the counter next to where Snell had measured out a little sack full of coffee. "And he sure doesn't care who hears him. More the better, he'd suppose. Why not ask him if he'd fix your arm?"

Snell leaned forward over the counter, his voice dropping low. "Because those kind of doctors—any ache or pain, they want to cut you open. Bleed you if you're lucky, make you puke if you're not, and anything that can't be made to come out the vein or out the top or the bottom, they'll just lop off with the bone saw."

Sarah laughed. "You're more afraid of a doctor than you're afraid of a witch!"

"Because I've heard all about doctors. Sawbones and leeches!"

"That's why I'm gettin' the glue," said Sarah. "Anybody's arm gets cut off, you just send them up to Hope Hollow, and I'll glue it back on. 'Great Fastener, Nev-R-Un-Stick.' With a promise like that, how could you doubt?"

"I'll give it to you free of charge," said Snell, "and you can have the coffee, too, if you tell me what to do about the pain in my arm."

Sarah clicked her tongue. "You're not much of a shopkeeper, Mr. Snell. What's the missus going to think if you're giving away all your stock? You sure you wouldn't rather have Rebecca mix up a dram for you? I think she'd put willow bark and honey into a tea for the pain, and then she'd make a poultice of green leaf of something-or-other mixed with turpentine and goose grease and, I don't know, liver and onions."

"Still sounds much better than having my bowels rinsed out by a Hippocratic," said Snell. "But Rebecca's up in Hope Hollow, isn't she? And I'm not giving out free coffee if I have to go all the way up there. You're standing in my store right now."

"Convenience has always been my greatest talent," said Sarah. "Here, you take this red kerchief." She took it out of her pocket and wound it around Snell's upper arm, tucking it in and tying it off above Snell's elbow, visible on top of his shirtsleeve. As she tied, she pressed her finger on the knot so it would be tighter. The whole of the soreness was under pressure from the kerchief.

"Does it have to be so tight?" said Snell, rubbing the muscle again with his free arm.

"It does if I say it does," said Sarah. "Tighter the better. You leave it there all day, even after you go to sleep."

"And that's going to help?"

"Not enough," said Sarah. She put her elbows onto the counter, unloading her purchases. "You've got to wake up at midnight."

"That'll wake the missus."

"Tell her it's nothing, it's just your sore arm. You put on your boots and you go down to the spring. Take off the kerchief and soak it in the spring water. The midnight spring water. And you wrap up your arm again, tight as you can, in that midnight spring water."

"The midnight spring water..."

Sarah knew that's when the water would be coldest, and the night air would add to the cooling effect. "Three nights you do that, and on the third night, you won't feel the slightest soreness."

In three nights, thought Sarah, a little sprain would probably be gone all on its own, but if it was worse than a little sprain, the cold compress would help speed the recovery. Mostly, though, the patient would feel the power of the midnight spring water. That would always be better than ice, if there were any ice, because midnight had a mystery that ice never would.

"Now, do I get my coffee?" said Sarah.

Snell pushed the glue bottle and the coffee toward her. "Midnight spring water is a hell of a lot better than having Doctor Waycross amputate."

Sarah scooped up her prizes and turned to go. She didn't see the door open, nor did she see Ouida Bell walking in with a box wrapped in a pretty red ribbon, distracted by looking at the lithographs of the advertising beauties.

Only by an inch did they miss colliding with each other, but the jar of Hamilton's Great Fastener, the Nev-R-Un-Stick Glue, did not stay where Sarah had balanced it. It crashed to the floor, and Ouida Bell slipped on the white mess. She came down hard on her rump, and the box she was carrying popped open. Molasses balls rolled through the glue and to all corners of the store.

"Oh hell," said Ouida Bell, and then she put her hands to her mouth in modesty at her accidental oath. Glue from her fingers spread onto her lips, her cheek. "Oh gosh, oh gosh, oh hell. Just, oh hell. Those were meant to be for Mrs. Snell, those molasses balls. I can't think why she's mad at me, but she is, and those were meant to be for her, so maybe she wouldn't be so mad. I baked them up special, and now they're all ruined."

Sarah knelt down beside Ouida Bell. She no longer had her kerchief to wipe away the glue from the poor girl's face, so she used the sleeve of her dress. "Why, Ouida Bell, the boys are going to be stuck on you worse than ever."

Ouida Bell smiled through her distress, and Sarah thought it was an honest smile. It suited her well. Neither her ruined dress, her ruined shoes, nor her ruined present for Mrs. Snell could dampen Ouida Bell's good humor.

It was past nightfall before I'd finished inspecting and arranging my equipment. My glasses and vials had survived the journey. The copper tubing, alembics, flames, condensers, and crucibles were serviceable, too. I stood them all on a wooden plank balanced across two sacks of cornmeal. For a bookshelf, I had three fruit crates stacked atop each other. The surgery was a chair by the window. Starlight leaked through the drafty walls.

I'd purchased a poor supper of crackers and cheese from Snell, on credit. I found my pens and paper from among my supplies, and I drafted a letter.

To the Gentlemen of the Georgia Medical Society:

I find myself lured under false pretenses to a town on the far frontier. I came here to doctor, but it appears that all the doctoring is seen to by charlatans, banjo players, and granny women. All the locals are afraid of some polecat that they fancy to be a panther. The threat of rabies is no real threat, only a few mad dogs that have already been killed. My own connection to the disease made me pay it undue interest, and for that I blame myself. My finances do not permit me to extricate myself from my circumstances and return to Savannah. Please, if there is charity among you, collect for me the cost of a third-class trip back to Savannah. I should happily serve in any capacity until my debt is repaid. Only save me, a fellow of your society, from this backward and benighted place.

Yours sincerely—
Aubrey Waycross, Doctoris Medicinae

A letter would take at least two weeks to travel back to Savannah, and the response just as long. I was captured for a month, doctoring to hams and hogs.

I settled into the pile of straw that was my humble bed and struggled for a half hour before I was able to tamp down the prickly ends, but the bad memories only grew sharper. I hadn't faced the thought of so many charlatans since... since Eva's sickness. No doubt we would have tried Grove's Tasteless Chill Tonic and then called in the Winter sisters for their cobweb cures. Each time I pulled up my blanket to try to sleep, I saw poor Eva's sweat-soaked brow, her knotted hair, the intelligence fading from her gray eyes. Damn all the hucksters for their false cures and false hopes. The disquiet of my situation wouldn't cease. My brain was too unsettled by the incurable past.

In Savannah, I'd had a little garret apartment. Young, vigorous people lived in the rooms below me. They played whist and ombre, drank liquors, and sang under the influence of ether. These ether frolics were all the fashion. The host would provide silken cloths soaked in the chemical, and guests would fall into good-natured hysterics. While still at my studies, with an eye to my dwindling funds, I'd provided my downstairs neighbors or their acquaintances with the ether they needed for their guests.

I disdained their card games and liquors, but I approved of their ether frolics—or the ether, at least. Frail humanity is consumed by the need to find amusement, happiness, laughter, and repose. Ether is a hygienic and efficient enjoyment, without the maudlin moods of drunkenness or the hours needed to read a novel or knit the complicated web of social relations or learn the rules of ombre. I am not a religious ascetic or mirthless curmudgeon, but my conscience does not allow the frittering away of time. Medicine is long, and life is short.

I sprinkled several drops onto a clean cloth, placed it against my nose, and inhaled. The medicine showman, the slippery mayor, the rabid panther, the ignorant townsfolk...

Ether's sweet smell lingers long in the nose. It tickles the brain just at the front, above the eyes. The holes in the roof revealed small spots of stars, the lamp of the heavens shining down upon me. The straw was fresh. A breeze curled through the worm-riddled walls. Outside, hogs in good company murmured among themselves, and I fancied I could hear their jokes. The voice of an owl echoed, and the hogs and I found this a first-rate delight. I cuddled farther into the straw. Why, a man is just a hog with shoes on. I knocked off my boots. They fell down from the hayloft and rang out like fireworks upon the floor below. The stars exploded in reds and greens and yellows. Then, wonder of wonders, the window and roof fell away, and the whole sky spread out like a pasture before my eyes. In the center was the moon, the great hog-nosed moon! The hogs made worshipful oinks, and I joined in their chorus.

2

THE AGE OF MIRACLES IS PASSED

The next morning, I left my letter to the Georgia Medical Society with Snell. He could not make promises regarding when the next mail coach would come through. Lawrenceville does not enjoy a regular mail service. That is a luxury reserved for county seats, and the late rumors of the panther had made the inconsistent visitations even less frequent.

At the southwest corner of the muddy town square was a spring. It had been improved enough to ensure that the humans did not have to drink from the same place as the animals. A metal basin with a tin dipper held the water for the people. A knee-high trough caught the overflow for the animals. Several animals were struggling to satisfy themselves. A large bristly hog rubbed against my trouser legs.

Then I heard banging followed by a loud yelp—a man's cry of pain.

It is the doctor's burden that he cannot flee from cries of danger and anguish. Sensible citizens may run, preserving their own lives, but the doctor's obligation is to the suffering. I headed toward the sound, which was coming from the church. As I got closer, I noticed the church's unpainted boards had warped in the summer humidity, and its limp bell tower was listing by ten degrees. The entrance doors were off-center. The left, by custom, was for the men, and the right was for the women. Neither fit well into its frame. The church was sagging under its own weight. A man stood in the shadow of the tower, sucking on the fingers of his left hand. His ears stuck out prominently from his head, and he was wearing ragged field clothes stained with mud.

"Hallo, sir!" I announced. "Are you hurt?"

He smiled through his discomfort. "Ah, Dr. Waycross! It's not worth your trouble. I jammed my hand in the door. Caught my fingers."

Any injury was worth my trouble, as long as it paid a few pennies. "At least let me examine it, Mister..."

"Boatwright." He held up his hand, the bruised fingers drooping.

I flexed the fingers, squeezed the knuckles, and felt the movements of the joints.

"No broken bones," I said, returning his hand. "You'll be back to your fields in no time."

He stood up straighter. "I am no farmer. More of a shepherd. Of men."

"Pastor Boatwright, then," I said.

A Savannah churchman is never without his parson's frock. Boatwright did not look like a pastor. It was his addition to the letter, his insistence on the mention of rabies, that had lured me out to this forsaken edge of civilization, beyond any easy rescue. He'd persuaded the mayor to abuse my sympathy. His name meant nothing to me. I studied the man, but I did not recognize him. He must have known me, though, since he'd persuaded the mayor to contact me personally.

"If you'll pardon me, sir," I said, measuring my anger, "I seem to have misplaced our acquaintance. You know me, but I do not know you."

"You were only a stripling, Waycross. I do not expect you to remember. But the troubles of your poor sister I will never forget."

"Eva?"

"I was a newcomer to the cloth. I came at your mother's request—a last resort, I think, because I saw the bottles of patent remedies and smelled the incense of herbalists. Of course, I was too late to intercede. Only an extraordinary act of divine mercy would have saved her, but the Lord did not grant a miracle. We cannot blame Him, Waycross. I saw to her spiritual needs near the last. I washed her forehead, gave her shrift."

Then I did know him. He was the Protestant clergyman who had sat at my sister's side and done nothing for her. He'd prayed aloud, but his words had been lost in Eva's ravings. He shoved bread and poured wine between her clenched teeth, and she spat it back. She would not drink anything. He questioned Eva about her impure thoughts, her unchastities, her beliefs in false creeds and dark magic, but Eva was guilty only of loving me too much.

A tide of melancholy swirled in my innards, but I repressed the outward signs.

"I saw the letter you wrote the mayor," said Boatwright. "I recognized the name immediately. 'Well, that young boy's gone and done something fine with his life. Just the fellow we need in Lawrenceville.'"

When I received my stamps and seals from the Georgia Medical Society, I'd written to mayors all over the state. I promised them healthful constituents and solid Hippocratic cures. But none had answered me, save Lawrenceville.

"Because of rabies? Mayor Richardson said that no one has hydrophobia."

"Yet," insisted the pastor. "The mayor dismisses the danger. He's a nearsighted man. 'Just shoot the mad dogs,' he says. Well, we cannot shoot them all. We cannot kill a disease with a bullet, can we? And when a dozen children are suffering like your poor Eva suffered... Waycross, I never wish to see a sight like that again. Do you?"

I shook my head. Tears threatened to reveal themselves in the corners of my eyes, but I did not want the pastor to see them. I closed my eyelids long enough for the tears to dissipate, and when I opened my eyes again, my vision was no longer blurred.

"There are no human infections yet, thanks be," continued the pastor. "But three dogs in three months? It's breeding in the woods, among the animals. I think this panther is a rumor gone too far. But it's useful, isn't it, to keep people from wandering into harm in the woods? Some poor farmhand or field urchin will come down with the hydrophobia before a fortnight is gone."

"It's possible," I said.

"It's inevitable." Boatwright stretched his fingers, and a wince of pain crossed his face. "Hydrophobia and Waycross. These words are linked together in my mind, Doctor. I consider it more than serendipity that you wrote to Lawrenceville just as that very disease, so terrible a memory for you and me, is awakening in our midst."

"What do you suppose that I can do?"

The pastor knew, as surely as I, that no one, from Hippocrates to today, had been cured of rabies. There is hope for consumption, cancer, dropsy, and blood poisoning. Medicine has remedies for each—not infallible, but often effective. Rabies, though... Against rabies, we are all powerless.

"When the plague comes," said Boatwright, "you can offer comfort, Doctor, and perhaps I can offer a cure." He raised an outstretched right palm reverently toward the sky. "From there shall come our hope and deliverance. Not from Thumb's patent medicines and not from the Winter sisters' soups and swills. Rabies will prove them powerless. You saw it yourself, Waycross: the parade of hucksters and charlatans, each of whom wrought a particular failure upon Eva."

I did not like this man when he'd ministered to Eva, and I did not like this man now. He'd been one more charlatan among many. His Protestant prayers had done no better than a mustard plaster or turpentine tonic, but one cannot speak much against the dominant religion, even in our enlightened era.

I turned back to Boatwright. "So, I am here as a witness to the failures of quackery?"

"You've already begun. You'd been in town but five minutes before you inveighed against Thumb's spectacle. I was right to bring you here."

"I've already seen Thumb's game," I said. "But what kind of superstition do the Winter sisters favor? Patent medicines? Herbs? Incantations?"

"If only, sir. Songs and spirits are damaging to the soul." The pastor exploded into a full coughing fit. "But witchcraft—that's far worse."

"Witchcraft?" I bit my lip. "But there is no such thing as—"

"Potions!" His ears had turned bright red. "Candles. Dancing. Long silences. What would you call that?"

I allowed a long silence. "Children's games."

"It smacks of devilment and superstition, that's what." He paused to let his words sink in. "Those who pretend at witchcraft lead people into false beliefs, which are bad for their souls and bad for their bodies. Don't you agree?"

I traded my weight from foot to foot in silence.

"The hags' influence was stronger before I came," said Boatwright. "They were living here in this town. My predecessor in the pulpit did not take a hard line with his congregation. He permitted shadowy dealings on the courthouse square. Well, I will have none of it. I haven't yet been able to eliminate their sway though I did see to it that they were run out of Lawrenceville. The more credulous townsfolk ascribe miraculous powers to these witches. Drawing out poisons and infections. Reattaching severed limbs. Making the lame to walk and the blind to see, I'd venture. It's idolatry."

"Hucksterism," I said. "No one can stitch an arm back onto a stump."

Perhaps those sisters once had a stroke of luck in treating an infected limb, and the story grew, through rumor and hope, into a miracle, but the age of miracles is passed.

"They are charlatans and heretics, and they will fail the test of rabies." He took on the stentorian tones of a sermon. "But you and I, we can help where they cannot. You treat the body, and I treat the soul. And together, we will stand against the lure of superstition."

The pastor stuck out his hand as though we'd negotiated an alliance. I do not care about souls—show me one in a glass jar. But

I needed an ally, even a flawed one. I took his hand and shook it in a limp, reluctant agreement.

Our business finished, I took my leave quickly and went back to my makeshift office. I passed the day organizing my books and bottles. My mind was not in my work, which was only useless rearranging. Boatwright had irritated the memories of Eva that I had thought healed. What if a case of hydrophobia appeared among the children of Lawrenceville? What if this supposed panther—certainly some other kind of woodland creature, for it was a scientific impossibility for there to be a panther in Lawrenceville, Georgia—put its teeth into human flesh? What if, in their benightedness, the afflicted went to the Winter sisters for treatment? These so-called witches might spread the contagion with some superstition about pouring out blood at a crossroads.

I held out hope of rescue back to Savannah. Still, I could begin the work of discrediting the Winter sisters now. I could earn the trust of some influential patients and cure them, and by their wagging tongues, news of the efficacy of scientific medicine would spread through the town. Furthermore, I should find out how these Winter sisters treated their patients so that I could hold up their cures as ludicrous superstitions. My remonstrations against Thumb had not gone well, but next time, I would not be caught unprepared and, perhaps, not up on a stage.

The only witnesses to my labors and ruminations were the hogs. I took pity on a runty one, paler than her kin, who was laboring in her breathing and leaking mucus from her nostrils. I treated her with a bloodletting.

When Sarah came into her and her sisters' cabin at Hope Hollow, the first thing she saw was Rebecca's rump. The eldest sister was leaning over their largest iron kettle, stirring the boiling contents with a wooden paddle. The odor was not pleasant. It smelled of too many herbs all at once, basil and rosemary mixed with an overpowering lavender, as well as the spiciness of rhododendron, the sharp tang of pine, and the musk of something decocted from a toadstool.

"Which poor fellow is going to have to swallow that mess?" asked Sarah. "And what's he sick with to need such doctoring?"

"You're the poor fellow," said Rebecca, straightening up. "And me. And Effie. It's dinner."

Sarah stuck out her tongue.

"You don't have to eat it," said Rebecca. "You can go hungry. You can get yourself a cold biscuit. Or shoot a pigeon and cook it up yourself."

Sarah went closer to the cauldron and sniffed again. The aromas blended together better—the lavender and rhododendron and pine were coming from other tinctures cooling in other places. The basil and rosemary were in the cook pot, along with tomato and some root vegetables in a kind of stew. It was still early for tomatoes, at least for most gardeners, but Rebecca's crop was ripe, and it would stay ripe all the way until November. Her success was owed to more than just the guano she used on the soil. It was cleverness.

"Effie's not going to have but two spoonfuls," said Sarah. "Why are you making up such a big pot of stew?"

"Effie will creep down at night and eat three bowls when she doesn't think any of us will know." Rebecca looked into the cook pot again and seemed satisfied. Then she crossed over to the kitchen table, where a dozen glass bottles, all mismatched, were set out. Each was filled with a different color of liquid. From these the variegated herbal odors were coming, oils and essences that Rebecca used in her work and occasionally in their supper.

"Why do you need to cook up so many medicines?" asked Sarah. "All a Hippocratic doctor needs is a lancet and a bone saw."

"Since when are you an expert on Hippocratic medicine?"

"I met the new doctor," said Sarah. "Remember, I said that they were sending for one. He's here now."

"You don't suppose he'll be any trouble, do you? Like the new pastor was?"

"Not any trouble. He's a fool, and not even a convincing fool." Sarah told her sister about the stage show, the spectacle with Thumb, and how the poor doctor was stunned into defeat by a banjo tune.

"He's your age, Rebecca, which is old enough to be married by now, but he isn't. And he's not bad-looking, if you don't mind that his hair is thinning up top and that his favorite pastime is shouting at medicine-show men."

Rebecca didn't say anything.

Sarah continued, "And what's more... he's a man of blood."

"What on earth do you mean?" asked Rebecca as a reflex, but her eyes betrayed that she knew what Sarah meant. "That scrying... that was a saw, and that meant Everett."

"Could have been any kind of blade, you said. And Effie said it was a man of blood, and Everett wasn't a man of blood. Now a doctor, there's a man of blood. And pus and puke and piss and every other fluid you can squeeze out of a man or woman. Who wouldn't want to marry a man like that?"

"You thought it was a silly game," said Rebecca. "You thought all of it was a silly game."

"It still is a silly game."

"Even when people die? Even when people run out of town so there's no more killing?"

Sarah fell silent, knowing that her needling had pressed too far, but she couldn't keep silent for long. "All I meant was I don't think we have to worry about this man of blood."

Rebecca nodded slowly.

"Where's Effie?" asked Sarah.

"I haven't seen her since this morning. Pendleton came up with a three-inch locust splinter in his arm, and it was hot with infection. I was two hours getting the splinter out and then cleaning up the wound. Honey to dry it out and keep it clean."

"I wish you cared about your little sister as much as you cared about every stranger that wanders up to Hope Hollow."

"Those strangers need doctoring," said Rebecca. "And she's not here to reattach an arm that's about to fall off or to drive out a blood infection or glumly stare the hydrophobia out of someone, is she? She's gone someplace—I don't know where. So while she's gone and you're out meeting the new doctor, the man of blood, then it's up to me to be making supper and making cures, isn't it?"

Rebecca cooks, and Rebecca doctors, thought Sarah, which for her amount to nearly the same thing. And if she quits either one, she leaves room for unrepeatable sadness to creep in.

By late afternoon, the heat of the day had made my office uncomfortable. I laced up my boots and pushed the creases out of my hat. A constitutional perambulation would clear my head and help me learn the land. As Galen wrote, exercise is good both for the evacuation of the excrements and for improving the condition of the firm parts of the body.

Which way should I go? Galen, I supposed, would have taken his constitutionals around the Forum and the Coliseum—urban places. Lawrenceville, outside of its clapboard courthouse, the four dirt paths bordering it, and a few stores, was wilderness. I sighed. Savannah was not Rome or London, but it was a city: orderly streets, rows of shopfronts, manicured parks, and a bustling quayside. It was not a place free from danger, but I knew those dangers. Here, I knew only that the woods, which began not three hundred yards down any dusty lane, might conceal any number of dangers—not a panther, certainly, but a mountain lion or rabid dog. Bandits. Cherokee. Belligerent farmers with shotguns and ideals about their property rights.

I decided it was prudent and in no way cowardly to confine my constitutional to Lawrenceville's square. I completed one perambulation and began a second, numbering the public establishments. The Rhodes Hotel on the south side. Next to that, a narrow storefront with a simple sign: Parr's Confectionary. A place called the Flowing Bowl. A tanning yard with open pools of chemicals oozing their vapors into the atmosphere. The catawampus church. A tree sporting three little straw poppets—perhaps to entertain children. A cabin with a red door, which might have been a school-house or a turkey hostelry, for all I knew. Wheelwright, black-smith. And back to Snell's Merchandise. The storefronts were no different on my third pass or my fifth.

Finally, I stopped in front of the confectionary, for that was the most unusual, a strange luxury for a frontier town. I peeked in the window. The cakes and pies and treacly concoctions displayed made my stomach rumble. Inside, a young girl was keeping the counter. Her curls were the color of daffodils.

"That's Mrs. Parr's daughter, Ouida Bell," said a Negro man, who sidled up beside me. "If I could get her to work for me at the Flowing Bowl, I'd be doing even better business. I think most of the candies that Ouida Bell sells, she gets back as presents from her suitors. She's what finally made you stop, huh?" As I must have looked puzzled, the man laughed. "You've been walking a circle around this square. I've seen you pass my window a dozen times."

Though it had been only eleven times, I did not correct him.

"I came out to see if you were all right or if you were looking for something. Maybe you lost your glasses or your dog."

"Nothing lost, sir." I tipped the brim of my hat and introduced myself. "Dr. Waycross."

"I know it. Can't keep the Flowing Bowl folks from talking, and it seems that, between them, they know just about everything, if you can sort truth out from the lies. I'm Renwick."

"What's the Flowing Bowl? An eatery?"

"Walked by a dozen times but didn't poke your head inside," clucked Renwick. "See, if Ouida Bell were working for me, you would have stopped. Yeah, it's an eatery. We've always got pork, biscuits, and whiskey." He fiddled with the ends of his shirt collar, which were starched and crisp. "The rest of the menu is whatever I think up that morning. Say, you're not one of those doctors that are on about the evils of drink, are you?"

I shook my head. "Drink, in moderation, can be beneficial for the constitution. It is hot and, thus, restorative for certain phlegmatic conditions. Of course, anything in excess can be destructive. Drink. Smoking. Exertion—"

"Walking around the square a dozen times. Don't you want a change of scenery, or is the sight of Ouida Bell what you're really after?"

I piqued under his needling. "No, not at all. I needed a constitutional, for my health. If I've offended you, Mr. Renwick—"

"Offended, nah. Doctor, I'm just looking out for me and my own, you know?" His jocular manner did not comfort me. "You're going to wear out our roads. They're already not so good. Drifts of mule shit and hog slop. Puddles big enough that a fellow can go fishing in them after a good rain. You keep going another dozen times, and there will be a rut right down the middle."

"I assure you, I won't dig a new Tallulah Gorge with my footsteps."

"Well, sure, sure." Renwick's friendly expression did not change, but he stepped closer. "But in the second place, Doctor, I don't want a teetotaler pacing back and forth in front of my store. Makes my folks nervous. Sometimes, Boatwright will stop in, raving about the costs of sin, or Mrs. Maltbie will make a fuss about her drunkard of a husband and how we're all leading him to perdition. But I've got every right to keep my store, and my folks got every right to drink there, if they like."

"Given that they drink in moderation," I protested.

"Or not in moderation," said Renwick. "A man can get liquored up if he's got the money to pay for it. It's a free country, isn't it?"

I wondered that a man of Renwick's race would call this country free. Nine-tenths of his fellow Negroes in Georgia were slaves.

"Just sayin'... be a lot more healthful if you were out in the forest, Doctor."

I started—the word "forest" was more menacing in Lawrenceville, for all its wild unknowns.

Renwick read the emotion on my face. "Oh hell, Doctor, I didn't mean it like that. I was only thinking that there's not so many of these hogs or tanning vats or cooking fires. The forest is healthful when there's not a monster in it."

"I don't credit those rumors, Mr. Renwick. Do you believe there is really a giant panther stalking the woods around us?"

"I ain't seen it, and I ain't talked to anyone that's seen it. But all of them at the Flowing Bowl have. Everyone's got a cousin, a friend, a farmhand who's got a glimpse of it. No paw prints. No fur. No teeth marks. There's been a couple mad dogs, but that's not the same as a panther, is it? Raccoons can be rabid, and no one's going to hide under his pillow because a raccoon might be after him."

I did not think myself a cowardly man. A person cannot be prisoner of a rumor. I would not be afraid of this panther until I'd seen it with my own eyes.

"And so what part of the forest should I go to, Mr. Renwick? There's forest all around."

"If you follow this road," he said, indicating a footpath that extended past Honest Alley, heading east, "it's nice and flat—shady, too. That'd make a nice walk."

I looked at the path out of town that headed east. "And there aren't any Indian war parties that take this same constitutional? Any bandits or robbers?"

"No, all the Cherokee are north of here. And the robbers—I keep them liquored up at the Flowing Bowl." Renwick stepped away and put his hand on the door to Parr's Confectionary. "I'll tell Ouida Bell you said hi."

I did not want to seem suspicious, and I especially did not want to seem lecherous toward this Ouida Bell. True, she was comely, and she was surely the object of every young fellow's desire here in town, but I had never been one to seek out companionship, marked as I had been by sadness. No one was as kind as Eva or as noble or as tragic, and while I was engaged in my studies, I needed the solitude to master my discipline. A sip of ether came to my aid whenever a pang of loneliness distracted me, ether being far quicker than courtship. I had no wish for a dalliance in Lawrenceville—to love and leave is worse than not to have loved at all.

So I decided not to perambulate the town square anymore lest others think I had intentions other than the improvement of constitution. I passed Honest Alley on my right and followed the path Renwick had shown me.

Lawrenceville's civilizing influence ended half a mile from the town square. Fields and pastures surrendered to aboriginal forest. Ash and elm and chestnut knitted into a verdant canopy. Low pines and rhododendrons and scattered spiny bracken lay on the forest floor, unkempt and untamed. With more industry and ingenuity, the people of Lawrenceville could transform these woods into useful land: fields, pastures, cabins, and orchards. The little rivulets could be dammed to drive a small wheel, enough to mill corn or turn a lathe. Lawrenceville need not be such a monotonous smear of nature. I kept a sharp eye on the underbrush and an ear tuned to the sounds of the forest, but they found only the regular features of the wild. Nothing, nothing to fear.

I met a turnip wagon headed toward town. I stopped to salute the driver, and the mule yawned broadly in my face, its breath smelling of turnips.

"Where're you headed for?" asked the driver, who'd given his name as Pa Everett.

"Just a little farther up the road, and then I'll turn back," I said jauntily.

"Just a little farther up the road, you'll hear a sound like an organ playing."

"What's that? A nest of bees?"

"Bees? Nope. Pigeons. Sight to see."

"I have seen a pigeon before."

"A pigeon, huh? Well, maybe you go a little farther up the road. Sight to see."

Pa Everett slapped the reins, and the turnip-breathed mule lurched into motion. As it moved its hind legs, it expelled a flatus that reeked even more strongly.

I watched the wagon disappear slowly back down the road I'd traveled. I didn't have any interest in a pigeon that sounded like an organ playing, but nor did I want to turn around just yet and follow behind that mule. I thought it best to see what this pigeon was all about. That would allow time for the air to clear, and I'd see what passed for genuine spectacle in the countryside.

A quarter mile farther, I started to hear the organ sound. It grew louder as I continued, but the pitch remained constant. A single pigeon couldn't keep up a song like that. Was it a geological feature, water echoing through a rock? The canopy cleared above me, and I emerged into a glade. The sound was all around me now. What could it be? Then, looking upward, I realized that, roosting on every protrusion from the gray trees, were pigeons, thousands upon thousands. What I'd thought at first glance were leaves and branches were wings and beaks. Pigeons stood on top of other pigeons. Pigeons collided in the air with other pigeons. Pigeons roiled and mated and snapped and scratched. The ground was snow-white with their droppings, and the ammonia made my eyes water. Their calls blended into one continuous hum. It was indeed a sight to see but unnerving in its immensity.

A single pigeon poses no danger, but a thousand little beaks? They could tear me into bite-sized morsels. I willed my breathing to slow down, moved my right foot back an inch, and repeated the motion with my left. I eased backward, never blinking, mesmerized by the millions of black eyes.

Then, musket fire crashed through the glade, and dozens of birds fell from their places. Bodies raised puffs of desiccated excrement where they fell to the forest floor. The bullet sent the assembled millions into chaos. Beating wings raised a gale of droppings and feathers. The whole sky was squalling. I dropped to my haunches and covered my head as birds flew past my ears.

"Whoo-whee!" shouted a voice above the din. "Hodgson, I got twenty in one shot!"

"What's that, Pearson?"

"Twenty, I said!"

Pearson's footfalls were coming nearer. The wings thrashing above my head did not permit me to make any response.

"Eighteen, nineteen, twenty! Wait, twenty-one! Whoo-whee, one better!"

The ground rumbled with the nearness of his bounding leaps.

"Aw, shit," he said, and all the bounding ceased. "That ain't a pigeon."

"It's the damn doctor. You shot the damn doctor, Hodgson."

"I didn't shoot him. That was you! You shot your twenty pigeons—"

"Twenty-one," said Pearson.

"Twenty-one pigeons and one doctor. That's some kind of record, but some kind of felony, too."

The sound of the pigeons faded, and my heartbeat quieted. I took my arms off my head.

"Wait, he ain't dead," said Pearson.

"You ain't gonna hang after all," said Hodgson.

The pair was standing right over me, blocking out the sun. Both men were tall and wiry, their legs like cornstalks. Pearson's head was covered in dirty blond curls. Hodgson's complexion was much darker. He had a waxed black mustache. Pigeon blood and streaks of fresh droppings spattered their clothes. Feathers were tangled in their hair.

I struggled to my feet. Neither Pearson nor Hodgson offered to help me up, but they stepped back to give me room.

"Doctor, I didn't mean to shoot you," said Pearson. His hat was against his chest. "I was aiming for them birds."

I took off my jacket so that I could beat the pigeon shit out of it, and with each whack, I remonstrated with the duo. "It's irresponsible, sirs. This is a traveled road. What if a pigeon carcass had hit me on the head? What if I'd had a heart palpitation and dropped dead right here?"

"We weren't thinking," said Hodgson. His eyes were downcast, and he scrawled in the white dust with the narrow toe of his boot.

"Well, see that it doesn't happen again." I slipped my jacket back on and tugged at the hems so that it snapped against my shoulders. "Wait—what the devil is that?"

A black shape moved behind Pearson and Hodgson. They turned to follow my gaze.

"Pearson, Pearson, it's that panther!" said Hodgson. His voice was a whisper, but it filled the glade. The noises of the pigeons had vanished.

In an instant, the rumor turned to sinewy muscle and knotted flesh. It was no mountain lion. It was far too large. For a moment, I could not believe the evidence of my own eyes, but if a man of science cannot believe his own eyes, his own senses, what can he believe? I had thought this panther an impossible tale, a ghost story grown large on the credulity of simple folk, but I should have heeded them. Now the panther was there, and my life was the price I'd pay for my arrogance.

Its jaws hung open, and great strands of white foam trailed from between its fangs. Its eyes bulged from their places, dark swellings half clouded with its disease. I am a doctor of only a single animal, the human animal, but I could see in that creature the same affliction I'd seen on Eva. Maniacal thirst. A quivering violence, coiled and ready. Poison, infection, affliction. The panther snuffled along the ground, approaching some of Pearson's slain pigeons. Hodgson sighted down his musket barrel. The creature was ten yards away, an easy shot. He pulled the trigger, and half a dozen birds dropped from the trees.

"Damn it, Hodgson! You missed him." Pearson threw his hat to the ground.

"Got six birds, though!" Hodgson bumped his fist against his companion's shoulder. "Wasn't even trying."

"You ain't gonna get to eat them, idiot. That panther is gonna get them."

"Damned if I'm gonna let it make off with my kills!"

Pearson fumbled at his belt and pulled out a knife. He rushed at the creature, which turned its head toward us. The creature hadn't been startled by the gunshots. Its hunger or malice made it deaf to danger.

Pearson, slashing the air, stumbled. The creature lunged and missed. The two opponents moved past each other. Hodgson had reloaded his musket. He fired again, missing both beast and birds. That time, though, the creature had enough. Its natural instinct overpowered its inner rage. With still enough sense left, it turned toward the woods and fled, its pawfalls kicking up clouds of pigeon guano so that the beast left behind a trail of what seemed like white smoke.

"You better run, you damn meat sack!" Pearson shook his knife at his fleeing enemy, but the gesture of defiance made him wince. He pressed his free hand against his arm then pulled his arms toward his chest, doubling over.

"Did he bite you, Pearson?" asked Hodgson.

"No, not a bite. Clawed me."

Hodgson peered at the arm Pearson was holding up. "Aw, quit your moaning. That's a scratch."

I was still rooted to my spot. The sanguine rush filling my head put a pounding pressure on my temples. "That was a panther. A rabid panther. Not a mountain lion or a wild dog."

"Yeah, doc, it sure was," said Pearson.

"But there is no panther. And yet it bit you. Maybe infected you."

"Not bit. Clawed. I've been clawed and bit enough to know the difference, and this is a clawing. Hurts like the devil."

I had to put the upheaval in my mind aside, because poor Pearson needed my attentions. The panther—the impossible panther—had fled, and the danger was past, and a man needed my help. I willed my bowels to obey me.

"Let me see," I said.

"Doc, it's only a scratch," said Hodgson, dismissing his partner's wound. "I've had worse from a tomcat."

"Only a scratch?" said Pearson through gritted teeth. "Why don't you get scratched like this? Then you can tell me it ain't nothing."

I put weight on Pearson's shoulders, guiding him to a sitting position, and knelt down beside him. The claw marks were there, and they'd broken the skin, but claws can't pass rabies. That's not where the infection lives. It lives in the mouth, in the bite. Mad dogs had mauled people, but unless the people were bitten, they hadn't been infected. If only that dockside cur had scratched Eva instead of putting its poisoned teeth into her leg...

That is what my doctor's training told me, but it also told me there should be no such thing as a panther in the Georgia mountains. I could take no chances.

"I need to bleed you," I said. My hand went for my jacket pocket, where I kept a small traveling kit: a lancet and a few essential chemicals. My fumbling fingers, still perturbed by the recent traumatic events, untied the bundle with difficulty.

"Naw, Doctor." Pearson's eyes grew wide. "No bleeding. I've got an ointment."

I thought I'd misheard. "Ointment?"

"Yeah. Stinky, oily stuff. Last month, I put a nail through my foot. Went up to Hope Hollow for it, before all this panther stuff started up, when folks weren't afeard to make the trip. Rebecca Winter mixed it up. I've got some left. Much better than bleeding."

"You can't put a balm on this, man! This is an actual flesh wound. It needs debridement. Stitches. Laudable pus—"

"Ointment worked on my foot just fine," said Pearson, curiously defiant for a man who'd just been attacked by a rabid panther. "You're not going to bleed me."

"Maybe I can talk it out, Pearson," said Hodgson. "Read it Ezekiel."

"Dummy! No, you can't." Pearson lifted himself up. "A doctor's got to do that. Doctor, do you have a Bible? Know Ezekiel?"

I did not carry a Bible in my traveling kit. A fine Southern Protestant would never ask for last rites. "Why a Bible?"

"Ezekiel will stop the blood faster than stitches," said Hodgson. "I've seen it, Doctor. Sarah Winter did it for my momma. You know Ezekiel?"

I swallowed my reaction. My feelings on religion were best not to air. "I think, sirs, that we should save prayer for more dire circumstances."

"Then maybe we do nothing," said Pearson, as if it were an equal option among a menu of treatments.

"Yeah, we do nothing," said Hodgson, nodding. He sat down beside us with a whump, sending up a cloud of white pigeon dust.

"Nothing's the worst you can do, Pearson! Don't give up hope, man. I'll bleed it to get the poisons out. I'll blister your feet to get the sanguine humor flowing away from your arm. Sulfurous phosphate to cauterize the incisions. That will bring up a laudable pus, which we'll keep flowing so that the humors—"

Pearson shook his head. "None of that, Doctor. Next, you'll be amputating."

"I refuse to permit it." I folded my arms, and as soon as I did, I regretted it, for the gesture made me look like a petulant child.

It wasn't their fault. They hadn't half a cup of sense between them. The blame rested on the Winter sisters. I pleaded, I lectured, and I scoffed, but in the end, I was made helpless by their ignorance. Pearson leaned on Hodgson as we hobbled back to Lawrenceville, and the only role left for me was carrying the slaughtered pigeons. I spent the entire walk stoking the fires of my anger. Since the panther was real and the rabies was real, that made the threat of the Winter sisters a reality too. I could not ignore their superstitions, knowing what I knew now. I would confront these sisters and make them answer for their lies.

3

HOPE HOLLOW

E ffie shouldn't be out there all by her lonesome," said Sarah.
"She's not a child," said Rebecca, blowing out the last
candle and leaving the room in full darkness. "She's old enough to
know what she should and shouldn't do."

Sarah huffed and pulled the covers off Rebecca. "You get up
and help me look for her."

Rebecca grabbed the quilt and tucked herself back in. Sarah
clenched her fists.

"Get out of the damn bed, Rebecca. Get your boots on."

Rebecca sat up. Sarah could barely see the outline of her face in
the meager moonlight that came into the cabin.

"I wouldn't be any help," said Rebecca. "Listen, if you don't find
her in an hour, come back and get me."

"I'm taking the gun," said Sarah.

"You're afraid? Of what?"

"Just... not anything."

Sarah left the cabin door open behind her. If Rebecca wanted
to keep the mosquitoes out, she'd have to get up.

The woods were still. Sarah liked the sounds of animals, the
sounds of life, when she could understand the woods and what was
moving in them. But, when the wind stayed silent, and the pigeons
and the owls and the cicadas kept to themselves, and the deer and
the foxes hid in their homes—those were menacing woods. Silence
was mystery.

Sarah held up a hand around her mouth to amplify her voice.
"Heya, Effie! Get your bony little behind to bed!" Nothing moved,
though: not an owl and not Effie.

She checked the clearing by the scrying bowl. She checked
the cornfield and the lemon-tree grove. She scouted around the
shed where their nameless mule slept. No sign of her. Effie had

wandered out late several times since they'd fled Lawrenceville, but Sarah had always found her close to the cabin. She'd been counting the fireflies among the sweet-potato vines or threading her way through a labyrinth of tousled rocks over the ridge, but not tonight.

Sarah swore aloud, vigorously. She wondered if she oughtn't go back inside for another candle, but that would be giving up too easily. She had hated how easily they'd given up in Lawrenceville. She could have shut that preacher's mouth with a single bullet even through all the smoke and cinders.

Sarah followed the path from Hope Hollow out toward the river. Cherokee feet, then the white settlers after them, had kept the path worn down to the dirt. Even after that spectacle in town, the sisters had a regular traffic of rheumatics and bleeders and croup-whoopers—rotten hypocrites, all of them. When the pastor had hung up those awful effigies, he'd had everyone in town behind him, but since the Winters had fled back to Hope Hollow, Boatwright's loyal parishioners got their hurts fixed there, where the pastor couldn't see.

She came to the ford at the Alcovy, and at last, the forest was not so quiet. The water ran among the rocks just the same at night as during the day.

"There you are," said Sarah. She'd spied Effie sitting cross-legged on one of the granite boulders sticking out from the shallows.

Effie's gray hair had caught the moonlight and helped Sarah spot her. Effie was the youngest of them, but her hair had started to turn silver when she was a child, and now that she was eighteen, almost all the black was gone from it. Her gray hair would have given her an aura of wisdom, had it been well-kept. Before Everett, Rebecca had helped Effie to brush it out, which gave it a little luster, but now, it was unkempt—clean but ill ordered. Sarah might have taken up brushing Effie's hair, but that was not Sarah's way. She looked after her sister in more profound ways, searching her out in the night when she'd gone a-wandering.

"How long have you been sitting here?" said Sarah.

"Since supper," said Effie. She was facing upriver, away from her sister.

"You didn't show up for supper. I kept a couple biscuits and some ham for you."

"Then it must have been since dinner."

Sarah nodded. "See anyone on the road?"

"Yes, but not yet. We'll get a visitor tomorrow."

"That panther's been scaring them all away. You think that someone will brave the bogeyman of the woods?"

Effie nodded.

"I should have killed that panther a week ago," said Sarah. "Ain't that the right thing to do? That way, all the little biddies and the goodwives can come up here for their sassafras beauty faces, get their hemorrhoids washed away, and have no fear for it. And they can turn up their snouts at us when we go into town."

"You aren't going to kill the panther," said Effie. "Not ever."

"You think the rabies will kill it before I will? Seems a safe bet. But I'm not going to let you wait here all night just to see or wait up for tomorrow's visitor. It's time to come home. Get to sleep."

Effie didn't move.

"I sure as shit am not going to stay here until sunrise," said Sarah. "You want me to throw you over my shoulder and carry you back home? Get off that rock. Make sure you don't fall. It'll be slippery."

But Effie still didn't move.

"Goddamn it, Effie. I'm going to get my boots wet, and it'll be the devil getting them dry before the morning. I hate walking around in wet boots." Sarah left her gun on the shore and stomped into the shallows. She was used to crossing the ford. She knew where little dry rises offered better footing. She got to the rock where Effie was perched. "What's your fascination with this stupid rock?"

"Not the rock, the river." Effie pointed upstream.

In the cane bracken was the carcass of a deer, a young buck. Sarah could see, despite the twilight, that the creature had been mauled and mangled.

Effie nodded. "The panther caught it up there, by that oak. Tore into it. But the deer got away and ran for the river. The panther didn't follow it."

Sarah felt the knotting of guilt in her stomach. "Why didn't you run away? Come get me?"

Effie tilted her head. "I was safe on this rock."

"A panther can swim a creek. A panther can climb a rock."

"It was afraid of the water. It wouldn't come down to the river even to get its kill."

Sarah understood—hydrophobia. Rabies.

Effie glanced at her sister then looked back toward the deer. "I watched it die. There was still life in him—no more than in a plucked twig of belladonna berries, but still, enough. I brushed my fingertips on the surface of his existence, and ripples flowed across the waters of life and death. And then he slipped below the water, and I did not reach out to pull him back."

"You can't tell this to Rebecca," Sarah said quietly then shook the thought away. She had never before been afraid of her little sister. "Effie, you're exhausted. You don't know what you're saying. I'm tired of standing here and getting creek water between my toes. Go on back home. Go to bed. Now."

Effie climbed down from the rock and pattered back to the creek side. She looked back, but Sarah hadn't followed her. "What about you?"

"I'm not going to leave this deer carcass in our river. I've got to clean up this mess."

"That panther's still around here."

"Yeah, that's why I've got the gun and why I want you to go home. Now get on, Effie."

Effie lowered her head.

"I want to get to bed," said Sarah, "so let me clear this deer carcass and get on."

Effie walked back out into the creek. Her feet were bare and kicked up sprays of silver water wherever they fell. She moved quickly and was soon beside the mangled deer. Effie put her hand on its flank, next to a terrible wound from the panther's claws.

"Effie, you'll get blood all over—"

Sarah stopped because the deer stood up and shook its horns. It peered down at Effie, its black animal eyes dumb and uncomprehending. Sarah didn't understand either.

"Let it die somewhere else," Effie said.

The deer turned away from the cane at the riverbank. It ran strongly on its mangled legs, ascending the hill and disappearing among the closing chestnuts.

"What in the hell was that?" said Sarah. "What in the hell was that?"

I'd come to Snell's store to buy a walking stick, but he had none in stock.

"Just pick up any old stick in the woods," he said.

Any old stick from the woods would not do, though. A proper walking stick, with a brass tip and the right heft to it, would help the miles pass more quickly, and I wanted to confront the sisters as soon as possible, while my righteous fury was still at its height.

"Then I want some provisions for the trek to Hope Hollow. Something invigorating."

"What would perk you up, Doctor? Some coffee? Turpentine? A dram of Grove's Tasteless Chill Tonic?"

I shook them all away.

"Maybe some ginger nuts from Ouida Bell at the confectionary?"

I had no time for that, either. "Just cold water, then."

"Water's free. Out by the spring."

"Is there nothing you'd sell me?"

Snell laughed. "You don't have any money, Doc! What could I sell you? Listen, why are you so hot and bothered now?"

I told him, as quickly as I could, about Pearson and Hodgson and that the panther was no myth and how the beast had raked its claws down Pearson's shoulder. "That won't spread the disease, but think... That's even worse. The panther attacks Pearson, but he doesn't get hydrophobia. And you will all think it's because of an ointment or a Bible verse. But it's because of the animal, you see. Not a bite, but a claw. And the sisters' reputation will grow even higher. But real hydrophobia, when it comes—because I've seen it now, I've seen that panther—won't be cured by an ointment. It doesn't listen to Ezekiel."

"Listens to nothing," said Snell. "But what can you do?"

"I can put them in their place, these pretend healers," I said. "I'll go into their dark house hung with vines and crepe and skulls."

"Skulls?" Snell looked at me. "I've never seen any skulls."

"Herb women, fortune-tellers, supposed alchemists. Always of a type, as if they've studied the same Durer woodcut. Sunken eyes. Wrinkled fingers. They make their faces ugly to scare away the demons—as if illness can be frightened! Old women, acting as if wisdom and power comes with age."

"I don't know how old the Winter sisters are," said Snell, frowning. "They've been here longer than most all of us, but we've only been here ten years. It's the frontier, remember."

"They cultivate an air of mystery," I continued, "as if that increases the power of their cures. Rubbish is what it is. Real medicine doesn't care if it's worked in an operating theater or a hog shed."

"You sure you don't want a bottle of Grove's Tasteless Chill Tonic?" Snell had one in his hand. "I think it'd be mighty fine for what ails you."

"What ails me are lies and superstitions. How do I get to their house?"

"Seven miles," said Snell. "You can take my mule if you'd like."

"I don't suppose riding a mule would save me from a rabid panther, would it?"

"A gun would serve you better," said Snell.

"I've never shot one," I said.

Snell's face blanched whiter than I imagined mine had the day before. "What do you mean, you've never shot a gun? You wouldn't have weaned off your mama's breast out here before you shot your first gun."

"Ways are different in the city, if you can credit it, sir. I wouldn't know the first thing about how to shoot."

Snell lifted a rusted tube of metal, oil-streaked and neglected, from behind the store counter. "You point this end at the critter you're wanting to kill," he said, "and then you pull this bit here to do the killing." He extended the battered old weapon toward me.

I could have taken the gun. It would have been better protection than taking nothing. It might even have served as a walking stick, but what if I tapped it wrong and the thing blew up in my face? And what would the Winter sisters think if I arrived at the door bearing such a weapon? They'd suppose me a mob of one or a bandit. But I meant to confront them on the sound basis of science—no gun for me.

"It's daylight," I said, "and the beast is likely to be asleep. If it spies me and thinks me likely prey, I am spry enough to run or even climb a tree. And if I had this gun, I am as likely to miss it completely as hit it somewhere far from its vital parts and send it into a rage. No, I shall leave the gun behind."

Snell shook the rifle insistently.

I shook my head. "I am on an errand of mercy, not of death."

"That sounds like a damn fool superstition," said Snell.

As the road descended from the higher elevations of Lawrenceville, it became less and less of a road. What had begun as a track of packed earth traced by the wheels of mule carts became a dusty path. The soil was red, of the famous Georgia clay, and more boldly colored there than at any other outcropping I'd seen. The wear of feet kept the gash fresh, showing the earth's bloody heart. Fear of the panther hadn't let the grass grow on this path. The sick and infirm still took this road to Hope Hollow though no one was out that day.

Perhaps if I were to be mauled by the panther and fight it off, the encounter would redound to my credit. Rumor would grow the event from a skirmish to an epic struggle. I, the conquering doctor, would tell my tale, and the folk would hearken to me.

My ears, sharpened to every sound, distinguishing songbirds from pigeons, squirrels from chipmunks, heard a low growl. So faint yet so close—rhythmic, like breathing, rise and fall. The growl continued, its rhythm increasing but its volume no louder. It was so very close, as though it were just at my right ear, but I felt no presence there and saw nothing. I willed my head to turn toward the sound, and willed it slowly, for whatever lay there was waiting for my movement, waiting for my mistake before it would make its strike. When I turned my head, though, the sound moved with it, just as much as I moved. It was too clever to be a panther. It was... it was a phantom! A spirit of fear and trembling had taken up on my shoulder to whisper terror into my ear. A gun would do me no good. I'd blast a hole through my own head, so near was this sound, which could only be a panther about to pounce, a ghost, a—

Then I knew what it was. It was the sound of my own breathing. My right nostril, half clogged with the rheum of the season, had settled into a snorting, rasping rhythm coinciding with my respiration. That was the growl I heard, the phlegm rattling in my skull. I'd been so afraid, heightened to every sound.

"Bah!" I cried into the wilderness. "Bah and foolishness!"

A pair of pigeons, startled from their lovemaking in a branch overhead, flapped away. Their stupid cooing I took for laughter at my expense.

As I set off again, rain clouds built in the sky when I neared the Alcovy River. Whoever had named it a river had never seen the Savannah or any other watercourse of consequence. The Alcovy was a creek with delusions. The road crossed it where the water was shallow and broad, running over an expanse of worn granite. I was still bothered and distracted by my foolishness, how I'd been spooked by my own breathing. I would not let a river scare me. I did not slow my pace as I stepped into the current but went with confidence. White-tipped water flowed around my shoes, and my legs slipped from under me like a buffoon's in a lowbrow comedy. I came down hard on my coccyx. The impact shot up my spine and out my teeth. I gritted them together, suppressing an oath as I dragged my sorry carcass to the far shore. I was soaked. My handkerchief was sodden, useless for wiping off my face. The current had stolen my hat. I saw it downriver, entangled in a jam of sticks. A forked branch had impaled it through the crown.

Could I really appear hatless before the Winter sisters? A hatless man cannot be taken seriously. At least I could conceal my foolishness at being startled by my own breathing—no one need know about that, least of all the Winter sisters—but a man cannot hide if he is hatless. The very item that he might hide under has been taken from him.

I tried a few tentative steps and felt no broken bones, but the ankle was sprained. I needed to bleed the joint so that I could release the excess fluids. I felt for my traveling kit, but I didn't have it. I'd taken it out of my pocket to treat Pearson. Had I left it behind in that pigeon-blighted grove? Or had it fallen from my coat into the river? I looked around me, peering into the shallows, but I saw no sign of my lancets, blistering plasters, or prussic acid. I was useless for my own complaint. This was worse than the embarrassment of the fall, the loss of my hat, and the discomfort of my wet underdrawers. I considered turning back. I could ford the river again, hobble on my bad leg the six miles back to Lawrenceville, drag myself into the hayloft, and recuperate with ether. But then where would I be? Back in town—damp, defeated, and useless.

No, I would go on. A little water never hurt anyone.

I passed a quarter hour, chasing the sunlight as afternoon slipped into evening on the last part of the walk. My damp clothes gradually dried into smelly wrinkles. Nothing would restore my hat, which was lost forever. I hadn't thought the journey would take so long. I thought I would have reached Hope Hollow, excoriated those pretended witches, and been back in Lawrenceville in time for supper. Now, though, I would miss supper, and what's more, my return trip would be through the darkness.

Someone was coming the other way, a young woman. She was coming down from Hope Hollow. Not to meet me—certainly, it was a patient leaving. Few times had I seen anyone so sickly. The woman was no more than a scrap of rag—thin, waiflike. Her skin was pale. A little black was left in her hair, but most of it looked to be prematurely gray. I could see the woman was no more than eighteen or twenty, despite her paleness and gray hair, but her pallor was so poor. Her humors were textbook phlegmatic though no textbook would have illustrated so extreme a case except in a chapter on cadavers. And this was the state of the patient leaving the care of the Winter sisters!

"Good evening, mademoiselle," I said. "Is it much farther?"

"Is what much farther?" she said meekly, sickly.

"Hope Hollow. The Winter sisters. I have... an appointment."

I cannot say why I lied. Perhaps it was compassion for this patient. To tell the truth to her, I would have had to explain the futility of the treatments she'd undergone with the witch doctors. That would spoil any of her hopes for a cure, hope being the only value she could have taken from an encounter with the Winter sisters. The chill of shame, wet clothes, and the evening air had taken all my anger.

"Then I won't keep you, sir." She started to leave, but I held out my hand, and she stopped.

"You will be careful, won't you?" I said.

"Of what?"

"Of what? Of a thousand things, but chiefly of that rabid panther that's terrorizing the countryside!"

"Oh, I shouldn't worry in the least about him." Then she turned away, at the same time drawing her arms up and tucking her head down toward her chest, as if she caught a sudden chill.

The pitiable creature... I should have asked to see to her condition. I should have asked what was wrong. I should have done so much just at that very moment, before all the other moments to come, but I did nothing, for I did not have my medical kit or my traveling bag, and I felt a sopping, limping, dreadful fool.

I came around two more bends in the path and saw my destination. Hope Hollow was a clearing curled up in the shadow of a rocky hill. The violet light of the evening sky was just enough for me to survey the place. The trees gave way to a farmstead: corn, pole beans, sweet potatoes, and watermelon vines. The house was a simple dogtrot cabin. A common roof connected its two little structures, forming a breezeway between. A chimney on each end puffed smoke. Low fences kept the vegetation away from the swept dirt yard. A kitchen garden bloomed with tomatoes, eggplants, kale, and collards. Four orange trees were there, improbably alive and fruit laden at this latitude. A doe-eyed mule was finishing its supper from a wooden bucket. The farm was in splendid order, ready to settle into night. Fireflies winked in the distance. The first stars appeared over the trees.

Had I come to the right place? Where were the atmospheric crows? The eerie wisps of Spanish moss and spider silk? I'd met a patient on the road, so that must have been Hope Hollow.

I climbed the steps to the cabin's porch. The door was open, spilling candlelight into the purple evening. My hobbled footfalls were louder than a knock. I stepped up, forward, and inside. A weathered pine table filled much of the room. Two benches flanked it. They were yellow and decorated with vines and little purple flowers. Lanterns hanging from the ceiling burned cool and white. On the mantel were corn-husk dolls, some fresh and green, others moth-eaten, which depicted men and women at their labors. One chap pushed a straw broom. An older woman peered down the sights of a rifle. Flanking the fire were iron implements: the standard poker, pot handle, and spoon, but also a wicked serrated device three feet long and a polished scythe a full head taller than me.

Drying on a rack near the fire was women's laundry, including the unmentionables. Before I could avert my eyes, I heard movement. A woman was entering through the back door. She was no more than thirty. Her hands held her apron up before her, into which she'd gathered a dozen yellow-speckled eggs. She started when she saw me, but she didn't drop the eggs.

"I'm sorry, the door was open," I said, stepping back toward the threshold. "I shouldn't have—"

The servant woman composed herself and dismissed my apology. "No, it's all right. We have people in and out at all hours. Middle of the night, sometimes."

Her face was angular and fetching. Her nose—straight, sharp, a bit long—introduced intelligent brown eyes that had stared too long at small jobs. When she saw I was lost for words, her expression turned kindly. I suddenly wished she were a town lady rather than a housemaid for witch doctors. Would that I could make her acquaintance in more fitting circumstances.

"Let me put down these eggs, and I'll help you," she said.

"But ma'am, I'm not here for help. Dr. Aubrey Waycross, at your service."

"The new doctor." The woman put the eggs into straw-lined containers. She worked very deliberately, taking great care with each egg. Something about her work was ominous. "Did you come for supper, then?"

"No, not that either." I shifted on my feet, which reawakened the pain in my joints.

"Well, I'll be serving supper soon. And if you don't need any help..."

My righteous anger had survived the long walk, the dousing in the Alcovy, and the off-puttingly pleasant appearance of the house, but then it caught in my throat. "That is, ma'am, I don't believe the Winter sisters should be giving out any help. They need to leave off their practice. Let the townsfolk get proper treatment. This is what I mean to tell the old women. Where are they?"

"Mm-hmm," she said. Her voice held a minor lilt of curiosity, as though she'd discovered an unusual red corn kernel in a pile of yellow ones. She brushed her hands on her apron. The blue and white checks in her dress were vivid and sharp. When she moved, I caught a flash of iridescence, of firefly wings.

"What happened to your leg, Doctor?" she asked while studying one of the eggs. It was too small to be a chicken's. Partridge? Quail?

"I fell in the creek," I said. "Now, please, I need to say my piece to the Winter sisters."

"You already have."

"Ah, but... What?"

"I'm Rebecca Winter." The young woman fixed me with a hard stare. "My sister Sarah's upstairs. And Effie is... Well, who knows where Effie gets to."

I felt like I'd been hit by a dockside boxer. "I am so sorry. I didn't know that you... I thought you were granny women. I'd heard from the people in Lawrenceville, and I had a particular vision in my head..."

"You're not the first one to make that mistake, Aubrey." She turned back to her work, freeing me of her transfixing glare. "And you're not the first one who's told us to take our evil herbs and get out of town. Others have been much more intimidating than a damp doctor. But we get a lot more patients than protests. I think, on balance, that the town would rather we stay around, so long as we stay up in Hope Hollow."

"Yes, but—"

"Mm-hmm?"

"The town isn't sensible enough to know what's best for itself." My sally against the Winter sisters was fizzling just as completely as my sally against Thumb. Fortunately, it was less public. "I don't intend to be intimidating, only rational."

Rebecca picked up a rolling pin. I was alarmed until she applied it to a mound of dough.

"Mm-hmm," she repeated.

The dough stuck to the rolling pin. Rebecca tossed on more flour. The puff of white issuing from her fingers was like a trick of prestidigitation.

"Aubrey, I need to finish supper, which I can't do while you're here. But I also can't let you limp back to your hayloft like a wounded deer."

I did not want to be eaten. And how did she know that I lived in the hayloft? I supposed no distance was too far for gossip.

Rebecca left her cooking and perused her shelves. Above some molasses and coffee were other jars, whose contents I could not identify. She took a squat glass container down from a high shelf, unscrewed the top, and smelled it. "Slippery elm, peppermint leaves, apple vinegar, and red-oak bark. The poultice doesn't smell so good, but it will help."

"I don't believe, mademoiselle, that such a cataplasm will work for me. And I haven't come for treatment. Quite the opposite, Miss Winter..."

Rebecca already had a glob of the thick brownish goo on her fingertips. "Aubrey, if it's medicine, it doesn't matter whether you believe in it or not. Now, take down your trousers so I can apply the poultice."

"Miss Winter, I cannot! We've hardly met!"

From above us, a paroxysm of laughter exploded between every plank in the ceiling. It felt as if the whole house was laughing.

Rebecca's expression turned stormy. "Sarah!" she cried.

Above us was a dancing of feet and sliding sounds of stockings on wood. Boards creaked. A mist of dust came from the floorboards overhead. Then a younger sister came down the ladder, touching none of the rungs, only sliding down the rails. She alit on the tips of her feet and then turned on them, facing us.

"You called, Sister?" asked Sarah. Her blond hair looked like flaxen straw on a broom. Sarah looked at least five years the junior of her sister. I could read that from the skin around her eyes. She had a small nose and small eyes. I would not have immediately marked her as Rebecca's sister. Even their coloration was different, but I did have a flash of recognition. This Sarah had been the one hiding behind a red handkerchief at Thumb's medicine show. She'd stuck her tongue out at me when she caught me staring.

"Dr. Waycross is suffering," said Rebecca. "Don't make my patient feel worse."

Sarah grinned wickedly. "Your patient, is he? Well, he's not behaving like one. Nor much like a gentleman, either. Wouldn't it be better, sister, to kick him out on his rump? Then he could try coming in again, and with the benefit of practice, he might make a better first impression."

"It would do no good. He sprained his rump falling down in the creek."

"But what do you want me for?" said Sarah. "He's not the sort for my remedies. You can tell that just by looking at him. By the company he keeps. I saw him talking with Boatwright."

I held up my hand. "The town's doctor and the town's pastor must be acquainted, mustn't they?"

"You're the town's doctor already, are you?" said Sarah. "How many veins have you bled, and how many limbs have you lopped off? Any fevers broken? Any dyspepsia eased? Nothing. Can't even cure your own sprained ankle. And you won't let Rebecca do it. And you won't trust my remedies."

"What sorts of remedies are those?" I asked. I was unable to defend myself on any of the other charges.

"Horseshit," said Sarah.

"Beg pardon?" I said.

"Horseshit," she repeated, exaggerating each vowel. "Though not actual horseshit. That's Rebecca's medicine."

Rebecca lifted a finger. "Sheep nanny tea is—"

Sarah cut her off. "It's much better to go to a real doctor, right, Aubrey? A Hippocratic who'll bleed you out of your feet and rinse your asshole with ipecac."

She was trying to rile me up with her foul mouth and uneducated opinions. I diagnosed her with a bilious humor, likely to manifest as a sour stomach and persistent joint pains, besides her acid temperament. "If by 'Hippocratic,' you mean a student of rigorous medicine, and if by 'ipecac,' you mean a scientific and time-tested remedy, then yes, it is much better to go to that sort of doctor." I took a breath. "We bleed and blister because it's what our patients need to get well. I wish I had my lancet with me right now. Extracting a few ounces of blood would put me right again."

Sarah grinned. "Everybody thinks his horseshit is the only kind that doesn't stink."

"That's enough, you two," Rebecca interrupted. She'd wiped the glob of medicinal goo on the corner of her apron and had picked up the fire poker. She broke a cindered log with a sharp jab, sending sparks up the chimney. "Aubrey, she talks that way to be provocative. She succeeds only in raising arterial pressure."

"Which is good for you, isn't it, Aubrey? Makes the heart beat faster, fonder?"

I nodded. She was right, unfortunately. I tried to put my weight on my injured leg and vainly hoped again for my lancet.

"Has he seen Effie yet?" Sarah asked.

"No," snapped Rebecca. "No, he hasn't. Is she even here?"

"She came back. She's outside. Look, he's not going to be the type for breaking chicken bones with me and burying them. And if he won't take your herbal poultice, then it's either Effie or he goes away with a bum leg and a busted rump."

I started to mention how they'd let that poor waif with the gray hair go, but then I stopped. I supposed not all ailments could be cured in a single visit. Perhaps they'd given her a poultice on her rump, and all had supposed that to be a good cure. Good intentions, bad medicine.

I didn't know what choice I had. I couldn't permit Rebecca to apply her poultice, and Sarah's cursing wasn't going to cure anything. Dare I suggest that either Rebecca or Sarah escort me back to town? I daren't. It was unthinkable, a gentleman and a lady alone on the road at night. Nor could I ask for lodging. A gentleman staying overnight, unchaperoned, in the home of strange women was a greater scandal. I would have to take my chances on the road. Even with wild animals sniffing at my heels, that was preferable to dishonor. I wished then that I'd taken Snell's rusted gun.

Rebecca fixed me with her eyes, considering. "All right, go see Effie," she said, exhaling. "Tell her to come in for supper." She indicated the back door with a nod of her head.

"Thank you, Miss Winter." I bowed to her. How improbable my thanks felt. I'd stormed down with notions of driving out the Winter sisters like serpents from the Emerald Isle, yet there I was, meekly agreeing to meet Effie rather than exiting with dignity.

"If she prefers to," Rebecca added.

"Excuse me?"

"If she can," corrected Sarah, with strange insistence.

Sarah's words did not placate her older sister, and I could make no sense of them.

"Come on, city doc, come meet the youngest." Sarah opened the back door of the cabin, inviting me to leave.

I took the invitation, not at all sure what I would find there.

"Hey, did you see a deer on the way up here? Dead deer, dying deer?"

"Nothing of the sort."

Sarah nodded slowly. Then she called into the night. "Effie. Someone to see you." She didn't wait for a response. The cabin's back door closed behind me.

The purple evening had vanished, replaced by a denser air. The stars were weak behind the mist. The yard around the Winters' cabin was lifeless. The animals had gone to their folds.

A girl was sitting at the edge of the porch, her legs dangling so that her toes brushed the ground. She leaned against the horizontal rail, her chin placed upon her crossed arms. Beside her was an enormous washtub filled to the brim with water.

It was the woman I'd seen on the road to Hope Hollow, the one I took for a patient, so sickly did she look. This was Effie, the third sister, and supposedly a healer! She couldn't cure her own phlegmatic humors, so how was she supposed... but then I remembered how I could not bleed my own swollen ankle, and I exhaled, letting out my surprise and confusion.

"Good evening," I managed to say to her.

Her graying hair was pulled back in a bun. She would have achieved a more haunting effect had she let it fall in loose, dirty waves past her shoulders.

"I hadn't known we'd meet again so soon. You were going the other way, you see..."

"Did Rebecca and Sarah send you?" she asked, not turning toward me.

"I'm not sure," I admitted. "I believe I have been swept here by confusion."

"Lots of people are."

For a moment, we contemplated the evening side by side. Last year's withered leaves crinkled beneath the hoof-falls of deer. A flashing white stripe showed the trail of a skunk. Up in the canopy must have been thousands of birds, or millions, but they were silent and invisible. In front of those, fireflies circled and traced the breezes.

"I thought you were a patient, not a healer," I confessed. "You looked so—"

"Are doctors never sick, Dr. Waycross?" Effie untangled herself from the railing and stood up. Unfolded, she was taller than me and taller than Rebecca. Her color was better, too, or she'd found a better light. She looked more ordinary.

"I'm sorry, Aubrey. I've got to go in for supper," she said.

"I don't mean to trouble you. I've got a long and limping return to Lawrenceville ahead of me—"

"I hope you feel better." Effie started toward the door.

"But you haven't... What I mean is—not that I would accept—your sisters told me you were going to offer me some type of cure? For my swollen joints and bruised coccyx. It's nothing, my leg will hold out, but—"

"Nothing's good for you," said Effie.

For the first time, she turned to face me, and I caught my breath. Her eyes—I knew her eyes. They were the same pale gray as Eva's eyes. The face and body around them could not be more different, though. Eva's red hair and sanguine constitution would have evaporated Effie's phlegmatic humor like a puddle beneath the noonday sun, but in their eyes, they were the same, the very same, down to the faint lines of yellow that traced the outlines of the irises.

I said nothing. Her pronouncement had no rational reply. Wordlessly, Effie went inside for supper, and I was alone in the night.

The doctor was gone. The sisters had eaten their supper. Effie had only two spoonfuls, and Rebecca had eaten even less than that. They were cleaning the dishes out on the porch in the candle- and starlit twilight. Sarah watched Effie fetch the water up from the spring in two enormous tin pitchers. It was confounding to see such a slight girl carry so much weight without wrenching her arms out of joint. Effie set the pitchers on the porch, and it felt to Sarah as if the cabin groaned with the weight.

"Thank you," said Rebecca. "That's more than I need."

"I can do the washing up," said Effie. "It's no trouble."

A faint color touched Effie's temples. The doctor's visit had disturbed the delicate equilibrium of her mood. Sarah's own balance had been disturbed ever since that deer. The deer had been dead. Sarah knew a dead deer from a live one even better than she knew a dead person from a live one. No animal could come back from such a terrible mauling. But when Effie had knelt beside it, the creature had stood up and gamboled away.

"No, Effie," said Rebecca as a breeze came unexpectedly from the mountainside, tousling the trees. Loose leaves fluttered. A pigeon started from its roost. Its neighbors cooed and scratched.

"Oh, let her do the washing if she wants," Sarah said.

"You could help," said Rebecca, who picked up a serving platter from the pile of dirty dishes. "With your hands, I mean, and not your opinions."

"I never saw much good in a plate," Sarah said. "Best thing is to throw 'em into the woods and let the squirrels lick 'em clean." She glanced at Effie then tucked her thumbs into her elbows and puffed up her chest, to speechify. "A plate doesn't do anything that your hands can't do just as well. Give 'em a quick rinse, wipe 'em on your sides, and what dishes have you got left? Nothing, that's what."

Effie picked up one of the pewter plates and dipped it in the washbasin.

Rebecca reclaimed the plate from her and began working it with a cloth. "How very civilized. Why do we even bother to cook our meat? We could gnaw it right off the bone."

"Nobody would care," Sarah said.

"I would," said Rebecca. "Mother would if she were here."

A feline howl broke the night. Ten thousand unseen birds took wing, and the wind, which had been blowing down from the mountain, reversed as the pigeons fled from the sound.

"Why," Sarah said, "there's Mother now. Think she's using a plate?"

Effie dropped a cup. It bounced twice against the pine boards and rolled off the porch.

"Aw, Effie, I didn't mean—"

Effie folded her fingers together and brought them close to her face. Sarah knew it wasn't a prayer. None of them knew how to pray.

"That is why I don't want her to do the washing up," snapped Rebecca. "She can't keep her mind on it."

Sarah hopped the porch rail and grabbed the cup from a mud puddle. "Not broken!"

"Give it here, Sarah." Rebecca reached out her hand. "I'll wash it."

Ignoring her, Sarah held out the cup to Effie, whose hands were still in front of her face.

"Give me the cup." Rebecca moved to grab it.

Sarah tossed it into the washbasin, splashing soapy water onto Rebecca's apron. "I wonder if Waycross is any better at washing up than at doctoring."

"Maybe next time, we'll see."

"You think he'll come back? He's too much of a fool to come back."

Rebecca plunged both hands into the washing. The sodden remnants of potatoes, biscuits, and greens swirled against her forearms. "Foolishness is pathological. He's only ignorant, and fortunately, ignorance is curable."

"You still believe that? After what happened? You didn't succeed in curing it when we lived in town."

"In some people, ignorance is planted far deeper." Rebecca caught hold of a fork and used a fingernail to pick away the burnt crumbs stuck between the tines. "Just go, both of you."

Sarah looked at her older sister: the candlelight from the open door cast a hard line across Rebecca's face. An oily shimmer of grease floated on top of the gray, soapy water. The panther howled again, the sound softer and farther away.

As I climbed out of Hope Hollow, the moon rose above the encircling hills. I could see well enough to stay to the path. At the Alcovy ford, I proceeded with great care. I used two oak limbs as staves to keep me from falling headlong into the black current. I took comfort in the small noises of the forest. My pace synchronized with the rhythmic chanting of crickets. The chirrups of small mammals skittering away told me that they smelled no creature more dangerous than myself.

I ruminated on the Winter sisters. They hadn't asked for money. That thought startled me, and I immediately patted at my pockets, feeling for my coin purse. Foolishness: I didn't have any money in it anyway. The only dollar I still possessed was secured in the sole of my damp left shoe.

What did their spurious cures offer that my true cures could not? Was Rebecca truly trying to heal me with an ointment? Sarah wanted a rise from me, but to what end: my improvement or her amusement? As for Effie, I could not hazard a hypothesis. I scratched at my temple, where a mosquito had begun its feast.

The townsfolk's belief in the Winter sisters seemed even more perplexing since I had met them. Simpletons would always fall for the easy tricks of hucksters and granny women, but the Winter sisters were neither of those. I couldn't classify them, and that itched worse than the mosquito bite.

My left foot caught the edge of a root, and I stumbled. It was only a missed step, and I was on good footing again in an instant, but I realized that I felt no complaints from my knees or bruises, even in those contortions. I took a moment to consider and realized I was almost back to Lawrenceville. I'd gone miles without noticing the soreness of my spine or the sprains of my joints. I hadn't needed a bleeding after all, nor a red-oak cataplasm. Time was the correct cure, helped along by mild exercise and cool air.

I strained my eyes to catch a glimpse of the courthouse square, the off-kilter steeple of the church, or the brass sign at Honest Alley. All I saw was featureless vegetation. The dull glow of the sky did not penetrate the foliage. The woods were a solid expanse of black.

Then a part of that blackness seemed blacker. Solid. Large. Moving.

The flash of a firefly reflected from the creature's eyes. I held my breath, hoping to disappear from its attentions, but when I stopped, I heard a change in its throaty respiration. It had seen me.

I could run but didn't know if I could outrun whatever was in the underbrush. My heart shuddered. My palms turned to ice. I had to run because to do nothing meant giving myself over to destruction.

Then the darkness coughed and swore.

"Damn it, just the doctor again," said Pearson, standing up from his hiding place, still holding his gun.

"You're never gonna get that panther," said Hodgson, crawling out from beside him.

I'd never been more grateful to see two utter fools.

4

AND THE MOON IN A SILVER BOTTLE

Sarah waited in the glade with her gun. She'd left a brace of dead pigeons in the center of the clearing, but the panther was too clever for that. Perhaps it wanted its meat fresh. The pigeons in the trees above carried on with their noisy lives.

If a deer came by, Sarah decided, she would shoot it and clean it for the meat. If Boatwright came by, she'd shoot him too, but his carcass would go to rot. Even a rabid animal like the panther would turn up its nose at preacher meat.

Clumsy steps approached from the distance, and Sarah surrendered any hopes of a kill. She took her finger off the trigger of her rifle but didn't emerge from her blind. Better to see who was coming her way. The smart money was on some hunter: Pearson, Hodgson, or Pa Everett. Possibly, it was Waycross again, lost on some errand, or the medicine man leading his wagon to the next town.

"Hallo, Miss Sarah? Are... are you here?"

"Ouida Bell?"

As Sarah came down, two dozen pairs of white wings went up. Ouida Bell pressed her hand to her chest in surprise. Her bonnet was a bright and pretty thing, bedecked with flowers. The birds cooed at it.

"Why, Ouida Bell, I don't believe I've ever seen you without... without anybody around. Seems like you always have a crowd. Or you're sitting in a whole bottle of glue in ruined clothes."

Ouida Bell tucked a loose blond curl back into her bonnet. "That's... Yes, that's very true." She twisted the toe of one shiny leather shoe in the earth and, too late, realized it was half an inch deep in pigeon droppings. "I've been up to Hope Hollow, and Miss Rebecca said you'd be out here."

"You came all this way by yourself?"

"Yes."

"And you weren't frightened?"

"I wasn't very frightened. I've got to live, panther or no panther, haven't I? Life goes on."

"I'm figuring," said Sarah, looking the girl up and down, "that you've got an itch that a vegetable compound can't cure. Need something to get all the glue off, even from underneath your underdrawers?"

Ouida Bell swallowed a grimace. "I need a kind of medicine... not truly a medicine... I told Rebecca about it, and she said it was your sort of doing."

"I see," said Sarah.

For all her faults, no one could accuse her older sister of being a miser of patients. Rebecca knew there were troubles—people, rather—who would not be cured by witch hazel or mustard seeds. "I don't have anything here but a gun. Is this a trouble I could shoot for you?"

"No! I mean, I suppose it would work, but I don't want to hurt anyone. It's the suitors—"

Sarah spat. Her mother had done a fair trade in love charms. "No magic in making a boy fall in love with you, Ouida Bell. Your dress unlaces in the front, don't it?"

Ouida Bell laughed. "It's too many suitors. Jimmy. Randall. Pendleton—though he's ten years too old for me—"

Sarah narrowed her eyes. Few wooers found their way up to Hope Hollow. Not even Everett had gone up there when he was courting Rebecca. She had dragged her sisters to town for his sake.

"—the other Jimmy, crook-nose Jimmy. Crogan. Pike. Perry and his brother. Philip."

"My heart is breaking for you, pretty girl," Sarah said, cutting her short.

"But what can I—"

"Tell 'em to stick it in the horseshit."

"But I—" Ouida Bell nearly fainted in protest.

"Not exactly those words. Just tell 'em to go sniff up some other tree."

"My mother. My mother doesn't want me to offend a soul. I couldn't say anything like that."

"The cruel truth is better than a cruel lie."

"But can't you give me something that's not so—"

"Cruel?"

"Well, yes."

They stared at one another as the pigeons cooed and crapped around them.

"The quickest way to lose your reputation," said Sarah, biting her lip, "is to be seen whispering with a witch."

"Maybe that would scare off the goodwives," Ouida Bell said. "Maybe it would scare my mother. But the boys wouldn't mind it a bit. Nobody sensible is afraid of witch stories."

"Yet you believe I've got some charm that can help you in your current predicament."

"A trick, maybe."

Tricks, charms—Sarah's mother made charms. Not so many love charms as "loveless charms," sold to goodwives who didn't want their husbands to press other children on them. The men-folk always wanted another hand around the fields, but the women knew a child took more than it gave—in raising, in feeding, in love and worry—and mothers knew the perils of childbearing, leaving the older children motherless and the husband alone to find some younger bride. They also knew the pains of a child's early death. Women sunbaked by fieldwork would come to the Winters' door in the twilight hours, and Sarah's mother gave them sachets of herbs or drams of black liquid or twine curiously knotted into a shape a bit larger than a thimble. Sometimes, they were wrapped in scraps of paper, decorated with writing. Sarah could never decipher them, but she loved the heavy black lines and the sharp angles: Old World workings or maybe just figures copied from books. Effie wasn't but a little thing back then. Sarah had been able to keep her close. Sarah shook her head. Ouida Bell wanted a loveless charm. Her work was not like her mother's. Her mother was dead, buried, rotted, and returned to the soil.

"I thought maybe I could get a skunk," said Ouida Bell. "For the smell. But I work in a candy store, and that wouldn't be good for business."

Sarah pursed her lips. Many tricks came to mind, but not all suited Ouida Bell nor her own sense of entertainment.

"What about a toad, then?" asked Ouida Bell. "Maybe warts on the end of my nose, and if'n I want to start sparking with someone for true, I could have you take the warts off, Miss Sarah."

"That's a damn fool old story," said Sarah. "You can't get warts from a toad."

"But doesn't—"

"Try it all you like." Sarah threw up her hands. "Take all kinds of toads and rub 'em on your forehead, on your arms, wherever you please. It'll never come up a wart." She leaned forward and spoke conspiratorially: "I've done it to myself and to lots of other people." Sometimes even in their knowing. "Never come up a wart. And nothin' gets rid of a wart but time."

Ouida Bell shook her head. "My momma will steal a dishrag and wash the warts away with it. Seven times a day for seven days. I've seen it."

Your momma just wanted a reason to steal dishrags, thought Sarah. Then an idea appeared. "You need to steal someone's underdrawers."

Ouida Bell blushed again, but not as crimson as before.

"Not just someone," Sarah continued, barely able to hide her glee. "Boatwright's. Get Boatwright's underdrawers. And you gotta hang them up in the window. Nothing will put a boy off more than the preacher's underdrawers hanging in your window."

"But... how will I get them? And what will Momma—or anybody—say? About me or the preacher? They'll think vile things."

So vile they'll run the preacher out of town, and so much the better for us all. "I'll steal them for you. No extra charge."

"I can't do it, Miss Sarah."

"But fancy you could. What a trick that would be."

"I couldn't do it."

"That's your whole trouble, isn't it?" Sarah frowned. "You've got to find a little meanness. Even a dram."

"If'n I can't?"

Anybody can find meanness, thought Sarah.

"What am I to do if I can't find my meanness?" asked Ouida.

Sarah sighed. "Well, we'll put unpleasantness into your suitors' minds."

"How?"

"We'll grind up something foul. You'll give 'em a glass of water when they come courting, and stir in your special powder. They won't feel it until later, when they puke. And then, when they think of you, they'll feel queasy. No affection can overpower nausea."

Ouida Bell nodded. "Not anything that would hurt them, right? What will we grind up? A frog?"

Sarah made a sour face. "You ever tasted a frog? Tastes almost like a fresh-plucked hen. Folks love frogs' legs when they're fried in good, rich fat. No, go ask my sister for some asafetida. Tell her you've got a cold you can't shake in your lungs. But don't hang the leaves around your neck like she tells you. Mash them up, and soak them in clear liquor for a week. Give the bottle a hard shake three times a day. And that's what you'll put into the boys' water glasses. You think you can manage that?"

"Reckon so!" Ouida Bell gave Sarah a spontaneous, affectionate squeeze. "What do I pay you?"

Intertwined pieces of red, white, and blue cloth made a banner over the courthouse door. The bare boards of the floor were painted in alternating squares of black and white, like a chessboard. I could not help but focus on imperfections in the execution—squares not on the square, drips of white paint on the black. A dais at the front supported an ordinary table and a Windsor chair. Fruit crates were stacked up for a lectern. Draped on the far wall was a flag of the United States showing twenty-one stars. Lawrenceville hadn't kept up with the times.

"Hear ye, hear ye! Let's all take our seats!" said Mayor Richardson, climbing onto the dais. I found a place in the third row.

"Fellow townsmen, wives, and assorted guests," Richardson began, "I wish to present the latest intelligence from Milledgeville on our bid for the county seat."

Richardson had gotten a letter. Mine, then, must have gone out on the return route.

"Hell with Milledgeville!" somebody shouted from the back row. "What are you doing about the panther?"

Richardson shifted on his feet. I noticed that now, unlike when I met him in Honest Alley, he was wearing shoes. "A pair of huntsmen, Pearson and Hodgson, have been engaged—"

My snort of derision was as loud as any of the others among the assembled crowd.

"Nevertheless, they are huntsmen, and either they will kill the creature, or the creature will die on its own time."

"And what are we supposed to do while we wait for it to die?" shouted someone else. "I can't make it to Hope Hollow for my trick knee. It was always too far, and now with the panther, I'm afeared."

I stood up. "I am a trained physician, operating from the... facilities... located just behind Snell's store. I would gladly treat your ailment, any ailment."

"Sawbones here would fix your trick knee all right," said a woman whom I wished I could have identified. "He'll lop it off in twenty seconds and give you your trick knee back as a souvenir. 'Put it up on the mantelpiece. It won't trouble you there.'"

There was laughter, and I sat down, red-faced and chastened. I should have replied with a clever retort, a verbal riposte to turn the laughter back at them, but I am not so clever on my feet, and I did have, among my possessions, a rather large bone saw.

"Ladies and gentlemen, may we please get back to the Milledgeville letter?" asked a flustered Richardson. "The panther is another matter for another time—"

"How can we be the county seat if we're all sick and dying because we can't get to see the Winter sisters?"

"How can we be the county seat if we're suffering witches in our midst?" That was Lizbeth Samples. Her tone was the same as when she'd berated Snell in front of me on the day of my arrival. "I think this is all their doing. Part of their scheme. The panther is their demon familiar."

"Pastor didn't run them far enough out of town," said Mrs. Maltbie. "Should have run them farther, I think."

Mrs. Snell puffed up. "Eula Mae Maltbie, I know that you've been to see the Winter sisters for your summer complaint. How can you be against—"

Richardson held up both hands. "Now folks, I have to read this to you because that's the purpose of this meeting, and the Milledgeville folks won't be pleased if I haven't done the democratic process, or some such. Panthers and Winter sisters aside, please, just for the minute, then you can go out into the hog yard and tussle."

"Really, Mayor, this matter is far more serious—" started Mrs. Maltbie.

"You will remember, I'm sure, that the petition of April twenty-second was well received, but so was the petition from Rest Haven. Our committee has learned..."

Richardson's speech failed to overcome the musk of too many bodies in too small a space and the hum of horseflies. The emotion was too high to keep silence: the matter of the panther, of the Winter sisters, all commingled. Women whispered behind me, and my ears wandered to the gossip.

"It's what I've been telling you all along." A quick glance confirmed the speaker to be Miss Lizbeth Samples. "Witches. That's the reason my cows get the tremors. My boys, too."

"Maybe it's just sour milk," said Mrs. Snell.

"Sour something," said Mrs. Parr, Ouida Bell's mother.

"I saw the middle one, in her red kerchief, walking past my yard. She stopped and picked something. And right then was when the cows went blinky, and the milk. I knew they were witches, but none of you believed me."

Their conversation was attracting glances, but Richardson droned on like a schoolmaster.

"Milk just goes sour sometimes," said Mrs. Parr. "Witches or no witches."

"But this milk is more sour than sour. It's poison, baleful poison."

"Now, really, that's nonsense," said Mrs. Parr, blowing a dismissive breath out her nose.

"Just 'cause you don't believe it doesn't mean it ain't true," said Mrs. Maltbie, raising her volume.

"Just 'cause you do believe it," said Mrs. Parr, "doesn't mean it is true."

"Not true? My cow's tail fell off." Lizbeth stood as she spoke, and the weight of her presence loomed over both doubters and believers.

All eyes turned from the mayor to the woman seething with righteous fury. Richardson couldn't keep up his speechifying.

"My cow's tail fell off," repeated Lizbeth, and she produced from her apron pocket a shrunken piece of brown leather tipped with white hairs. She whipped the object to the floor and hit the boards with a sharp crack. "Believe or don't believe. It doesn't put the tail back on a cow. Tell me that's not witchery."

Boatwright was absent from the meeting. He was preaching a circuit in Jefferson, and I was grateful for his absence. He might have seized Lizbeth's dramatic moment to launch into a sermon even worse than Richardson's speechifying.

I was compelled to speak. If the town were to be cured of its fascination with the Winter sisters, the idea of the Winters as powerful witches first needed to be dispelled.

"Miss Samples," I said as the crowd's eyes all turned toward us, "I assure you that you needn't resort to supernatural malice to explain these incidents. Any number of natural causes might spoil milk, and there are one or two that cause a cow's tail to fall off. Chronic bovine bubo comes to mind."

"Are you a physician of beasts, Dr. Waycross?" growled Lizbeth.

"No, but we share many of our infirmities with our farmyard companions."

"That's a worse heresy than denying the witches," said Lizbeth. "You went to Hope Hollow, I hear. Have they ensorcelled you?"

"Quite the opposite, Miss Samples, but I still must defend them on charges for which they are wholly innocent. No one's poisoned your cow, and there are no such things as witches."

Lizbeth fumed in her own anger, and I fancied I could see wisps of smoke coming from her pores. Then the tolling of a bell shattered the fragile silence. The ringing seemed to strike at the top of my spine. It was not the church bell, nor was it a fire bell. The air was fresh with the aroma of smoked ham.

"No sense keeping on here," said Richardson from the podium. "We'll get to our business when the doctor doesn't have some speech to make and when our huntsmen get that panther. Go on, then, see to that bell."

"I'll bet it's the medicine show," said Snell.

We all trotted out to Honest Alley with a sense of relief at the escape. The medicine show had indeed returned, braving the specter of the woods, though Salmon Thumb had abandoned his banjo. He was now dressed like a Quaker, all in black, save for a white wig and a few silver buckles on his hat and shoes.

"Friends, friends," he said, his open arms reaching to us all. "No, I should say, 'fellow mortals.' For it is our sad, sad lot, you and me, that we will die."

His audience, as one, looked at their feet. His appearance and demeanor were so changed from before that I was startled into silence. I supposed I should intervene when his speech made its turn to inevitable hucksterism, but for the time, I wanted to see how it unfolded.

"You want me singing and dancing for your entertainment," said Thumb. "Someday, I will again pick up my banjo and play for you. But this morning, I come with a message such as your pastor might preach. Though I'll be less long-winded and more interesting."

That raised only a meager chuckle out of the crowd, which was still pensive from the revelations of Lizbeth Samples and her cow's tail.

"We are mortal, friends. How many husbands lose their wives on the joyous day of birth? And how many wives lose their husbands to the thresher or to cold lead shot? How many of us have scars from smallpox where lovers once planted kisses? Oh, friends, my friends, few and evil are the days of our lives." Thumb turned his eyes to the sky. "It is the sad truth, my friends, that we are born to die, and the dead cannot be brought back to life."

He must have been surprised at the power of his words, to have put us so quickly into a somber mood, but we'd brought our somber mood with us to his show. Thumb took off his hat and put it against his chest. His gray hair was messy. His entire face seemed to be slumping.

"But I bring you something new. Different. Unexpected. Wonderful!" Thumb's voice rose in pitch and enthusiasm with each staccato sentence. "Listen! Don't miss out! Investigate! Place your finger here"—he touched his nose—"to assure you of your senses. Pinch the soft skin of your elbow, here"—and he did—"so that you know you are awake. For my news may seem like a dream."

I could hear the collective heartbeat of the crowd thumping in time with his rhythm.

Thumb opened his black Quaker vestments and revealed a pocket with ermine lining. From this, he took a bottle as large and wide as a port decanter. It seemed far too heavy to lug around in a cloak pocket. He held it aloft in both hands. His arthritic pinky finger stuck out at an odd angle from the rest of his fingers.

"This, my friends, is the best thing that has ever happened."

I burst out in laughter, but I was alone. The rest of the crowd was enraptured. I thought Thumb looked right at me and winked. He and I were the ones laughing, though for different reasons.

"My friends, this is the Elixir Salutis: the Choice Drink of Health, or Health-Bringing Drink, Being a Famous Cordial Drink. A long name, yes, but if all its wonders were listed on the label, we would be here an epoch to recite them."

Finally, the product emerged from the pitch. It was a strange new way to sell the same old swill. What was in this formula that was not in Grove's Tasteless Chill Tonic? For all their promises, these medicines couldn't even take the rheumatism out of Thumb's littlest finger.

"I am asking for your belief, friends. How much does that cost you? Not a penny. To believe is light and easy. It is harder to doubt because to doubt, you must flounder while, all around you, your friends and neighbors are drinking of the elixir of life. You have nothing to gain by doubt but everything to lose. For sure results, have faith."

The group started to move forward like the tide. I'd waited too late to make my rebuttal. Thumb's unusual delivery had kept me silent—or spared me the embarrassment of another ineffectual tirade.

"The Elixir Salutis: the Choice Drink of Health, or Health-Bringing Drink, Being a Famous Cordial Drink will not make you immortal, friends. For we all must die. But no longer will you lament that your elders were taken before their time—nor your children before their prime. Your days will be many and merry. Who loves a dollar more than he loves his life?"

"Not me!" said the crowd.

"No one!" cried Thumb. "No one will go away unblessed. If you are too poor to buy, and if your neighbor will not love you as he loves himself and buy a bottle for you, then I will give you one from my own pocket. For sure results, have faith!"

A great cheer went up from the crowd. Whenever a free bottle—small and brown, sealed with a bit of wax and marked with a plain paper label that read, simply, Elixir—was bestowed, there was joyful weeping and words of blessing.

I stayed in Honest Alley until the crowds thinned. I wanted a word with Thumb without the masses looking on. Finally, all the customers were served. Thumb scratched his mule behind the ears, helping it to settle down. The creature showed its contentment under his ministrations by flopping its ears and yawning, which proved contagious. I yawned in sympathy. Thumb patted the mule on its muzzle and stepped away. He rolled up the funerary backdrop and secured crates of glass bottles with twine. I approached and held out a dollar. It was my last one, wrinkled and wet and ill smelling from its hiding place inside my shoe.

"Hiya, Doc. You want to buy my hollow promises, easy cures, and impossible hopes?" He took my dollar, wrapped it around a bottle of Elixir, and handed both back to me. "Good for what ails you," he said.

"What if what ails me is an arthritic pinky finger?"

Thumb smirked. "You noticed, huh? That's what years of playing the banjo will get you. Reaching way down the neck for those highest notes. It's not a natural way to move your fingers."

"A change of climate would help, as would leaving off the banjo playing."

"That's just what you'd like, isn't it? Have me skedaddle to the desert or at least stop with my ditties. Well, I can't leave off the banjo for too long. That's my only trick. What do you think of the Elixir Salutis?"

I uncorked the bottle. It smelled of alcohol and sugar and flowers, but it tasted of nothing at all. I took another sip, holding the liquid in my mouth and then in my throat. "Nothing."

"Maybe there's nothing wrong with you, Doc." Thumb smiled.

I laughed heartily. "What's in it? A narcotic?"

"It's good for what ails you," repeated Thumb. He took a comb out of his pocket and arranged the hairs on the flanks of his mule.

"A melancholic acetate? Sublimated tincture of white vitriol?"

"Maybe." Thumb worked on a tangle along the mule's neck. "Maybe not."

"I won't spill your secret formula to any of your competitors." I put my finger up to my lips. "Not even the Winter sisters. What's in this bottle?"

"Couldn't say." He didn't meet my eyes.

"The ingredients aren't the important part. You're selling promises."

Thumb slapped the sides of his mule. "I can't tell you what's in it because I don't know. I buy it wholesale from Milledgeville. There's a fellow that gets it from Charleston."

"Doesn't that cut into your profits? Can't you brew up any old thing and put a label on it?"

Thumb looked offended. "Then it wouldn't be the Elixir Salutis, would it? It would be Thumb's Theoretical Tipple. Doesn't have near the ring to it."

"Who'd know the difference?"

"I would," said Thumb. He looked down the swaying back of the mule. "Holtzclaw here would."

"Why's that? You don't feed your mule your patent medicines, do you?"

"Surely, I do when poor Holtzclaw needs them. A sick mule makes your own heart sick. And he's the proof of the medicines. If he gets better, it's because of the ingredients, not the show. Poor fellow can hardly read a label, can't pay attention to a speech. Ain't that right, buddy?"

The mule gave no sign of disagreement.

"We've tried them all, Doctor. Holtzclaw spat out Avery's Celebrated Radish Medicine. Couldn't swallow Edgar's Invigorating Lineament Tablets. He took two draughts of Dr. Pepper morning and night for a year, and he never got any better. But Grove's, we like. Elixir Salutis, we like."

"So you and—Holtzclaw?—believe there's good in these po-tions?" Thumb's face seemed earnest, but he was well practiced in faking honesty. "As much good as you promise?"

Thumb drew in his lips and then let them out with a pop. "No, not that much. But some."

"Then, why not leave off the huckstering? Let your medicine sell itself for what it is?"

Thumb sighed and seemed to crumple. "Wish I could, Doc. But people want a show. Banjos and crazy promises and the moon in a silver bottle. And what I've got is great stuff. So I sing and dance and pontificate and speechify to help them so that they'll take a chance on the few drops of good that I can do for them. You see, Doc? You see?"

He was like the Winter sisters. He wasted good intentions on bad medicine.

Three days after Thumb and his Elixir Salutis had moved on to the next little town, a different gathering occurred in Law-renceville. Two dozen people assembled in front of Parr's Confec-tionary. The window display generally drew them—or the sight of Ouida Bell Parr—but that day, it was the presence of two visitors: Rebecca and Sarah Winter. I could see them myself through the glass, making selections from the confections on offer.

In a few moments, I gathered the sentiment of the crowd. I worried that a mob had gathered to heckle the Winter sisters, and certainly, some in Lawrenceville would have been all too glad to shout curses at those supposed witches, but the people I knew to be partisans of that faction were absent. Perhaps they were mass-ing their forces with Pastor Boatwright. Instead, everyone gath-ered there was sick. Ailing folk of every sort were loitering nearby, hopeful for an audience.

I mingled with the crowd, and all around me, I heard wheezes, eructations, and sharp inhalations of pain. A few bottles of Elixir Salutis and Grove's Tasteless Chill Tonic were passed around, as well as whiskey, turpentine, and spring water. The sight of one man in the crowd chilled me. His illness could bode far worse for the town than any other person's.

"Pearson, what's happened with your panther wound?" I wondered if he might be there to seek treatment for hydrophobia even though it had only been a clawing and not a bite.

"Healing up all right, Doctor," said Pearson, scratching under his cap. "But I've got an itchy trigger finger. All my fingers, really."

"Poison-ivy leaves," said Hodgson.

"Damn it, they weren't poison ivy. Not the right shape. I keep telling you."

I questioned him for the signs of rabies. "No fever, then? No tremors? No fear of water?"

"Naw, Doctor," said Pearson. "Just itchy, like I said."

"Well, good, good." My relief was only provisional. "So, poison ivy. The scientific remedy is to blister the feet, followed by a week of fasting."

Pearson made a sour face. "I'd rather the Winters make up a poultice for me. Hurt a lot less."

I swallowed my rejoinder. Let the silly fellow have his poison-ivy poultices. I did not care what cure he put to his nuisance condition as long as the real danger was in check for the moment.

I noticed a woman who hopped up every time she tried to sit—hemorrhoids. A lancet would dispatch those with satisfying speed, but the woman had suffered her hemorrhoids rather than consulting with me. They should have been my patients, yet they were lined up, in sight of my office, for the Winter sisters.

I clasped my hands behind my back and swayed on my feet. I noticed a ruddy-faced man, his face slicked with the perspiration of fever. He kept his eyes fixed on Rebecca and Sarah. An old man was nearby, using his cane to keep the weight off his trick knee. A bleeding would set him right, but when I caught his eye, he looked away.

"Sir," I said, venturing to address him, "I can have your knee—"

"You'll just cut my leg off, sawbones, and call it a cure," he spat.

"Never! Amputation is only recommended in cases of infection or blood poisoning..."

But he'd already limped away from me on his cane and trick knee, preferring the folk medicine of the Winter sisters to my time-honored Hippocratic cures.

The crowd waited respectfully, but I went inside the store. I was... not angry, precisely, but vexed, confused, indignant: all rare emotions that I did not like. A tiny bell signaled my arrival in the store. The inside of the confectionary was covered in lithographs advertising Pharaoh's Flour. They were beautiful, if mercenary, works of art. A laughing Amenhotep stood before the Great Pyramid, letting milled flour flow from his fingers like desert sands.

"Can I help you, Doctor?" asked Ouida Bell. She pointed at the cases. "Molasses candy is just out of the kettle. Did you want peanut nougat? Horehound drops? Creamed walnuts?"

"Oh, I'm not..." I sputtered. "I haven't thought about it."

She understood and turned back to her paying customers. "Anything else for you ladies?"

"Ginger nuts," said Sarah.

Rebecca gave her sister a puzzled look. "We've got ginger snaps at home."

"A snap isn't a nut, is it?" Sarah rubbed her mouth with the back of her hand.

"No ginger nuts." Rebecca rummaged through her coin purse for what she needed.

"Am I a child?" asked Sarah. "Who are you to tell me what I may and may not have?"

Rebecca glared at her sister. "Sarah, what are you trying—"

"I'll buy the ginger nuts," I said, trying to hush the argument. I had a more pressing issue. "How many would you like, Miss Sarah?"

"Aubrey, you don't need to," said Rebecca. "She doesn't even like ginger nuts."

"Three pounds, Dr. Waycross!" Sarah clapped her hands. "Wrapped in ribbons."

"As the lady wishes," I said, looking toward Rebecca.

Ouida Bell smirked as she measured the ginger nuts. I had the dollar Thumb had returned to me, and I gave it over. We watched as Ouida Bell secured the nuts with a handsome knot of silk ribbons.

Sarah accepted the wrapped box with a wide grin. "Why, thank you, Aubrey. I'm glad I could help you feel better."

"I don't understand."

"You want to make a peace offering," Sarah said. "Show us that you feel like an imbecile about your visit. But you can't say that. Too stiff an upper lip. So, thanks for the ginger nuts."

She walked to the shop windows and pressed her nose against the glass. People in the crowd looked up her squashed nostrils.

"Let me pay you for the nuts, Aubrey," said Rebecca, blushing.

"No, it was my choice," I said, not at all certain that it was.

Through the glass, I could hear children's laughter. Rebecca looked uncomfortable. In her demeanor, I saw the symptoms of shyness, care, and intelligence. It was a shame that she'd never had the opportunity for a proper medical education. The Savannah Poor House and Hospital would not allow her as a doctor, but perhaps as a ward nurse or a midwife. I could see her pressing a cool cloth to a fevered woman's forehand and the woman finding relief in Rebecca's calming presence. I imagined her seeing the sores of a suffering child and debriding them with the gentlest touch, causing not the least bit of pain.

"Keep them, please," I continued. The business of the ginger nuts had put me off my distemper at the crowd outside. "A peace offering, as Sarah said."

"Effie likes ginger nuts," said Rebecca. "She'll eat them."

Sarah snorted, not turning around.

"Why didn't she come to town with you?" I asked.

"She never knows what to pick. If she picks the pecan roll over the molasses ball, she's hurting its feelings," said Sarah.

Ouida Bell disappeared into the back room, beckoned by her mother.

"I am sorry about our last meeting, Miss Rebecca. My injury robbed me of my gentility. I hadn't meant to be so..."

Rebecca smiled. "Well, you made it back to Lawrenceville, so there's that."

"Yes, there's that."

"How is your leg?"

"Oh, it was feeling much better the same evening."

"So Effie cured you."

"She... she didn't do anything, Miss Rebecca. And, in my particular case, doing nothing was a fine treatment, and certainly the least troublesome. Time heals all wounds, they say."

"All but the fatal ones." Rebecca sighed. "We'd best see to the crowd, Aubrey. I don't want to disappoint them."

"But, Miss Rebecca," I ventured. "I wish that you wouldn't."

"What, see to the crowd?"

"Don't you suppose that I should treat them instead? I do have the credentials and the training. They should be in my office for their cures, not loitering in front of the candy shop. You're only here for a shopping trip, not a medical mission."

Rebecca frowned. "If someone needs my help, I wouldn't refuse it."

"It will take time for them to trust the Hippocratic cures," I continued, "but they are the correct ones. It prolongs the pain if the townsfolk see you working here."

Rebecca took my arm and turned me toward the picture windows. The thrill of her hand on my arm consumed a goodly portion of my anger and my sense. "Do you suppose, Dr. Waycross, that there would be so many patients here if our cures were only pretend?"

"I don't know," I muttered. To utter those words caused me gastralgia and shame. I wished for a little dram of ether so that I might quiet my internal turmoil and answer Rebecca Winter with reason and decorum.

"I don't know," I said again. "Perhaps... perhaps I could be permitted to observe—"

"Aw, hell," said Sarah. "Boatwright's here."

The other faction of the townsfolk was coming. I did not think they would stay away from the scene. The crowd shuffled as the pastor insinuated himself among them. The glass muffled his words, but his tone was clear. Sarah let out a series of uncomplimentary expressions underneath her breath. Rebecca sighed again, more wearied than worried.

"Is there a back door?" I said. "You could slip away without entangling yourselves in his sermonizing."

"I'm not chickenshit," said Sarah. "I'll go out the front door."

Rebecca nodded. "Our patients have been waiting to see us. I won't abandon them."

"Pastor Boatwright isn't going to let you do your... works... here today," I resolved. "The sick will just have to go to Hope Hollow, panther or no panther. The pastor never follows you up there?"

"He's afraid of the place," said Rebecca, "like he's afraid of the gates of hell."

Sarah spat onto the floor and smeared the globule with her foot until it vanished into the wood. "He thinks we don't forgive those who trespass against us."

"Nevertheless," I said, "you'll accomplish nothing while the pastor's haranguing you. I'll talk to him, and you'll be able to get away safely."

Sarah shrugged. "Talk's cheap enough."

I went out the front door alone, leaving the sisters to escape from Boatwright's moralizing another way.

"And is it not said that, in the end of times, demons will hunt your children for prey and that witches will walk among you?" The pastor searched among the indifferent faces. "Ah, here comes our doctor! Tell them, Waycross! Tell them the horrors of the hydrophobia. How it will spread from the panther to the animals and then on to the weakest and then to the strongest. Tell them how your sister died, a gnashing demon trying to kill her beloved brother."

How dare he turn my sister, who had been all softness and kindness, into a caricature for his show?

"Pastor, not another word," I growled.

"See, the memory is too painful, even for our stalwart man of science. You were inside with the sisters, were you not? Have you excoriated those witches for their deceptions? For bringing their iniquities into our midst?"

I said nothing, for the sight of the pastor had suddenly caught my professional eye. Rivulets of sweat fell from his ears, soaking his collar. His forehead was as crimson as his cheeks, and his fingers were alarmingly pale. Even the anger I'd felt toward him was held in check for a moment. This man was sick.

"Pastor, are you quite well?" I asked.

I put my hands onto his neck. The lymph nodes were like walnuts beneath my fingers. His blood pounded in his jugular.

"Truthfully, I am not," said the pastor.

"Choler has flooded your face, sir. A consequence of your displeasure. I fear apoplexy if you don't let out some of your poisoned humors."

The crowd murmured its interest in this turn of events.

"I haven't time for it, Waycross." Boatwright stepped out of my hands and set his eyes toward the confectionary. The Winter sisters hadn't left yet. They were watching the proceedings from the windows.

"You haven't time to save your life?" I countered. "Pastor, please. Come to my office. You need ten ounces of blood taken out posthaste."

Boatwright looked from me to the Winters, who were still watching us. Why wouldn't they leave? He put his own hand to his forehead.

I put my mouth close to his ear to whisper, "Show your flock that you trust me."

Boatwright put his arm around my shoulders, and I reciprocated. The crowd offered mild applause, and the pastor raised his free hand, palm extended. "Here's real medicine," he said. "Not spells and incantations."

We stumbled toward my office, locked in step, supporting each other. I threw a glance back toward the confectionary. The Winter sisters hadn't fled. The townsfolk were lining up for their attentions.

I held Boatwright's arm fast, leading him to my offices. He dragged and scraped at every step. Whether he felt compelled to meddle in the proceedings down at the confectionary or whether he was afraid of the medicine, I wasn't sure.

When we passed through the barn door and he saw the alembics and retorts, the bottles and tinctures, his resolve seemed to break, and he became more pliant. Nausea passed across his face. I guided him to the surgery chair.

"But what about the sisters?" he said. "Have they gone?"

"It would do you no service to drop dead of an apoplexy," I replied. "Never mind them for the moment. We'll balance out your humors, and then you may return to your usual pursuits."

Boatwright nodded. I pulled a wooden crate up to the front of the chair. In the Savannah Poor House and Hospital's surgery had been a bed that adjusted to raise and lower the feet. No such luxury was here.

"Take off your shoes, Pastor, and put your feet up here."

"Why, sir, am I taking off my shoes?"

"Because I am going to bleed you from your feet." The scientific principle was simple: bleeding from the furthest extremity would pull the blood from the whole body, giving the best chance for restoration of balance to the humors. An amateur physician would more likely bleed from a source closer to the point of excess, perhaps taking blood from behind the pastor's ears. That would effect an immediate relief but not a lasting one.

The pastor had not yet removed his shoes.

"I cannot bleed you through your boots," I scolded.

"Must you bleed me?"

"What are your alternatives, pastor?"

I clamped down hard on his leg so that he would not jerk away and ruin the good of the lancet cut. I'd put the blade between the big toes and the next largest, in the soft skin there, but that was, alas for the pastor's comfort, only a preliminary incision, just to waken the veins in the pad of the foot.

"It hurts, Pastor Boatwright, but it is a hurt that heals. You must be strong, not only for yourself but for your flock."

"Then go on, Doctor. But a little warning next time!"

Warning, we are taught, is not the physician's friend. A doctor works best on definitive, quick action and on surprise. The patient's fear can tense muscles and close veins, prolonging the operation or ruining it altogether, and the longer the work, the longer the pain and the greater the chance for mistakes: blood poisoning, a slip, or an infection. That is why we are taught to amputate swiftly when we must amputate: speed is the most humane way to take off a limb.

The pastor continued, nattering to distract himself from the pain. "There might yet be time for me to interrupt their workings down at the confectionary."

"Leave them alone today, for the sake of your health. There will be other days."

"Understand, Doctor," said the pastor, "that when I was given this pulpit, I made it my mission to see those witches abandon their practice in this town. There was a fire, a very nasty piece of business. There were romantic entanglements, jealousies. Nasty, nasty business. I shouldn't wonder that one of the witches set the fire herself. A promising life was lost, but I think it was a blessing. Because of that fire, the town burned with a revival spirit. But now, that spirit has faded in Lawrenceville, and I hear their names more and more. Winter this, Winter that. The hydrophobia, the mad dogs—perhaps it is another blessing."

I traced the vein that runs from the ankle down to the very base and center of the left foot, and there I opened the blood flow. The pastor bucked, but I still held his leg fast.

"What happened with the fire?" I said, keeping up the distraction while trying to work as quickly as possible. "Tell me, won't you?"

The blood was sluggish, and I used the lancet to open the vein a little wider. This, I knew, multiplied the pain of the first cut, but it was necessary. An audible grinding came from the pastor's teeth. I did not like causing this pain, even to one such as Boatwright, but it was necessary pain. Boatwright only had to receive the pain and play the victim. The doctor, who causes the pain, bears the heavier burden.

"Doctor!"

"Why don't you tell me about the fire?" I said again, for it was all I could think to distract his mind.

"It was at the corn mill. Spontaneous combustion. I've understood from the locals that the wheels can grind the corn so fine that it hangs in the air, like a fog that will not dissipate. And when the air is dry and the weather is hot, that fine dusting of corn in the air is like tinder. It readies the very air to burn. One spark, and it went up like a tinder box!"

"And there's no way to prevent such an accident?" I tilted the pastor's foot to try to draw off more blood, but the flow was still sluggish. The blood was dark and thick, a result of poor diet and a lack of post-dinner constitutionals.

"I think it was no accident," continued the pastor. "I think it was providence. Had it been anyone else but Everett caught in the inferno, I suppose that I should not have been able to incite the town to the action that followed. But Everett was entangled with the Winter sisters. Sweet mercies, Waycross! Must you keep digging with that thrice-cursed blade! This is all gossip—among the sins of my parishioners, gossip is a prominent one, but by turns, it brings useful information. After the fire, they took the burned and bleeding Everett to the Winters' house and then to the graveyard.

The Winter sisters could not save him. If they had, again perhaps I would not have been able to draw up the crowd that pushed the sisters out of town. As I said, providence."

So Rebecca had had a suitor. She was not consigned by choice to solitude or to a maidenly life with her sisters. If she loved this Everett fellow, perhaps she would again... but that was an idle dream.

"Waycross! What are you doing?"

My attention had slipped. The end of the lancet was twisting in the pastor's foot. I snapped back from my mental wanderings at his words.

"So," I said, "in the wake of tragedy, in which poor Rebecca's suitor was killed, you blamed the Winter sisters for the fire. And you used that blame and fear to bring together a mob of the townsfolk and hung effigies of the sisters in their yard, and with torches and pitchforks caused them to flee their home here and hide away at Hope Hollow?"

The pastor nodded. "See? It was all providence, the visible hand of providence."

More than a lancet would be needed to purge the pastor of all the corruption he held inside.

Sarah watched with pleasure as Waycross led Boatwright away from the crowd. She imagined the cures the doctor would apply to the pastor—a purging emetic, a clyster to rinse out his bowels, and other painful and ineffectual attempts at medicine. Too bad the enemas didn't really work. Boatwright could sure stand a thorough scrubbing from the inside out.

Coming to town together, without disguise, as themselves, for the first time since the fire—it was a risk. Rebecca had insisted that they try and that Sarah not bring her rifle, and Sarah was surprised to see that so many patients were waiting for them. They were mobbed not out of evil, but out of need. The pastor's latest sermon hadn't scared anyone away. Waycross had taken him away before he could work his wiles.

"It's quite a crowd for us, isn't it?" said Rebecca. She sounded smug. "We'd best get started."

"There's no cure for what they've got," muttered Sarah. "A pandemic of goddamn hypocrisy. Ready to burn us one night and pleading for our help the next."

"They were wrong. They've learned they were wrong. Now, are we going to help them?"

"Why should I?" Helping Ouida Bell had been all right—Ouida Bell had sought her out—but those lazy hypocrites were another matter. "Why in the hell should I?"

"Because I will. Because Effie would."

Sarah would not break that bond. "It's not so far to Hope Hollow," she said. "They're all too lazy to come see us."

"Or too sick," admonished Rebecca. "Or scared."

"More lazy folk than sick folk."

"Which one are you, Sarah? If you don't start helping, we'll be here until sunrise."

When Rebecca opened the door of the confectionary, the crowds cooed and pressed in closer.

"A line, please, an orderly line," said Rebecca, turning to a father and child and taking them into her confidence.

5

IT'S A HELL OF FUN, GENTLEMEN!

One large glass held ethanol, the other sulfuric acid. I increased the heat of the reaction by adjusting the screws, which lowered the bottoms of the vessels nearer to the flames of the brazier. Bubbles rose in a steady stream to the top of the glass. I watched the rainbow shimmer on the surface of each bubble. When they popped, they released whiffs of ether's heady, pungent aroma. It smelled of happiness and honest chemistry. I slowed the reaction by a fraction with a tiny move of a screw. To keep everything in balance required perfect attention. To let one's mind wander might mean catastrophe, an explosion, a fire. When Snell tapped me on the shoulder, I was so startled that I nearly upset all my instruments.

"Man, you nearly gave me an apoplexy!"

Snell snorted. "I've been trying to get your attention, but you've got your nose stuck so deep in that stuff that you weren't paying me any mind."

I reassembled my composure. "What can I do for you, Mr. Snell?"

"It's not me, it's the wife." Snell smirked. "She's screaming and wailing. Thinks she's been poi-soned." He stretched out the word in derision. "Think maybe you could give her a doctoring? She didn't get to see the Winter sisters when they were in town last week."

I tried to hide my delight. I made sure the ether reactions were out cold, with no pockets of heat left in the glasses, and poured the coals from the brazier back into the hearth before I collected my traveling kit.

Snell and I walked north on Patterson Street. "Hope Hollow's a long way to go for a fool sickness like this one," he said, "especially if I have to go with her and take the gun. She's on about the panther, of course. I can't shut down the store every time the wife gets poisoned. And it takes five bottles of Grove's Tasteless Chill Tonic to get her to simmer down, which is five dollars cash. You work for less than that, I'm sure. I convinced her she ought to see you since that's what the pastor's on about."

Coming to the pastor's aid in front of the crowd had redounded to my credit. Curing Mrs. Snell would be even better than curing the pastor. A shopkeeper's wife makes it her business to know and be known. Gossip flows faster from her than from any other fountain.

Snell took me to his fine house on Oak Street, on the ridge north of town. Their porch had a pleasant overlook. I left Snell sitting there, enjoying the breeze, and went through the front door. The drawing room was well-appointed with pine furniture and long white curtains—fine luxuries for a frontier shopkeeper.

Mrs. Snell sat beneath a black lace veil. Tears and other fluids oozed down her chin. When she heard me enter, she began coughing.

"Good morning, ma'am," I said. "And how are we feeling today?"

"Horrible! Plagued!" she croaked. Drops of phlegm splattered from her mouth. "Poisoned! Cursed!" She clutched at her throat with both hands and made retching noises.

"May I be so bold as to examine you?" I knelt beside her chair and put the back of one hand to her forehead.

She swatted it away. "You don't need to," she said. "I know what's going on. I got poisoned by that"—she paused to cough— "Ouida Bell. Yesterday, I was walking toward the spring with my bucket, and Ouida Bell was coming the other way, laughing. Laughing about me. And so, I gave her the stink eye, you see, and what did she do?"

I thought the pause was rhetorical, but Mrs. Snell expected a response.

I ventured, "Ouida Bell poisoned you?"

"Mr. Snell thinks I'm mad, but I'm not, I tell you, I'm not."

"Did she put something into your water pail?"

Mrs. Snell's voice dropped, and she leaned in close. Her breath was bilious. "A frog."

"A frog?" I said.

"Yes, a frog. I didn't know I swallowed it." A spasm of coughing sent bits of spittle onto my cheek. "Maybe she ground it up real fine and it put itself together in my stomach. But now, I've got a frog down there, and it's going to be my mortal blow."

No species of poisonous frog was native to Georgia, and if someone wanted to poison Mrs. Snell, there were easier ways.

"I can promise you," I said, "that unless you dropped the creature down your own gullet, there's no frog inside you. And if you did swallow one, it would expire in minutes and not do the least bit of harm."

"So, you think I'm being foolish too." She daubed at her mouth with a handkerchief.

"My training tells me—"

"Your training wasn't out here on the frontier. We've got ailments that city folk don't get. Indian curses. Old whispers in the mountains. Poison frogs. The Winter sisters know all about them. I should go up and see them, but Snell's too lazy…"

"Every place has its peculiar miasmas," I said, "but none of them are borne on curses or whispers. They're chiefly dependent on the weather."

"I didn't think a fellow like you would understand."

Mrs. Snell fell again into a fit of rich, unguent coughing. Her skin was cold and wet. Her perspiration smelled acidic. She was ill. A frog was not poisoning her, but something else was: a spoiled piece of meat, probably. She needed an emetic to turn out her bowels, but an emetic wouldn't be enough. That might turn the bad food out of her stomach, but it wouldn't break the superstition's hold on her mind, and unless I could convince her that the curse was gone, she'd make herself sick again with coughing and moaning and fear. It was nonsense but nonsense that needed a cure.

The Savannah Poor House and Hospital did not teach us to cure with anything but lancets, emetics, enemas, and blistering agents. Four tools, four humors, four temperaments, four elements, four cardinal directions: a perfect and logical system, recorded in Attic Greek. Those were sure to cure all the infirmities of the body—excepting, of course, hydrophobia.

While Snell went to get a bucket, I hurried to a nearby marshy spot. A slow spring halfway down the ridge welled up between the roots of old trees. Turning over a few leaves, I found a tiny common toad. Was I brave enough to work this cure? I knew Mrs. Snell needed it, but it was very close to superstition. I reassured myself that it was the best cure for the patient. It was not Hippocratic, but perhaps it would work.

Back in the cabin, I measured ingredients with shaking hands as Mrs. Snell continued to press her case. "Folks grind up all kinds of baleful creatures," she said. "Scorpions, turtles, earwigs. Nasty stuff."

"Here's your draught, ma'am," I said. I handed her the cup. "A third part ipecac, the rest ordinary rum, with a dose of sugar for indigestion." The rum and sugar entice the patient to finish the whole dose.

Mrs. Snell swallowed it in a single swig. Her eyes bulged. "Sure is enough rum."

"Medically essential, I assure you."

She settled back into her seat, and I waited. Borborygmic rumblings rose from her churning bowels. Her head swayed.

The emetic began its violent action, and Mrs. Snell bent over the basin. An ordinary person would find his own stomach turned when in the presence of odors and fluids like those. Nausea, like yawning, is contagious, but physicians cannot permit squeamishness. Vomit, blood, urine, feces, and pus are our best clues to a patient's internal state.

True to my discipline, I peered into the basin to examine the colors and consistency of the expelled humors. At the same time, I let the frog fall from my hand.

What would the fellows of the Georgia Medical Society think? If they called me to answer for my actions, I would say I was only reassuring the patient with a piece of prestidigitation. It was good medicine mixed with superstition to make it more palatable to the patient. Still, I was nervous. Would I pull off the trick, or would I be caught in the act? Which was worse?

When Mrs. Snell looked up from her purging, her color was already better, but it improved a further two shades when she saw the frog swimming through her yellow effluvia.

"You see, Doctor?" she said, her excitement limited by her depleted condition.

I smiled, perhaps not proudly, but with some satisfaction. "Ah, you were right about the cause but not the malefactor. This is not a cursing frog, for... well, that is... the cursing ones are always black and vile, don't you know."

"Hmm, yes, yes," said Mrs. Snell, who then retched again into the basin.

"But this little fellow is the color of dirt, the sort that dwells around springs. I think that he must have worked his way into your drinking glass, or maybe he crawled into your mouth while you were asleep. And so, yes, you were cursed by a frog, but not with ill intent. You are a victim of bad circumstances. Please, do not blame Ouida Bell. I think she is innocent on this occasion."

Mrs. Snell nodded. She was too nauseated to argue. I bowed to her before taking my leave. When her pallor improved, she would be out in the shop, first thing, to tell one and all about her illness and recovery, and she would tell how she'd been right, that it was a poison frog, but it wasn't Ouida Bell or the Winter sisters who'd afflicted or cured her—it was that nice Dr. Waycross.

Out on the porch, Snell clapped me on the back. His hand came down like a hammer blow, and for an instant, I thought I might be under attack, but Snell meant this as a gesture of affection. He shook my hand, and a dime was between his fingers.

"All right, Doc. You did all right."

Yes, I had done all right. Ipecac had worked some cure, but I felt that the rapidity and totality of her cure was not because of the medicine. It was the damned frog, which I had caught, hidden, and prestidigitated. Should I now carry frogs in my medicine kit next to the lancets? Or leave behind the lancets? My hand quivered, and my head ached. I took a small dram of ether to steady my nerves. Yes, I had done all right—I was sure I had done right—but it was not the sort of right that my peers would have accepted. Do they have courts-martial in the medical profession? How would I defend my deviation from my training, from two thousand years of tradition?

The proof was not in what they'd read in Hippocrates. Being written does not make an assertion right. The proof was in the improvement of the patient, and in an hour, she was fully restored to health, with no mention of any poison or any curse. The illness was not only cured but forgiven and forgotten, a cure in body and in mind. This frog was not science, but...

No, it was science. If science was the observation of cause and effect in the natural world, then I had performed a perfectly scientific cure. Trusting only what is written in two-thousand-year-old books, even if those books were written by Hippocrates and Galen, would not be science. That would be superstition. That would be faith.

For my success and for my nagging doubt, I deserved better than my usual lonely bowl of cold porridge for luncheon. I wondered what ten cents would get me at the Flowing Bowl—perhaps a full meal or even a whiskey. As I entered the establishment, lewd jokes and coarse bodily noises interrupted the sound of sloppy eating. Renwick kept order among the tureens of stew, barrels of whiskey, and clientele.

The serving counter was full, but the burly farmhands and sawyers each scooted an inch so that I would have a place to rest my rump. Far down the table were Pearson and Hodgson. They had tall tankards of water for rinsing down the homebrewed whiskey, and they drank their fill. No signs of hydrophobia yet, then.

"The special, please," I said when Renwick noticed me. I didn't know what the special was, but I wanted to pretend that I did.

"Sure, Doctor." His instant, bright response boosted my mood.

My neighbor turned to me. Against etiquette, he was still wearing his floppy straw hat inside. Sawdust and leaves sprinkled from its brim into his food like seasoning. "Doc Waycross, is it?" he asked. "Fulton, log man."

I shook his hand. "How do you do, Mr. Fulton? Pleasure to meet you. Log man, eh? Does that mean you chop down trees?"

"Naw," said Fulton. "That's an axman. I clean up the logs as they come down the chute. Square them up if we're making planks or lop off the knots to make the log more round if it's going into a cabin."

"Why, with all those squares and circles, you could call yourself a Euclidean geometer."

"Yeah," said Fulton. "I like the sound of that. A geometer."

The special appeared in front of me: smoked pork, green onions, carrots, corn, a dinner roll the size of two fists, and a tumbler of whiskey. I salivated, and so did Fulton. He was looking at the whiskey.

"Mr. Fulton, you'd do me a service if you'd take this beverage and put it toward your health." I slid my glass toward him.

"A teetotaler?" said Fulton.

"No, sir, my geometer friend." I was warming to the place, the people. "Whiskey is good for sanguine temperaments. But it makes me sleepy, and I need to keep up my wits, should a patient have need of me."

"Much obliged, Doctor." He looked into the whiskey for his own reflection. "Doctor, if it's not too much trouble to disturb your dinner, I wondered if I could ask you about a sickness that's been hurtin' me."

Joy blossomed inside me. "I would be delighted!" The clientele of the Flowing Bowl turned toward us. "Ah, would you prefer to continue in my office?" I said, abashed.

"Ain't nothing these folks don't already know about," said Fulton. He glanced left and right down the counter as all ears in the Flowing Bowl followed our conversation.

"Hey, Fullie! You showing him your scales?" called a compatriot.

"I'm eatin' here, Fullie! Put 'em away," said another.

"Don't turn my customers off their supper," said Renwick, running mugs of coffee to scattered tables.

"My office is more private," I repeated.

But Fulton removed his hat, and his hairless pate was covered with cracked green skin. I kept my reaction in check.

"What do you think, Doc?" he asked.

I hadn't the slightest idea. Perhaps a frog might help.

"There was this lizard, one of the little green ones, and he got under my hat, and I whopped myself on my own head to get rid of him 'cause I was surprised, you know? I got lizard guts all over my hair. Do you think that's the problem?"

"Hmm," I said. I knew less about lizards than frogs.

"I shampooed twice a day with Grove's Tasteless Chill Tonic, but it didn't do any good, and I think the bathing was doing me harm elsewhere, so I stopped."

"Quite right," I said. "Better to keep one's own oils as a barrier."

From three seats down came a long eructation then guffaws of laughter at the splendid timing. I smiled in harmony with the humor of the Flowing Bowl, the challenge of a diagnosis, and the new confidence the town had in me.

"Mr. Fulton," I said, "we should treat this like a poison, as if the blood of your local fauna has irritated your skin. Come on up to the office after you're finished eating, and I'll make up a preparation. Tar, I think, for the base, then white vitriol to cleanse the affected flesh. And a moderate bleeding from the feet, which will draw the poison down out of the body."

"Why, that would be right kind of you, Doctor," said Fulton.

"It's my pleasure, the least I could do." I shook his hand again then ran a chunk of dinner roll through soft yellow butter.

"But if you get all fixed up, Fullie, who're we gonna laugh at?" asked a bar mate.

"I don't give a right damn. Maybe Buck, with his gimpy leg. Buck, do us a dance."

A white-whiskered oldster rose from his stool. "Maestro?" said Buck.

The men at the bar began clapping. They already knew the rhythm. Then Buck started his dance, a one-legged clog. His floppy right leg followed his left in exaggerated, loose motions, the way a rider flops along with his runaway horse. Then Buck threw the leg over his shoulder so that his foot flopped beside his ear. The Flowing Bowl shuddered with the applause.

"Another turn, Buck?" asked a farmer to my left from beneath a fine mustache.

"Naw, P, I'm worn out," said Buck. "Let me sit a spell."

"What's P short for?" I asked the man with the fine mustache.

"Nothing." His mustache turned upward to reflect the grin beneath. "My daddy said that the clerk who was writing down my name dropped dead right there in the county office, and he'd written only that one letter."

He laughed at his own fate, and I joined in. P and I shook hands, then I shook hands in turn with two dozen fellows. I caught a few names then though I would come to learn them all: Masters, Neal, Curtis, Patterson, Maltbie, and Born. Half a dozen of them offered to stand me a whiskey. I offered the same. Cards and dice came out, and while I didn't lay any stakes, I followed the games as if my fortunes hung on them. We told tales of great horses and greater fish, fortunes stolen and squandered, women desired and despised. I was astonished by the easy camaraderie I had with the men. They did not seem to hate me more than any other man nor fear me nor think me an outsider, a city mouse, or a foreigner. The loquaciousness the liquor evoked was certainly an aid.

When everyone's taste for ordinary spirits had waned, the best wares appeared from below the counter. There was a fifty-year-old cognac and some clear potion that, when held up to the light, shone a luminous blue. Men drained tall bottles of Grove's Tasteless Chill Tonic in single, satisfied draughts.

"Gentleman, gentlemen!" I said. "I have a dram better than Grove's Tasteless Chill Tonic."

"What, a kind of medicine, Doc Waycross?"

"No, not medicine: entertainment. The latest science." I refrained from telling them that it came from high society in Savannah. This crowd would consider that pedigree a black mark, as if one's whiskey came from New York City or one's cloth was woven in an English mill.

"How much does it cost? I've only got a dime."

"No charge," I said.

"First bottle gratis," said Renwick. "That's what they always say at the medicine shows."

"No charge, sirs," I repeated. "Not now or ever. Consider it my gift, a presentation of the merits of chemistry. Ether's a lot better than tobacco because it doesn't yellow your teeth. And no persistent headaches the next day, as with alcohol. Neither wife nor preacher could object to a substance so good and mild. Perfection through science, sirs."

My audience looked from one to another, parsing my pitch.

"It's a hell of fun, gentlemen," I said. "Hell of fun!"

I dashed back to my office and obtained the largest bottle of ether from among my shelves.

"Doctor, this isn't going to cut into my whiskey business, is it?" asked Renwick as I returned with my burden.

"If anything, it will make your clients more thirsty," I said.

I doused a cloth heavily with the spirits, and we passed it around among us. The fine houses in Savannah likely passed a silken handkerchief using tongs and a silver tray, but our rustic application had no adverse impact on our joviality. A friendly spirit took hold of the company. We clapped each other on the back, shook hands like fast friends, and ran ten-step footraces between the bar and the far wall. Men stood on chairs and balanced on one foot, and there was laughter—gales of it. Ether is a hygienic happiness. The teetotalers should have been pleased that I had enlivened the drunks with chemical cheerfulness. Maltbie crashed into Argyle, and both sprawled to the floor, giggling like children.

"Watch out, that's my refixed arm," said Argyle. "Don't want it coming off again."

"Tell the doc," said the crowd, who already knew the story. "Tell us one more time."

Argyle rolled up his sleeve to show his forearm and a bright-pink scar. "Board saw," he said. "It went clear through me. Didn't hurt none because I didn't have an arm left. I got to Hope Hollow an hour after my arm did. But that didn't make no matter."

"Bullshit," said Renwick.

"Ain't, neither," said P solemnly. "I was the one who found the arm."

"And the Winter sisters reattached it?" I said, incredulous. That was beyond the medicine of superstition. It was a tall tale grown too tall.

Claggers slipped out of his boots and wiggled his ten pale toes. "Effie got it stuck back on there. Find a feather, and I'll show you that it's ticklish."

"I ain't tickling you," said Renwick. "Tickle yourself."

"Can't tickle yourself," said Argyle. "Scientific impossibility."

"I bet you a double whiskey you can, too, tickle yourself," muttered P. "Somebody got a feather?"

"How?" I asked.

"How what? Reattach it? Why does that matter, how? If I don't know how, it's because they don't want me to know how. And I don't much care how."

My mind could not be satisfied with ignorance, though.

"I still think it's bullshit," said Renwick.

Claggers asked, "How many stumps do you see in Lawrenceville?"

"Portman's only got one arm."

"Never grew," said Claggers. "A defect from birth."

"How about Gartener?"

"That leg was lost at King's Mountain. British cannonball blew it off."

"So why didn't he just put it in a burlap sack and save it till the Winters could stick it back on?" demanded Renwick.

Claggers had an answer: "Nobody was in any shape after King's Mountain to find all the pieces."

Even through the ether, a thought troubled me. A town the size of Lawrenceville should have a dozen maimed men and women wandering its streets. In Savannah, which was not as fraught with rifles and sickles and board saws, many people were missing a limb. They were daily sights in the markets and on the squares. People in Lawrenceville were no less skilled at injuring themselves, but they did not suffer the consequences. Here were men, ether-frolicking men, who told me their limbs had been reattached by the Winter sisters. In vino veritas, it was said, but I've come to no conclusion about ether.

"Pass us that towel, Doctor," said Argyle. "Don't hog it all for yourself."

I took in a deep draught and passed the ether rag to my fellow men.

6

WHETHER I BELIEVE IN IT OR NOT

W aycross, grab that pigeon!" shouted Boatwright.

Poor sleep had left me feeble and my head aching, and the bird escaped my fumbling grasp. It settled upon a rafter and peered down at us with unblinking eyes. The top of the animal was white, but it was gray underneath. As the bird shook its wings, it shed flakes of white.

I glanced around the church. Ten rows of pews faced a lectern and a simple wooden table. The walls were white, the pews unpainted. Above the final rows of pews, set apart for slaves, Cherokees, and half-breeds, was a rickety balcony, which I would not have ascended even on a bet.

"Hang it all," said Boatwright. His frock coat was streaked and disheveled.

"Begging your pardon." I paused to consider my question before I asked it, but I saw no reason to turn back. "Did you paint that pigeon?"

"The Bible does not speak of pigeons," the pastor answered. "It's always doves. I was trying to make this little fellow perform. It appears that he has other motives."

The pigeon stretched out its wings, unfolding farther than I expected. "They're the same animal," I said.

"Doves are clean and holy. Pigeons fill the woods with droppings."

"So you did paint the pigeon," I said.

"I gave it a coat of whitewash, yes. So that it would better illustrate my sermon. I wanted a boy to release it from the rafters at a pivotal moment: give the congregation a spectacle since that's all they seem to be interested in."

The painted pigeon started a song and then, distracted by its own biological needs, paused to let loose a series of white streaks onto the floor.

The farce cleared my dark humor, but I did not let my levity show to the pastor. "I don't read any trouble in your complexion, so if I cannot be of service to you, I'll take my leave."

"No, Waycross, stay. I need to speak with you."

"Do you need more blood taken? Are your bowels in order?"

"Never mind my bowels." The pastor gritted his teeth. "I heard from Mrs. Maltbie that the Winter sisters handed out herbs and vocalized magical utterances for two hours while you kept me imprisoned in your surgeon's chair for that bloodletting."

"You were in danger of apoplexy."

"And I have also heard that you polluted the Flowing Bowl with a new kind of narcotic last night."

"I haven't..." I was bewildered. "Polluted? Narcotic?"

"Ether," said Boatwright, exhaling the word like tobacco smoke.

"A fundamental error," I said. "Laudanum is a narcotic. Ether is not. Chemically, it's—"

"It is a poison!"

Boatwright's voice startled the pigeon, which flew to a farther rafter.

"I did not summon you here to intoxicate my flock, Waycross. You are meant to help me put the fear of witches and quacks into this congregation. Tell them that quacks are powerless against the devil's diseases." Boatwright picked up a clod of earth that a farmer's boot had tracked into the church. "Because that demon panther is out there, its fangs dripping with disease. It answers only to one master, or rather three masters... the Winter sisters. It is their pet, their familiar. How else could you explain a panther in north Georgia?"

He was raving, caught up in his own superstition. I studied the white tufts of hair emerging from the pastor's ears. He was going to throw himself into another apoplexy.

"Instead, you are consorting with the enemy. Quaffing Thumb's patent medicines." Boatwright looked at me as he might a spider just before flicking it into the fireplace. "You are being drawn into their evil, sir."

He threw a clod of dirt at the pigeon, but the clod disintegrated in the air and scattered dust over the pews.

"I have shouted and fulminated and roared my displeasure to my flock, but they love their singing medicine man. They worship their miracle-working witches. What entertainment do I have to offer them in return? A painted pigeon? A phlegmatic doctor anxious to chop their limbs off?" He studied the white splotches on his sleeve. "Waycross, a congregation must not resent its pastor. They mustn't think me boring or worthless, for the good of their own souls. Your lancets and clysters and bone saws mean you will never be beloved, but that's no matter, is it? They heal no matter how the patients fear them."

Then I thought of the frog and how the patient must be cured in mind and body. "Sir, you are mistaken. It's vital that—"

The pigeon flew over our heads, and a flurry of feathers rained upon us.

Boatwright swatted at the air and the cascade of feathers. "Confound it all! Why our Lord should choose such a foul and unruly symbol, I shall never know. Why couldn't the Holy Spirit have descended as, say, a begonia?"

Boatwright took off his left shoe and chucked it at the enemy. The painted pigeon dodged nimbly and, in the resulting moment of confusion, made its escape. It flew between the pastor and me—I might have caught it if I'd had my hands out at the right moment—and darted through the doorway and into the world beyond—to rejoin its flock, I suppose. I would look for it the next time I took a constitutional. One white pigeon might stand out in a grove of a million.

The pastor fumed incoherently. He retrieved his shoe, sat upon the first pew, and replaced the shoe on his foot.

"Waycross, come here," he said.

I didn't care to sit next to him. His violence and buffoonery did not impress me.

"Waycross, come here!"

I placed myself in front of him but did not sit down.

"Understand, Doctor, that evil compels people to seek out the good, to vigilantly purge evil from their midst. It is like a bleeding for the soul, Dr. Waycross. A cut that cures."

"The metaphor, sir—"

"I will cut as deeply as I must, Dr. Waycross. I will bleed this town until its soul is healthy again."

Sarah sat in front of the fire, whittling a piece of hickory until the wood fell apart in her fingers. At first, she didn't notice when the hickory was gone. The bright red of her own blood startled her, and then came the delayed shock of pain, muted because the knife was so sharp.

"Damn it," she said.

"What's wrong?" asked Rebecca, who didn't look up from the sewing.

"I cut myself."

"Hmm."

"Well, don't feel like you have to drop everything and help." Sarah stuck her finger in her mouth.

Gloom still pervaded Rebecca, the smoke and darkness of the mill fire and Everett's death. Sarah didn't know how long one was supposed to mourn. She'd never had to mourn. Their mother just... went away, and there was no fit mourning. Everett had been a decent sort but not more decent than Effie, who was of one blood, one bond. Wasn't six months long enough?

Sarah took her finger out of her mouth. The bleeding hadn't stopped. The cut was narrow but deep, and it wasn't binding itself. Sarah held it up to Rebecca, but Rebecca didn't move.

"Maybe I should go into town," said Sarah, "ask Doctor Waycross if he'll stitch me up."

"He would encourage the bleeding," muttered Rebecca, "for the sake of your humors."

"Naw, he'd stitch me up. They have to teach about stitches in that doctor school, don't they? It can't all be amputations and bleeding."

"I suppose."

"It was nice of him to take Boatwright away, wasn't it? Maybe we both go into town, and you thank him for his kindness. I'm sure he'd appreciate it."

"Why do you care, Sarah?"

"Because you can't stay mad at Effie," said Sarah. "You can't keep on mourning."

Rebecca put down the stockings she was working on. "I'm not mad at Effie—"

"Well, good. All fixed, then."

"You wouldn't understand, Sarah."

Sarah put her free hand around her finger and squeezed, applying pressure. Thin rivulets of blood trickled out from between her clenched fingers. "I think you and Aubrey Waycross should see more of each other. Because maybe the wax didn't mean Everett. Maybe it meant Doctor Waycross, man of blood. And there's nothing better to forget one man…"

"Than to swap him for another?"

"I didn't mean it like that."

"And then Effie and I will be happy and whole again if I've got a new man in my life? Sarah, how can you be so simple? So facile?"

"Then enlighten me."

"Why didn't she heal him, Sarah?"

"Maybe she couldn't heal him," said Sarah, but even as she said it, she knew it wasn't true. She had seen Effie raise a deer back to its feet, seen the deer flee into the forest with all its life back in its veins. If Effie did that, she could have healed Everett, but she hadn't.

Rebecca shook her head. They sat in silence for several minutes. Blood fell from Sarah's finger and onto to floor in slow, heavy drops.

Finally, Rebecca spoke. "Did you need some help with that finger? I think spider silk would close up the wound fastest."

Later, Sarah stared at her finger, contemplating the cooling embers of the fire. Her finger hurt too badly to sleep. Rebecca had wrapped up the cut in spider silk, but that hadn't taken away any of the sting. Sarah had a handful of good cures for pain, but her cures didn't work on herself. Reading out of the Bible, jumping a knife, burying a bloody bandage by the crossroads: these were all for people who believed in such magic, not for the people who worked it. She should have asked Effie to fix her up. She could have done better than spider silk if she'd wanted to.

Sarah climbed the ladder to the upstairs room, with their one large bed. Rebecca and Effie were both sleeping. They got along well enough to sleep beside each other. If only their waking hours could be so peaceable.

Effie could have mended the wound. Sarah was sure of it. Effie's works were subtle. Sarah couldn't say how they accomplished her ends. The most terrible of wounds had come to Hope Hollow. That man with the nearly severed leg—the bone was whole, but nearly all the flesh was separated. Effie wrapped it up in wet cloths, and that had been all he needed. Also, the girl with blood poisoning—Effie had sat with her, and before the night was gone, the girl's pallor became ruddy and hale. But no one else had been like Everett, so badly injured in the mill fire, clinging to a feeble breath when he'd been brought to Rebecca.

Sarah worried at the spider-silk bandages. The cut stung. She wondered if she shouldn't wake Effie, but she was afraid. What would it mean if Effie healed her cut? What if she didn't?

Maybe Waycross needed some encouragement in his wooing. Perhaps one love does not replace another, but certainly one love is better than none.

My dealings with Boatwright made my dreams more solid. They did not dispel until late in the morning and left behind a fearsome headache. I relived the moment of meeting the panther. In my nightmares, the creature put its fangs into my leg, and I could feel, in the haze of my sleep, the poison of hydrophobia run into my body, like an injection of prussic acid. If not of the panther, my dreams were of fire. Flames rose from greasy torches, and three effigies hung in the willow tree—I'd seen those effigies. They were still hanging by the burned-out cabin. I saw Rebecca, only ever she, fleeing into the darkness in bare feet and a night dress, and I wanted to reach out to her, but she was too fast, and the smoke clouded my vision, and I woke coughing and sputtering.

I bled myself, the usual treatment for nightmares. I took three ounces from my left arm, and on alternate days, I took four ounces from my right. That was not enough, for the dreams kept coming. Ether helped to ease me to sleep, but it lost its efficaciousness before the morning. What I really needed to do to settle my dreams and resolve my headache was take the blood from lower down in the circulation, where the humor was coagulating. It's a quirk of anatomy that the sanguine humor collects at the chordate root, better known as the anus.

My office door did not have a lock, so I wedged a chair beneath the handle to secure my privacy and threw a blanket over the window. The mirror I fetched to help me work showed a gaunt face with sunken cheeks, an illusion caused by the gloom. I was certain I did not look so bad in daylight.

My treatment was unpleasant under even the best circumstances, but that I had to administer it to myself posed greater problems. I lowered my breeches and bent forward, far enough to clasp my ankles. Then I took out my lancet and tried to find an angle that would open a vein just inside the anal opening. I made a cut, but it was shallow and hesitating. No blood flowed.

No sooner had I set the blade than a knock came at the door. Startled, I tried to right myself, but a sharp pain took the wind out of me. My lancet blade was stuck into my buttocks.

"Anybody in there?" someone asked.

I'd made a terrible mistake. I'd jammed the door handle by wedging a chair beneath it, but a chair would not stop anyone determined from getting inside. My buttocks waving in the air—I'd be the laughingstock of the town for the rest of my days.

The knock sounded again, more insistent. "Aubrey?" The voice was a woman's—so much the worse!

"I'm indisposed!" I shouted. The lancet clattered to the floor. "Please, come back later."

"Do you need help, Doc? Got your foot stuck in a bear trap?"

Then I recognized the voice. It was Sarah Winter. What did she need? What could possibly bring her here, at this least opportune of all moments?

"No, but thank you for your concern!" I said, forcing a chuckle. "I can't see any patients at the moment. Please, I crave your pardon, Miss W—Madam."

"It'll only take a minute, Aubrey." A hand was on the door handle. Wood creaked.

"Please, I beg you, come back later!"

From the other side of the door came a muffled, angry sound. Sarah Winter retreated. I could not make out her words, but the tone, passing through the walls well enough, suggested vivid, foul oaths.

I shuddered in revulsion, muttering oaths of my own. Slowly, I found my composure. The shallow cuts were not so painful once washed with a little cold water, but my headache was worse than ever. Each heartbeat sent a fresh jolt of pain across my skull. I winced against the exertion, the surprise, the shame... but most of all, the stupidity. What if Sarah were not acquainted with this Hippocratic treatment and instead only saw a supposedly learned man putting a lancet into his own asshole? To cure a headache! It was more bizarre than any old wives' cure I'd heard for headaches: mustard plasters, cabbage juice, a good night's sleep, a frog slipped into an emesis basis. She'd never let me hear the end of it. She'd torment and tease me for as long as I stayed in Lawrenceville.

I slumped into a chair, but a shot of pain made me leap up again, so I had no choice but to stay on my feet. A constitutional would help my circulation and perhaps restore my heartbeat to its regular pace.

I couldn't take my constitutional in town. My gait was lopsided, owing to my own failed treatment. Passersby would have awkward questions, and I had no wish to answer them. I did not think the details of a lancet to the buttocks would persuade anyone to seek my cures, no matter how my reputation might be improving, so the forest was the only option. I would stay close to town, where the panther was not likely to be lurking. And if he was? Perhaps a dose of fear was the cure I needed for my mind, as the constitutional would be a cure for my body. Boatwright's belief that the panther was the sisters' demon familiar was catching. I'd heard Mrs. Maltbie repeating it to Lizbeth Samples. Some proof of the foolishness of that assertion would be helpful. Maybe I would come across the creature dead from its disease. That would dispel the rumors.

I followed paths as they twisted around chestnuts and between close-pressed poplars—the marks of hunting trails, turkey-driving runs, and the wanderings of furtive lovers on their sylvan rendezvous. I set my course by the sun, aiming south.

I wondered how Hippocrates had persuaded the first patient to submit to a bleeding from the buttocks. Perhaps his reputation excused any proposed cure, no matter how ludicrous, or perhaps learned men of the time decried his foolish treatments, but their objections have just been lost in the ages since. Why haven't we physicians, in two millennia, found a treatment for a headache more suited to human dignity? A dram to swallow or an ointment applied to the forehead? I wondered if some cure existed that I could trick myself into taking and believing—swallowing a frog or a bottle of Elixir Salutis.

I emerged from a rhododendron tunnel and saw a shadowy figure crouching at the base of a stunted tree.

"Aubrey?" The shape shifted, and a sharp nose and angular features were silhouetted.

"Miss Winter, is that you?"

It was Rebecca, kitted for an expedition. Leather sacks and satchels hung around her shoulders. She stood and dusted debris from her skirts. "What brings you to the deep thickets?"

"A constitutional," I confessed. "I have a headache that's plagued me for days."

"Did you lose your lancet?"

I clenched my buttocks. "It might be time to try something else. Anything else." I looked around. We were alone in the forest—no hunters, no gossips. "What would you give?"

"Even a remedy that you don't believe in?"

"If it's medicine, it will work whether I believe in it or not." Nothing in her pharmacopeia could be more demeaning than the Hippocratic cure.

She nodded, a smile touching her face. Then she rummaged through her satchels, withdrawing a cinched leather pouch. She untied the knot and measured out half a pennyweight of gray-brown powder. "Willow bark. Stripped, dried, ground, sifted."

"And I swallow it?" The powder was light in my palm, like a heap of ash. It couldn't be worse than being caught with my britches down.

Rebecca offered me her waterskin, and I recalled the apothegm, "If she shares her cup with you, that's as good as kissing you." I felt my face stretch with a wide smile—then I grimaced involuntarily as I swallowed the bitter powder.

"Willow bark's not an instant cure," Rebecca cautioned me. "Let it work half an hour."

"Half an hour would be a joy," I said, fishing the flecks of powder from between my teeth. "I've struggled with this headache. Even ether can't make me forget it."

The space between us fell silent. A bird overhead made a short, sharp, and unmusical noise. In the far distance was the report of a gunshot.

"Would you walk with me for a ways, Miss Winter?" I asked. "If I may steal you away from your herb gathering? To make sure I don't faint from the willow bark. Or get eaten by..."

"It would be dangerous to faint out here in the woods," said Rebecca, taking my proffered arm. "There are bandits and panthers and strange women everywhere."

We followed no particular path in our stroll or in our conversation. Talking was a relief. It allowed the pent-up troubles of my weeks in Lawrenceville to ooze out.

The pain across my brain seemed to dissipate as I spoke. "If the sick won't come see me, should I be making house calls? Do you venture out from Hope Hollow to attend to your patients?"

"Not usually," said Rebecca. "That day at the candy store—that was an exception."

"You were certainly very popular," I said.

"Thank you for distracting Boatwright and his faction. As for house calls, people don't want us to visit them. They will take the witches' cures, live or die by their advice, but they won't have them over for supper."

"But there's no such thing as witches," I said.

"There are people who believe in them nonetheless." Rebecca turned her head and stared into the distance though one could not see but a few hundred feet before brush and bracken and hill and valley obstructed the view. "That does them more harm than a real witch would."

I risked an impertinent question. "Rebecca, do you enjoy living in Hope Hollow?"

"It's where we've spent most of our lives. The walls are painted thick with memories. It is quiet, but I have plenty to read." She considered her fingers. "Sometimes, I might wish to have more visitors."

"There's no reason that you should live in exile unless you prefer it. Wouldn't it be simpler for you and for your patients if your practice was in town?"

Rebecca skipped a step in her gait, and I stumbled to match her pace.

"We have tried before, Aubrey, but I'm sure you heard what happened."

I had heard the whole sad matter, and I nodded. "Boatwright told the story, but from his slant. He told me about the fire, about the mob, about how he made you leave town."

"We chose to leave town," said Rebecca, "because it seemed wiser. Because there was nothing left for us in town. No reason for me to be there, since—"

"Since Everett?"

Rebecca's pace slowed.

"I'm sorry," I said. "That was a tragic accident, I understand, and Boatwright exploited it shamefully. I won't say any more about it. But I must tell you, there is something else that he's exploiting. He's telling a story that this panther is a demon familiar, a servant to witches. It's utter foolishness, a blackguard lie, but it's bound to be received by certain people and spread with the speed of any vicious rumor."

"How do you suppose we quash it?"

"If you lived in town again, I think, the superstitions would not find any fertile ground in which to grow. Even the most credulous would see that you and your sisters are not strange women. Not witches, certainly."

Rebecca started walking again. That thought seemed to brighten her face, but it clouded again in a moment. "Many of the townsfolk don't want us nearby."

"They are wrong, though," I said. "They are a splinter spreading infection to the rest of the body. Root them out, and I think you'll find that you are, on the whole, loved by the town. Doesn't the crowd at the confectionary prove that? You aren't witches because there's no such thing. Why let these few scare you away? You should not let a man like Boatwright be victorious. He still revels in his success, that he was able to drive you away."

"I thought you and Boatwright were allies. You said a town's doctor and a town's pastor ought to be."

"Boatwright means to exploit superstition while I mean to cure them of it. Do not call that man my ally. We are at contrary purposes at every step."

"But I thought you have a much longer acquaintance than your time here in Lawrenceville."

I flushed. "And even then, we were at odds. He did nothing efficacious for my poor sister. He prayed for her, which is as good as nothing, and he berated her for her sins, of which she had none. I think he was the worst of all the hucksters and quacks my mother begged for aid, because we were supposed to believe him, believe his superstitions above all others, for they have the greatest force of tradition. Poor Eva. Nothing could have saved her—no doctor, no herb, no miracle. She was doomed. But he needn't have given us false hope."

Rebecca and I were walking arm in arm, and she placed her other hand on top of mine. "I'm sorry about Eva."

"I'm sorry about Everett."

"Will you tell me the whole story someday, when you are ready?"

"If you promise the same, Miss Winter."

She nodded.

We walked on several paces farther, passing under a high bower of chestnuts.

"I would like, Miss Winter..."

Eight weeks had passed since my letter was posted to the Georgia Medical Society, with no response. What deliverance could it promise: some third-rate post as a corpse washer? My prospects in Lawrenceville, though not shining, were not so dim. I was a doctor there, with patients and cures. I was settling into the story of the town. I cured a woman with ipecac and a frog. There was a drama there yet to be played, one that involved the pastor, the panther, the Winters, hydrophobia, and the credulousness of the town.

Rebecca gave me a cockeyed glance. "Like what, Dr. Waycross?"

She had spoken lightly, in jest, yet I stumbled in my reply. "It's only that... it would be nice to... have the company of a kindred spirit in town."

"Are we kindred spirits?" said Rebecca.

"I treated Mrs. Snell for a cursed frog," I confessed.

Rebecca arched her eyebrow. "How?"

"By emetics. To cure her real symptoms. But a bit of prestidigitation convinced her I'd solved her false symptom, too."

Rebecca laughed as I explained how I'd hidden the frog in the basin. "What would the medical men of Savannah say?"

My smile faltered. "What would you have done, in my place?"

"I might have chosen a gentler emetic, probably Seneca root. They call it mountain flax around here. It's also a valuable treatment for snakebite, on much the same purgative principle. Being foreign to the body, Seneca root is expelled by our organism, taking with it the poison."

I felt a quiet thrill when she said "emetic" and "purgative" and "organism."

We came under the branches of a vast oak. Its arching canopy spread out above us, and the ground beneath our feet was level and clear, starved of light by the shadow of the ancient tree. We were in a theater of branches, woven just for us. Rebecca and I walked three turns around the perimeter of the oak's shadow, saying nothing.

"Miss Winter," I began, "I would like to ask you if... if you would consider..." But I couldn't go on.

Rebecca smiled, but her eyes revealed her disenchantment. "How's your headache?"

I hadn't thought about it in several minutes. "Why, it's much improved. Do I owe that to the willow bark or the charming company?"

"The willow bark," said Rebecca.

"Either way, Miss Winter, you have saved me a bleeding."

"Keep your blood inside you, Aubrey. It does more good there."

Sarah rested her chin in her hands and her elbows on the railing of the porch. She watched Effie circumambulate the rocky bald, a little ways away, where an old stump and the scrying bowl still stood. Effie kept her eyes on the ground, and every so often, she'd pluck up a green shoot, sniff it, frown, and toss it away into the woods. Sarah watched the display for a quarter hour before she finally went out to meet her sister.

"It's the onions," said Effie. "I don't like them."

Sarah was relieved. That was a minor folly, one of the eccentricities by which she'd always known her sister: a girl who didn't like onions and didn't like eggplant, who would rather sit quietly on the porch than chase after the chickens.

"Not something Rebecca planted, is it?" asked Sarah. "Rebecca wouldn't want you to be rooting around in the garden. Even I've got the good sense to stay out of there."

"No, wild onions."

"I guess she can't be mad at you for pulling up wild onions."

Effie turned back to her work. She lifted her eyes to a cluster of chestnuts growing closer to the water. "There's a whole passel of them there. They haven't pushed up yet."

"How do you know?"

Effie tapped her nose. She scurried to the chestnuts and rooted in the dirt with her fingers. She brought up three brown, fleshy nubbins, each about the size of an egg.

"Those are onions?" asked Sarah.

"No. I don't know what they are. I'll give them to Rebecca. She'll know. Maybe they're medicine."

Rebecca was returning just then. Effie had heard her first, and Sarah knew the rhythm of her footsteps. No animal moved like any other, their noises as singular as their flesh. Rebecca trotted right past Sarah and Effie, not noticing them.

Sarah picked up a granite pebble and slung it sidearm at Rebecca's feet. It bounced off her boot heel, and Rebecca whirled around.

"Not even going to say hello?" asked Sarah. "Look, Effie's got something to show you."

Effie hesitated. She brought the three little objects close to her chest, as if to shelter them.

"It's all right, Effie." Rebecca moved her satchel to the other shoulder, shifting the weight, and met her sister.

Slowly, Effie unfolded her palms. "What are they?"

Rebecca touched one. Its flesh yielded under her fingertip. "Garlic bulbs, but they're rotten. Weevils got to them."

"Will you take them?" said Effie.

"I don't have much use for bug-ridden garlic, Effie."

"But... you can take them. You might need them."

Rebecca took the offered bulbs and placed them into a pocket on her satchel, among the fennel and the sassafras and the ginseng. "The woods were full today. I even ran into Aubrey."

Sarah concealed a smile.

"He had a headache," said Rebecca, "and thought he could walk it off. I gave him some willow bark, and it seemed to do him right."

"Hell, a headache is simple," said Sarah. "Half an hour will cure just about any headache, willow bark or no. You could have had more fun with him than that."

"We were fine, Sarah. Aubrey said something else, though. He said that Boatwright is trying to poison the town against us again. The pastor's saying that we've, I don't know, summoned this demon panther as our familiar, our servant to spread fear and pestilence and evil in the forest."

"Rat bastard," muttered Sarah. "Some of those idiots are going to believe him, aren't they?"

"Such people were never our friends," said Rebecca. "But I wonder if the best solution isn't the direct one."

"I kill the panther and put its head on Boatwright's stoop? How's that for direct?"

Rebecca shook her head. "No one's been able to kill it yet, not even you. That's odd, isn't it? You two come on in. Wash up while I get supper on."

Effie trotted at Rebecca's heels while Sarah lingered behind. Everett had been trouble, no question. In life, a little. In death, so much more. He'd made a wound that couldn't heal, but Waycross might be a salve for Rebecca's pain. There was no better cure than forgetting.

Late that evening, Pendleton rapped at my door. I recognized him from the Flowing Bowl. The man was in obvious pain, and in deference to his discomfort, I hid my satisfaction that he was entrusting his health to me.

"Pendleton, good fellow!" I said a touch too brightly. "How may I be of service?"

He held his forearms up, palms toward his face. They were bloody and wet like raw meat and filthy with dirt. "Rifle blew up in my face," he said between gritted teeth. Removing his hasty dressing stirred fresh blood. "I had sight of that panther. Pulled the trigger, and it's Yorktown all over again, right at my nose."

"Oh, not so bad as Yorktown," I said. My headache had vanished completely—Rebecca's willow bark was remarkable—and my spirits were high. "Fellows at Yorktown had their arms blown clear off. No danger of that here, good sir. Go to the light over there. Let me get a little water."

I brought an ewer of spring water and a length of clean cloth. Beneath the blood, Pendleton's arms were in good condition. Most of the damage was superficial: ordinary abrasions and a few splinters of metal. Less happily, one piece of debris had traveled up the left forearm, leaving a long gash and then opening a cut in the thin skin near the elbow. Dirty black powder was mixed into the ragged flesh. I could see through the epidermis and fat into the muscles below. They pulsed with crimson droplets in rhythm with Pendleton's heartbeats.

I placed my finger into the forearm wound, which made Pendleton yelp as though it were a red-hot poker. "The pain is an excellent sign. It means that your sensations are intact." I repeated the experiment by digging my fingernails into his palm on the same hand. Pendleton winced, but it was a wince that brought us both relief.

"So, what will you do?"

"Debridement first. Then I'll clean the wounds with a solution of carbolic acid, and then I will remove any tissue at risk of necrosis with the scalpel."

"Will that hurt?"

"A good deal," I admitted. "If it did not, we would wonder if we'd used enough carbolic acid."

I asked Pendleton if he wanted a swallow of whiskey before we began. He shook it away. I made Pendleton lean forward and brace his forearms against his knees. He turned his head so that he wouldn't have to watch the operation. I didn't blame him for this weakness. He kept his reserve and let me work without flinching or screaming. It was a textbook debridement. The sizzle of the chemicals was the sound of cleanliness, of harsh purity.

I waited a long time, many minutes, until the bloom of pain started to fade from Pendleton's face. Then I poured a measure of water over his forearms, washing away the acid, and Pendleton's eyes thanked me for it. The flesh was clean, the large part of the dirt removed. Next, I needed to trim away the dead skin so that necrosis would have no chance of setting in.

I placed my nose close to his quivering muscles as I worked along the gash. My position blocked my light, but I did not need to see. I felt through my scalpel, the living portions resisting the blade and the dead portions yielding to it.

The flow of my work was interrupted by a sudden resistance. My scalpel blade was entangled with the tendons of the elbow. I'd pushed too far into living tissue. I pulled the blade back, and it scraped against raw bone. I finished the operation with closer attention, flicking away the pieces of dead skin and metal splinters, and then leaned back to admire my work. The deep red of dried blood and the ash of the powder were gone, replaced with the moist pink that promised regeneration and health.

"Pendleton, I commend you on your stalwart composition," I said, wiping the scalpel blade clean. "I've seen hardened criminals bawl their eyes out on the operating table. You've comported yourself admirably."

"I thought you hadn't started yet, Doc," he said, turning and seeing, with surprise, the change in his wound. "I felt a few little stabs at the beginning but then nothing."

"I had a blade up against your bone!" I said. My face must have turned ashen because Pendleton's did the same.

We repeated the experiments from earlier, and he showed no sign of feeling. The arm was dead. A putrid humor rose in the back of my throat. It was my slip of the scalpel, a bit too much living tissue taken near a nerve, the misvoyage into the bones...

A dead arm, besides being of no use to its owner, is ripe for necrosis. It is no longer an arm but a sack of corruption waiting to spoil and spread.

"Pendleton—" I started.

"You can't cut it off, Doc." He commenced shaking in his chair. "Couldn't we wait? See if it cures itself?"

"I'm so sorry, Pendleton. But it's hopeless. What's dead cannot be brought back to life."

Pendleton kept talking, but I couldn't hear his words—only accusations, guilt, and failure. I was a failure at my chosen profession, clumsy and foolish, inexperienced and overeager.

The amputation was a terror. It required three strong men from the Flowing Bowl to hold Pendleton down. He thrashed under the bite of the bone saw. My guilt made me hesitate when I should have been decisive, hack when I should have sliced. The hogs squealed as the patient cursed his fate, his doctor, his Lord, and his life. Long after his stump had been cauterized and he had been helped to the boarding house, after I'd buried the arm beneath a pine tree, after I'd climbed into the hayloft and tried to settle my mind with ether—long after, I could hear those animal noises, echoing.

Ouida Bell came running into the clearing of Hope Hollow. Effie looked up from her washing. Rebecca put on water to boil and brought out clean cloths for compresses. Sarah ran out to catch the terrified girl and bring her in.

"What's happened? What's happened?" asked Sarah.

"Just... and the panther..."

"What with the panther?" Sarah sighed as Ouida Bell's full weight crumpled into her arms.

"It... it bit me..."

"It bit you?"

"I was coming because... and then there it was, in the rhododendrons, and I was rooted... and it bit me."

"Where?" Sarah got Ouida Bell up the steps of the cabin. Rebecca had already spread a large white sheet across their only table. "Where did it bite you? I don't see any blood." Sarah helped Ouida Bell onto the table. "Where?"

"I'm afeared to show you."

"Damn it, girl," said Sarah, "we're doctors. If you're not going to show us, then you can just bleed to death."

Rebecca hissed at her sister, "You'll scare her all the way to death." Turning to Ouida Bell, she said in a measured tone, "there's nothing indecent. We need to see."

Ouida Bell flushed and lowered the waist of her skirt, revealing her right buttock. Four dull red puncture marks stood out against Ouida Bell's pale white flesh, but no blood was there. The bite hadn't broken the skin.

Sarah whistled. "That's hardly even a bite. I thought that panther was going to have mauled you to an inch of your life. What's all the fuss for?"

Rebecca hissed again, "Don't you know how to shut your mouth?"

"But look at it. It's not even bleeding. Does it hurt?"

Ouida Bell pulled her skirt back up. "No, I suppose it doesn't. I was... frightened. I still am."

Sarah hopped up onto the table, sitting beside Ouida Bell. "Now, you listen to me. I think you're just about the luckiest girl that's ever lived. People have been fearing that panther for months. They know it's rabid. But it's only gone after one man, and that was when he shot at it. Didn't bite him. Only clawed him. Self-defense, you'd say. Then, the panther sniffs you out. Smells your peculiar scent of woman and chocolate."

"I won't stay to listen to this nonsense," said Rebecca, heading for the cabin door.

Ouida Bell's eyes were each wide as the full moon.

"Chocolate, ginger nuts, molasses," continued Sarah, "all scents unknown to this wild creature. It only knows rotten flesh and bird shit and moldering leaves. But here's this girl, this beautiful girl, smelling of all the sweetest smells, and her blond curls like corn tossing in the wind as she flies to Hope Hollow on some—"

"I wanted to—"

"Hush up, I'm telling a story." Sarah held up her hands. "And for a moment, the wild beast comes to its senses. Its waking mind comes out from the terrible demon of hydrophobia. And it doesn't want to attack. It wants to know. It sees, it smells, it hears, but that is not enough. It wants to taste. And so it reaches out with its mouth and it tastes. Like a suitor. Like a lover."

Ouida Bell laughed.

"And that's why I think you're the luckiest girl in the world," said Sarah. "Because the panther that everyone is afraid of is in love with you."

I went to the burned-over lot and cut down the three straw effigies from the willow branch. They'd hung there far too long. Then, I did not know what to do with them. Burning them did not seem right, nor burying them, nor throwing them to the ground to rot. Instead, I took them to the river where the current was fast and shoals turned the water into a froth. There, I untied the thread that kept the effigies together, and I threw the unbound pieces into the current. The water took them away. I wondered if there was forgiveness there, in the places where our unbound pieces go. That, though, was a long time hence, a country from which there was no return, and I meant to find absolution here.

Diagnosis

"We must observe his paroxysms, his stools, urine, sputum, and vomit. Observe, too, sweating, shivering, chill, cough, sneezing, hiccough, the kind of breathing, belching, wind, whether silent or noisy, hemorrhages, and hemorrhoids. We must determine the significance of all these signs."
—Hippocrates

7

THE LONELY PETUNIA IN THE

ONION PATCH

JUNE 1822

Lawrenceville was in a panic over Ouida Bell's mauling. Of course, Rebecca had told me the truth, that it had only been a little nip that hadn't even broken the skin. A hangnail was a worse wound than what Ouida Bell had suffered from the panther, but rumor and fear had elaborated the attack into a full mauling, with Ouida Bell, bloody and clinging to life, staggering to the Winter sisters' door and them knitting her flesh back together so that one could not even see the signs of the mauling upon her. The more fervently Ouida Bell denied that this mauling or miraculous healing had taken place, the more fervently the townspeople believed that it had. Perhaps Ouida Bell could have put the rumors to rest by showing them the actual wound, the little nip on her buttocks, but she was too modest.

Boatwright pounded from the pulpit in rhythms that grew louder with repetition. The panther was not a natural scourge. It was a demonic familiar of the witches, a symbol of the town's wickedness. What more proof did they need than that the panther had attacked the most innocent and beautiful of us all? Evil hates beauty the most.

I was in disgrace. I'd sworn I was not a sawbones, but I'd taken off a man's arm because of my own mistake, the first amputation in as long as Lawrenceville could remember. No one wanted my medicine, believing that I would slice the patient, lance him, bleed him, and scour him with emetics and clysters so that pain and effluvia ran from every orifice. And for what? An amputated arm, a miserable failure. I'd done my best cure in Lawrenceville with the Winter sisters' medicine, with ipecac and a frog.

I went into the Flowing Bowl for supper and found no welcome. The patrons at the counter did not scoot to make room for me. No one would lend me a chair. I ended up eating a cold biscuit while standing in the corner. When Pendleton came in, his sleeve pinned up to his shoulder, I felt two dozen pairs of glaring eyes turn not to the wounded man, but to me, and I made my exit.

I took my constitutionals around the town square, and each time I passed a sawyer or a farmer or a hunter, he'd cross to the other side of the lane, as if my very aura would separate people from their limbs.

Thus, no one would come to me for curing. But for fear of the panther, no one would go to Hope Hollow, even with a gun. No one wanted to tempt the panther with another sweet treat nor bet that the Winter sisters, powerful as they were, could work another wonder.

The ailing and ill roamed the square in Lawrenceville. The streets looked like the wards of the Savannah Poor House and Hospital. If Boatwright was doling out healing through prayer, it was not to the general population. I saw women suffering from summer complaint and men clutching their bellies against the gravel because they'd overimbibed. Parsons had a fearsome sty in his left eye that made it seem as though he were gazing through fire, and children ran from him. The palms of Renwick's hands sported fat boils that caused him great pain when he tried to grip a saucepan. Any of it I could have treated, but no one trusted me. They trusted only the Winter sisters.

I did not trust myself, either, and like the townsfolk, I could not contain my own wonder at the Winter sisters. I hadn't seen the wound myself. What panther would only have nipped at Ouida Bell without pressing the attack? How could a wild and rabid animal have left behind only a few teeth marks, not even breaking the skin? Perhaps the Winter sisters had done something to treat the girl. I believed Rebecca when she said there'd been nothing to treat, yet... I wondered at the power of their medicine, which cured without pain, without amputation, without heroics. Furthermore, its power was proven because, in the absence of its availability, the town descended into the ordinary unhealthiness of its people and climate. The town needed the Winter sisters.

I returned to Hope Hollow on a gray Wednesday morning. The sky was low, and the tops of the trees disappeared in the descending mist. The sound of a musket shot rattled the air. In response to the thundercrack, a cloud of black wings arose from the grove of a million pigeons. The birds rose no higher than the mist at the treetops and churned and swirled like smoke until their panic settled. Failing memory or exhaustion compelled them to return to their branches, and the crack of a rifle came again. Another hundred birds were slain.

If I wanted any sort of redemption from this mistake, I would need to follow the Winter sisters' cures, at least for a time. I had to humble myself before whatever skill had kept this town's limbs intact, its teeth glistening white, its fevers few, and its graveyard empty, save for that sole tombstone for Everett.

What if, instead of treating Pendleton, I'd taken him to Hope Hollow and presented him to Rebecca, Sarah, or Effie? What would they have done? Would they have taken more care? Would they have put on a poultice or ointment to debride the flesh without the dangers of the lancet? What could I learn from the sisters, and how could I show the townsfolk that I had learned? Only my guilt and humility would atone for my failings and help me to correct them.

Fording the Alcovy presented no troubles. I moved from stone to stone without conscious thought. I realized I'd crossed it only when I was on the other side. The fields and swept yard around the Winters' cabin were silent.

I spent several minutes considering their door.

No, this is a mistake.

I took two steps backward and hit something moving and soft: a sheep. I tumbled into confusion, getting tangled up with wool.

As I tried to find my footing, I sensed more shoes than I anticipated from an ovine altercation, and the smell was better.

"Aubrey, Aubrey, wait!" said Rebecca.

We were in a frightful knot. She twisted her torso to release my
legs, and by turns, we untangled our ribbons, cravats, bonnets, and
shoelaces and found ourselves half-sprawled, half-seated on the
hard-swept red clay.

"I was coming back from gathering." Rebecca's bonnet had
come loose in the tumble. She tucked her hair up under it, and
dust fell into her face. "I saw you in the yard. I didn't want to
shout. I thought I might startle you."

"Well, good you didn't," I said, straightening myself. "It seems
I'm not too steady in the best of circumstances. Quite a comedy."

"Yes, quite a comedy."

I saw no use in backing away then. "Seeing as how we did run
into each other... I have an important question for you, Miss Winter. A proposal."

"A proposal?" she said, her voice sharp with surprise.

"Yes, and if you will permit—"

"Aubrey, please, let's consider this somewhere, anywhere other
than the dirt?"

I clambered to my feet and stooped to aid Rebecca. The fingers
of her ungloved hand wrapped around my proffered wrist. I felt
the warmth of the blood in her veins.

Rebecca led me up to the cabin, where two chairs sat in the
breezeway between the halves of the dogtrot home. We settled
into this comfortable, sheltered passageway.

"Now," said Rebecca, "this proposal?" Her legs were crossed at
the knees, and she leaned forward in her chair.

"Yes." I had to present myself scientifically. "I've considered at
length." I did not want her to think a rush of humors had led me
to rash action. "I haven't known you long, but I've had occasion
to observe your character and habits, and I think them excellent."

Rebecca nodded. She kept her expressions hidden.

"And though we have different beliefs, I believe that we are of similar temperament." I cleared my throat. "To the crux of the matter, then. What I want to ask is... would you consider joining up with me?"

"Joining up? Is that the city term?"

"A partnership," I clarified.

"Aubrey." Rebecca exhaled, a slow deflation from pursed lips. "I am not the kind who believes in instantaneous attraction, and I don't believe that you are either. People are not magnets. Their polarities are not plain. Attractions and repulsions have to be tested."

"But what better way to experiment?" I leaned forward, gaining excitement. "If you are in Hope Hollow and I am in Lawrenceville, it's more difficult—"

"But what about my sisters?" Rebecca looked down at her feet. I saw the top of her hat, which had been sullied by my bootprint.

"Your sisters are welcome, too," I assured her. "I want to know you all."

Rebecca lifted her eyes straight up to mine. She glared, and I felt like a bug, impaled. "That, Dr. Waycross, is most untraditional."

In a flash, I reheard what I'd said. "Oh, hell." My bilious humor drained to my feet, and blood rushed to my cheeks. "A proposal, yes, but not that sort of proposal. Miss Winter, I'm so sorry."

She continued to glare.

"I've heard the frontier demands hasty courtships in some circumstances. Not our circumstances. We are rational people and don't find ourselves in such straits."

Rebecca's cheeks flushed. My churning biles and phlegms turned me insensible. "Miss Winter, I do not suppose that you harbor any affections toward me. I am not worthy of them, and I would not propose to claim them. That is, I may wish it, but I meant—"

Rebecca held up her hand. "Suppose you tell me about your proposal."

"I want us to share a medical practice. In town. Waycross and Winters, physician and healers. Your cures are not without merit. The loyalties of your patients prove it. Their good health. Their intact limbs. I cut off Pendleton's arm. You wouldn't have done that. You would have saved him."

"Aubrey—"

"I don't understand your cures. I don't know why they work or how much good they can do. But I won't stay ignorant."

Rebecca's cheeks were fading from scarlet, at which I took heart.

"Do I enjoy letting blood?" I continued. "Get a spiritual lift from giving enemas? Do I want to lop off arms? That is medicine, as proven by the great forefathers of the profession. But even they have their limitations. And if we can ascertain the mechanisms of your healing, separate substance from superstition..."

A tangle of hair came loose and fell across her face. Rebecca tucked it back. I knew she was either weighing my proposal on its merits or crafting a gentle rejection.

"Are you staying for supper, Aubrey?"

In the center of the table was an enormous roasted potato. It was the largest specimen I'd ever seen. Five or six must have unified underground. The amalgamation resembled a human form. It was a trick of the brain but unnerving, a giant potato that looked like a little man, served up for dinner.

"Sisters, Dr. Waycross is joining us for supper," said Rebecca. She scavenged an extra, mismatched place setting: a tin plate, a wooden spoon, and a fork with the handle twisted.

Sarah stood over the vegetable homunculus, holding an ornate knife with a bone handle. Effie occupied three inches of space at the end of a bench. She glanced toward me, and that time, her eyes did not put me in the mind of my sister. Effie's were gray, true, but the light of the room was different, and the intelligence behind them was strange.

"Sometimes, this gets messy," said Sarah as I laid my place setting next to Rebecca's.

"Messy?" I asked. "How—"

Sarah made an incision, and skin peeled back from the wound. The potato writhed and squealed with the escaping steam. "This one didn't explode," she said. "Sometimes, they explode."

"One exploded." Rebecca glared at her sister. "I told you it would explode. The skin was too thick. It got too hot. Will you never leave it alone?"

Sarah made a farting noise. "I'd rather talk about the one that exploded than the thousand that didn't. Much more interesting, isn't it, Aubrey?"

I made a noncommittal noise.

Sarah slapped a crosswise slice of the roasted potato onto my plate. Its flesh was a vibrant purple, a strange hybrid. Three hot droplets of sauce splattered on my shirtfront, and I wiped them away, leaving grease on my fingertips. Sarah dished out equal portions to her sisters and herself, and then she took a seat nearest the fire. They waited for me to take the first bite because I was the guest.

"Sarah, may I borrow your knife?"

Sarah considered my request for longer than I'd anticipated. Then she took the knife from the table, spun it in her palm, and offered me the handle. "Don't cut yourself, Aubrey. I'm serious. Do not cut yourself with this knife."

"Or what?" I asked, shocked. That was my first impression of gravity from her.

"It's Effie's," said Sarah.

I wasn't sure why that would make any difference. Ownership does not imbue a blade with spirit or poison. I held my portion of the potato fixed with my fork and drew the knife across its surface, making a crosshatch of pieces. All the sisters watched me work, Rebecca judging my skill as a surgeon by the way I handled my cutlery. Thus, I tried to make a show of it, cutting very close to the skin of the potato. Suddenly, the table lurched—a kick from underneath, I thought, though I could not see who'd done it. The knife scratched across my plate, and the blade bit into the skin of my left index finger.

"Aubrey!" said Sarah with a sharp inhalation.

"Nothing, nothing. A clean nick is all. Look, not even any blood." I extended my hand to her so that she could reassure herself by inspection, but I could not see the wound. The pain was quickly fading, the cut already invisible, as if it had never been there at all. Sarah studied Effie with a fixed stare.

"It appears that Effie's knife is rather kind," I said, aiming for levity. "Especially to clumsy folks like me."

Rebecca frowned. Sarah watched Effie, riveted. Effie sat still.

"But you cut yourself with it," said Sarah. "I told you not to do that."

"Why? What's one knife instead of another?"

"Aubrey, it's no matter," said Rebecca, picking up a biscuit. "It's only Sarah playing a trick on you. Eat before it gets cold."

I picked up my fork, ordinary and less dangerous. The potato would fill the stomach of a hungry laborer, but it would never become a culinary rage in Savannah. "It's good," I said.

Rebecca recognized the diplomacy and appreciated it more than undeserved praise.

"Nightshades are full of hate," said Effie into her water glass.

"Yet you eat them." Rebecca did not look at her sister.

"Who am I, that I should have the right to choose?" said Effie.

The table fell silent. By the motion of Sarah's gums, I could tell she was running her tongue over her teeth, chasing particles of food.

"Sisters," said Rebecca, breaking the silence. "Dr. Waycross has brought me an interesting proposal."

A piece of potato caught sideways in my gullet. I'd used that word, fraught with romantic connotations, unwittingly. Rebecca must have known how it would affect her sisters.

Sarah's eyes widened, and she folded her arms on the table. Effie's attention was on her supper.

Rebecca looked from one to the other until they acknowledged her. "Aubrey has asked us to move our practice back to Lawrenceville."

"Hell, that's a step, at least," said Sarah.

Effie writhed in her white cotton dress.

"Well, I think it's a splendid idea." Rebecca's tone was bright.

I was delighted. A gas bubble tried to escape from me, but I held it back with pressed lips. Rebecca was the eldest, head of the household. Her decision would be final.

"Witches live in remote mountain hovels," added Rebecca. "And we are not witches."

Sarah sniffed. "They sure believed us last time—"

"Are you afraid of them, Sarah?" countered Rebecca.

"I don't give a squirrel fart about them!" Sarah exclaimed. "Just that, when tempers get hot…"

Rebecca's face darkened.

"Perhaps you'll agree," I said cautiously, hoping to diffuse the energy, "that healers should live where they are most useful. Particularly with this crisis of the panther. A city does not put its hospital in the hinterlands."

"Yes, precisely. More useful," Rebecca said.

"And convenient," I said, taking a biscuit from the platter Rebecca offered.

"Yes, convenient."

"Rebecca needs some cockle-doodle-doo," said Sarah. "She's lonely in her Hope Hollow."

"Sarah, that is vulgar and insulting." Rebecca snatched the platter of biscuits from her sister so that the plate hit the table hard, and I jumped at the noise.

"Aubrey, are you sure about this?" Sarah grabbed a biscuit and tossed it in the air with her right hand then caught it with her left. "Rebecca can't tell the difference between plants and people. She's the lonely petunia in the onion patch."

"Rebecca, Sarah," said Effie. "Please, don't fight."

"All three of you will be under my auspices," I said. "And you have more friends than you realize. Think about everyone that was lined up outside the confectionary for you. Everyone you've helped with your cures. Boatwright and his adherents are a loud minority. The gratitude of the majority is silent but far more powerful."

"Every human being is a skin sack stuffed up to the neck with greed and flesh and stupidity." Sarah scowled. "And what spills out of their face holes are delusions and mistakes."

"Then why do you help them?" shot Rebecca.

"I don't!" Sarah threw the biscuit hard, and it smashed against the ceiling. A sprinkling of crumbs fell over us like snow. "I make them do foolish dances," she continued in measured tones, "but they get better anyway. And then more of them come."

"We are healers," said Rebecca, "and we should be where we can do the most good. We're going to Lawrenceville with Dr. Waycross."

Sarah's innards twisted with each bag she helped to heap onto the mule cart.

"What are you going to do about your garden, Rebecca?" she said.

"Wild herbs are more efficacious than tended ones," Rebecca said. She placed the enormous granite pestle she used for grinding into the cart, and the wagon's axle groaned under the weight.

"And what about the house?"

"It's a wild house." Rebecca shrugged.

"You're not thinking—"

"About what?" snapped Rebecca. "Because I have, about everything you are going to say. I am not afraid, Sarah. I didn't think you would be."

Sarah didn't want to see a dozen people before breakfast and ten times as many before supper. Most of all, she didn't want those fear-riddled hypocrites to come to Rebecca at all hours of the night. In Hope Hollow was the protection of distance, of wild animals. She did not want to lead Effie back into a town of ordinary mortals.

"You're not thinking about Effie. If there were another tragedy or, worse, a miracle, what would Boatwright make of it? What frenzy would Boatwright shout into his sheep about such a happening? There wouldn't be enough bullets to settle them all."

"We won't let that happen again. We won't be frightened away. Aubrey says we have friends. The town is trying for respectability."

"But what about Aubrey? What if he suspected a miracle, a wonder cure? It would fascinate him."

"I wouldn't care," said Rebecca, too suddenly. "This wasn't that sort of proposal. It's not a romantic understanding. It's a partnership for medicine." Rebecca turned to go back inside.

Sarah called out to her, "Wait."

"What?"

"There was a deer. I found Effie with this dead deer by the creek. I think it was dead." Sarah hesitated.

"And what was she doing with this dead deer by the creek? Giving it a bath?"

"I... don't know. The deer got up. It ran into the forest."

"Then it wasn't dead, was it?"

Rebecca turned away again, and Sarah did not call her back.

I made arrangements with Mrs. Snell to put up the Winter sisters in the Snells' garret. On the day of the move, I helped load their essential possessions into a mule cart, a weather-worn relic of pioneer days. On the surface of the pile, I could see glass vessels—some fluted like a flower, some squat like a melon, some stuffed with varicolored powders, and some empty. An apothecary's chest was wrapped in a bolt of cloth. Wooden drying racks were wedged among shears and hand scythes, mesh strainers, pill presses, and drinking vessels of copper, clay, ivory, and stone. Rebecca had packed an enormous mortar, deep enough to bathe a child. I offered her the use of my own, but she insisted that certain instruments were personal, like a chamber pot.

Sarah's contributions included a silver bowl and matching silver ewer and another pair in pewter. She had knives ranging in length from needle to rapier. Canvas sacks were crammed with threads and yarns—not only cottons and wools in crimson, saffron, and black, but also cords that looked like dried vines and threads so fine that they must have been spider silk or human hair. She had a wooden case of pins, tipped with gemstones. A trio of animal skulls stared back at me: a ram, a raccoon, and an unknown carnivore. Strangest of all, though, was an iron cage containing a common passenger pigeon. I wondered why Sarah needed to keep one when nature provided a limitless supply just down the path.

Effie's belongings must have been at the center of the pile, either less fragile or more structural. What is she bringing? That question supplanted the mystery of passenger pigeons and animal skulls.

The mule knew his own way. No one needed to drive him. Rebecca and I walked ahead of the cart. We couldn't see Sarah. She was sulking on the rear running board, behind the mountain of their possessions. Effie was using her entire body to keep the pile from tumbling, pinning down a threatening tower of cooking utensils with her left elbow while holding back a carved wooden chair with her right foot.

The cart creaked in distress whenever the angle of the road changed. We trundled over a knot of hemlock roots, and the cart shuddered.

"Oh!" said Effie.

I turned in time to see a burlap sack beginning to fall. With unusual alacrity, I leaped forward and caught it. Glass clinked inside.

"What's in here?" I asked.

"Bottles," said Rebecca, smiling. "So many bottles."

"A fellow collector. Wonderful! I look forward to showing you my cut-glass phials. The Venetians have refined glassmaking—"

Sarah rolled her eyes, and the mule kicked the dirt and started again.

I motioned to Rebecca that we should hurry ahead of the cart to talk in privacy. "Sarah hasn't threatened to quit her practice, has she?"

"Every hour. But she can no more leave behind her work than you or I can."

Rebecca and I were the first to round the chestnut-shaded bend and see the Alcovy creek, where another wagon was about to start the crossing, coming the other way.

"Ahoy, ahoy!" It was Salmon Thumb and his medicine-show stage. "You've saved me the trouble of crossing. I was coming up to see you."

"You have found me, sir." I swung my hat in greeting as I called back across the waters. "How may I be at your service?"

"Flattered, Doctor!" shouted Thumb. "But I meant the Winters. Though it's ever a joy to see your smile."

Rebecca chuckled, but I was less amused. What business did he have with the Winter sisters?

Thumb left his mule on the north side of the river and hustled across the creek to meet us, churning up white foam around his knees in his haste. "I'll take your fella from here. What's his name?"

"He'd only need a name if we had more than one mule," said Sarah.

Thumb took the bridle from where it dangled beside the Winters' mule's face. "Why, that's no good. You'd still have a name even if you didn't have any sisters, now wouldn't you?"

The question hovered in the air like smoke, and several moments passed before the wind took it away unanswered.

"I'd give him a name if I were you," said Thumb. "What do you think, miss?" He looked up at Effie, perched upon the mountain of possessions, and smiled. If he was being a showman, I knew no purpose in it.

Effie pressed the palms of her hands together and put them below her chin. She seemed to be hard in thought, but the thoughts conducted her only to further silence.

"What about 'Sonny'?" asked Thumb. "Lots of mules named Sonny. He wouldn't feel like a stranger. He wouldn't stick out. Just a nice, ordinary name. What do you think about that, Miss... Effie, right?"

Effie moved her hands to her lap. "Yes," she said.

"Sonny it is! Better than no name, anyway." Thumb clapped his hands. "Let's get you across this river, Sonny." The mule recognized in Thumb a better master than any of us, and he traversed the river, shallow and swift, with ease. "Now, that's a good boy," said Thumb, piloting our crossing. Not once did the stack of possessions threaten to topple. Effie rode in tranquility.

Thumb scratched Sonny behind the ears as he climbed out of the water and onto the northern bank. "Good boy. Isn't Sonny a good boy, Miss Effie?"

"Yes," she said.

I still had no answer for why Thumb had been on the way to Hope Hollow, business or courtesy. Perhaps he was suffering with some ailment that Grove's Tasteless Chill Tonic couldn't cure in either man or beast.

"I hope you're well, Mr. Thumb?" I asked.

"Doctor, I'm right as rain," said Thumb. "Not a complaint in the world."

"So why—"

"Questions, Doctor! There's no reason, really. I'm just being neighborly." He steered Sonny and the wagon to a shady place beside the stream, and Thumb's mule, Holtzclaw, followed of his own volition. "Now that we're across, I'd be obliged if you'd sit a spell and have a little refreshment. I've got Elixir Salutis. Good for what ails you, especially if what ails you is hard work on a hot day. No charge, before you even think such a thing. No charge at all."

"Well, good," said Sarah. "Let's sit a spell. I'm parched."

Thumb opened a wooden crate at the back of his wagon, and bottles clinked against each other. He tossed out libations with a high lob and a flourish of the wrist.

Provisioned, Rebecca found a dry log beside the water, and I joined her. The river sparkled as it ran. Pebbles beneath the water shone like jewels. To sit in such a place with one as charming and intelligent as Rebecca Winter—the scene belonged in a pastoral novel.

Rebecca faced the water, and glimmering sunlight framed her head. Loose wisps of hair near her ears were illuminated and resplendent. I placed a hand upon her shoulder. I tried to alight with no pressure or force, as though I were a bird landing on a fragile limb. In my fingers, I felt a quickening of her pulse. She leaned toward me, accepting the light embrace.

We turned as a pair toward the wagons. The mules Holtzclaw and Sonny were gossiping together. Upriver, Thumb squatted on his haunches next to Effie, who was seated on the moss at the edge of the riverbank, her legs turned demurely to the side. I saw her lips move and his head nod. Then, Thumb poured his Elixir Salutis into the river. The wind caught the narrow falling stream and swirled the patent medicine into mist. Effie poured her bottle out then filled and emptied it again, rinsing it clean. Then she and Thumb unloaded the rest of his stock from his wagon. They threw the bottles one by one into the river, where the glass shattered against the rocks.

"Thumb, all your medicines!" I cried.

"Who needs 'em?" He held up his hands, and I saw that his once-crippled pinky fingers were straight as young saplings. The rheumatism was gone.

"Has Effie done that?" I asked, amazed. Rebecca squeezed my hand, pulling me backward.

"Such a clever lady!" Thumb beamed as bright as a hog in sunshine.

The Elixir Salutis was an oily smear on the face of the water, and as the roiling river broke the bottle glass into finer and finer shards, the water blazed with light. I could not stand to look at it, so bright and wonderful and vast was the destruction.

8

DID YOU HURT ALL THESE PEOPLE ALREADY?

The wind brought wave after wave of heavy rain, and Sarah could almost imagine it as a creature on the roof—pacing, scampering, leaping in the night.

Yet she was pleased that not a drop fell on them through the ceiling. Unlike at Hope Hollow, the Snells had put tar paper under their pine shingles—no leaks. The Snells also had other fine luxuries to offer: two windows with glass in them, a free-standing wardrobe with cedar drawers, a washstand with a ceramic basin, and a fat iron stove with a chimney piping away the smoke—and all this on the second floor, in the spare bedroom. A spare bedroom itself was an extravagance, and to have such excellent and expensive things put up there was a marvel. Sarah admitted she had not thought that any in Lawrenceville lived so well.

Waycross had been abashed when he'd seen just how fine the Snells' spare bedroom was. And why shouldn't he? Sarah thought. He'd been living in their hog barn for months.

"I'm quite used to the hayloft now," he'd said three or four times, failing to convince anyone.

Mrs. Snell had offered no explanation or apology. "You three ladies will be very snug and tidy here," was what she said.

They were indeed snug. The bed was not as big as they were accustomed to. Rebecca took the side nearest the windows, Effie laid herself on the farther side, and Sarah took the middle. Rebecca told Sarah to sleep on her side rather than her back so that they would have more room.

"I can't sleep on my side. All my humors will pool up. I'll get a cataplexy. Hey, I bet Waycross has plenty of extra hay if you want to go cuddle up with him."

"Quiet, you."

"We moved all the way down the mountain so you two love-birds can be closer, and now you stop in the last hundred feet? Go on. The last six inches are the hardest, so I've heard."

"That's indecent and rude. I would not participate in anything so shocking—"

"Fine." Sarah couldn't see her face in the darkness. "Did you believe Mrs. Snell when she told us it'll be handy having us so close by?"

"I believe she thinks Ouida Bell puts hexes on her. So yes, she'll find it handy having us as her guests."

"The old bat. Said to our faces she 'thought it terrible' what happened to us last time we lived in town. Said 'superstition got the better of a bad lot.'"

"Yes?"

"Well, later, when I was passing through on my way to the out-house, I overheard Mrs. Snell talking to her husband."

"What did she say?"

"She said, 'if there's a scene like the last one, what should we do? Turning them out's not charitable. But I'm not letting a mob tear down our house.'"

The sisters waited each other out in silence. When they'd last lived in Lawrenceville, they hadn't needed to be guests in anyone's home. They had the cabin Everett had built them, but that was a burned-out wreck now. Someone had cut down the effigies from the willow tree. Sarah wondered who had finally done it.

The rain swelled again, washing down the roof and spattering against the window glass.

"Sarah, if you'd just roll over..."

"I'll sleep on the floor," said Effie, shuffling.

"If anyone, it's Rebecca who should sleep on the floor," said Sarah. "She's the one who thought it was such a fine thing to come back to Lawrenceville."

"You didn't have to come," said Rebecca. "Nobody's put you at gunpoint. Stay up in Hope Hollow, for all I care."

Then they stayed quiet for a long time. A single, distant rumble played against the driving wind of the rain. Effie's breathing caught in her throat. She'd fallen asleep and was snoring.

"You and Effie would combust if I didn't keep between you," Sarah whispered.

Effie's snoring stood out against the rhythmic ebb and rise of the rain, a harsh counterpoint.

What if it had rained that day when the mill caught fire? What if the rain had purged the air of the fine, flammable dust, ready to take to any spark? Then it would have caught fire some other day. The mill wasn't the first to suddenly catch flame like that, and it wouldn't be the last.

But the townsfolk muttered, of course, whispering, "It must have been a lover's quarrel. Rebecca's anger set into fire. Spontaneous combustion, a hex of witch's fire, the evil eye set alight."

Their stupid hypocrisy made Sarah burn. They couldn't see a simple matter for what it was, an accident.

What had come after, though—Sarah didn't know if that was an accident or not.

Effie inhaled sharply, snorting, and Rebecca rolled out of the bed. Sarah heard her foot bump something metal—the chamber pot. Rebecca swore. Sarah rolled into the warmth Rebecca had left behind, and Effie settled among the folds of the quilt, which quieted her restless breathing. Rebecca muttered, pulled on her shoes, and left the room. Sarah imagined her sister's discomfort with piss drying between her toes.

I awoke to the sound of a hundred hogs trying to wriggle their way into my office, or so it sounded. When I dressed and descended from the hayloft and slid open the door, I saw not a collection of curious hogs but a crowd of people.

When I appeared, a hush fell across them. I should have combed my hair, but I'd thought I was going to be shooing pigs, not seeing patients. I was overwhelmed—at first flattered but then fearful.

So many cases appearing all at once could only be an epidemic: cholera, diphtheria, malaria, hydrophobia. Has it finally struck?

Then my sleepy brain cleared, and I realized the crowd of patients was not there for me but for the Winter sisters. As at the confectionary, a crowd had assembled for them. It was no epidemic, only the gamut of ordinary and seasonal discomforts that afflict us all.

"Good morning, Doctor," said P, and two dozen others murmured likewise.

"Good morning, ladies and gentlemen," I said. "The Winter sisters aren't here yet. I can see to you while you are waiting." I stepped forward and took P by the shoulders. I looked into his eyes and pushed his forehead back so that I could look into his throat. "What are the symptoms? Weakness? Trouble breathing?"

P stepped out of my examination's reach. "Just the weather in my hip. Begging your pardon, but I ain't going to let you saw my arm off because my hip is hurting me."

I winced at the accusation, but it was not new.

As if summoned, the Winter sisters rounded the corner from the square into the hog yard outside my office door. The crowd's attention turned. A babble of voices and noises started again: coughs, sneezes, wheezes, rales—a cacophony of illness. That was what I had wanted ever since I'd come to Lawrenceville: a bevy of patients, with the usual complaints, seeking my honest and scientific aid. Really, the patients were there for the Winter sisters' cures, but now, they couldn't have one without the other, could they? A quiet thrill of accomplishment curled my toes. I could turn the herb women from superstition to medicine. I could prove to them to leave off their more nonsensical cures and work into our joint practice any of their medicines that could be shown, in the ways of science, to have a good effect. I stood at the edge of discovery.

"Aubrey, did you hurt all these people already?" chimed Sarah above the din. "It's not even eight o'clock in the morning."

Her bite could not wound my spirits. "I haven't hurt anyone," I protested to the back of the patients' heads. "I haven't had the chance to examine them."

Rebecca took the hands of a woman I didn't know, whose child complained of stomach pains.

"Please," I said, "can all of you form an orderly line?"

"Have you drawn up any water yet, Aubrey? Lit a fire? We'll need some boiling water for infusions." Rebecca led her patient into my office—our office.

"I've only just woken up," I said meekly to her back. "I'll fetch some."

Effie looked flushed to me. A little color would be a sign of health for her phlegmatic constitution, but not that shade. Her forehead was dappled with perspiration, as if she'd exerted herself with more than just the short walk from the Snells' house.

"Miss Winter," I addressed her, stepping up into the circle of patients surrounding her, coaxing them back with my arms. "Are you quite well?"

"It's nothing," she said, but barely had she gotten the words out when her spindly body jolted forward, and she took a step to catch herself. An instant later, a second blow. My hands were spattered crimson.

"Witches! Witches and demons! Mistresses of the panther that stalks us all!" hissed someone, or several someones, the voices unrecognizable among the shouts of indignation and shame. "Now their demon familiar will come right into town, stalk you in your homes!" People retreated in every direction, fleeing the scene in the panic of the moment. No one stepped up to defend the Winter sisters, whom they would otherwise trust with all their mortal frailties.

I dashed forward to catch Effie, but she'd already regained her balance. Her right side and her back, the two sites of the impacts, were red and sticky with... with the juices of rotten tomatoes.

"I'm all right, Aubrey," she said. Her color, perhaps in contrast to the tomato skins plastered to her, looked better. She was her customary shade of unnatural paleness.

Her gray eyes softened, and I saw Eva again. A memory of helplessness overcame me, but this time, I was not helpless.

"A very foul act," I said as I pulled out my handkerchief to remove the worst of the stains from her face and hands. "I shall tell the mayor at once. If he has any sense, he'll find a respectable fellow to act as constable and bring the matter to justice."

"Tomato is a nightshade," she said. "Nightshades are full of hate."

My handkerchief was only smearing the mess, not removing anything.

"I'll fetch that water, and we'll get you clean." I grabbed two buckets from the hog yard and trotted toward the town spring.

To my thinking, the whole axis of the problem had turned. The Winters weren't the ones who traded in superstition. Those were the pastor and his adepts. They were the fearmongers and falsehood spreaders.... and now fruit throwers, too.

When I came back holding a brimming bucket in each hand, I couldn't find Effie. The waiting patients shrugged their shoulders when I questioned them. I went inside my office.

"Effie?" I asked.

Sarah, standing nearest me, poured a clear, pungently alcoholic liquid into a shallow bowl. "She's with a patient," she said, gesturing upward with her eyes.

Luckie Maddox and Effie were sitting in my hayloft. I couldn't hear them. The shadows of the loft covered their faces. Only a few shafts of dusty sunlight came through the gaps in the chinking, illuminating in spots and streaks the crimson, indelible stains on Effie's dress.

W hat was wrong with Luckie?" asked Sarah as soon as Luckie had gone.

Waycross was attending Rebecca on some herbal poultice.

"Luckie misses his dog," said Effie as she climbed down the hayloft. "It was one of the dogs that got bit by the panther. It was rabid. He had to shoot it."

"And you didn't... bring his dog back to life, did you?"

The far corner of Effie's mouth curved upward in an approximation of a smile.

"Because if he misses his dog, that would be the easiest way to cure him."

"Don't be silly, Sarah."

"So what did you do for Luckie's melancholy? Bleed him, like the city doc? Chop his arm off?"

Effie shook her head. "No cure for sadness."

There are a million cures for sadness, thought Sarah, and some of them very good. "Effie, you can't... you can't stick out here in town."

"Never in my life have I stood out," said Effie.

"Right, because that's what I do. I'll be outlandish. I'll be mocking and provoking. And you, please, just... stay safe."

"Nothing will—"

"People will be watching you more closely. Waycross especially. Don't do anything that fascinates him."

"But I didn't."

"You didn't mean to, I know. But they'll all be watching you, Effie. They'll be knocking on our door, day and night, for hangnails and bunions. If you think you're going to bring anything back to life, just don't. Say you can't."

"I don't understand, Sarah."

"Then never mind. Just... never mind. Those bastards and their tomatoes."

Effie took her sister's hand, holding it in her small palms. "Are you all right?"

Sarah took her hand back. "Cowards. I wish I knew who did it. I'll find them. Hell, they'll probably show up here with a wrenched elbow and ask you to cure them. You'd fix them, wouldn't you, Effie? You'd know them, and you'd fix them anyway?"

Effie shook her head. "I wouldn't know."

Sarah thought, How can she be so good? The world is a poison to goodness. Next time, it won't be tomatoes. It'll be rocks and, the next time, knives.

The pastor summoned me that afternoon, sending word by way of a messenger boy. The parsonage was a tiny white house in the shadow of the shoddy chapel. The windows were caked with mud, and green trails of grime leaked down the facade. The Lord cares for the sparrows, but he doesn't always give them three-story nests. The child opened the door without knocking, and I stepped into the gloom. From the shadows came the pastor's voice.

"Waycross, you have been a great disappointment to me."

"What's the trouble, Pastor?" I said this in my most hospitable voice. "Loose pigeon?"

"No."

"Cough? Dry heaves? The hell-roarin' trots?"

"Waycross, do not bring your bowel-related blasphemy in here."

"I beg your pardon, Pastor. I should have said 'the squirts.'"

"You should have said and done much differently, Waycross. You should have been in church this morning. Everyone should have been in church this morning instead of queuing up to see our hometown witches."

Is it Sunday again?

I crossed my arms. The pastor rose from his chair, walked to the fireplace, where a few cinders were smoldering, and took out a red-ended brand. He used it to light a candle and settled back into his chair. Then he appeared as a disembodied head floating in a circle of yellow candlelight. The parsonage was eerily dark for the daytime.

"I thought you were going to bring us bleeding and blistering and other cures more painful than prayer. But, instead, you've brought three witches and their demon familiar and their magic right onto the town square."

"Have you seen the panther around here?" I said. "I haven't heard the first growl. How can you think that the Winters have anything to do with that panther?"

Boatwright ignored me. "You've sold your soul to magic and superstition, to potions and herbs and the perversion of religion. In your fallen state, polluted by ether, you've opened your soul to their enchantment. Pray for your redemption, and help me drive them away, back to the hollows where they belong." His talk was far worse than any I'd heard from patent-medicine salesmen.

"Drive them away? Certainly not. And it will take more than tomatoes. Were you the one who threw them?"

"No, but I bless the soul that dared to. And with courage, there will be more to follow."

My mouth felt dry. The corners of my lips clicked as I spoke. "The sisters are under my auspices and protection. I am a scientist and healer, and I would not permit them to do anything that was harmful. I'm looking for the truth underneath the superstition, to use it for the benefit of all who are afflicted. How can that be evil?"

"You're raking through stinking manure, looking for a pearl. But why would there be a pearl in that filth? The Winter sisters are quacks and herb women, the type that permitted your sister Eva to die. And you are apprenticing yourself to them."

The Winters were not that sort of quacks and herb women. The Winters did not trade in false hopes but in the essence of true ones. The more the pastor inveighed against them, the dearer the sisters felt to me. They were not the kind that would have just let Eva die. Rebecca would have soothed her with a poultice, and Sarah would have spun some tale, and Effie, looking at Eva with the selfsame gray eyes, would have... I didn't know yet, but I was going to find out. She would have at least done something. I wondered if it would have done Eva any good.

"All paths can lead to knowledge if they are carefully trod." I glanced behind me to see if I could open the door and let in more light, but it was already ajar, and the light it permitted didn't scare away the darkness.

"Not all paths. Some lead straight to error and perdition. The devil can't be tricked, Waycross."

"I don't believe in the devil, sir," I said.

"Enough!" The pastor's chair suffered a blow from his fist. "Waycross. I know what you and those witches are doing in your hayloft. Fornication. Vulgarity. Impiety. Fornication."

"You already said fornication."

"Such is the gravity of the sin." The pastor's skin stretched tight around his mouth. "Waycross, I brought you here to Lawrenceville," he leaned toward me, his eyes glowing amber in the firelight, "because I hear the devil whispering at night."

I kept my composure until I'd descended the steps of the parsonage and rounded the front of the church. Then I erupted. I stomped, kicked up rocks, and fumed in wordless syllables.

"It's all right, Doc," said someone from behind me.

I looked up from my shameful display. "Thumb?"

"In the flesh." Thumb held up his palms for investigation. He was wearing the Quaker clothing—black hat, white wig, buckled shoes—from his last spectacle. "I've got a little shopping to do. A few folks to meet. Doc, if you don't mind me asking, what has you so hot?"

"The pastor has swallowed a wasp or three. He's swollen up over my peddling superstitious cures for the devil. He wants me tarred and feathered."

"Tarred and feathered is no joke," said Thumb gravely. "Tar hurts. Can't scrub it off without taking part of your epidermis."

I was instantly uncomfortable at the idea that Thumb was speaking from experience, that he had endured more than a tongue-lashing from enemies of his work.

"Come on, Doc, let's get some grub."

We did not go to the Flowing Bowl, as I'd expected. That was a relief. The crowd there was still not welcoming to me over the hurt I'd caused Pendleton. Instead, we went to Molly Rhodes's boarding house, which was less popular than the Flowing Bowl because Mrs. Rhodes insisted on temperance at her table. Her biscuits were higher and softer, her pork smokier, her sweet-potato soufflé made with more molasses than sweet potato. But all she offered to wash it down with was buttermilk.

Thumb drank his buttermilk lustily, three full glasses. That should have inverted the stomach of any man, but his constitution seemed peculiarly immune. "Boatwright's a blowhard," he said. "Don't fret over what he says, so long as you feel you're doing right. Goodness knows I'd have been run out of every town there is if I hadn't played the banjo till the naysayers changed their minds or gave up. Like you."

I nodded. "Words I don't fear. Tomatoes I don't fear. But what if Boatwright whips his congregation into a mob? Whoever threw the tomato could be taught to throw fire."

"Well, that's what you'll just have to wait and see. And watch out for. But you've got friends. The whole town is not against you."

"When are you lighting out again, Mr. Thumb? I should miss your reasonable counsel."

"Not for a while yet. I'll be here to help if you need me to catch any tomatoes."

"Why stay put? I can't imagine that the sisters and I have left much business for your tonics, I'm sorry to say."

Two crimson patches rose on Thumb's cheeks, and I had an answer.

"A lady friend?" I said, leaning in conspiratorially. "Who's the lucky lass?" A chord rang in my brain—the crossing of the Alcovy, all his elixirs spilled into the river. "Surely not Effie?"

Thumb nodded, his mouth turning up at her name.

"She's too young for you, Thumb." I shook my head. "Her gray hair notwithstanding. She can't be any more than eighteen."

Thumb smiled, ignorant of my distress. "How old do you think I am, Doc?"

His skin looked as though it was peeling away at the hairline and behind his ears. I would've said fifty, but few on the frontier lived that long.

"Forty-five?" I asked.

Thumb exploded with laughter. A good minute passed before his barking subsided enough for him to catch his breath. "All part of the show, Doc. Folks would rather buy medicine from an old fellow than a young one. They get confused between age and wisdom."

Thumb took off his Quaker hat. His white locks came with it, revealing a close-cropped, healthy head of jet-black hair. He scrubbed at his temples, and to my astonishment, skin came away in great globs. His jowls melted like wax, and the cracks around his eyes smoothed out. What remained was a face pink and fresh.

"Doc, I'm twenty-one. Not too old for anyone, especially not Miss Effie Winter."

9

A CURE HE LIKES

The myriad materia medica of four healers, all crammed into my office, was a dizzying spectacle. Rebecca's enormous mortar and pestle took up the table I'd dedicated to my laboratory equipment. The shelves sagged with powders, unguents, saps, oils, milks, mucuses, and miscellaneous effluvia. Sarah's pigeon cried from its cage. We'd hung it up with the hams in the rafters. Happily, none of the sisters wanted to undertake purposeless beautification. No one insisted on carpets, curtains, lace, flowers, or wall hangings. A spray of lavender branches and a fresh layer of sawdust by the window were the only new niceties.

I had precious little space left for my own living. My personal effects got crowded into the hayloft with me. This is how a homesteader must feel when, having ordered his cabin just so, he decides to take a wife—except that I had three, and they weren't wives.

I was taking my supper cold in my office. The sisters took theirs with the Snells. The gossip-starved townsfolk might consider Rebecca and me dining together an undue, premature familiarity, and we wanted to be respectable.

In my supper bowl were pork and sweet potatoes. I eased the digestive action of the heavy food with a bottle of Grove's Tasteless Chill Tonic, which was, as promised, tasteless. The bowel movements that it produced were regular, strong, and healthful. As a cure, it was useless, but it was satisfactory as a digestive.

I let out tasteless eructations as I reviewed my hasty notes from the previous week. They were not proper case studies. There'd been so many that I hadn't had the time to turn my jumble of ailments, adjectives, and arrows into a narrative. I'd circled "red-hot poker" for a reason I couldn't recall. Next to "catarrh," I'd written "juniper," but I had learned that juniper had leaves, seeds, roots, berries, shoots, and sprouts. They could be crushed and ingested, steeped, smeared on as a poultice, or smoked and the vapor inhaled. For the time, it was enough to remember that juniper might be useful.

Even after Rebecca, Sarah, and Effie had seen to all the visitors on their first day back, an equal crowd appeared the following morning and the next. I found Rebecca's treatments the most attractive, for they seemed the most like my own—an active principle applied to the affliction—therefore, I spent the most time standing close to her, observing. The patients, though, diagnosed another reason for our closeness besides curiosity, and thus was the knowledge of a romantic understanding between us communicated to the town at large.

At Rebecca's prescription, the millers suffering from summer complaint took arrowroot and cinquefoil in copious quantities of water. This flushed the complaint from their bodies faster than my purgatives. Eliza Green, Pendleton's niece, was wasted to skin and bones. Rebecca ordered a regimen of sassafras tea and sorghum molasses, which started to restore healthy flesh to the young woman's frame inside of a week. She cleared up two acute cases of quinsy with goose grease rubbed on the throat. Parkerhouse had a fearsome case of gravel, and I couldn't stand the thought of all the delicate lancet work needed to clean out the man's urinary passages. But Rebecca had all the gravel out in three days with corn-silk tea. The silks, mind you—not the kernels or the husks but the silks, boiled in water with a little cream and sugar. Every gentleman on Earth would prefer tea, no matter what kind, to a prolonged surgery on his genitals.

Just as I was considering that, a knock came at the door. Other people might rest from their labors at mealtime, but a doctor never can. I remembered the last time a knock had come like that. It had ended with the amputation of Pendleton's arm, my shame and disgrace. My meal suddenly sat heavy and cold in my stomach, all the humors of digestion rushing elsewhere, to my head and my bowel, but I could not ignore the knocking. I opened the door.

Rebecca was there, holding hands with one of P's scampering children. The anxious parents, P and Catherine, were just behind them.

"This little one's got a broken leg," said Rebecca. "They came to the Snells while we were at supper, but I said that Doctor Waycross is the one to set a broken bone straight."

I took two steps backward. "Rebecca, you needn't... It's only... but I'm sure you could see to it."

"That's right," she said, "Doctor Waycross will set it right. Now, Doctor, will you see to the bone while I make up a draught that will help him sleep?"

The parents lifted the boy into the surgery chair by the window, not that the window afforded any advantage since it was dark outside. Rebecca brought over more candles before she went to work on the soporific dram. The fracture was simple, only a single clean break, from what I could feel with my gentlest palpations. No bone protruded from the skin. The limb was of good shape and color. I set the bone in the Hippocratic way, a bandage stiffened with flour and water, and I showed Catherine how to change the dressing daily.

Rebecca returned with a steaming drink of chicory and spices. The boy wrinkled his nose, but P shook him by the shoulder, and the boy drank. He was asleep before I'd finished giving all my instructions to Catherine.

They left, P carrying the boy and Catherine close behind. As soon as I'd slid the door closed behind them, I turned to Rebecca. "You needn't have brought them here for a simple fracture."

"No, Aubrey, I did need to. They needed to come to you. They didn't want to because of—"

"Pendleton," I finished. "But I was hardly saving this limb. It was a simple treatment. And one limb doesn't atone for another."

"One doesn't, but a hundred do. And this is the first. Lawrenceville must trust you, Aubrey. You're the right one for so many cures. I cannot do surgery. I cannot bleed or balance humors. There is good in your hands."

I reached out and touched her arm. Her dress was warm from where she'd been making the hot draught at the fire. When I touched her, she stepped a little closer, into my touch, and my heart quickened.

Sarah felt peevish, for all that day, she'd seen only warts. Children, old folks, didn't matter—a wart is a wart, damn ugly, and Sarah could do nothing to make them disappear. Effie, maybe, could wipe one away like a smudge of dirt, but no one asked for her anymore when it came to warts. Folks seemed to have decided that they shouldn't trouble Effie with minor ailments. They asked for Sarah to fix their warts. She could tell them the only real cure was to wrap it up and don't pick at it, and it would get better in six months if they left it alone, but folks never want to hear that the only cure is time. They mistrust your important cures if you tell them there's nothing you can do about a little wart.

Thus, the best cure was to tell a patient to steal a dishrag, wash with it then tear off a strip, wrap the wart in that strip of dishrag, and not take it off but once a week. The other part of the dishrag they should bury at a crossroads until it rots away. In Sarah's reckoning, no one would call the constable over a stolen dishrag, but the act of stealing was enough transgression to clarify the mind, to bring it to attention. The part wrapped around the wart keeps the patient from picking at it, and the rest, buried in well-trod earth, rots away in about six months, just when the wart goes away on its own. That was a neat solution, not in the least painful, and much preferable to Waycross's cauterizing iron.

The fifth time Sarah told someone to steal a dishrag, she still enjoyed the idea of the dishrag crime spree she was unleashing, but by the tenth time, she was bored. Folks would just be stealing each other's dishrags back and forth. She started tearing strips from a rag at hand and making up tales to explain its healing properties.

During a lull in patients, she decided to slip away. Rebecca wouldn't notice she was missing. Rebecca's patients had a hundred complaints from pestilent to priapic, and Waycross was glued to her side. Sarah had seen his eyes sparkling with delight whenever Rebecca smashed some lard and sulfur into a raw rash or steeped linseed tea for a whooping cough, and she noticed her sister was thrilled when Waycross lanced a boil and the pus came out clear, as if that was a talent possessed only by the city doctor. Sticking knives into people didn't take any skill—everyone knew that. By then, all their patients had seen Waycross and Rebecca mooning over each other.

Sarah put an apple and a bottle of Grove's Tasteless Chill Tonic into a sack, provisions for her excursion. She wondered if she should leave Effie. What if the tomato-throwers come back? Boatwright was fuming. He'd told off Waycross. He'd kept to his fairy tale about the panther as the Winters' familiar, and the rhetoric was hot. He might try some subterfuge, but they'd been there for weeks, and Boatwright hadn't mustered much righteous anger in the townsfolk. Lawrenceville and Effie would be safe from each other for a few hours.

Sarah set off into the forest. The fear of the panther ensured that no one would bother her on her constitutional—on her walk. "Constitutional" was Waycross's word, and Rebecca had taken to it as well. They took their "constitutionals" together in the evening after supper, walking ruts in the roads around the town square.

A little ways west of town was the Yellow River. Most rivers had decent Cherokee names, like Altamaha or Chattahoochee or even Alcovy. The Yellow River had to spoil it, which was a damn shame. A yellow river was something that should flow into a latrine, not a lake. Maybe that's why folks stayed away from the Yellow River. Like the Alcovy, the Yellow River wasn't any good for boats or fish—too shallow and too rocky. One of the rockiest sections nearest town was called Hurricane Shoals. A dozen rivers had their own Hurricane Shoals. Another was up in Jefferson, on the Oconee, but the Yellow River's was particularly unpleasant. The swift main channel spurted erratically and noisily between jagged granite boulders. The lesser flows swirled in slower side eddies and moist pools. Pine pollen lay thick on the slow water. Maybe that was why it was the Yellow River. Mosquitoes clustered there, too, along with pieces of bone and fur and half a gnawed fish. It smelled of mud and rot. Sarah didn't like Hurricane Shoals, but at least no warts would be there to trouble her.

A shallow-rooted pine had fallen over just upstream of the shoals. She clambered over the root ball and sat down on the truck to let her feet dangle over the white spray.

"Stinks out here."

Sarah whirled around and saw Thumb on the eastern bank, coming out of the woods.

"What in the hell are you doing out here?"

"I've been trying to get your notice ever since I saw you leaving the square," said Thumb. "I was calling your name for a quarter mile. But you must have been lost in your thoughts. And you walk so fast I couldn't keep up."

"So you followed me all the way from town? Got a wart that couldn't wait?"

Thumb reddened. "Not a wart. I've got a question. A favor, really."

"One that couldn't wait?"

"If you want me to go, I'll go. I don't mean to be a bother."

"You're more of a bother when you keep blabbering on. Just tell me what you want, I'll tell you to screw off, and then you won't be a bother anymore."

"I don't know what I did to get on your mean side, Miss Sarah. Maybe I'm wasting my time asking for favors from you."

"All mortal flesh is on my mean side, Salmon Thumb. Don't think you're special."

Thumb took a step forward and hooked his thumbs under his suspender loops as if he were about to speechify. Sarah knew how long his speeches could be. She held up a hand.

"Short as you can, sir."

"I want your blessing to court your sister," he said.

"She's swollen up like a pumpkin for Aubrey Waycross. You could probably duel him, twenty paces with pistols, but I think Rebecca wouldn't be much impressed by that."

"I meant Effie," said Thumb quietly.

"I know you did, but I wanted you to say it."

Thumb flushed.

"I saw you at the river," said Sarah, "when you tipped out all your medicine. I've seen you sulking around the square when you ought to have taken your mule and your banjo and moved on to the next town."

Hurricane Shoals gurgled beneath her. She'd eaten her apple down to the core and threw it into one of the stagnant pools, startling a pair of dragonflies.

"Why are you asking me?" said Sarah. "Rebecca's the oldest."

"While I've been sulking around," said Thumb peevishly, "I figured out that Rebecca's not the one to ask, not when it comes to Effie."

Sarah felt a deep quaking in her bowels, a sudden nervousness. Their mother had drawn them into a circle together. She'd bound them together in a promise of protection for them all. When Rebecca had stepped from the circle before, that was Everett. Now, it was Waycross. With Thumb wanting to court Effie... an acrid memory of smoke came back to her.

"Effie can choose for herself whether she wants you courting her or not," said Sarah.

"Is that your blessing?"

"It's not a blessing, and it's not a curse. Two people can do whatever they damn well please, if'n both are willing."

"So, it is a blessing?" Thumb grinned.

"I can take your head off your neck from a hundred yards," said Sarah, "and I won't regret it. I'd only need one word from Effie. You'd never see me, never see the bullet."

Thumb tipped his cap to her in reverence and in thanks.

Wouldn't matter if I did shoot his head off, thought Sarah. Effie would just stick it right back on if she preferred.

I'm supposed to quit drinking," said Maltbie morbidly as he came into our office.

He looked like a sack of corn, his body lumpy and overstuffed, with stubby arms and legs. A peek out the door confirmed that he'd arrived like a sack, too—on the back of the blacksmith's wagon. The smith must have loaded him up behind the Flowing Bowl and sent him to us. Maltbie's wife would have scalded and tanned him had he arrived back home in his state—better to deliver him to the doctors, where we would, first, do no harm.

"And how successful have you been in quitting drinking?" I asked, helping him to a seat. His pungent breath, rich enough to set me on fire, answered the question.

"Not drinking is powerful," said Sarah, playing up a rural manner. "It works much heavier on a drunk than a drink does on a teetotaler."

"That's the truth," said Maltbie. He collapsed into the chair. "I get these headaches. Damn, the whiskey, it's my medicine for the headaches. I tell that to the missus, but she won't have it. That's why I started in the first place, and now, it's why I can't quit." Maltbie held up his fingers and wiggled them. "What if a bird's gotten hold of me?"

"That could be serious," said Sarah, nodding. "If a bird gets hold of your hair and builds a nest with it, you'll never have peace until that nest is abandoned."

Maltbie nodded in agreement.

"Meantime, the chicks' peeping, pecking at the nest, twisting your hair around—all that comes back to your head. That would give you the worst headache of your life."

"But that's nonsense—"

The twin stares of Sarah and Maltbie fixed upon me.

"I mean, that's nonsense because, sir, you have rather little." I scratched the top of my head, near my own thinning spot.

Maltbie reflected the gesture. His only hairs were a few stragglers behind the ears.

"And what could you do?" said Sarah, wrinkling her button nose. "Shoot every bird, knock down every nest?"

"There's millions of birds here," said Maltbie. "I'd never find it if a hair had gone missing. It could be in any one of a hundred thousand nests in that grove."

"Nothing we could do unless we burned the forest down," I said dryly.

"We'll try that if it comes to it," said Sarah, "but until then, let's suppose it's not a bird that's got hold of your hair. Because if we suppose that, there might be a way we can help you."

"Yes, suppose that," said Maltbie. "Then what can we do?"

Sarah put her hands behind her back and strutted in thoughtful perambulation. She stopped and was about to speak but started up her pacing again. At an arbitrary moment, she spun around to Maltbie. "What does it feel like, when you're having your worst headache?"

"Like someone putting a nail through my skull. Right here." He put his finger on his temple near his left eye.

"Then, that's where we'll work." Sarah dashed over to a reinforced tea chest in the corner. She threw open the lid, keeping her bent form positioned to block any view into the chest's contents. After a minute, she righted herself and closed the chest with her foot. In one hand, she held a hammer, in her mouth, an iron nail, and in her other hand, a human skull.

"Where on Earth did you get that skull?" I demanded.

"Take this one, Maltbie," said Sarah. "I have plenty."

"Where on Earth did you get plenty of skulls?"

"Folks will part with a skull if you ask," said Sarah. "People that don't need theirs anymore. Now, Maltbie, watch me." She put the skull on the table indelicately. "Take this nail and line it up right where you feel the headache. If, one day, your headache moves, line up the nail there instead. And then—"

Without looking, Sarah brought the hammer down on the nail aimed at Maltbie's surrogate skull. The sound of splintering bone was unmistakable, known to all physicians.

Sarah withdrew the nail from the skull. The hole it'd made was round and clean. Only a few hairline fractures had spread from the site of impact.

"I'm glad I'm not him." Maltbie whistled his dismay.

"When this skull gets too full of holes and comes apart into a thousand pieces, that's what you want. Means you've broken through your own headache. It might take a week or a month. Keep going."

Sarah handed him the skull. Maltbie held it up and looked into its hollow sockets. "Sure glad I'm not him," he said again.

He left the office with his useless cure. I stood beside the window and watched him walk round the hog yard and wave to the friendly animals. His gait was unsteady, but he didn't need a wagon to get him where he was going.

"Do you believe you did him any good?" I asked Sarah, who was jostling against me at the window.

"Maltbie does, and that's enough. I found a cure that he likes."

"Isn't his wife one of Boatwright's most ardent partisans? She's not going to like her husband bringing home a human skull and pounding it with nails, is she? She's going to think that's witchcraft."

"So we should have given him a benediction and sent him home with nothing?"

"Isn't it dangerous to incite one of his supporters like this?"

"Dangerous? To make a little busybody like Mrs. Maltbie angry? Because she might go whisper about it to Boatwright and her friends at the corn shucking? I'm not going to give up on a good cure because Mrs. Maltbie might be mad. What's the worst she could do?"

"She might throw more than a tomato," I said.

10

GRAVEYARD DIRT

A library is an identity in linear feet. A phrenologist would do better to read his patient's library than his skull. Rebecca and I chose to intermingle our books on the office shelves so that we might both consult them. I fretted over the matter before committing to the arrangement. The mingling of her books with mine—or mine with hers, for she had far more than I did—was a profoundly intimate act.

Once resolved, we integrated them by theme. Rebecca's notes on Indian physic, copied from missionaries' diaries, leaned against my Galen and Avicenna. Her old almanacs accompanied my astronomical tables. A good many of her cures came from those notes and books. I perused them all, committing to memory all that I could, but many more of her ways and wiles were not written anywhere, excepting when I wrote down what I saw. Those cures she'd learned from her mother, or she'd perfected herself, or she'd heard from someone: an ancient Cherokee or a young Creek mother, a German homesteader, an itinerant Irishman, or a English goodwife recently arrived to the frontier. She had a vast intellect to collect, sort, remember, and refine all these superstitions into cures. That was just what I hoped to do with the Winter sisters' cures, but passed through the alembics of my own scientific and logical reasoning.

The greatest delight in combining our libraries was finding duplicate volumes between our collections. She had a Culpeper herbal older than mine. Her Paracelsus was in German, the relic of an Old World immigrant, while mine was in Latin. We compared the volumes and found intriguing differences. A handsome Trismegistus in her possession smelled of fire, which gave it an authority that my schoolbook edition lacked. She had no Hippocrates, but that was no great matter. I had all the Hippocrates we needed inside my own head. That we shared several volumes, that some of our cures sprang from the same pages, gladdened my heart.

Nowhere was there any mention of prestidigitating a frog. That had been my own invention, and I still felt rather proud of it. I could write it into a pamphlet with my own name on the front. Rebecca, of course, could write a much longer volume, but the frog was mine.

After weeks of working side by side, we had fallen into a rhythm. Most days, we all saw to the early-morning patients, then from afternoon through evening, Rebecca and I stayed close to the office, tied to our materials, while Sarah and Effie went their own ways.

Thus, that evening, Rebecca and I were alone. We had no patients waiting on us, but we had every reason to be together there, in privacy—a respectable time for courtship.

I looked over the rim of my cup at her. "I've been thumbing through your books for cholera."

We were sitting in the shadow of the bookshelf, gathering near it like a hearth and drinking coffee. Mine was brewed from Arabian beans. Hers was an amalgam of nuts and herbs that pretended to the title of "coffee." She was habituated to the imitation, so the genuine tasted false.

"There are many contradicting cures and twice as many theories as to the cause," I said. "What do you think it is?"

"Bad water," she said, as though that were not a puzzle that had bothered the brightest minds since the days of the pyramids.

"But what is 'bad' water?" That was a familiar debate from my apprenticeship at the Poor House and Hospital. I knew my evidence. "Cholera has broken out in new settlements, where the water is clear and sweet. It's broken out in brackish places and dry places and cold places, winter or summer. So, if we cannot agree on the character of this bad water—"

Rebecca stood up to refill her bark brew, and the argument faded inside me. I didn't want to talk about cholera, either. I was sitting there, in privacy, with a young lady of my own age and temperament, with whom I had a romantic understanding. I should not have been debating cholera with her. We should have been talking about... whatever constitutes normal conversation.

She sat down again across from me with a fresh cup. "So, what else have you found?"

I looked over the shelves to refresh my memory.

"I don't mean in the books." She smiled to cover a flicker of exasperation. "Or not only in the books. In Lawrenceville. In the woods. Anywhere."

She had a specific topic in mind, which she meant for me to divine from the atmosphere. Cholera came again to my mind, but I pushed it away. I could offer praise for her feminine qualities. I could not remember when I had done that. I tried to arrange some compliments in my head. Her cheeks were rosy, like an acute dermal infection of erysipelas. Her teeth were the pure white of a perfect blister raised from mustard oil on the smooth skin of the underarm. Also, her secondary sex characteristics showed admirable development...

I scrambled for another topic—mountains, fauna, flora... a fact or fancy, new and surprising, that would show that I cared about the world outside my office.

She scratched at the back of her neck. I'd never seen her do that before. Her attentions, for a minute, seemed far away. "Dr. Waycross, I've heard that respectable people, all the best houses in Savannah and Milledgeville, share a most respectable pastime."

"Ombre?"

"No, one that you know better than ombre."

I brought down the bottle of ether from its place among the anatomies and lectures. When I uncorked it, the bottle exhaled its sweet smell, the vapors almost visible in the air. The smell is too sweet to be pleasant, like a mountain of blueberries left to rot in the sun.

"Are you sharing, Dr. Waycross?"

I gave her the bottle. She inhaled, and then I took my turn.

A tide of good feelings washes over me, drenches me. It swirls in my ears and splashes between my toes and gets into my nostrils. Nature crawls in through the holes in the roof and the cracks in the wall. The cawing of the night birds blends into a symphony of forest sounds. A sleepy turkey calls from a thicket. The whoosh of skittering squirrels, desperate for their nests, scatter pine needles.

There is a hog under the laboratory table. Together, we shoo it out and chase it around the yard. We try to ride it. Soft breezes make the trees to sway, opening the canopy of the forest to columns of moonlight. Crickets sing their love songs, each to each. The sky turns dark and light a thousand times, as we watch stars and planets and fireflies and clouds and ages play out above our heads.

Rebecca begins buck-dancing alone, following a melody that only she can hear. I sit on the floor, crossed-legged, as I haven't sat for years, and clap to the hypnotic rhythm of her footfalls. When she kicks up her heels, I can see black riding boots, laced high up.

A galaxy of purple spots stutters and winks close to my face and grows and shrinks and changes hue from midnight to lilac and back, and they buzz like bees, but they are singing. Rebecca has a sack filled with flour, or straw, or the feather pillow from my bed, and I have a similar one, and by swinging it, I shoo away the purple spots, which giggle and scatter. Rebecca strikes me over the head, causing me to stumble in glee, and I retaliate, and she falls over, and I catch her.

I do not fall in love with Rebecca because of chemicals or purple spots. The rise of a lover's affections is more mysterious than the workings of ether. I fall in love with her cleverness, her kindness, and her nature that is kindred to mine. We have both lost people that are dear to us. We have both turned to medicine as a cure for our own hurts. But all these abstracts are forgotten. When her library meets mine and mingles, I know that it is true.

W hat you need, Ouida Bell, is some graveyard dirt."
Ouida Bell had hiked up her skirts, unashamed that time, so Sarah could see the rash—a field of angry red dots scattered discontinuously over her legs. Sarah ran her hands over the damaged area. There was no tender inflammation, no raised wounds. The worst of the rash was near where the panther had bit her, but that wound, which had been only a playful nip, had healed weeks before. It was a coincidence. The rash certainly was not blood poisoning from the animal bite since no fever was present. Nor was it erysipelas or ringworm. It also wasn't... that other disease, the one Sarah shook out of mind the moment it blinked across her imagination. No, the rash was a symptom of hand-foot-and-mouth disease. If Waycross or Rebecca were treating the girl, they would say it was of no real concern. Like warts, hand-foot-and-mouth always goes away on its own, but Sarah never felt that kind of answer was good enough to satisfy a patient—especially Ouida Bell. Also, to her mind, the more folks digging around the churchyard, the better.

"What will happen if I don't put grave dirt on it?"

"Climb up your legs," said Sarah. "And then you'll see it on your palms because you can't leave your legs alone and you're itching at them. And then the pox will be crawling out your mouth, all around your lips and nose."

"Oh, God!" Aghast, Ouida Bell put her hands to her mouth then shrieked. She held her hands out in front of her and shook them as if flinging off plague water. "Is it scarring?"

"Not usually, but you can never figure on it. Anyway, why worry about some pox marks on your lips? That'll help keep the boys away."

"I haven't had trouble with the boys since I started with the asafetida. So, it's graveyard dirt for this... this rash?"

"Yes. And not just a little bit, either. I think we need to bury you."

"Bury me?"

"Under the cover of moonlight. You and I must go to Lawrenceville's churchyard. We will dig a hole five feet deep, wide enough for your shoulders. And then you will strip—"

"Why must I do that?"

"For the cure to work, you must be naked as the beasts of the woods, naked as the lilies of the field."

Ouida Bell scratched nervously at her legs then pulled her hand away, blushing.

"Then you will climb down into the hole, standing up, and I will bury you up to your neck. You must stay there until the coldest hour of dawn." That whole time, you won't be able to scratch.

"When can we do it?" whispered Ouida Bell.

Ouida Bell brought a lantern. Sarah had half a dozen tallow candles and two narrow-bladed shovels. They met at the Parrs' cabin. Though she'd been its only human victim, Ouida Bell did not confess any fear of the panther in the twilight gloom. She'd survived one attack, and Sarah had brought her gun.

"If this panther really is your demon familiar, like Boatwright says," teased Ouida Bell, "then you didn't need to bring your gun. You could just tell it to sit, roll over, play dead, couldn't you?"

Sarah smiled. "But I did bring my gun."

Unlike confectionaries, graveyards do not call out to passersby for their custom. Lawrenceville's graveyard was a quarter mile from the town center, set back a good ways from the road and hidden behind a small rise. Four granite stones marked the corners, but the rest of the fence had never been built. A wooden scaffold there held up an iron bell: the burying bell. It tolled to summon the town: men to dig the grave, women to mourn, children to leer, the pastor to intone about the fragility of life, ashes to ashes, dust to dust.

Lawrenceville's graveyard bell had rung for Everett. Afterward, the funeral crowd marched, in a mass, to the Winters' cabin, with Boatwright at the head of the procession. Sarah had her rifle. She could have lined up graves next to Everett's: for Boatwright and for anyone else that spoke hate against her and her sisters, but Rebecca did not want blood to follow blood. Life is not restored by death.

"Right about here ought to do."

Sarah sank her shovel blade into the earth about ten feet from Everett's headstone. The town didn't have a funerary mason, so the headstone was actually a boulder in which was artlessly carved "Evrt." Rebecca had done that. She was worthless with a chisel.

Ouida Bell picked up the other shovel and joined in. Their blades clanged against each other immediately, sending sudden sparks up against the lantern light. "Sorry," Ouida Bell said.

"We've got to find a rhythm, else there's no good two of us working on it."

"It's my cure, so I don't mind doing the digging." Ouida Bell paused to push up the sleeves of her evening gown then attacked the loamy top layer of soil. When she reached the red clay, she slowed. Each shovelful was heavier.

"Let me take a try now," Sarah said.

"You're going to be burying me and digging me back up, right?"

"So?"

"So I'll do the digging now." Ouida Bell grunted. "I don't want you plum tuckered when it's time to get me out."

Sarah leaned on her shovel and watched. Three feet down, Ouida Bell started having a hard time with the angles. Sarah should have thought to bring a bucket. Truth was, she had never buried anyone in the churchyard before. Usually, just the threat of a burying was enough to stay anyone from scratching, and that's all that Ouida Bell needed to do: not scratch it, even when it itched like the devil. If only people could control themselves, half of the world's curing wouldn't be needed, nor half the world's guns.

Ouida Bell heaved up a sprinkling of red clay. Clay is cool and close, damp from the nearness of water. "It presses against all the itching at once," Sarah's mother had always said. "It calms all the nerves. It immobilizes the fingers so they can't scratch and spread."

"This better work," muttered Ouida Bell.

"Nothing's better than a graveyard burying for what you've got." Sarah started to pity the poor girl, smeared with clay, dirt running in sweaty streaks from her forehead.

"What if it scars? What will I have then?" asked Ouida Bell. "What if it scars my lips?"

"Folks have scars and live a fine, full life."

"But I won't. If I don't get rid of this hoof-and-mouth—"

"Hand-foot-and-mouth. You're not a cow."

"If my face gets scarred up, I will be. I'll be like some animal. All I have is my face, Sarah. My momma says, 'She's the prettiest one in town,' and all the boys say, 'Why, isn't she the belle of the ball?' and the church ladies coo and pet my cheeks. They twirl my hair, and I think maybe they'd really rather pull it out by the roots. Because that's who I am: pretty Ouida Bell, prettiest girl in town." Her shovel bit in deep. "If there's no pretty face, then there's no Ouida Bell."

"Plenty of menfolk don't care about a pretty face if the rest of a lady's parts work hard enough." Sarah regretted the jibe. It was too harsh. "You could learn to play the piano. Start a sawmill or a liquor still. There's a thousand useful things—anything you like."

"What if I want to stay pretty? Just as good a choice as playing the piano."

Sarah peered into the hole. "Maybe with two shovels."

Together, in half an hour, they finished the hole five feet deep. It was clay down to the bottom, where the granite started. A little water was pooling in the hole already.

"Ready?" Sarah asked.

Ouida Bell nodded and slipped her evening gown over her head. The fine hairs of her flesh glimmered in the candlelight. She folded her arms across herself against the night air. Ouida Bell climbed down into the hole.

Sarah scooped the first shovelful of dirt back into the hole and then a dozen more, working quickly as Ouida Bell shivered. "Is it cold?"

Ouida Bell nodded. "But it gets warmer the more dirt you add. And it tickles. It's the strangest feeling. Like nothing else I've ever felt."

"I'd wonder if it were familiar. Who else is going to be burying you in graveyard dirt?"

They chattered and laughed while Sarah packed in the dirt around Ouida Bell, and when the work was done, Sarah lay down beside Ouida Bell's head and rested her chin on her hands.

"Do you know, Ouida Bell, that I've never prescribed a graveyard burying before, much less had the patient consent to it? They've taken a little graveyard dirt but never been buried up to their neck in it. You are a brave woman."

Ouida Bell tried to nod, but she bumped her chin on the ground, which sent both her and Sarah into gales of laughter. When Ouida Bell laughed, the earth around her trembled from the movement of her body beneath.

Sarah saw a light bobbing on the road. The sun was not yet on the horizon, but the eastern sky already had the milky gray of dawn.

"What in the devil is this?" cried Pastor Boatwright, running up to them.

He dropped his lamp in shock. All he saw was an animated head upon the ground and Sarah beside it. She waved him a fine toodle-oo, and Ouida Bell grinned with all her teeth.

II

A SLAP WITH OLD BREAD

Eudoxia Everett came to us in the arms of her father, who'd run all the way from their farm. The ten-year-old had been splitting wood, he said, and the new ax blade wanted its taste of blood. It had jumped a locust log and sunk itself into her leg. That was not the trouble. Pa Everett could clean an ax wound. Eudoxia, bandaged up, was back to her labors within an hour, but the next day brought fever and pain. The leg was hot to the touch. Pa Everett feared blood poisoning.

When I unwrapped the dressings, I knew infection was already deep in the leg. The bandages dripped with pus—not the laudable, flowing sort, but the sweet-smelling pus of putrefaction. The edges of the wound were black and ragged and crusted with vile matter. If I didn't take her leg, she'd die. If I did, she'd be a burden, unmarriageable, a source of sorrow to herself and to her family. Pendleton's disembodied arm returned as if in a vision. What if I mangled the poor girl's leg as badly as I'd mangled Pendleton? The family had already been visited by tragedy. They were the father and youngest sister of the late Everett, Rebecca Winter's suitor, who'd died in the mill fire.

"The best course is debridement and scouring by carbolic acid," I said, intending to ease them into the truth of the situation.

But as I rose to fetch the carbolic acid, Rebecca stopped me. "Let me see her," she said, her voice wavering.

Eudoxia smiled when Rebecca came to the side of the examination table. Rebecca smiled back, but the smile quivered just as her voice had. Rebecca put her fingers close to the black edges of the wound. I knew she could feel the heat of infection, the pulse of corruption. She knew the treatment needed to be as terrible as the wound.

Rebecca squeezed the girl's hand and stepped away from the table, then she disappeared behind some shelves. I took that as a signal that I was to administer the treatment. Rebecca, perhaps because of her affection for the family of which Eudoxia Everett was a part, hadn't the stomach for inflicting pain, even when that pain was necessary and curative.

Before I could begin, though, Rebecca reappeared, holding a slice of mold-covered bread.

"Now, this won't hurt a bit, Eudoxia," she said.

In my astonishment, I forgot about the carbolic acid. The mold was hoary blue-white fuzz interspersed with dark-green circles. She wet the bread with water from a pitcher, then she wrapped the whole of it, injury and bread, in clean bandages.

I was speechless, dumbstruck. I wondered if and when I should intervene, for surely no doctor would consent to the use of moldy bread for an infected leg. Such a bizarre superstition deserved to be ripped from the pages of whatever cursed herbal Rebecca had found it in.

While Rebecca worked and I gaped, Eudoxia talked. "I miss you, ever since Henry. You should have come by to see us. Pa misses you, too."

"I'm sorry, little one," said Rebecca. "It's... not so easy."

"Who's Henry?" I sputtered.

"He never liked his given name," said Rebecca. "We never used it. He was just Everett."

"Henry," said Eudoxia weakly.

"Shh, don't you worry about it," Rebecca told her patient.

"Why don't you come up to see us?" asked Eudoxia. "We used to see you all the time."

Rebecca flushed. "You're feverish, little one. Just rest. Dr. Waycross will be up to see you in a couple days."

"Not you?"

Rebecca shook her head. "I'll come by and by. But Dr. Waycross will see to you. He's a nice man."

"What's his whole name?"

"Aubrey," I said, interrupting at the sign of Rebecca's distress. "You can call me Aubrey if you like."

"Aubrey sounds like Henry," said Eudoxia.

The work finished, Rebecca nodded at Pa Everett. I thought they might exchange a few words, but it wasn't needed. Pa Everett—given name unknown—returned the respectful gesture. Evidently, he trusted enough in that strange moldy treatment, or in the healer administering it, that he did not question it. I, on the other hand, was festering with doubt.

I could barely wait until Pa and Eudoxia had left. I had made many discoveries with Rebecca during the last few weeks—willow bark, balm of Gilead, witch hazel, valerian—but she had not applied a wholesome botanical. It was moldy bread. But Rebecca acted quite precisely. She gave no explanations. She applied the bread, wrapped the leg, and sent Eudoxia away with a smile.

"Rebecca, you know that I have every trust in your cures, but this particular one, given the severity of the girl's condition—"

She heard the accusation in my voice. "It often effects a full cure. It depends on the mold, I think, but I'm not certain of the difference yet. The whitish growth, as on this bread, seems very promising."

"But maybe your affections for the girl have clouded your judgment. I know that you don't want to inflict pain on a family that has already had so much, but think of the consequences."

"I have considered them. I trust this cure more than I trust your carbolic acid."

I wasn't satisfied. "I feel that, by doing nothing, we've increased the chances of amputation. And please trust, my dear, that I have seen your cures perform good works, but moldy bread? How can it debride the flesh or rebalance the humors?"

"Neither of those are necessary," said Rebecca. "And it's not nothing. The bread will be enough. It sees to the infection."

"Dear, in almost a third of cases where the cut is inflamed like Eudoxia's—"

"And don't think that 'dear' and 'darling' and other sweet nothings will convince me to give up on my cures. Have more respect for me than that."

"Rebecca, then. Miss Winter. As I meant to say, in up to a third of cases, the carbolic acid prevents blood poisoning by burning away the necrotic flesh and avoiding amputation, even in the most severe cases."

"A third?" said Rebecca. "If a third of the ax wounds that came to Hope Hollow turned to blood poisoning, this would be a ghost town."

A dark choler swirled in my stomach. The town had not yet forgiven me for what I'd done to Pendleton, nor did they trust I would not amputate in every case that I saw. But there I was, on the cusp of mangling this poor Eudoxia Everett because I did not trust what Rebecca said was a good cure. If I were really to learn, to humble myself, I must trust her medicine not only in the smaller matters of warts and dyspepsia, but also in cases of life and death.

"As you say, then," I said to Rebecca. "As you say."

When I traveled up to the Everetts' farm two days later, alone, I was not going with the hope of performing an alternate cure. Either Rebecca's moldy-bread poultice had saved the child's life, or I would be attending at a deathbed.

The cabin they lived in was slipshod and rotting. The uneven cuts of its logs made the facade slump to the west. Two chickens, gone savage, were struggling with each other in a tussle of wings and beaks and feathers. The steps by the door were coated in slime, and as I tried to ascend to the porch, I saw a woman huddled against one of the corner posts. She wore a night garment soiled at the hem with red clay. Tears streamed unbidden down her cheeks, wetted her dark hair into slick strands, and stained her fingers.

"Ma'am, can I help you?"

The woman lowered her hands and opened her mouth. Her terrible cry of agony shattered the evening with a high, single note. I'd heard such a scream two other times. The first was when I'd watched a master surgeon remove a tumor from a woman's abdomen. She expired on the operating theater's table. The second was from Eva, mad with hydrophobia.

The wailing woman was coming toward me as the door to the cabin opened. Yellow light spilled across my vision.

"I thought I heard a noise out here," said Pa Everett, yelling over the terrible wails. "Is that you, Doctor?" He motioned toward the woman with a nod and said into my ear, "We're not going to say anything about that, Doctor. We're going to go right inside."

The cabin accepted us into its glow, and the door closed. The keening ceased as soon as we were out of sight.

Inside, I saw a hearth, a table, a rope bedstead, and a ladder up to a loft, as well as a few bags, boxes, and a wooden chest. They were ordinary objects, but I could not make sense of them as the cry of the woman was echoing inside my head.

"Can I get you a drink, Doctor?" asked Pa Everett "Coffee? Cup of sugar? We already ate our supper, and the children finished every crumb, but there might be a biscuit hidden away."

There was no possible way I could eat. He was behaving as though porch banshees were an everyday occurrence.

I steadied myself against a chair. "But who? What? What in the hell—"

"Doctor, we're not going to say anything about it."

"But, sir—" I stammered.

"Not one word more. What would you like to drink?"

"I'd take... a coffee if you have it ready."

Small wonder that Rebecca had not been a frequent visitor. That grief-stricken mother, or banshee or whatever it was, howling in Rebecca's face...

Pa Everett went to the hearth, where a percolator was hanging low over the embers. While his back was turned, I took my flask out, stole a sip of ether, corked it, and hid it away. A veil of tranquility fluttered over my mind, and a gauzy vagueness covered the memory of... out there.

I winced as I took the scalding cup Pa Everett handed me. Not wanting to offend, I drank. The ether must have had a numbing effect on my tongue. The coffee was neither molten nor offensive.

Pa Everett sat at the bench next to the dinner table. "You didn't come up all this way to chitchat, now, did you?"

After sitting beside him, I tented my fingers and rested my chin upon them to look studious. I was giving the ether a little more time. Pa Everett let me ponder through another three swallows of coffee.

"I came to ask after Eudoxia, sir," I said.

"Eudoxia always had a shine for Rebecca, too," he said, clearing his throat. "Looked up to her. When she and our Everett were courting."

"I am so sorry about your son," I said.

"You don't have to tiptoe around dead folks, Doctor. You'd always be on your tiptoes."

Still, we gave a moment's reverence to Everett's memory. Then I inclined my head toward the door, toward the crying woman. "Is she—"

"We're not going to say anything about that, Doctor."

"But—"

"That's something else. Someone else. I don't know what that is." He sprang up from the bench. "You wanted to see Eudoxia."

He called up the loft ladder, but he needn't have bothered. All the children were listening above us. Eudoxia scampered down on her own two feet and across the cabin floor. The motion of air through my lungs ceased.

"Eudoxia, go ahead and show him your leg," said Pa Everett.

She tossed the heel of her right leg up onto my knee. My hands were shaking, despite the ether. Her skin was all fresh and pink— no tenderness, no inflammation, no fever. I couldn't see a trace of the wound, the ragged and raw flesh, the foul-smelling pus.

No words would come to me. Was this magic, a miracle? Neither was possible. The cure was a good one, but that was faint comfort to me. My educated brain had wanted Rebecca's ridiculous cure to fail, as it should have. Hippocrates had never mentioned moldy bread, and Galen must have thrown in the garbage heap a remedy that could have saved gladiators and emperors. The best and ancient minds of medical science would have maimed this child with surgery or let her die of blood poisoning because no other treatments were available. Evidentially, though, they were wrong.

"Hell of a thing, ain't it?" said Pa Everett. "Moldy bread. I'll try it myself next time."

Pa Everett shooed Eudoxia away with a wave of his hat, and she fled, giggling. "You tell that Rebecca she doesn't have to be a stranger," he said. "Don't have to wait on a visit until somebody needs a slap with old bread."

When I stepped onto the porch, a rush of darkness came toward me, and a black shape was right at my ear, screaming and howling. I felt cold breath and flecks of spittle land on my cheek. The wail was a blast of lightning. My temples lit up in electrification and pain.

"Keep right on walking, Doctor," said Pa Everett, over the rending wails of the crying woman. "We're not going to say anything about that."

12

THE ELDEST LEADS

I'd memorized the rules of ombre and practiced a dozen hands with Rebecca. That fashionable game of Savannah had never been played before in Lawrenceville, but if Lawrenceville wanted to be the county seat, it needed to be ready to accept fashionable people. We were ready to introduce the respectable pastime to the town. Mayor Richardson and his wife offered to host the game, and I asked Mr. and Mrs. Snell to join us. That was a fitting party of six, but then I thought Effie belonged there, too. It made the pairs awkward, but Effie needed more exposure to decent people, and decent people needed to see her. I invited Sarah, as I felt I must, but was glad when she laughed in my face. She wouldn't keep her wit in check long enough for respectable company.

I'd reconciled with Rebecca after seeing the wonder of her cure, and she hadn't blamed me for my doubt. That was only my nature, she said. Rebecca was dressed in vibrant yellow, the color of a sunflower. Her bonnet was trimmed in peerless white lace, and she wore white gloves that came to her elbows. Mrs. Richardson's gloves were not so nice. Mrs. Snell's kidskin gloves only reached her wrists. Mayor Richardson looked as though he would have preferred to sleep. Snell was up for a lark. He mocked the way I shuffled the cards.

"Don't just smash them together," he said, laughing. "You look like a schoolboy. Riffle them like this." He took away the deck, and the cards clattered in an orderly manner among his fingers. "There you go, Doctor. Safe to say you're not a gambling man."

We chuckled out of duty, and I dealt the cards among us. But the presence of an audience, even a friendly one, made me uncomfortable.

Rebecca picked up her hand and said, "Wait, Aubrey. You are supposed to take the eights out. And the nines and tens."

"Ah, drat, that's right."

Her foot found mine under the table, and she placed her boot atop my shoe, a gesture that simultaneously showed affection and calmed the nervous tapping of my toe.

I collected what I'd distributed so far and searched the deck for the eights, nines, and tens and started again. "Now, the eldest leads with the first trick. Who's the eldest?"

Mayor Richardson looked at his wife, and she looked at Snell, and in the uncomfortable pause, Effie placed the three of clubs into the middle of the table.

"Ha, well that's fine!" I blurted. "The youngest, of course! Much more polite than the eldest."

No one else seemed to share my delight at the fine solution. Even Effie wrinkled her brow. Richardson, who was sitting to Effie's right, inched his chair toward his wife.

"Now what, Doctor?" said Rebecca.

"Ah, the ombre, which I suppose to be Effie, may call for 'ask leave.' That is calling a king to seek a partner, but if none is found, then she proceeds 'solo.' And she must win five tricks while the rest of us seek to thwart her."

"Doctor, I don't know what in the hell you just said," snorted Snell.

Mrs. Snell flicked his ear for the vulgarity.

"Put a higher card on top. She has to top it to win the trick," said Mrs. Richardson.

"I think she's going to win anyway," said Snell.

His wife flicked him again.

"Waycross will tell you if you do something wrong," teased Mayor Richardson, to a loud general agreement.

After she played her card, Mrs. Snell asked, "Mayor, any news from Milledgeville?"

He scratched behind his left ear, and one of his shirtfront buttons came undone. "These things move rather slowly. It's terribly important to us, you understand, but for the men in the House, only a trifling affair. They have the Cherokee to the north, the

Alabamians to the south, the British still sailing off the Savannah coast."

"Not even a rumor about the county seat?" I asked.

"Rest Haven is making a campaign, and they have a strong case. They're suited well on Suwanee Creek, which can take small boats to the Chattahoochee. They've a greater population, too. But Lawrenceville is in the center of the county. And we have promising industries. The tannery. The sawmill. Several excellent farms. And not one, but four doctors."

"Hear, hear," said Mrs. Richardson. She passed a plate of molasses balls to Rebecca.

"Boatwright came to me, fuming," confessed Mayor Richardson. "He thinks unorthodox healers in our midst is a travesty. Burying our virtuous girls in the graveyard. Actually, he used words much less polite."

"What did you tell him?" I asked.

"That as long as there was more good than harm, I saw no reason to interfere. And that I didn't want any trouble... from him or from you. Though I must say that putting people in the graveyard in the middle of the night sure sounds more like witchcraft than medicine."

"We are doctors, sir." I said. "I cannot explain all of Sarah's methods, and she has a certain mischievousness that I think may be inseparable from them. But above all, because we are doctors, we do no harm."

"You sure have a lot of lancets for doing no harm." Snell laughed, and the rest of us were supposed to laugh, too.

Mrs. Richardson brought in a plate bearing delicate wafers topped with fruit compote and a sprinkling of rare white sugar. Effie took one, then I noticed the tray circulated around the table without anyone else taking a wafer. Neither Snell nor Richardson nor their wives took one after Effie had served herself. I wondered if we hadn't run afoul of some country taboo, where the guests were supposed to politely demur to the host or to the person of highest social standing, or what have you. It was all foolishness.

"These look splendid," I said. "Rebecca, won't you have one?"

"No, thank you, Aubrey."

I was burdened with no such need for gentility. I just ate. "More for Effie and me. Effie, we'll have to eat a dozen each, won't we?" Then I said, "Boatwright doesn't know how much this town benefits from four doctors. How much all of medicine will benefit."

"You were up at the Everetts the other day, weren't you?" said Mrs. Richardson. "How is poor Eudoxia?"

"Cured! And all thanks to moldy—"

Rebecca's eyes widened. I read her expression, which said, "Hush your mouth, Waycross."

I wanted our hosts to know of Rebecca's accomplishment, which was a thousand times better than graveyard dirt and better even than the lancet for this poor girl. I wanted them to know how clever Rebecca was, what talent she said, but Rebecca, I supposed, did not want them to know. Perhaps moldy bread did not belong in polite company as it felt too much like a superstitious cure.

"Those poor Everetts," said Mrs. Snell, trolling her voice slowly. "They've had enough pain, what with their boy and the mill fire, and the mother before that."

"What happened to the mother?"

"Ma Everett died of puerperal fever a week after a stillbirth," said Rebecca.

"But if it's not Ma Everett on the porch, who is it?"

Richardson scratched his head. "Her ghost, I suppose. She came with the rest of the family, moved right along with them."

"But that's nonsense. It isn't a ghost. Rebecca, tell them it's not a ghost."

"I haven't been to the house in ages," she said. "I couldn't say." The weight of her boot pressed down onto my toes, showing her displeasure and desperation.

I coughed, and the table looked at me. "Mayor Richardson, I believe it's your turn to play," I said, recovering.

Richardson played a king with a leer, but Effie tossed down the ace of spades, collecting another trick. She pulled a card to start another, but I held up my hand. "That's the fifth trick you've taken, Effie. I think that makes you the winner."

"Didn't I tell you she'd win?" said Snell. "Put us out of our misery, Miss Effie."

Sarah tipped the cup, and the dice clattered onto the old board. A hundred years of falling dice and fast fingers had finished the wood to a smooth, dark surface.

"Double threes. That's all right, isn't it?" She advanced two of her red checkers toward Ouida Bell's black ones. "Should I do that?"

Ouida Bell leaned forward to watch Sarah's move then flopped back against the pillow. The backgammon set was an heirloom. A paper label in French was barely legible on the front side. It probably gave the rules, but Sarah couldn't read French. The Winter sisters didn't have a backgammon set, just as they didn't have a deck of cards, and Sarah had never learned the rules. Ouida Bell had promised to teach her, so while Waycross and Rebecca and Effie were busy with their ombre party, Sarah had gone up to Ouida Bell's cabin.

She found Ouida Bell in bed, heaped over with blankets. She had a fever and muscle weakness. Her fingers were tingling, which made even picking up the dice a chore. Sarah looked her over, peering into her throat and her nose, checking her neck, and squeezing her toes. All seemed well. The rash, for which Sarah had prescribed graveyard dirt, had cleared up fine. Sarah brought down the backgammon board from the shelf, and they started playing, but Ouida Bell's heart wasn't in the game.

"I'm sorry, Sarah. I just can't think straight right now."

"Well, never mind," said Sarah. "You can teach me later. It's probably a summer cold. And don't let anyone say you caught it from the graveyard. That's a damn lie. Colds don't come up from graveyards."

Ouida Bell closed her eyes for a moment. "What do you give people for summer colds? Same as for winter colds?"

"For most folks, I'd say to get a potato. Keep it in bed with you for a week, and then put it in your pocket while you go about your living for a second week. And then don't eat the potato! Don't let anybody eat the potato. Throw it in the river."

Ouida Bell laughed, which tickled her throat and made her cough.

"Does the potato do anything?" asked Ouida Bell.

"Four times out of five, a person with a potato gets better faster than a person without a potato. Waycross would say that's not scientific. It's not Hippocratic. How could it be? The ancient Greeks didn't even have potatoes."

"They didn't?"

"No, ma'am. We came up with potatoes on the new side of the ocean."

"Well, I never figured that." Ouida Bell sighed and leaned back again. "No potato for me, though?"

"I ruined the cure by telling you about it. Now you won't believe in it, so it won't work." Sarah fiddled with the checkers on the backgammon board. "The only real cure for a summer cold is some rest and some time."

"But that's no fun," said Ouida Bell. She closed her eyes.

"I know. Not near as fun as burying you in the graveyard and scaring the living daylights out of Pastor Boatwright." She chuckled at the memory, and Ouida Bell did too, which started her coughing again.

"I'll bet they're talking about it down at their ombre party," said Sarah. "Richardson is shaking his finger at Waycross and Rebecca. 'Can't you two keep your sister from stirring up trouble?' But it's not me they've got to worry about."

"What do you mean?" asked Ouida Bell.

"Nothing, nothing," said Sarah quickly. "Just... nothing."

She couldn't tell Ouida Bell about Effie. Rebecca and Waycross and Snell and Richardson and the rest were fooling themselves, playing at manners and society and fashion, when sitting at the table, pale and cold, was a marvel of ancient savagery in the person of Effie Winter.

"So, what kind of remedy would Rebecca cook up for a summer cold?"

Sarah grinned. "Fried earthworms."

Ouida Bell tittered. "Really?"

"Fried in butter with garlic. Mashed up into a paste. Mix it with a little milk. And spread the paste all over your neck."

"That's so disgusting!" Ouida Bell smiled.

"It's supposed to be. The smell crawls into your nose, tickles your brain parts, opens up your ears. You hear the earthworms sizzling. You hear their little fleshy bodies go pop! pop! pop! in the hot butter. Their gray goo gets right here." Sarah pressed at the hollow of her throat, just at the bottom of her neck. "You smell it for days. It soaks into your skin. Everywhere you go, people smell it on you, the earthworms and the garlic. And in two weeks, you're all cured." Sarah shrugged. "It's a crock of shit, just like the potato. I think that's all we have, Rebecca and me. Waycross, too. It's all right for little cures, like a summer cold or dyspepsia or gravel or the hell-roarin' trots. But there's nothing we can do about the real troubles."

"Lucky for me that all I've got is a summer cold." Ouida Bell propped herself up on an elbow. "You should just make up a big lie."

"What?"

"If it's all lies, then the bigger the lie, the better the cure. Tell just a huge crock of lies. A miracle cure." Ouida Bell's voice rose in excitement. "Good for all that ails you."

Sarah sniffed. "Like a medicine show?"

"Yeah, a medicine show. You've got no competition. I've seen Thumb around, but he hasn't gotten up a show in weeks."

Courting Effie has distracted him, thought Sarah.

"I'll bet you can do it. Get up a crowd. Make it disgusting. Tell them about a potato or fried earthworms or whatever. Really get them going. Then, it'd cure just about anything."

Sarah imagined the crowd, drawn up close. They believed her. She could use that. She'd charm an affliction out of them. "Ooh, Boatwright would hate it."

"Sure would." Ouida Bell giggled and blushed. She didn't cough that time.

"Why, that'd be some fun," said Sarah. "Some fun."

13

LIKE HOGS IN A HAILSTORM

I was returning from the confectionary with a box full of ginger nuts. Passing by Honest Alley, I was startled to hear my own name being called, and not in greeting.

"Dr. Waycross thought that Baxter had stomach poisoning, but you know what we have here, right, fellows?"

Sarah Winter was holding her own show in Honest Alley. I was shocked to see her before the crowd. I'd never consulted with her on a case of food poisoning. I wondered if I should protest.

"So, Baxter said, 'What can you do for me, Doctor? My stomach is one big puffed up sack of wet slush. If I could stick a pin in it, all the goo would come out, and I'd feel right again. One huge fart would make it right.'"

She grinned at the disgusting details, and so did the audience.

"I knew what it was, though. Worms. A worm." Sarah rolled her hands as though unrolling thread. "Not indigestion. Not nerves or exhaustion. Waycross wanted to give a syrup of ipecac to scour out the stomach. But that would kill him."

"Damn right, it would kill him!" said a man. He drove his fist into his palm to emphasize the fatality.

"Purges work on city worms," said Sarah, "but our worms are nasty sons of bitches. They're all barbs and teeth. If you puke 'em, those worm hooks will bring your insides out."

The gathering laughed.

Sarah drew strength from the collective praise. "So, I said, 'We'll charm that worm out.' I poured a bottle of milk into a pot over the fire. I told Baxter, 'Whatever happens, whatever you feel, you're going to sit still. Put yourself right in this chair. Grab onto the edge of the table. Keep your mouth open. Don't shout, don't shake around. Don't move your hands. Stay still.'"

"Boy howdy, ain't no way he knows what's coming," said a thickly bearded mule trader.

"I made Baxter sit down at the table, tilt his neck up so that it was in line with his throat." Sarah pantomimed this to the audience, squatting in the air to mimic sitting at a table. "Once that milk got hot, I sprinkled it with spices. Have to make it smell delicious, not like you smelly whoresons. Cinnamon, cloves, maple syrup. And then Waycross and I scooted back from the table because we didn't want to be near this thing."

I had no idea what thing my fictional self was supposed to fear.

"'Do you feel the worm, Baxter? Feel it shimming up your throat?' He was going to say, 'Na,' but he hushed up because a big purple head was coming out of his mouth. A giant purple turd as big as his mouth, bloody and chunky, and it was getting bigger."

The audience grinned with disgust.

"Baxter's shaking in terror. Now, that purple turd was two feet long, swaying around. It swayed over the milk, sniffing it in. Baxter's turning blue because he can't breathe. And Waycross has got his hair in his hands. He's not seen our worms before. Now, that worm dunks his head in the milk, so for just a second, it can't see me, can't hear me. I jump for it"—she jumped forward, and the crowd gasped and fell backward—"and I grab that worm with two hands around its neck or whatever a worm's got instead of a neck. I yank it down like I'm yanking a sheet off a bed, and the tail snaps like a whip crack. But it's slippery. It gets loose. Its spikes come out, the spikes it keeps in its head so that it can stick itself inside a body. It turns to look at Waycross, and it hisses, all blood and teeth, and it's coming right for him—"

Sarah threw something purple and long and fleshy to the ground—rope or a pig's intestine, or the tail of Lizbeth Samples's cow. The crowd squealed like hogs in a hailstorm. They stumbled backward until they fell over each other, scrabbling in the muck and manure for footing. Then Sarah stepped down on it with her boot.

The guts of the thing popped out of its skin and spilled out into the alleyway. Slime and sinew covered the lower hem of her dress.

"See, I told you," said Sarah. "Our worms are nasty sons of bitches."

I didn't wait for Sarah to emerge from the crowd's adulations. My part in the tale, such as it was, was finished, and I returned to the office, wondering if any patients would follow me, their own minor stomach ailments grown by hyperbole into worm infestations. The show might drum up some business for us, but I wished she were less flamboyant. We did not need to advertise, especially with such grotesqueries, which our detractors would take for superstition and monstrosity. Perhaps Sarah wanted more of my attention, and that was her method of asking, casting me into her spectacle.

Rebecca and Effie were both in the office when I arrived, and no patients were there at the moment. The sight of the two of them together gave me pause, for I couldn't recall when I'd seen just the two of them without Sarah. They sat in queer tension, in opposite parts of the room. Effie was washing some of my surgical implements in a basin of clear water. Rebecca tended to a tray of seedlings, which she'd been raising under glass. Each planting plate had sprouted five or six young shoots, far too young to tell what sort of plant they were, and from each grouping, Rebecca culled all but the strongest. The plucked shoots were gathered in her hand. She would toss them on the trash heap or into the fire because they'd grown just a bit slower than their siblings.

"Your sister is telling the wildest tales at Honest Alley," I said, putting away my hat. "Luring out stomach parasites with warm milk. And dramatically illustrated, too. She's never really done that, has she? Charmed out an intestinal worm?"

Rebecca sniffed. "All for show. It's easier to give the patient an anthelmintic draught. I make a tea of chamomile and pumpkin seeds, strong enough that the patient can barely tolerate the bitterness, morning and evening for five days. A sure cure."

"Or a hot clyster," I added. "Takes care of worms in three days. Anthelmintic is a fine, fine word. Where did you learn it? It's not in Hippocrates even though it's Greek roots."

"I know many fine, fine medical words without having read a word of Hippocrates. I know Culpepper and Trismegistus and a hundred others."

Effie splashed her fingers in the washing basin and dried her hands against her dress. "There's a letter for you, Aubrey."

"From who?" I could think of no one at all who would have written me.

"I haven't opened it." Effie produced the envelope from her pocket and gave it to me.

The paper was damp from Effie's fingers and battered from its journey. It was addressed to "Dr. Waycross, Fellow of the Georgia Medical Society, Lawrenceville."

When I broke the wax seal, two dollar bills fluttered to the floor. Rebecca regarded them with interest. "Who sent you money?"

I said nothing.

"Go on and tell us, or I'll think the worst," said Rebecca teasingly.

I moved to fold the letter and put it away, but Rebecca grabbed for it and got it out of my hands. "'Honorable Dr. Waycross,'" she began, making her tone more formal to match the language and writing. "'We are saddened to hear of your straitened circumstances in Lawrenceville. You went thence on a noble mission, furthering the aims of the high society of physicians, and to find the place bedeviled with granny women and superstition must have come as an unpleasant revelation. These granny women, or witches, as we suppose they style themselves, ought to be prosecuted for their fraud. Alas, the frontier gives rise to many fraudsters of their ilk—'"

"Rebecca, please, that's quite enough," I said, mortified.

Rebecca laughed. "I suppose we are the granny women, aren't we, Effie? The frauds to be prosecuted?"

"This was before I had met you. I posted the letter my very first night in Lawrenceville."

"Before you even knew us. Based on rumor. Doctor, that is most unscientific of you." Her voice began playful, but as she spoke, her hurt grew. "To have come to a conclusion about us without having made any investigation or personal observation. To tattle on us to your society friends in Milledgeville—"

"Savannah," I corrected.

"In Savannah, the fine gentlemen that you so admire, to give them rumors and gossip and superstition. Well, I don't think much of that at all, Aubrey. Why did they send you the money? Here's more. 'Give every effort to the eradication of these quacksalvers and to the edification of your new home. We have taken up a collection among ourselves for your support. Herewith is enclosed the proceeds to encourage you in your fight against the ignorance that these women represent. Do not use this money to abandon Lawrenceville, sir, for it was not collected for that purpose. You are a physician of excellent character and good standing, and we have no doubt that you will prevail. Excelsior, sir. Yours cordially,' some name that I cannot decipher. The doctor's handwriting is terrible."

I looked at my feet, near which lay the two dollars collected to support my persecution of superstition and ignorance. "I wrote that letter in a very dejected spirit. As you said, I didn't know the truth yet."

"No, you did not," said Rebecca.

Effie looked through the window, watching the hogs cavort in the muddy yard.

"I shall return the money to the Georgia Medical Society. I have no need of it." I gathered the bills from the floor, where they'd fallen near Effie's feet, and pressed them into my pocket.

"And when you return the money, will you write about your changed impressions?" asked Rebecca. "How you've learned from the witches? Become their pupil? How you've seen a girl's leg saved by moldy bread?"

"They wouldn't believe me." I shook my head. "Not unless I could explain the mechanism. What balance of humors did the bread alter, and how? I cannot say."

"You can tell them that the world is more than the sum of its bloods, phlegms, and biles." Rebecca paced away from me, saw Effie, and turned back. "That the tens of thousands of plants in this sublunary world do not all obey the laws of Hippocrates."

"That, my dear, the medical men would never believe. To revise the fundamentals of their art, throw over three thousand years of evidence—it's impossible."

"Every idea, if it lives long enough, is proven wrong," said Effie.

Rebecca snapped at her sister, "And so you'd rather have no ideas at all?" She turned back to me. "It has been possible for you to overthrow your beliefs in the face of truth. Or am I deceived in that as well?"

I nodded, but then I thought I should have shaken my head. I wished for words to describe my thinking, but my mind faltered. In the space where an answer should have been was but a cottony haze.

Rebecca continued, "Well, are you leaving us? Back to Savannah? To your medical men and their convictions?"

I'd never supposed myself to be a country doctor forever. Lawrenceville and I had needed each other in a time of desperation, but once all that was settled, shouldn't I find my fortune somewhere more civilized, prestigious? Savannah and Milledgeville and Charleston were the capitals of the world as I knew it.

"I wouldn't leave alone." I lowered my eyes, not courageous enough to deliver my intentions directly.

"You would," said Rebecca. "If you left Lawrenceville, you would leave alone."

She was courageous enough to fix me with her eyes, no hesitation in her reply. The quickness and conviction struck me like a blow to the stomach. Had I known and feared this all along? That to be with Rebecca, I had to be with Lawrenceville, too?

"Is this ungrateful town more important to you than... than your own happiness?"

"Yes," she said.

"Why?"

"Because, in another place, I would not be the same person. I am my roots. My vegetables. My leaves and herbs. I know where they bloom, year after year. I know when they die and when they come back to life. For what I have sown and nurtured all my life, I shall remain to reap."

So I could not have both Rebecca and the life of a city doctor.

Though I knew she would not be the strongest ally in my defense, I had no other. "And Effie, would you ever leave Lawrenceville if there was good fortune or prospect or sense in it?"

Effie turned to us, seeing my cheeks red from embarrassment and Rebecca's red from the force of her conviction. "I would prefer not to." She turned back to the window and the hogs.

14

IT LETS THE DEVIL KNOW WHO TO HUNT

I didn't see Rebecca for three days following the incident of the letter. She hadn't appeared for her medical duties. That fact was no great matter for the patients, who had other doctors, but it was a great concern to me. Sarah said Rebecca was out harvesting late-summer roots and collecting the leaves that would wilt when the season began to turn for fall. If I went looking for her, I was likely to be eaten by the rabid panther, said Sarah, and I didn't doubt her. I could not move in the woods with the grace of its native—or adopted—daughters.

She was testing my heart or forcing me to test it myself. Would her absence make my heart grow fonder? It did. I hadn't appreciated how much Rebecca's kindred spirit had helped to ease my days. I could find her sharp intelligence and her kind affections not in Savannah or Milledgeville or Charleston, but only there in Lawrenceville. My head pounded with consequences. The sanguine humor that flooded my brain, driving such emotional responses, hissed and sputtered in veins accustomed to the cold humors of reason and thought. Ether was the only balm I could give them—chemical quietness. I could not sleep without it, and I woke up dry mouthed, off my appetite, itchy, and irritated, which another dose of ether helped to quell.

I'd run through a gallon of the stuff by the time Rebecca returned. She entered the office with her herb satchel stuffed with greens. I peered down from the hayloft, my vision blurred, my thoughts groggy, filled with a happiness I did not ascribe, entirely, to the prodigious quantities of ether.

"I wouldn't miss P's corn shucking," she said as explanation for her reappearance. "The first of the season is always the best party."

When a farmer declares his harvest ready, the corn has to be shucked the same day so that it does not rot in its web of wet silks. P was of Hungarian extraction, and he and his wife, Catherine, kept several practices that conflicted with the general opinion. Every year, he announced he would harvest his corn early, just at the end of August, before the homunculi got it. Fellow farmers knew his real motive: he wanted the first corn shucking. In theory, every farmer cuts on a different day, and everyone contributes to each other's harvest, but in practice, Rebecca told me, the later the season, the fewer the workers. The first shucking always has a splendid turnout. It is as much festival as farmwork. Men and boys walk the fields, plucking corn and throwing the cobs into passing wagons. They take breaks to shoot at squirrels, hoot for the best hits, and jeer at the flagrant misses.

I knew I was not fully forgiven for the letter to the Georgia Medical Society, but on the day of the first shucking, Rebecca and I went to P's swept yard together. All the sweethearts went.

The August evening was fine, with a long twilight that filled the sky with orange and reflected health onto those below. Young girls tore open the husks and pulled out the silks. The women, sitting in a circle around the growing pile of corn, tended to other necessary affairs: soaking the husks, stacking cobs, patching, quilting, debating news, rumors, and tales, and putting aside their piecework to rehearse the forms of a square dance. P and Catherine had to feed the masses. P fretted over a whole hog roasting over an anemic fire as Catherine tended a dozen boiling cauldrons, borrowed from neighbors. Their children scrubbed potatoes, cleaned beans, peeled apples, and watched stewing cabbages. Effie hovered at the rim of the cauldrons as the cabbage boiled down. Sarah was out with the sharpshooters, collecting squirrels for an after-dinner pudding.

A good number of the cobs were rotten with fungus, and those the youngest boys collected with delighted squeals. They stomped the rotten cobs flat, rubbing their toes in the soft leavings, and some they set alight with a brand taken from the bonfire. The rotten cobs took the flame greedily, and the boys heaved them into the cow pond. Sounds of hissing and popping filled the air.

Pastor Boatwright watched their antics from near the lakeside, frowning. He appeared to be studying the boys' game for a sign— not the unavoidable burned fingertips or eyebrows, but a more menacing one. Rebecca and I left him alone in his reflections. We'd profit nothing by confronting him.

Rebecca joined the circle of women. I stood nearby, catching passing threads of talk dealing with preparations for the seasons— pickling and brining, getting salt out of the dirt in the smokehouse floor—supplemented by romantic gossip. Rebecca laughed and smiled and retorted and rejoined, as lively as any of her peers.

"What's happening to your garden now that you've come down from the mountain?" asked Old Elizabeth. "Are you letting it go fallow?"

"I left the nightshade in charge," said Rebecca. "Nothing misbehaves for the nightshade."

"Ha ha!" I laughed too loudly so that the women in the circle would think she'd told a joke.

A grubby adolescent, who'd done his best to scrub away his grubbiness, approached the women's circle and addressed Mrs. Parr. "Ma'am, where's Ouida Bell tonight?" His hat was between his hands. "She wasn't at the store today. I wanted to buy her some peanuts."

"Why, Stephen, she's feeling under the weather, so she stayed back at home," said Mrs. Parr. "But I'll tell her you were asking after her."

The adolescent flushed. "Nah, that's all right, ma'am. You don't need to tell her. Think flowers might make her feel better? What's the name of the purple ones? Prosies?"

Mrs. Parr and Old Elizabeth and Young Elizabeth and Liza Jane and Rebecca all laughed, and the boy scuttled away into the roil of dust and games and anonymity.

"My, you have a handful with all the suitors for your Ouida Bell," said Old Elizabeth.

"She doesn't encourage it, but it can't be helped," said Mrs. Parr. "It's the way of boys and girls."

"Ouida Bell's so fetching," said Young Elizabeth. "Prettiest girl in town, I'd say."

Mrs. Parr shot a cold glance at the compliment.

Seeing the perplexity on my face, Rebecca whispered into my ear, "Evil eye. Never praise or boast. It lets the devil know who to hunt."

"And what are you two whispering about over there?" teased Old Elizabeth.

"Oh, nothing," said Rebecca.

I shifted in my shoes. Rebecca's shoulders pulled back. She tore the silks from an ear of corn with both hands. The naked cob dropped into her lap.

"Sweet nothings, I'd guess," sang Mrs. Parr.

I put my hand on Rebecca's left arm, a public gesture of allegiance and support for her. Yes, the whole town supposed they knew our circumstances, but I wanted Rebecca to know as well. I meant to stay with her. Words were a poor apology. Actions were better.

Lizbeth, of the tailless cow, coughed conspicuously from across the circle. "Mrs. Parr, what's Ouida Bell got?"

"I don't rightly know," said Mrs. Parr. "A seasonal complaint, I figure. Weakness. Feeling puny. She'll be right in a few days. Sarah's been by, but she hasn't seemed to do much."

"If you'd like, we'd be happy to call on her," I said. "Rebecca and I can visit in the morning."

"Maybe you've already been out to the Parr's," said Lizbeth darkly. "Or maybe you just did it while she was walking home from the confectionary."

"I don't follow your meaning—" I started to say, but Rebecca hushed me with the swat of her arm.

"Pastor's told me about Ouida Bell," said Lizbeth, enjoying her ominousness and the attention it brought. "It's an evil creeping on her, an evil that Dr. Waycross knows very well."

Old Elizabeth tutted. "Lizbeth, really, you oughtn't to spread such gossip."

"A hex. A poison. A witching. On the prettiest girl in town. Everybody thinks it was Sarah that worked the evil charm, what with that burying in the churchyard, but I know it started with the panther's bite. It's still your magic, though. The panther is your familiar, your dark hand reaching from hellish places. Why'd Sarah command the beast to bite Ouida Bell? Jealousy? No, pure wicked delight, I figure. All of you are just like her, haunting after the sick. Who'll be the next victim? I wouldn't touch this corn if I were you, after her kind's touched it. Maybe they've hexed it, just like they've hexed Ouida Bell."

"Lizbeth, hush yourself," said Old Elizabeth.

"Ma'am," I said, fuming, "of course you know there is no—"

"Tell that to Everett." Lizbeth stood. "Ask about when all the doors and windows locked up tight on his cabin for three days and nights and nobody could get out. About the milk that is making me sick."

"Your cows are eating white snakeroot, Miss Lizbeth," said Rebecca. "I've seen it growing in your yard. It harms their circulation and comes out in their milk. Stop letting your cows eat poison."

"I'll bet you know all the poisons of the world," she said, venomous. "Snakeroot? I believe you planted it."

"Lizbeth," said Old Elizabeth. She flailed with one hand as though trying to fan out a candle. "She's trying to help you. Let's not spoil a nice evening."

Lizbeth stalked off into the fields, uttering dark prayers to herself.

"There's no pleasing some folks," said Mrs. Snell, who'd been drawn by the commotion. "I knew it was the snakeroot that was to blame. I have Snell pull it up from our yard. Isn't that right, Mrs. Parr? You don't have any snakeroot, do you? It's not milk sickness for Ouida Bell?"

Mrs. Parr shook her head. "Not that. I don't know what. Just feeling puny. Shaking, like she's cold, or sweating."

"Shall we see her in the morning?" I asked. "I'm sure that, among us, we'd find a suitable remedy for her affliction."

Mrs. Parr wavered, though. Lizbeth's superstitious words had slipped into her ears. The silence lasted only a few moments, but I'm sure Rebecca felt, as I did, the tension among the members of the party. The talk at the circle drifted back to prognostications for the coming season, the thickness of caterpillar fuzz, the prevalence of butterflies in the noonday meadows. Rebecca joined in when she could, and she laughed as she must, but the animation had gone from her voice, and the silks she ripped from the corn cobs fluttered lifelessly to the red clay beneath her feet.

Then, when the memory of Lizbeth's unpleasantness was just at the edge of our minds, the sour woman returned with reinforcements. She'd stormed off to find Boatwright by the cow pond, and she brought him to the firelight. I took Rebecca's hand as a reflex, wanting the weight of my office to protect her from shame.

"They laughed at me, Pastor," said Lizbeth.

"Now, no one laughed—" Mrs. Parr said.

"They didn't listen. They don't see the danger. Tell them what you told me."

The pastor waggled his fingers. He was not courageous enough to repeat what he'd said to his most faithful congregants in front of those he accused. Rebecca's pulse beneath my hand was fast. She kept quiet, but not out of fear.

"Tell them how the devil's been whispering," said Lizbeth. "How he told the Winter sisters and their familiar, the panther, to bring death to the beautiful because we spill more tears for the beautiful."

"Yes," said Boatwright, "yes."

Mrs. Parr's face drained of blood. I worried she might faint and, in her fainting, fall into the fire. I stepped closer to her, but she was startled by my gesture. Boatwright took her fear for his strength.

"You see?" he said. "You feel the devil, too."

"I don't feel anything," said Mrs. Parr. "What is it? Do you know what's afflicting her?"

"The pastor doesn't know," I said. "We doctors shall examine her in the morning. And we doctors shall take every necessary measure." My hand tightened around Rebecca's.

"You won't be able to do any more for her than you could do for your own sister, than any mortal could do for your sister. Death is inevitable, and the hydrophobia proves it."

"Hydrophobia?" said Rebecca, breaking her silence. "There are a hundred ailments more likely than rabies. Surely, it's not rabies."

"But it is, just like Eva's," said Boatwright.

I released Rebecca's hand and clenched my left fist, feeling the bite of my overlong fingernails in my palm. "I forbid you from ever speaking of Eva again."

"Who are you to command and forbid, Waycross?" asked the pastor. "Can you heal a mortal soul of death? No, you cannot, no matter how much you love them."

Mrs. Parr cried out, and Mrs. Snell wrapped her in her expansive arms.

"Pastor, if you do not speak more plainly—"

"Ouida Bell. Go see her, Doctor, and tell me if I'm mistaken."

The pastor stepped closer to the fire. His eyes lit up yellow, and his lips drooped with shadow. Sparks from a snapping piece of greenwood threatened to set his hair alight. "I think you know. I think you understood the devil took your sister. Instead of quelling the devil, you've incited him, you and your women. You've played with twigs and teas, and all the while, the hydrophobia has been stalking Ouida Bell. She will die, like Eva died, and she will not be the last. This wicked town will burn, burn, burn."

"This isn't Salem, sir."

"Would that it were, Waycross," he said. "Would that it were."

The next morning, Rebecca and I went to see Ouida Bell at the Parrs' cabin. Mrs. Parr was in tears, for the disease had turned sharply worse overnight. Ouida Bell lay in darkness, barely moving.

"Are we sure it's hydrophobia?" Rebecca stepped back from the bedside and joined me against the wall of the cabin.

"The symptoms fit," I said, nodding.

I had hoped we would see only a complication of the hand-foot-and-mouth disease, which Sarah's scandalous treatment had, despite my horror, seemed to alleviate. The red pox had gone away, but it's not impossible that the disease, or some other impurity caught from her descent into the clay, had created an excess of phlegmatic humors. I saw immediately that my hopes were in vain. I should have known better than to hope. She'd been infected ever since the panther's bite, and we hadn't seen it, and she was dying. Ouida Bell Parr's face was flushed red with fever, and the corners of her mouth were smeared with saliva. She thrashed beneath her blankets. Mrs. Parr laid cloths dampened in spring water on her daughter's forehead, but Ouida Bell didn't bear them well. Her neck would spasm, and she'd fling away the cloth, adding it to the growing pile beside her bed. I had seen it before, through a child's eyes, which record impressions with greater color and clarity than the clouded eyes of an adult. I had seen those spasms in Eva, and I knew what they foretold.

Boatwright had been right. He'd diagnosed rabies in Ouida Bell, and I hated that he was right, hated him more than the panther or the disease.

Rebecca leaned in closer to me. "Have you examined her?"

"I thought you should do the examination," I said.

I could not examine Ouida Bell's necessities without breaching decorum. A Savannah doctor would never dare to examine a woman's person beneath her clothes. A physician relied on outward signs, examination of effluvia, and perhaps the use of an ear trumpet to listen to breathing sounds without pressing an ear to the female's chest.

Rebecca studied the horror on my face then said, "For goodness' sake."

I left her with Ouida Bella and Mrs. Parr.

As I waited on Rebecca, I circumambulated the Parr house and yard. A trio of chickens followed behind me, taking me for their leader. We wandered behind the spring house then back. I picked up my pace, and the chickens followed. Two contradictory humors alternated through my temples. Each brought its own clarity and its own sharp pains. I was fearful, of course. The prognosis of rabies is a medical certainty, leading always to death, and where one case is found, many more may follow. I was afraid of how the pastor would use Ouida Bell's death for his own gains against the Winter sisters—and against me, their benefactor and ally. But growing against the fear was a sanguine excitement. The rhymes of life had delivered to me a patient like my lost sister, but now, I had the hope of curing her. In the Winter sisters, I had seen cures I'd never thought possible.

The door clattered, and I came to a sudden halt. The chickens that had been following me crashed into my legs, and my trousers got soiled with chickenshit.

"It's certainly the same bite," said Rebecca grimly as she came out the door. "The one I saw when she said she'd been nipped by the panther. Healed over, but that's how the rabies got in. The bite, even though it wasn't deep, and the rash, and then the summer cold, and now—"

"How do you propose we should treat it?" I said. "Moldy bread?"

"Are you making fun of me, Aubrey?" She stepped right up into my face.

"What? No! It worked for Eudoxia's leg. I'd call it a miracle, but I know it's not. And if you can reattach a severed foot to its owner—"

"I've never reattached a foot," said Rebecca. "That's a tale gone too far."

"But there must be something like moldy bread that you use for hydrophobia," I insisted. I was talking too fast, and my tongue tripped over my words. "A rabies rum or some such."

"Nothing that I have seen work. Nothing that I trust." She turned and walked several paces away from me.

I ran through the herbs of the past weeks. "We could try Seneca root. You said it draws out poison. Or we could pack her wound in a plaster of lobelia and cider vinegar, like in that Cherokee—"

"No."

I held my ground but raised my voice. "Nature has stuffed the world with millions of flowers and shrubs, but none of them is a cure for hydrophobia?"

"None of them," she barked back, frightening the chickens in the yard.

"Then what do you give hopeless patients?" I spoke more tenderly as I approached her.

"I never treat hopeless cases. The age of miracles is passed."

"We don't need a miracle, Rebecca." I touched her shoulder. "Hydrophobia is not a demon, no matter what Boatwright preaches. The universe would not be so imperfect as to afflict us with an incurable disease."

"Hydrophobia is incurable."

"That's what they taught me in my schooling. And Culpepper and Hippocrates have remedies, but they are futile. So what do the old wives' tales say? What do the savages say?"

"Madstone," said Rebecca sharply, pushing my hand off her shoulder. "That's what the Cherokee say."

"Show me, please." My hands were folded together in petition, but it might have looked like a prayer. "I'm dying to see it."

Rebecca frowned. "You're not the one dying."

Then perhaps she realized that part of me had died that day when Eva died. I knew as near the pain of hydrophobia as any living mortal. I'd seen that terrible suffering written in Eva's eyes, and for me, not for Ouida Bell or for Eva, Rebecca's expression softened.

She undid a collar button, and from her dress, she took out a leather bag, which had hung around her neck by a braided strand.

"Hold out your hand." She opened the pouch and dropped its contents into my upturned palm.

It was a single white, wrinkled spheroid, about the size of a hazelnut, though lighter. It rolled on the lines of my palm.

"Where does it come from?"

"Why does it matter?" said Rebecca.

"I want to know."

Rebecca retrieved the madstone from my palm and put it back into the leather pouch. "Sarah took it from the stomach of a deer."

"The deer swallowed it?"

"A madstone is an accretion of calcium," said Rebecca. "But it's rare. Sarah's killed a thousand deer, and she's only found one. I make her check every stomach."

"How do we give it to Ouida Bell? Does she swallow it?"

"No, no. That might choke her. Or lacerate her bowels. Or it won't do anything." Rebecca scratched at the back of her neck. "Aubrey, I don't think there's any use to it. Madstone is for poisoning. Rabies isn't a poison."

"But old wives and savages believe in it."

"They throw mysteries at mysteries. They put too much hope in strange things."

"We must try. Either the madstone does nothing and humanity is none the worse for our experiment, or the madstone cures her and we celebrate a victory over death."

"It is a hopeless case."

"Then why not try?"

"Because the last time I put hope into a hopeless case, I was broken. He died, Aubrey. I couldn't help him."

"Everett?"

Rebecca nodded, barely perceptibly.

"Then perhaps we ask Sarah," I said. "Or Effie. If you do not believe in the madstone, then we can bring Effie and ask how she might treat poor Ouida Bell. I don't know what she will suggest, but it is better than nothing, than hopelessness."

Rebecca stood in thought for what seemed like a very long time. The trio of chickens that had followed me before regained their courage and started to explore my feet.

"What about Effie?" I asked at last.

Rebecca shook her head. "Let's try the madstone."

Rebecca moved Ouida Bell's thin shift so that the bruise on her leg was visible. Ouida Bell did not resist. She was like a corn-husk doll, papery and limp. The wound was not oozing, as Eudoxia's had been. It was nearly invisible, only a barest shadow of a bruise. Rebecca took out the madstone, telling me to hold it against the bruise. I demurred, citing decorum, but Rebecca insisted. I touched the madstone against the skin ever so lightly.

"Harder," said Rebecca.

I pushed on the stone with all my strength. The wound turned white from the pressure. My wrist complained about the awkward position, and Ouida Bell made whimpering noises. I kept pressing the stone into the wound, and she wriggled her legs in discomfort. I changed my position to keep the angle and the force. The thrashing might have been a sign that the medicine was working. The body is not healed by gentleness, I reminded myself.

Suddenly, the bed was a mess of toes, blankets, and drops of sweat. Rebecca and I dodged kicks aimed at us. Then Ouida Bell fell back to her blankets, spent.

Rebecca tapped me on the shoulder, and I let up. She'd put a bowl out on the table and filled it with sweet milk. I carried the madstone to her, holding it out at arm's length from my body. I set it down into the bowl of milk as instructed, and it bobbed on the surface. Rebecca watched the madstone as though watching for the first green shoot of spring to rise from the earth. Her nose was almost in the milk itself. I watched her and the madstone with equal intensity, not knowing what signs I should be hoping for. Then Rebecca swore under her breath. The madstone was sinking, taking on weight. In a minute, it had disappeared completely.

My hopes sank with the stone. "What's happened?"

"Nothing, Aubrey," she snapped. "If the madstone had absorbed any poison from Ouida Bell, we would have seen it ooze out into the milk."

She fished the madstone from the bowl and shoved it into her pocket. Then she marched from the cabin, away from the darkness and the stink, away from me.

S arah hadn't believed, so she went to see. She waited until Mrs. Parr left the cabin, then she stole in, using an old nail to lift the wooden latch. She opened the door just enough to let herself in, keeping out the sound and light of the afternoon. A chicken tried to come in at her heels, but Sarah kicked at it, and the nosy bird squawked and fled.

Mercifully, Ouida Bell was asleep. Sarah reached out to put her hand on Ouida Bell's shoulder but stopped. She couldn't let herself touch that skin, pale and sweat soaked and covered in gooseflesh. That wasn't how Sarah wanted to remember.

A rash. A summer cold. Sarah cursed herself. What foolishness. What utter, hopeful foolishness. She should have known from the start that Ouida Bell wasn't suffering from a simple ailment. It had to be that rabid panther. If only she'd been able to kill it weeks before... but it had eluded her. Of the three sisters, only Effie had seen the animal. Effie could have shot it, but Effie didn't carry a gun. She didn't kill.

Sarah slipped back outside. Her legs failed her. She fell to the earth. The chickens flocked around her. Sarah let them come. They pecked around her toes. Their wings brushed her cheeks, her face. When the shadows moved with the changing sun, and a beam of dusty evening light crossed her face, Sarah picked herself up. She wiped away the memories from her eyes.

"We're not going to say anything about that," she told the chickens.

Chapter 15

A DISEASE ONLY FOR THE WICKED

I staggered through the town square, my arms wrapped around an enormous melon. It was, incredibly, the smallest one at Almonton's patch. I had accepted it because Almonton was grateful for his treatment, which had been a welcome and easy distraction from the weightier plight of Ouida Bell, and he had no other currency with which to pay me except watermelons.

Even the hungry hogs ignored me as I carried it. They'd had countless watermelon rinds added to their late-summer feed, and familiarity bred contempt, but my affection for the watermelon was growing. I liked the neat bands of green that alternated in rhythmic, regular patterns. I knew what was inside—pink and goo and seeds—without having to crack it open. Neighbors along the road said, "Sir, that's a nice watermelon," and I said, "Madam, thank you."

After walking for several minutes in contemplative silence, I heard angry voices behind the Brambons' house. Picking up my feet, I hied toward the noise. I rounded the back of the house, still carrying my watermelon, and I stumbled. I rebalanced the fruit from my right hip to my left, and I saw Effie. She was sitting on a cracked stump. A brown-and-blue crockery pitcher, decorated with abstract vines, sat on the earth beside her. She'd been on her way to fetch water or on her way back. Her legs were drawn up close to herself so that she was perched, sparrowlike.

I also saw three men in Sunday clothes though I was fairly certain it was Thursday. Each had on his best brown trousers and black suit coat, and they all had shirts with cufflinks, but they were not respectable men. I did not recognize them and took them for visitors from Hog Mountain or Jug Tavern.

Effie was wearing an orange calico shawl over her shoulders. I'd never seen her with that garment before. The three men surrounded her in menacing postures, but they stepped back a pace when they saw my watermelon approaching them.

I dropped the melon, which bounced on the pine-straw-covered earth, and undid my cuff buttons to roll up my sleeves. "Are these men accosting you, Miss Winter?"

She shook her head. "They want what everyone wants. I'm not hurt."

"We need her help, and she's not listening," said one of the men.

I glared him into silence. "But are they troubling you?" I asked.

Effie closed her eyes. "People are not the trouble. People cannot help what they are."

I walked toward her and knelt. I wanted to catch her hands in mine, to reassure her that I would defend her, but she'd hidden her hands in the folds of her clothes.

"Tell me, plainly," I said.

"These men are sick and want a cure," she said.

I looked at the men, who had folded their hands behind them like soldiers at parade rest. I stood and addressed them, continuing to keep my body between them and Effie. "Come to my office, sirs. I am a doctor. I will see you in the ordinary course."

"It's not a trouble you can cure, Doctor," said one of them.

"I will be the judge of that," I said. "I'll give you my advice, free of charge, and then you will leave Miss Winter alone."

"French gout," they said into their shoes. "Fireplugs. The rising pins and needles."

"Only syphilis?" I said. "You couldn't find a doctor in Jug Tavern to give you calomel?"

One of the men lifted his Sunday hat, and I gasped. Beneath irregular patches of hair, his scalp was covered with blisters. He was as good as dead. Once the affliction had advanced to that stage, it had already conquered the brain. Under that man's skull, his brain was coming apart in meaty chunks.

The other two took off their hats. They had the same degree of affliction. I'd never seen such a pitiable sight, even in the charity wards of Savannah. "What, all three of you? How did you—" But then I decided I did not want to ponder their immoralities. "Sirs," I said, regaining a diagnostic calm, "I will give you all the mercury I have. I will bleed you. But I fear that you have come looking for a miracle."

"That's why we came to Effie Winter," said one of the men.

I knelt down again to Effie's side and spoke softly to her. "Can you help them, Effie?"

Effie drew her arms into herself and said nothing, which was no answer, and the men saw it. But whether Effie would help them or not was not for them to decide. I wasn't even sure if it was for Effie to decide.

I stood up and addressed the men. "All I know is calomel, gentlemen," I said, showing them my empty hands. "Do you want it or not?"

The three dying syphilitics shook their heads. They'd staked their faith on Effie Winter, and when they realized that nothing was there for them, that Effie was unmoved by their pleas and sorrows, they slunk away. Like men to the gallows.

Effie and I watched them go.

"Don't blame yourself, Effie. No medicine could cure those men. They are too far gone with their disease." I offered her my arm to help her stand.

She took it and rose from the stump, then she brushed splinters and sawdust from her dress. Her hair was dirty. Her eyes were wet, not as if she'd been crying, but as if they were irritated by the slicing of an onion. I saw the resemblance of her eyes, again, to my sister's, perhaps because, in my remembrances, I always see Eva through tears. I wished I could ignore that superficiality. Effie and Eva were not the same. Likely, Eva had died before Effie was born. They'd never even shared the Earth, but the sympathetic workings of my mind could not be made sensible.

"Those scoundrels brought their death upon themselves," I continued. "Syphilis is self-inflicted. It's not a disease that can afflict the innocent."

"I'm glad there is a disease only for the wicked," said Effie.

"Of course, we would not refuse to treat anyone, wicked or not," I stammered to my defense. "It's only because those men were hopeless that we did nothing for them. But there is less sadness with syphilis, I think, than consumption."

"Or rabies."

Effie knew about Ouida Bell. That's who she meant.

"Or rabies," I echoed. "I do not hold out hope for a miracle, but whatever can be done to ease her suffering."

"Yes," said Effie. And we stood in silence, respectfully, until a moment had passed.

"Come now, Effie, are you going back to the office or to the Snells'? I'll see you the way, lest those men come back."

"Aubrey, your watermelon." She gestured at the enormous fruit, which sat intact on a heap of pine straw.

"Ah, this silly thing. What I am going to do with it, Effie? You wouldn't want some, would you?"

"Yes, please."

I'd so anticipated a refusal that I thought I'd misheard. Only a moment later did I say, "We'll slice it up when we get to Mrs. Snell's."

"Why not now?" Effie took out her knife, which I had not supposed she carried everywhere.

I wondered what else was hidden in her pockets. That was the same knife I'd used at their cabin in Hope Hollow, the knife Sarah had warned me not to cut myself with, yet I had. No trouble had come from that injury, despite Sarah's fear.

"Why not now?" Effie held out the knife handle to me, her own palm wrapped around the blade.

I ate my fill of watermelon, as did Effie. I'd never seen her eat so much food. She always ate like a bird, a spoonful or two, but she ate far more of that watermelon than I'd supposed would fit inside her little frame.

Later that evening, after I'd left Effie and the remnants of the watermelon in town, I met Rebecca. We had plans to prepare a meal, just the two of us, and even though I was full of watermelon, I was glad of the chance to pass an evening with Rebecca.

"That's a good job," Rebecca said, inspecting the potatoes I'd peeled.

They were rosy and spherical, apples from the earth. Each matched its siblings in size and character.

"A scalpel and a kitchen knife are not so different." I put my surgical experience into removing every scrap of red peel. I excised the brown eyes as though removing tumors. It was soothing to the mind.

Using a much larger knife, Rebecca cut the potatoes into perfect cubes and scraped them into a pot that hung over the fire. Two weeks had passed since we'd shared any but the hastiest meal together. Rebecca had arranged for the Snells to be out at the Flowing Bowl this evening so that she and I could be together, and I was grateful. Even if we'd been in Savannah, with a theater for us to attend or boxwood gardens for strolling, I would have chosen an evening in the kitchen with Rebecca over any lecture or performance. If Lawrenceville and Rebecca were of a piece, then I would take them both together.

Mrs. Snell's kitchen had a wide hearth, provisioned with a complicated series of pot hooks to hang food at different temperatures. Creosote blackened the ceiling. As befitting the kitchen of a shopkeeper, the shelves displayed commercial cooking and cleaning aids, all with the labels facing outward: Charming Charlie's Chicken Seasoning, Edgar's Amalgamated Soap, Popular Potash, Scientific Pure Italian Soda, Limewater Liniment for Meat Tenderizing and the Relief of Corns, and a viscous black goo cryptically called The Almighty Hammer. A bottle of Grove's Tasteless Chill Tonic was also there. When Rebecca uncorked it, the room filled with the smell of vinegar.

"Just reusing the bottle," she said.

"It's a nice bottle," I replied. "Almost worth the price of the medicine."

"The bottle and the story," said Rebecca.

She cut pats of butter into flour, working the mixture with her fingers, breaking the butter into pea-sized pieces. "Do you know this is no ordinary butter?"

"Isn't it?" I picked up another potato.

"It's suffer butter, salted with tears," she said. "The milk comes from cows that have broken legs or rheumatism. They must also have lost their calves to newborn fever. Otherwise, the butter is not sweet enough."

"A rare and terrible treat." I nodded.

"And the cows are part of a failing herd, a few staggering animals haunted by the memory of their deceased sisters. They pasture on the grasslands of Yorktown and Saratoga. Their hay tastes like gun smoke."

"But that isn't enough, is it?" I replied, warming to the spirit of the jest.

"No. The milking boys are all youngest sons who suffer the beatings of their elder brothers and know that they will never share in the inheritance of their labor. And the milkmaids who do the churning are spinsters that once stood at the parson's door, clutching a bouquet of posies for a groom that never came."

"And what of the churns?" I prodded. "Were they made from thousand-year-old oaks riven by lightning bolts? And the carts onto which they load the butter—"

"Are also used to bring home the bodies of the dead. The spokes of their wheels are stained with graveyard dirt. And the carts are pulled by ill-tempered mules with ill-tempered drivers, cuckolded by their wives and scolded by their mothers."

"And why is suffer butter the most delicious butter?" I asked. "Why does it make the lightest biscuits and the richest cakes?"

"Because it is the most costly bought butter in the world," she said. "Aubrey, careful! Watch what you're doing."

In my distraction, I'd peeled all the way through the flesh of a potato, slice by slice, until I was about to peel into the skin of my palm.

"I think that's enough potatoes." Rebecca took the knife from me and chopped the last one into cubes and added them to the cauldron over the fire. "Now, we leave them to stew."

I hovered right at the hearth, my nose nearly in the soup. The mingling aromas reminded me of simpler pleasures.

"I need to put the lid on," said Rebecca. She tapped my shoulder.

"Oh, yes, of course," I said, but I wasn't yet ready to step aside. "I've always been interested in cooking. I've never had the time to learn."

"Well, I can teach you about biscuits and soups and getting out of the way." Rebecca still held the lid. I knew it was heavy, but I was captive to the smells.

"I shouldn't wonder that you're an excellent cook," I continued. "An herbalist's work is not that different from a chef's. Any doctor, really, is a kind of cook. Diagnosing humors and appetites. Brewing up courses of treatment."

"And chicken soup is a panacea. Now, I need to put the lid on, please."

"What is in here, besides the potatoes? I see eggplant and tomato."

"It's nightshade stew," said Rebecca.

That made me lean away from the rising steam, and Rebecca stepped in to place the lid on the iron pot.

"You can't be serious," I said.

"Potato is a nightshade. So is eggplant. Tomato. Sweet peppers. They are all cousins." Rebecca tapped on the side of the closed cauldron with a wooden spoon, ringing it like a school bell though the pot had no music, instead giving off a single muffled thud. "You need to know what parts of the plant to eat and how to prepare them. Potatoes must be eaten before the flesh turns green. A tomato's leaves and stems will sicken you."

"And you've put them all into this stew?"

"It's an herbalist's joke, I guess." Rebecca drew up her skirts and sat down on the hearth, the heat of the fire on her back. "Hilarious, isn't it." Her voice was flat.

My prying had taken the spirit out of her recipes.

"I'm sorry, dear," I said, and I was. I sat down beside her.

A log cracked behind her, sending a burst of steam and sparks up the chimney. Rebecca was unmoved. Wherever her thoughts had retreated, they were far away.

"I think it's..." she started, then she stopped.

"No, please. Go ahead. I'm listening."

She paused for a long time, and I could not tell what was transpiring behind her eyes.

"Rebecca?" I ventured. Was she angry with me or struggling with a delicate phrasing?

"I think it's time for seasoning," she said. "Salt."

"That wasn't what you were going to say."

She swallowed, a thin click to her dry lips. "I think that nightshade is perfect. If there were only nightshades in our world, that would be enough. They're food and medicine and poison. Potato, mandrake, and belladonna. What more do we need?"

I made no reply.

"And nightshades have invincible roots. They are hardy, perennial, vast, and spreading." Rebecca was looking into her palms. "I wish that I could graft nightshade onto our own mortal roots. I wish I could drain the blood out of our veins and replace it with the juice of nightshade's black pearls."

The heat of the fire blazed behind her, and the stew inside the cauldron, boiling vigorously, overflowed its container. Streams of broth ran down into the fire, where it vaporized aromatically. I could have been afraid of those strange sentiments, but I loved Rebecca.

"Plants are not like people," said Rebecca. "Plants return and return, never ceasing. They die, but their death is not forever."

"Would that Eva had been a flower, not a person," I said.

"Will you tell me about her?" Rebecca looked up with eyes shimmering from tears.

"I wouldn't... That is, we're here not for sad memories but a meal together, aren't we?" I thought I would not get through my tale without some tears of my own, and I did not want them to spoil the sentiment of the evening. I put my hand on top of hers. "Let's think about who we have, not whom we've lost." But I heard my words ring false and trite even as I spoke them.

Rebecca's hand moved beneath mine. She knew, too.

"Eva was nine years older than me," I said, drawing her in my memory. "She was... soft. Round and soft. A figure for a kindly person, and Eva, above all, was kind. Her hair was a profusion of ginger curls, unique in our family, and it made me think of fire..."

Sparks rushed up the chimney. A superstitious person might have thought... but I was not a superstitious person.

"It was April. I was newly turned six. She and I were walking on River Street. I think she'd bought me licorice because this memory has the scent of anise. It must have been candy for a birthday. And now, I cannot stand that smell. I held her hand. And then I saw the dog, a wharf-hardened cur, ragged and bleeding and vicious, and my sister lifted me into her arms. The dog bit her leg instead of mine. Her face did not change. Her eyes did not look away from mine. I knew that she'd been bitten only because I heard the sound of the teeth. I heard the skin breaking. I heard the change in the cur's growl as its muzzle pushed against Eva's plump calf. But Eva never showed me her pain or fear. She did not want to burden me. She'd meant that as a kindness."

Rebecca nodded. Her hand softened under mine. She turned her wrist so that our fingers would intertwine.

"A pair of sailors grabbed the animal, and Eva took me home. The bite was not a severe one. The teeth marks bled, but the leg was not badly hurt. My mother wiped the wounds clean with Tifton's Tincture of Turpentine and said a prayer, and none of us considered the incident again. I was a child. I couldn't have known the danger. And Eva said nothing. Because she was kind. Because she did not want to worry us. Not that there was any cure in Savannah for the infection that festered inside her. And it showed itself three weeks later. Eva would not drink. The sight of water made her nauseous. She could not get out of bed. She could not speak. I don't remember the last words she'd said to me. They were ordinary words, sibling to sibling, that I gave no importance because I had no inkling that they'd be her last, that her mind would die weeks before her body. My mother poured on more Tifton's Tincture of Turpentine. But, of course, Eva did not improve, and soon unceasing streams of saliva soaked her pillow. And this was when the parade of healers began. My mother summoned anyone with a pitch or a potion or a promise. But they were not bad people. I see that now. Even Boatwright, then, if he was one of the healers who attended us. Even he was not malicious. They were fighting an impossible battle with any possible cure. I should have given them more respect for their bravery in desperation, for the right intentions. But a body is not cured by good intentions."

"No matter how much we might wish it," said Rebecca.

"Then when it was far too late, my mother brought in a physician. A silver-haired man from the Savannah Poor House and Hospital arrived. He impressed me the most. I crept behind him into Eva's room. Eva huddled against one of the corner posts. She wore a night garment soiled with her own effluent humors. Her fiery hair was now greasy smoke, dark and knotted. Her breath came in halting sobs. I sat at her bedside and placed a cool cloth on her forehead. Eva's eyes turned to me, but their kindness was gone. They were now like an animal's, without intelligence or recognition. She attacked, bellowing with violence and agony. I jumped backward, out of range of her fingernails. The physician tied Eva's wrists to the bedstead. She began a howling, unearthly madness, thrashing against her bindings, her body contorted. She was the nearest thing to a demon that I had ever seen in this world."

I looked up at the ceiling, where nothing was.

"And he told us that she would die. That there is no cure for hydrophobia, for rabies. Any unguent, any incantation, any patent medicine, is only false hope, a poison. And because he told the truth, gave no hope and broke no promises, I admired this man the most. I wanted to be like him. An ordinary man—a chicken farmer, a grenadier, an emperor—lives only a single life. His value to society will never exceed the span of his own years. But a physician, by his lancets and his sulfur enemas, earns a portion of each life that he saves. I wanted to restore the flush to a pale woman's cheeks and send breath back into a pitiable infant. I wanted to see old men straighten up without their canes and grandmothers do a little jig on refreshed knees. I wanted to cure children of the ailments that robbed them of their enjoyment of the world."

"And you have," said Rebecca. "Dozens of times over." She moved closer to me.

I laid my head upon her shoulder. "But I wanted to see, one day, a girl delivered from the certain grasp of hydrophobia."

"We cannot do what is impossible."

The next day, I went back to the Parrs' cabin to see Ouida Bell. The day was filled with thunder. A hard rain scoured the bare soil from which the harvest had been drawn. The atmosphere was ominous to the point of being cliché, but that couldn't be helped.

Ouida Bell Parr was not dead. Her limbs jerked, and her head snapped back and forth, but she could still choke down a little water and eat a biscuit in her more lucid moments, which kept her alive. That meant she was strong, not only in her body, but also in her mind.

"Stinks in here," said someone from a gloomy corner. It was Sarah.

I hadn't known she was there.

"Her caretakers have had greater concerns than housekeeping or hygiene," I said. "You're welcome to come back with a broom, once matters of life and death are settled."

The damp blanket over Ouida Bell's chest rose and fell in irregular rhythms. Red splotches stood out from her sallow complexion.

"I always thought she was vain," said Sarah. "Always in a dress cinched too tight for any real work except flirtation."

"Except when you buried her naked in the graveyard."

"Yes, except for then." Sarah's face softened for an instant, and she looked back toward the bed, toward the feeble and dying patient that slept there, and her chin set into hard tension. "Let's go, Aubrey. Nothing we can do for her."

"But we must try."

"Horseshit. It's not going to do any good. Let's go."

"I thought you and Ouida Bell had a friendship."

"Ouida Bell, but not whatever this flesh-and-bones thing is."

"Sarah, please," I said in low tones. "Have a measure of compassion."

"Ouida Bell can't hear us if the rabies has gone far enough." She tapped a knuckle against Ouida Bell's forehead.

The girl shivered down her back. Her eyes opened. They were black, like the eyes of an animal.

I pushed Sarah away from the bed as I grabbed a cup of water. "Can you drink?" I asked. "It will help."

I brought the cup closer to her. Her breath hastened, each inhalation sharper and shorter than the last, an ominous sign. It reminded me of Eva huddling against her bedpost. Trembling, I put the rim of the tin cup to Ouida Bell's lips.

At the touch of the metal, Ouida's hand, rigid like a claw, smacked the cup from my grasp. My heart pounded as her back arched like a shell, and her limbs twisted at unnatural angles. Her sweat-soaked nightdress covered her like a thin layer of mucus.

I put my right hand, ever so lightly, onto her shoulder. Her neck snapped as her head spun, and she landed her teeth in the flabby skin between my thumb and index finger.

"Damn!" I recoiled from the sudden movement and pain.

I stepped back, and Ouida Bell came at me again, but her frail body couldn't keep up the attack. She fell backward into the bed as I was pressed up against the side of the cabin, heart pounding at the suddenness of the assault.

I looked at my hand and found a little blood from the bite marks. I took out my handkerchief and applied pressure. In a moment, the blood had stopped. I did not think of rabies then.

That was a disease spread by mangy curs and mysterious panthers, ragged in their flesh and mind, and Ouida Bell was still human despite the disease assailing her. I did not think of rabies, but I should have.

Sarah's expression hadn't changed from fixed annoyance. After the attack ceased, she sighed. "Why did you come here, Aubrey? What did you think you could do?"

"Because I'm a healer, and she's a person in need of healing."

"What are you going to do, then?"

"Nothing, I suppose."

I looked at the skin of my hand, where I'd been bitten. A droplet of blood squeezed out of my wound.

"What would you try, Sarah?"

"I have nothing. Rebecca's got nothing. You've got nothing. And Effie is the master of nothing."

"But if you could try anything, what would you try?"

"Why do you care?"

"Why do you not, Sarah?"

Sarah glared at me as though I were a perched pigeon—a vulnerable, stupid creature. Then she contorted her face into a hideous leer. Her jaw dropped and skewed to the left. She twisted up her brow so that one eye was bulging. "Affrat! Fraset! Frasset!" Her arms rose straight in the air, and she hopped from one foot to the other. "Affrat! Fraset! Frasset! Ferret! Farfat! Tafrat! Fatsat! Fartart!"

"What on Earth?" I put my hands over my ears. "Is that gibberish?"

"You begged me to do something. You can't complain if you don't like it." Sarah stomped around the perimeter of the bed, leering and howling and spouting spells. I thought she'd gone half mad herself. I'd never seen her so worked up.

Ouida Bell made no response, as of course she wouldn't, to this utter nonsense.

"What are the words supposed to do?" I asked through gritted teeth.

"Be believed. And people have believed in them since before the Ishtar Gate. They're Babylonian words. Prayers, maybe. Or curses."

"Sarah, stop it. Stop it. It's not helping."

She glowered at me. "Well, then, here's the best magic spell. The most powerful that ever there was." She fumbled in her pouch for a scrap of paper, and she borrowed a pencil from me. On the paper, she wrote out a grid of letters:

```
S A T O R
A R E P O
T E N E T
O P E R A
R O T A S
```

"Do you know this one, Aubrey? It's a palindrome, same up and down, left and right."

"Is that important?"

"No, of course not, except that a hundred generations thought it was. Gamblers put this square in their shoes for good luck. Kings etched it under their plates to save them from an assassin's poison. Dying men burned the paper and swallowed the ashes to cure their mortal wounds. Here, I'll wad it up and stick it under Ouida Bell's armpit."

Sarah lifted up Ouida Bell's right arm and shoved the paper into the fold of her axilla. The arm fell across Ouida Bell's torso at an unnatural angle, limp.

"Let's see if it saves her life," she said. "It's nothing. It's foolishness. I only do what I can get folks to believe in, what they already believe in. But when there's no mind left..."

"She has survived this long."

"And it's been torture. I would take her out and shoot her. Put her out of her misery." Sarah's eyes were red, and I knew enough of people, whatever else my ignorance, to see it as a sign of great distress.

"Bullets are not cures," I said.

"Any good end is a cure," said Sarah, "and death is the best end Ouida Bell has left."

"I did not think you were so heartless," I said, ashamed of the faint hope I'd entertained.

"I'm not heartless. It's only... Ask Effie. I can't..."

"Effie can cure her?"

"I can't. Rebecca can't. Neither of us could do anything for Everett, either. We put him in front of Effie, and he died. And maybe Effie could have cured him but didn't, or maybe she knew she couldn't cure him, and so she did nothing. But leave it to her. Let Effie save Ouida Bell's life or let her take the weight of her dying. Because I can't."

Sarah flew out of the cabin. The door slammed, and the walls shuddered. Ouida Bell, or the shade of her, struggled for her life in the darkness with me.

Chapter 16

ORDINARY WATER IN AN ORDINARY WORLD

Nothing resolved, nothing gained, but what could I have expected? I'd gone to Ouida Bell's bedside with no hopes of a miracle, and none was given. Sarah's behavior had been shameful, but she was grieving. I could not judge her. Also, I came away with an injury of my own, a shallow bite in the fleshy part of my hand. I did not think that such a bite could pass the contagion of hydrophobia, but as soon as I returned to my hayloft, I bled myself from my thumb and forefinger, taking far more than would have been needed, even for a snakebite.

The next day, and the next, I was relieved to take up station in my office, hoping for a few patients with ordinary complaints—gout, diarrhea, dyspepsia—that could be handled with ordinary medicine or an herbal concoction. I needed curable diseases to reaffirm my belief in my usefulness. I saw to them and felt restored. My hand was healing well, with no signs of corruption.

Effie was the only Winter sister attending with me at the office. Rebecca had been called away to an imminent childbirth. It was the first birth she'd ever attended, and she considered being invited a great privilege. No one would've invited a witch to be present at such a liminal event. One would invite only a trusted and respected healer. I was happy for her. Childbearing is the happiest sort of medicine, a painful condition that would soon be cured with smiles and laughter and handshakes and coos.

"Are you hoping to see many visitors today, Effie?" I asked, rubbing my hands together. I offered her coffee to shake off the chill. She'd placed herself upon one of the hams that still lingered around the office, reminding us all it had once been Snell's storehouse. Only the two of us were there, and Effie's hair was wet. I noted that not out of disapproval but because it felt strangely intimate. I'd never before seen a woman with wet hair except for my sister. My mother, in her superstitions, rarely bathed.

"I hope never to see anyone."

I coughed, hearing the indictment of my enthusiasm. "You mean, only suffering people come to see a doctor, and you would not wish suffering on anyone?" I brought her the coffee, and she held the cup close to her chest. "That's generous, but someone is always suffering. It's the mortal's lot in life, to suffer unto death."

She brought up her legs so that she was hugging her knees, making herself smaller.

"Not that we are hoping for a patient," I said, "but if the inevitable compels a poor soul to seek our expertise—"

Effie sneezed.

I waited to see if her single sneeze would turn into a series, then I continued, "If a patient comes in, my questions to you are because I'm trying to learn."

"I don't know how to teach."

"Don't teach. Just treat. It's my responsibility to learn. What can I have at the ready for you? An herb? A knife? A length of silver thread?"

"I'd prefer a glass of water," she said.

"Is the coffee too hot? I'll fetch you some cream."

"Don't trouble yourself. I'll get it." She unfolded herself from atop the ham and went to the ewer we kept near the laboratory glass.

Effie hadn't poured a full cup before the small door between our office and Snell's store opened. In staggered Mrs. Snell, bent double, supporting herself with two crossed canes.

I hastened to her side. Effie finished pouring her cup of water as I guided Mrs. Snell to sit in the surgery chair. If she were to faint, best to have her in position already, I figured. "Please, Mrs. Snell, what's the matter?"

"Oh, it would be faster to list what doesn't hurt." Mrs. Snell shuddered.

I took out my silver pocket watch and measured her pulse.

"I suppose that my eyelashes—the ones I have left—are all right, and I can't complain of any pain in my pinkie fingers. But everything else, ah, me!"

Mrs. Snell's pulse fluttered arrhythmically under my fingers. Her lymph nodes were swollen. She had a fever, and she winced as I asked her to flex her appendages. Her joints crackled like wet logs in a fire.

"I think half my troubles come from my guts," she said, putridity on her breath. "I have violent dyspepsia. When I walk, you can hear the gravel rattling. And it's mortifying to say this, but I must: my Snell says that I am issuing a vile, sulfurous flatulence."

"Gastralgia?" I asked.

"Yes, two of them! And I have pains in my extremities and my innards. My back hurts, and my toes hurt, and my neck hurts, and my heart hurts. They are all so tired of their work." She patted at her eyes. "And that isn't the worst. I have a terrible brain congestion, a fog that keeps me from saying any right thoughts and makes me think fearful ones. My head is all in a mist, and in the mist, I see ghosts. Some are people that I knew back in Louisville, but others I've never seen before. Some are monsters with teeth like pitchforks, but these are not so frightful as the ones that are sweet and kind. They are like angels, and they are telling me that I am not one of them. They have the most terrible smiles."

Such a torrent of symptoms. I looked at Effie. She had fallen back to the wall, her arms folded across herself, and she pressed her stomach as though troubled by her own pains.

"See, I am contagious!" declared Mrs. Snell, pulling her shawl across her face. "Dear Effie's coming down with my pernicious nostalgia."

"Mrs. Snell, please, it's all right," I said.

"No, I'm sure it is not. It will never be." Mrs. Snell closed her eyes as she spoke. "What can cure all my ills? I will not survive it. The bleeding for the fever would drive the dyspepsia, and the pills for phlegm would stoke the fever. Give me a clyster for the gravel, and you'll rip up my insides with fuel for flatulence. To say nothing of the ghosts, the nostalgia..."

A previous rendition of myself would not have been dissuaded from giving her a bleeding, despite all those symptoms, but I knew what a bleeding would do. I did not know what Effie would do. What could she do for Mrs. Snell, and what could she do for Ouida Bell?

I moved closer to Effie, meaning to unstick her from her place by the force of my presence, the same way a man can free up a bench by sitting too close to other occupants.

"Let Rebecca do it," she said.

Did every patient in Hope Hollow stir fear inside her? "Rebecca's with Mrs. Islington, who's just in her confinement."

"Then Sarah—"

"Sarah had to fetch some more human skulls."

Effie folded her hands. She pressed her fingers together so hard that the tips turned red. Mrs. Snell gave a series of glottal expulsions, hiccups of air driven by spasms of the lungs. Her head slumped to one side.

Effie stepped forward, her movements small and uncertain. She drank from the cup of water she'd poured for herself. Her nervous tremors caused a few droplets to spill, but she did not wipe them away. They slid from her cheeks and left tiny blots against her collar.

I held my breath to listen for the faintest whispers she might utter, be they prayers or spells. I watched every muscle for the slightest movement. I looked for her fingers to stretch out in therapeutic touch, but Effie's hands never moved from her sides. I kept a constant watch on her fingers, looking for signs of prestidigitation. I looked at Effie's eyes, pale gray and virtuous and memorable, in case mesmeric suggestions appeared in the rhythm of her blinking. But nothing was there to see.

Minutes passed. Mrs. Snell's eyes opened. She glanced around the room. "Do you know... I'm feeling a considerable lot better now."

I smiled. She was being kind to Effie's feelings. "Yes, good work, Effie. First, do no harm, right?"

Effie's right eye disappeared behind fallen strands of gray hair. She brushed them back over her temple. She made vanishing bows to Mrs. Snell and to me then hastened out to the pig yard. She gave no excuse nor backward glance.

Mrs. Snell grinned, showing more teeth than I'd ever seen her display before. They were in remarkable condition. Whiskey rots a tooth in a few years, but Mrs. Snell's teeth looked as white as a porcelain doll's. So many people in Lawrenceville had remarkably preserved teeth. How did they manage it? An herb, a mineral in the water? The Winter sisters?

Mrs. Snell pressed a weight into my palm. I pulled my hand back and examined what she'd placed there. It was a five-dollar coin, a fortune.

"I can't accept this," I said, dumbfounded. I held my palm out so that she could take her coin back. "You haven't received anything—"

"But I'm leaving with a lot less than I came in with. That's worth a fine price."

She curled my fingers back around the coin, which felt cold in my hand.

As she left, Mrs. Snell's heels had spring. Her shoulders were back, her breast puffed out. Her walking canes swished like batons at her sides.

What had Effie done? A trick of the mind? A sleight of hand? Executed a confidence game between her and Mrs. Snell, with me as the victim? I peered into the cup of water Effie had left unfinished as though it were a scrying glass. I saw only ordinary water in an ordinary world.

When she heard the distant movement, Sarah quieted her breathing. She raised her rifle and willed her heartbeat to slow. The barrel of the gun was perfectly steady, aimed at the animal sound.

When it was Effie, not the rabid panther, that stumbled from the rhododendrons and onto the forest path, Sarah kept the gun aimed for just a moment, just a moment longer. Then, she released her breath and her heart, and the blood rushed to her head.

Effie looked up at her. "Where have you been? We haven't seen you for three days."

"I've been looking for that panther again." Sarah dropped downward, branch to branch, scaring up a brace of pigeons at each move. "And looking for you."

"Have you been up this tree the whole time?" said Effie.

"Not always this tree. But some tree."

"I'm sorry," said Effie.

"For what? You haven't done nothing yet." Sarah alighted on the earth in a crouch. Leaves were in her hair and bird droppings and sap on her palms. Sarah wiped her hands on her skirt one at a time, tucking her rifle into the crook of her arm. "You're heading up to see Thumb?"

Effie nodded.

"It's a wonder Waycross let you go. I thought he would be just fascinated by you."

"He is, but I couldn't—"

"I think," said Sarah, "that you should go back. Thumb will be there tomorrow. But you need to see Ouida Bell."

Effie wrapped her arms over her chest, hugging her shoulders. She was making herself smaller as if she could hide inside her humility. Sarah flared inwardly at her sister. Whom did she think she was fooling?

"Go back," said Sarah. "If not now, then before daylight. Kiss your sweetie, and then go back to town."

"But won't it encourage Aubrey... and what about Rebecca?"

"Damn them both," said Sarah.

She knew the danger. If Effie cured Ouida Bell, Waycross would become fascinated with Effie, his natural curiosity tilting into obsession, and fascination was an affliction not easily cured. Rebecca would know the change at once. What would happen? More fire, more death? Life was a spiral, a spiral coiling in, but there was no way out if Ouida Bell was to live.

"You need to see to Ouida Bell," said Sarah.

"I would prefer not to."

"I don't give a right damn what you prefer or don't."

Effie shook her head.

"Maybe I sneak you in," said Sarah. "You cure her, and then you sneak away. No one knows it was you. The town doesn't know. Aubrey doesn't know."

"Do you think that will leave the town at peace?"

"No, no," said Sarah. "But I don't care. You have to cure her, Effie, if you can. And I believe that you can. You brought that deer back to life after the panther killed it. And Ouida Bell isn't even dead yet. That should be simpler, right? Wash away her hydrophobia."

Sarah wondered what Rebecca had said to Effie on the night of the fire. How had Rebecca pleaded for Everett's life? That could not have been so different from where Sarah found herself now, and Everett had died. Effie hadn't saved him.

Sarah had her gun, though. She had always defended Effie, trying to save her from all harm, but she had a gun. That was a terrible thought. Sarah should not value any life over the life of her little sister.

"You have to go back," said Sarah, and two tears threatened to fall. "You have to save her."

"Why?"

"Because you can, Effie."

The town square was swaddled in the purple blanket of evening. I could see the front facade of the courthouse. The rest was hidden in the night. Hogs and men and women appeared and faded like ghosts, stepping from shadow to illumination and back again. From a dozen glass windows, candlelight beamed. Snell's storefront was a wash of reds and yellows. The air was thick and humid. The evening was as sweaty as I was.

A hog came near me, the little sweet one. I hadn't given her a name because no one should name his future supper, but I recognized her upturned snout and the bristly burst of hair above her rear right haunch. Her tail was wagging a hearty hello.

"Good evening, madam," I said. "Worms or heart troubles?"

The hog snuffled at my shoes then scampered away, inviting me to play.

Ebullient laughter spilled from the open windows of Snell's house, along with enough light for a parade. As I climbed the porch steps, I saw Mrs. Snell was in a frolicsome mood, dancing with all four limbs flailing. Snell had a fiddle, which he was sawing with great concentration to stay on beat, if not on melody. Rebecca was dancing with them, her footfalls loud and gay. No one heard me climb the porch steps over the din of the music, so I put my face up to the open window, like a specter looming in.

"Whoo! Whoop, whoop!" Mrs. Snell bounded toward me, her great arms thrust wide. A kiss smashed into my cheek. "Doctor, Doctor, come on in! It's a party."

Snell stopped playing, but Rebecca still tapped out the rhythm with her feet.

I disentangled myself from Mrs. Snell's greeting. "What's the glad occasion?"

"Look at this!" Mrs. Snell arose on her toes and danced out a bounding rhythm on the floorboards. The house shook in her enthusiasm. Her heels kicked up so high that I could see the soles of her shoes were wearing thin.

Rebecca came up beside Mrs. Snell and mimicked her pattern, matching her leap for leap.

Mrs. Snell sprang higher, her energy increasing. She spun back to front, front to back. Rebecca was tiring. She couldn't keep up, and finally, Rebecca stumbled.

Mrs. Snell cackled with delight. "See, I can beat the whipper-snappers. Remember what I was like this morning, Doctor? A useless bag of bones. Now, whoop, whoop!"

It was a triumph, one that made me sick with mystery. Snell looked at me, and I wondered if he wouldn't ask later for a male cure of his own, so high were his wife's spirits.

"I'm glad at your health, Mrs. Snell," I said. "I wonder if I couldn't see Effie, please. Is she here?"

"What's the matter?" asked Rebecca, who'd settled into a chair to catch her breath.

Mrs. Snell clapped her hands twice. "Why, if I saw that girl, I'd hug her and squeeze her until her stuffing came out. I'd bake her up a chocolate cake and a mountain of cream, and I'd throw strawberries in her face until she plumped up enough to be pretty."

Rebecca stood up and crossed the room. "Aubrey, let's go outside for a minute."

I offered her my elbow, and she took it. The two of us, so joined, took a moment to navigate the doorway. I turned myself so that Rebecca could pass through first, but she misunderstood, and we ended up squeezing through at the same time.

Outside, we did not go far, just enough up the road so that we didn't have to shout over the screech of the fiddle. My elbow was damp with sweat where Rebecca held it.

"Aubrey, what's happened?" She took her arm from my elbow and picked up my hand.

"Mrs. Snell. Effie restored her so easily. By what manner, I could not say."

"What did you see her do?"

"She stared at Mrs. Snell for a few minutes. Then, Mrs. Snell was cured."

Rebecca's mouth narrowed to a small point. "Do you think she's a miracle worker?"

I scuffed my feet in the dust of the road. "This is only one case, but a fascinating—"

That word, fascinating, set Rebecca aflame.

"The graveyard is not empty, Aubrey. There's a tombstone for Everett." Rebecca turned to march back to the Snells' house.

"Please, wait." I dashed toward her and caught her sleeve. "It's not... whatever you think it is. I just... What is she, Rebecca?"

"She's an empty soul."

"You cannot leave me with that mystery! You are her sister. You know what she is."

Rebecca looked at me, and fire burned in her eyes. "She is evil."

I wound up at the Flowing Bowl behind a heap of biscuits and roasted pigeon and more whiskey than a soldier could drink in a week.

I stirred my food, watching the steam curl. The extravagance was supposed to lift my spirits, but I had no appetite.

The tavern was quiet. A few patrons played chuck-luck for dried beans. Buck debated the weather with his tablemates. P drummed his fingers and looked as though he were thinking out a difficult puzzle. Even Renwick was enjoying a moment of tranquility.

Then the door flew open so hard that nails popped out like a porcupine's spines. Framed by the doorway was the imposing Mrs. Maltbie.

"Savages! Whiskey whore-mongers!"

"Eula?" said Renwick. "What in the—"

"I've warned you not to sell to my husband. I've prophesied your doom."

"I haven't sold him any drink," said Renwick, lifting his hands in honest innocence. "He hasn't been in, except for the chicken and dumplings."

"And what's in your vile chicken and dumplings?" Mrs. Maltbie spat on the floor. "Rum? Whiskey? Unvirtuous spirits?"

"Worms is what's in 'em!" said Buck. "But Sarah Winter will take 'em out."

"I know you've been selling him liquor, you iniquitous devils!" said Mrs. Maltbie. Her fingers wrapped around the head of her iron-clad cane. "You impecunious tempters! You torpid jackanapes! You blighted roustabouts!"

I sat up straighter in my chair. "Mrs. Maltbie, if I may—"

"You mayn't! I will not be silenced. Your turpitude, Doctor, is as profound as theirs. Your ether is a poison no less pernicious than demon rum."

"I shan't brook an ill word against ether." My chest swelled, and the veins on my neck pulsed. "The fatuous sententiousness of your ilk—"

"If you two would take your tiresome words outside," said Renwick.

"How's this for a tiresome word, eh?" Mrs. Maltbie raised her metal cane and brought it down upon my table. It split like a stump beneath a mattock. My plates of pigeon and biscuits and chicken and dumplings shattered on the floor, and a spray of whiskey filled the air.

"God damn!" I cried, shielding my eyes from the spray of splinters.

At first, Mrs. Maltbie looked stunned, but she quickly recovered. "A righteous blow! The first of many."

Mrs. Maltbie whirled the cane and batted the cups and bowls from the length of the bar. Buck and P dove for cover, and Renwick lunged for her, but she riposted with her cane, catching him across the forehead. She shattered bottles of whiskey and beer and water and pickled eggs. The fragments rained down like grapeshot.

I fled. I couldn't stop Mrs. Maltbie by myself. I needed help.

I careened out of the Flowing Bowl and straight into the solid wall of someone else. The impact knocked me flat. My head hit the hard earth. My jaw was knocked out of square. My left buttock fell on a sharp rock, and I think my coccyx came loose. I tried to stand, but my body failed to obey.

"Aubrey, get up." The hand on my shoulder was Effie Winter's. She lifted me by the armpit with uncanny strength and set me on my feet.

"Lord Almighty, you've got to help," I said. "There's a mad-woman in there. She's raging."

"Ouida Bell?" asked Effie.

"What?" My head was still ringing from my fall. "No. The violence of her hydrophobia hasn't—"

The whole facade of the Flowing Bowl shuddered from a mighty blow from inside.

Mayor Richardson ran past us at full tilt, pumping his arms. "Don't just stand there, doctors!" He threw himself into the fray.

"Effie, come."

"I prefer—"

"I don't give a damn what you prefer," I said. "You have a Hippocratic duty. Well, perhaps you don't because I didn't make you swear to it. But I have a Hippocratic duty to render assistance in every case, and the best assistance I can render is you."

I took Effie by the hand and pulled her into the Flowing Bowl. She let herself be led.

Mayor Richardson was sitting on top of Mrs. Maltbie, pinning her to the floor. She thrashed, her fists clutching her cane, which banged on the wooden planks.

Effie knelt down beside Mrs. Maltbie. Quiet fell across the Flowing Bowl. Her breathing became calm and rhythmic. Then Mayor Richardson helped Mrs. Maltbie to her feet and guided her out with a stern hand on her arm. Effie lifted her eyes but did not stand up.

The Flowing Bowl awakened slowly to the sounds of men muttering curses as they picked splinters and glass from their arms. Renwick had a gash across his forehead that was dripping blood into his eyes. I couldn't see all of P's injuries. He was a pair of legs protruding from under a table. There would be two dozen broken bones. I hoped vainly that none would require amputation, but I knew that for compound fractures, sometimes no other choice was available.

I needed bandages, lancets, debridement acids... Along his forearm, Buck had one gash of particular concern. The skin had opened in a way that would be hard to close. The cut was deep enough that not much blood was flowing, which was a bad sign. That was a difficult injury. A piece of bread lay on the ground beside us. It wasn't moldy, but it was dirty, and perhaps that was just as good. I took the bread and pressed it against the cut.

"You'll be fine, Buck," I said though I was by no means sure of it. "Hold this on here until... until you get tired. Two hours, at least. I want to see you tomorrow. We'll see that you're on the mend."

I left him to ponder his treatment. Effie was moving from patient to patient, soaking clean rags in water and then wiping away blood and debris from the wounds. The labor was useless—a physician does not clean a wound unless it is for stitching or debridement or amputation. Better that the blood forms a crust to hold in the laudable pus.

As I fretted, Effie tended to the terrible gash on Renwick's head. As she cleaned the bloody wound, it became a thin white line across his brow. It hadn't been as bad as I'd feared.

P was bearing his full weight as he brought more cloths for Effie, not a broken bone in his body. The man at the chuck-luck wheel had taken a cane whack to the left side of his head, which might have been a mortal blow, but Effie washed away the blood, the bruise, the hurt, and the daze. He picked up the chuck-luck wheel from a puddle of chicken and dumplings and gave it a spin for luck.

I was not sure what I was seeing. I paid attention to every twitch and sign and quiver. I considered the position of her hands, the angle of her face, the way she daubed at the injuries, the pattern of stains on the ever-growing pile of dirtied rags. I would have accepted green sparks leaping from her fingertips or fire alighting on her hair or whispered songs of angels or the ghosts of ancient heroes returned from the dead. I would have believed anything, but nothing was happening. I stood in the doorway, lost, as Effie brought the wounded to their feet.

I woke that night to strange noises. The sound was an extended, wet scraping, like some creature with a long tongue licking the door. The window afforded no view. I saw only hogs in the moonlight, and peeking between the boards of the wall, I only saw slivers of light.

I listened and heard human breathing, intermixed with soft mumbling, angry words. My anxiety vanished. I slid open the door to confront Boatwright just as he lifted a paintbrush for another swath.

"Pastor, what are you doing?"

His face was frozen. Red drips of paint dribbled onto the threshold.

"Are you quite well, Pastor?" I said.

Boatwright flung his brush to the earth, causing a spattering of paint to spray his shoes and my bare feet. "Waycross, I am not all right," he fumed. "Mrs. Maltbie is not all right. This town is not all right."

"It was a terrible scene at the Flowing Bowl, sir," I said. "I don't know what possessed Mrs. Maltbie to such violence."

"You possessed her. You and the Winter sisters have possessed her. She was a faithful woman, always in church, always at prayer, always loyal to me. And your pernicious influence has driven her mad. It was that skull that you gave her husband. A wicked thing."

"The skull is used to treat his headaches."

"That's ludicrous, Waycross. Listen to yourself."

I crossed the threshold into the yard, my bare toes turning over straw and dust. In large red curves, I saw that Boatwright had painted flames on my door.

"The signs of heresy and hellfire, Waycross. They are a warning to all good people to stay far away from this cursed place. You've awoken the devil. Rabies in Ouida Bell. Savageness in Mrs. Maltbie. This wicked town will burn, burn, burn."

Boatwright talked fire, but he was only wind. "So, Pastor, what else do you have in mind to scare me, besides the painting?"

Boatwright's mouth flapped before his rage let him expel words, too. "I'll denounce you to the authorities. I'll write to the Georgia Medical Society and have them revoke your diplomas."

"Taking away my diplomas does not revoke my knowledge, Pastor. No one in Lawrenceville cares if our cures are attested by the academies so long as they work."

"I'll have you indicted for quackery. I'll have you deported from the county as disturbers of the peace. I'll tell all the legislators in Milledgeville that the county seat should not be granted to a town as corrupted and dissipated as Lawrenceville. What happened to my God-fearing, goodly people, Waycross? Why do my best congregants turn into raging demons?"

I scratched my chin and made a great show of pondering. "Too much blood and not enough sleep," I said at last. "Get away from my home, Pastor."

"You cannot command—"

"Get the hell away from my home."

"The hell, sir, is—"

I stepped closer to Boatwright, and he recoiled. Then he fled into the night, leaving behind footprints in red paint.

17

SO MUCH MYSTERY

At the Flowing Bowl, I had seen as near to a miracle as I dared to believe, and it was all Effie Winter's doing. Had she not come, had she not worked whatever nothings she'd worked on Mrs. Snell, I would have had to take the bone saw to half a dozen compound fractures.

If Effie was working wonders for Mrs. Snell, for Mrs. Maltbie, and for the patrons of the Flowing Bowl, could she not also work them for Ouida Bell? I had to see what would happen.

I found Effie at the spring, running cold water over her hands. The creases around her eyes deepened at the sight of me.

"We're going to Ouida Bell's cabin," I announced.

Effie continued her ablutions. Her hands, pale and wet, looked like ice. "I'd prefer not to," she answered, barely audible over the water bubbling from the spring. "You don't need me."

"I'll be the judge of that," I said sharply. "Come with me, and we'll talk about your misgivings."

Effie trudged behind me on the walk over, saying nothing.

Autumn had touched the earth. The chestnuts were aglow with reds and yellows, and the hemlocks flickered like candles under the leaden sky. The pines retained their verdant greens, so the character of the forest was dark and deep yet lit at turns by bursts of color.

The cabin was gray and still. Dark cloths were tied over the porch railing and drooped over the windows. The wooden steps sighed as Effie and I ascended. Nobody answered when I knocked, and I felt an ominous gravity. I cracked the door open, and Effie went in first.

A spirit was flittering around the hearth. It had Ouida Bell's face. It had Ouida Bell's eyes, full of intelligence and clarity. It threw the windows of the cabin open to the air. Sunlight poured in, and the room glowed with autumn light.

"It's kind for you to come all this way, Miss Winter."

Her voice was not at home yet in her body. Words stumbled strangely from her tongue.

The age of miracles had not passed. It was dawning new upon us.

"How did you heal her, Effie?" I'd kept my peace while we were with Ouida Bell, but as we returned along the path that followed the Alcovy river, I couldn't stay quiet any longer.

She jumped at my question. Our path back to town was taking us alongside the shallow shoals of the Alcovy, in the shadow of a bluff. The soil was thin beneath us, and in that clearing, the earth had eroded to the naked granite. Parts of the bluff had broken off through the years and fallen to the stone below. The orthogonal splits looked architectural and artificial, as if we were among the ruins of a sacred structure, a temple from times long gone.

"How did you heal her?" I asked again.

Effie stopped because I'd caught her hand. She shook me off then sat down upon one of the sundered stones, its flat top like an altar, but she made no reply.

"Ouida Bell was dying of rabies," I said. "Rebecca and Sarah and I could not have been mistaken. She was at the edge of death. And now, there is not a sign of the hydrophobia on that girl. The mad animal is gone. How did you cure her?"

"Why do you think it was me?" Her eyes were closed.

"Effie!" My voice burst loudly on the first syllable and cracked on the second.

She pulled her legs up from the stone and seemed to shrink. "I can't say. I can't tell you."

"You can't or you won't?" I sat down beside her and waited a moment until the world surrounding us was again heedless of our presence. "Whatever you've done or think you've done or don't understand or are afraid of, tell me. We will solve it together."

She shook her head.

"Am I not wise enough, Effie? Then tell me what to read. Am I not spiritual enough? Tell me to whom I should direct my prostrations and prayers and sacrifices. Am I not pure enough? Tell me how to wash away my impurities."

"What's your favorite color?" she asked in a whisper.

Taken aback, I answered truthfully. "Blue, I think. Sky blue."

Effie was looking past me, watching the river. "Everyone answers so easily. Rebecca's was lavender, then green, and then yellow. Sarah's always liked brown because she thinks no one else does. They made fun of me because I would not pick. But I've never had a favorite color."

"Why?"

"I would prefer not to. Who am I to choose?"

Patient delivered of hydrophobia."

When I returned to my hayloft, I wrote that on a clean square of paper, folded it, and sealed it with wax. On the front, I wrote, "Eva." As I had no other address, I placed the letter into the hearth, atop a smoldering pine log. The edges of the envelope caught fire first, and a ribbon of bright orange passed across the burning paper. Pale smoke rose up the chimney, taking the good news higher and higher, up to... but that is only a superstition.

Treatment

"A little knowledge about cleanliness and care can do more good than many costly potions from the apothecary."

—Nicholas Culpeper

18

REBECCA WINTER'S CELEBRATED
BRAIN SALT

SEPTEMBER 1822

The fat, full moon was low on the horizon, barely above the trees. It was orange as a pumpkin and just as large, plump and overripe and ready to be picked. In its eldritch glow, a dozen men and women, naked, were setting fire to the fallow field.

"Glorious, isn't it?" whispered Sarah, with reverence. "Like something from the Old World."

Ouida Bell, next to her, made no sound.

The naked men and women—Catherine, P, Maltbie, Mrs. Parr, and a dozen others—had dug a trench around the fallow field with harrows that Sarah had rubbed with mare's milk. They were lighting torches from a central bonfire and spreading the fire to the four corners of the field, touching the dry hay and wildflowers and chestnut saplings and rhododendron bracken until it sprang into sparks. Then they stood back in wonder at what they'd done, the orange moon reflecting the flames they had made.

"You didn't have to let my mother in," said Ouida Bell at last. "I didn't want to see her old dugs drooping down."

"I don't turn anyone away," said Sarah.

The farmers had come to her. They wanted good harvesting for this year and good planting for the next. Sarah thought of burning the fallow fields. Fire would wake up both the earth and the fire lighters. She'd told them when to assemble and what to bring. They passed the word in secret so as not to offend the pastor. Sarah regretted not mailing him an invitation. Word would get back to him, no doubt, of those pagan doings in the fields just outside of town, but hearing the tale is inferior to the whole effect: the twirling flames, the acrid scent of green shoots turning to smoke, the moon and the earth collaborating on the coloration. Perhaps he would come anyway, and the sight of so many of his congregants in the nude around a bonfire would seize up his feeble Protestant heart.

"Where's Effie?" asked Ouida Bell.

"She doesn't care for fires," said Sarah.

Ouida Bell's toes dug farther into the soil. "What do you think she'd do about the harvest? Not set fires. Not make my mother get naked and dance in the moonlight."

A wet branch exploded with a thundercrack, setting up sparks.

Ouida Bell kept talking. "She'd do something. I don't know what, but something, and better than this. What's a naked mother with a firebrand ever done for anyone?"

"If you're not having fun, then go home." Sarah put a silver-tipped measuring stick down next to her rifle. The measuring stick was an old trinket from the hayloft at Hope Hollow, covered in her mother's black letters. Sarah found it worked just as well for pointing or dowsing as any other stick. "Head on home. Go to sleep."

"I'd prefer not to," said Ouida Bell.

"Then be quiet. Your complaining is spoiling the mood."

Ouida Bell began to say something, but someone shouted. A disturbance in the bushes, a moan and a wavering—the panther rose from its resting place, which was alight. The creature looked exhausted. Its disease had nearly run its course, and all the viciousness had been sapped from its spirit. It stood on its four shaking legs and opened its mouth to roar, but no sound came from its foam-filled jaws.

"Hey, you damn pussycat! Git along now!" A naked man with a torch was standing in front of the panther, and it was the panther that was afraid.

"Scram, you! Scram!" said a naked woman.

Sarah had her gun in her hands and drew a bead on the animal, but the flames had frightened it badly. It was fleeing. In one leap, it cleared a gnarl of roots and a cowering Pendleton and the harrowed trench. The shot was an easy one. Sarah could have plugged it in the back of its skull at twice the distance.

"Shoot it, Sarah!" Ouida Bell flapped her arms.

The panther was rabid, a danger, but Ouida Bell had been rabid too, and Sarah had... She'd run away. Then Effie cured Ouida Bell. Perhaps Effie could cure the panther, too—if she supposed it worthy.

"Sarah, damn it, shoot it! Kill it!"

Effie had let Everett die, but Effie had not let Ouida Bell die. Why? What did Ouida Bell deserve that Everett did not? What did Sarah deserve that Rebecca did not? Sarah lowered her rifle, and the panther reached the far woods, escaping into shadow.

"Sarah, why didn't you kill it?"

"I'd prefer not to," said Sarah.

Mayor Richardson had fixed a late-September Tuesday for the census and an important referendum on the county seat. To lure his constituents away from their farms and to overcome the final lingering fears of the panther, which was weak and dying, Richardson arranged entertainments for all ages, sexes, and tastes and had them printed on handbills to be delivered throughout the county. The schoolhouse was hosting a literary event, which featured a debate between two pupils on the slavery question, a spelling bee, and readings from Shakespeare. A revival tent was erected down by the river, and Boatwright promised the water was still warm enough for baptizing. The First Daughters auxiliary was holding a cakewalk, and excellent doctors would be on hand to see to any troubles, free of charge.

I'd read the handbills three times before I realized the Winter sisters and I were the promised doctors.

The celebrated Tuesday of the vote began with rain, but that did not dissuade the influx of patients. Autumn is a hale time of year. The placid turn of weather makes for high spirits, and overindulgences rather than afflictions drove the infirmities we saw. P's flaxen-haired little boy ate too much green corn and got the squirts. Buck showed up with pitchfork wounds in his thigh. He'd found the tool in a haystack at a most inconvenient moment for himself and his lady friend. Old Elizabeth fell off her chair and needed all her bones reorganized. I lost count of the teeth I extracted. I put them all in a jar so that I could tally them later. My ears rang with shouts of pain, and my hands were slick with the drool and tears of dozens of people. Rebecca ran out of sassafras and turpentine. Sarah's hands were raw from mixing up graveyard-dirt poultices.

The evening fell clear and crisp. Flaming oil-brands had been stuck into the ground around the square. Skinny children roasted fat sausages, sweet griddle dough, and sugar apples over three heaping bonfires. Every person cast ten-foot shadows, so the earth writhed and wriggled with a thousand specters.

Rebecca and I had looked forward to an evening of frolicking. She wanted to dance, but I found I didn't have the spirit for it. I was exhausted from my efforts, the pain, and the cries.

"Go try the cakewalk," I said, not wanting to hamper her fun. "Win us a splendid cake."

I wanted only to go to sleep, to let the darkness take away the lightning storm in my head. The willow bark was useless. I should have asked Sarah for a skull to smash. I opened my flask of ether. Precious little was left, and I hadn't had time to make more.

Music and clapping and laughter and sweet promises filled the air, and their scent was thicker than the smoke. I excused myself from the expectant faces that approached me, more patients with more problems, and slipped through the gaps between dancers and frolickers, aiming for escape. A hand fell upon my shoulder.

"Hiya, Doc." Salmon Thumb had a vast grin connecting his earlobes. "A fine show you've got here."

"It's not a show. It's an appeal to democracy." I pressed a hand to my forehead.

Thumb whistled, and the high note traveled like a dart straight through my ear. Then Effie was standing next to him. She stood straight and tall, her feet placed symmetrically. She wore a bright-blue dress trimmed in yellow ribbon.

Thumb bubbled over with high spirits. "Well, Doc, we just wanted to say hi. We're going to join the frolics." In a flash, he scampered into the thick of the masses, leaping and dancing and whistling. He started singing at the top of his lungs, "Oh, I wish I was a lizard in the spring!"

"I should go see that he doesn't hurt himself." Effie followed Thumb into the masses.

I could not let her vanish.

"I wish I was a lizard in the spring!"

Effie was singing—singing!

When Thumb jumped and clicked his heels, Effie copied his movements. She leapt a little higher, clicked a little louder, and landed a little sprier. Thumb bounded closer, and then they were dancing together. His head was on her shoulder, a great heavy mass against her fragile collarbone. His lips were flapping, and she was nodding, and by the placement of her head toward his ear, I knew she was answering him. I couldn't hear over the din of the crowd, which swelled to a crescendo.

Thumb and Effie joined hands and spun around each other, heedless of anyone but themselves. Their trajectory sent them on a wild course. I followed in their wake across the square, out into the darkness beyond.

They fell together with a roar and splash. The stone trough of the spring had risen from the dark ground to catch them. They were drenched. Their clothes stuck to them, clinging in inopportune ways. Water dripped from Effie's hair.

Thumb gazed up at her, and he echoed the closing words of the song: "I wish I was a lizard in the spring!"

Effie made a sound of happy exasperation. She swatted her hand at the brim of Thumb's hat to push it down into his eyes. She clambered to her feet but slipped on the bottom of the trough. Her momentum took her body one way, but her leg went another. I was fifteen feet away, but I heard the snap of bone.

Thumb gawked. Effie made no cry of pain. She looked at her leg with curiosity.

A tremendous excitement filled me. How would Effie treat herself? I squinted through the darkness. I held my breath so that I could hear her incantations.

"Aubrey? I've been looking all over for you."

Rebecca's hand touched my shoulder. I did not feel it until she spoke, accusation in her voice.

"I... I saw Effie fall," I said, shame coloring my voice. "I think she's hurt."

Thumb and Effie heard, and Thumb came over to investigate. He stepped between me and Effie, and I saw nothing, nothing, nothing.

By the time the three of us turned to look at her, we saw only a superficial injury, no more than a scrape. Rebecca must have wondered what all the fuss was about. Thumb, if he had an impression of a more grievous wound, would not have trusted his senses, but I knew Effie had knit her own bones back together.

"You saw that, Rebecca—"

"I saw nothing, Aubrey, and you saw nothing, either."

"Let me go help her up."

"Thumb can do it, but she doesn't need his help."

Thumb did offer to help Effie out of the trough and to her feet, but she waved him away and got up by herself.

"What did you see, Aubrey," asked Rebecca, hurt and anger burning in her voice, "that you find so fascinating... that would lure you away?"

"I was only looking after her, your little sister, and then when she fell, there was the natural doctor's urge to help..."

My reply was unconvincing, though. I swallowed the rest of my words, trying hard to calm myself. I closed my eyes and saw everything again: the slip, the fall, the motion, the bone, and Effie standing up again, whole and unbroken.

"We're leaving," said Rebecca. She had her arm around Effie.

"Let us see you ladies home, at least," said Thumb, who was only a witness to the darker drama.

"We know our own way," said Rebecca, and Effie made no protest.

Thumb and I watched the sisters until they disappeared around the corner of Perry Street. A clot of choler rose into my throat. I wished I could swallow the rest of my ether to send me to sleep. As I wondered what Thumb was feeling, I looked at him. He was soaked from top to toe. The brim of his hat drooped low over his eyes. He was scratching his Adam's apple with a thumb and index finger.

"Doc?" he asked, his voice wide with wonder.

"Yes, Mr. Thumb?"

"If your sweetie and my sweetie are sisters, what does that make us? Sweeties-in-law?"

I've brought these for you," I told Rebecca when she answered the door the next day.

"They aren't very pretty." She took the flowers and held them in front of herself as though bearing a torch.

"They aren't meant to be," I said. "Look at them."

The yellow lady's slippers had been the hardest to find. The wispy fennel was slightly aromatic, but it could not overpower the stink of lobelia leaves, and sassafras would never be the belle of the ball, no matter how many fevers it broke. Taken together, though, they make an excellent nerve tonic. The bouquet was not a pretty one but a useful one.

That brought a faint smile. "Well, you have been paying attention, Aubrey."

"If you have water boiling over the fire, you can dunk this in it and drink the tea until I'm forgiven."

Rebecca exhaled, rattling the drying leaves of the flowers. "What's to forgive?"

"I mean—"

She raised a single finger, and I shut up.

"Let's take a walk, Aubrey."

We walked, side by side but not touching, for half an hour. Silence passed between us, but the woods were not quiet. Squirrels rustled among fallen leaves. Acorns fell like heavy raindrops. New bird songs passed from branch to branch. The summer birds had flown south, and northern species had taken their place.

The road curved to skirt a hillock of granite. We slowed as we passed over tossed and disordered ground. Ancient upheavals had broken stone from stone. Water had further confused the landscape. Two crows perched on a branch above us, and their calls passed back and forth as easily as a human language. I looked up at them then remembered that one should never look directly up at a bird.

"Come on, let's keep going." I pointed upward at the threatening tails as an apology for breaking the silence. "They have the high ground."

"Don't mind the droppings," said Rebecca. "It's a blessing."

"A blessing?" More than the sentiment, it was the specific word that surprised me.

"Sassafras loves a little sprinkle of manure. All herbs do."

I was no roadside weed and did not care to be shat upon by birds, but I didn't say that to Rebecca. I was so pleased that she'd spoken, that the tension of silence was slackening. She could talk about manure or the moon, so long as we were talking.

Ahead of us was the sound of water, a stream bouncing. The road met the river, their paths chasing each other over the Georgia foothills. Water ran over the wide, slick rocks, jumping up in spray where the flow crashed into a log or ridge.

At the water's edge, Rebecca headed upstream. I stayed close behind her. She brushed aside a thicket of fallen branches, and I saw chaos there that was not all nature's doing. A stone dam had been breached long before, and the river fell six feet through a crack in its face. The rest of the dam was home to lichens, moss, and assorted detritus. A breeding pair of towhees was perched on a hanging ledge. A separate channel, a millrace, ran parallel to the river. It did not carry any water, having long been cut off from the main channel. It was clogged with limbs, bracken, and bramble. Charred pieces of metal and rotten planks stuck out of the mud. A snarl of vines stretched out to draw the blackened stones back to the earth.

Rebecca clambered along the bank toward the ruins, and I followed. She entered the maze of burned-out foundations, respecting the old walls though they were no longer there. Wide granite slabs marked former thresholds. I recognized where the driveshaft to the waterwheel must have rested and where the millstones had turned.

She arrived at a chosen spot, a low stone that work and rain had smoothed. Around her were the picturesque ruins of the mill and the dark Appalachian woods. An artist could not have arranged the scene any better.

I sat down in a crumple next to Rebecca's pastoral perfection. No artist would paint it. The scene was only for us.

"There are rare specimens here," she said. "It's the fast water, the shady crevices."

"Hmm," I said.

"I've never seen any mosses like the ones that grow on the dam. I grind them up and put them into a tea for appetite. And the ash, well..."

"The ash from when the mill burned down."

"The millstones throw out so many fine particles of flour and corn that the air can carry a flame. One spark, and the room is an inferno."

"Spontaneous combustion," I said.

"Not spontaneous, but instantaneous." She bent over to draw her finger through the remnants at our feet. "And Everett..."

"You don't have to explain, Rebecca."

"No, I need to tell you." In her cupped hands was a clod of fragrant black mud. "Everett didn't die here. He was still alive when Paxton and Snell brought him to us. I did all I could, Aubrey.

Every salve and poultice and bandage that any witch or doctor has ever put to burned flesh, I tried. But I knew from the first that I couldn't save him. He needed greater medicine than mine."

"So you asked Effie." I knew the whole tale, though I had not heard it from her.

The muscles in Rebecca's cheeks tightened. "The last few times he'd come calling, it was to see her. He'd changed. Effie fascinated him, like a serpent fascinates its prey." She scooped a handful of ash and mud from the charred foundation.

Rebecca's jealousies and darkness suddenly had a new sense to them, and I breathed in sharply. My curiosity about Effie wounded Rebecca. It was an echo of love and loss.

"I wanted him to live. Even if Effie was the one who cured him. Even if that left him completely in her thrall. Hearts can change, but the dead cannot be restored to life." Rebecca let the mud fall back to the earth, but her hands were stained with the ashes of animals, vegetables, and mortals. "No, that is wrong. I admit it. I hated him in that moment, hated both of them. I hated that she had captured his mind, that he did not love me anymore, or if he did, that his love was second to his fascination. He did not understand Effie, and when he came to visit, it was not to see me, but to see her. Not to understand me but to understand her. But how can there be an understanding of a creature like Effie?"

I kept silent, for fear I would say the wrong words and betray my own total fascination.

"She did nothing, Aubrey. She did nothing, and he died."

"Do you think she could have healed him?"

"I don't know, Aubrey! If she could have cured Everett and didn't, that's as good as murder. Or it's a trick, a medicine show, and she's fooled us all."

"But the hydrophobia—"

"What about it?" she snapped. "What did you see? A person who was sick and then wasn't sick. That happens every day. A body heals itself most of the time, doctor or no."

A body does not heal itself from hydrophobia.

The flow over the dam was a thin, constant sound, more like wind than a waterfall. Pigeons stirred the air above us. The smell was stagnant, moldy, and decayed. The river did not purify that place of its history.

"If it was a miracle," muttered Rebecca, "why did Ouida Bell get one and not Everett? Why did she do it for you—for Sarah—and not for me? Was it because she had fascinated Everett? Was it because he'd thrown me over and Effie thought she was doing right?"

"I would not suppose that hydrophobia and burn wounds have the same remedy," I said. "Perhaps her cure is only specific for particular conditions."

Rebecca looked down at me. I met her eyes.

"Aubrey," she said. "I need to know if you were watching Effie frolic with Thumb out of... friendship, I suppose, and not out of fascination." Her voice was affectless, held by concentration and discipline. "And in everything. In her cures and her actions, in her person. Tell me that you are not fascinated by her. I need to know so that I am not destroyed again."

Neither Rebecca nor I were souls that could live with ignorance, and that made me love her all the more. "I swear to you, Miss Rebecca Winter, that my heart belongs only to you."

I sealed my promise by leaning toward her, but her face met mine before I was ready, and our lips mashed together. We were both surprised, but we accepted that we could not begin again. Too much was awkward and abrupt for the moment to be passionate, but it was heartfelt. Also, no doubt stood between us. We were a matched pair, two lovers twined. The wind picked up a handful of dust and ashes and scattered it across our shoulders. I heard prurient whispers in the rustle of fallen leaves, but I have never worried about offending ghosts.

19

GOOD FOR WHAT AILS YOU

The smells of balsams and burning candles were too strong in the office. Chemical odors set my chronic headache to throbbing. My arms itched from nervous agitation. I opened the window to let out the miasmas. A fine breeze was stirring the atmosphere, and the air improved. What would I do when winter's chill sealed us in with our stinks?

"Borrow a cup of sugar?" asked a loud voice, right at my ear.

I started like a squirrel at the crack of a stick. Thumb's head poked through the window.

"What did you say?" I asked with annoyance. "Sugar? I don't have any sugar, sir."

Thumb looked perplexed. "No, see, I was askin' if you needed to borrow a cup. Or wanted to have any. Sorry—I was trying to spare a word or two, get the message across faster, and now, look, I've been rattling on trying to explain what I meant. Here's the story. I bought fifty pounds of white sugar and figured you might use a bit. For your coffee. Or medicine."

"Fifty pounds of sugar? White sugar?" I was aghast at the extravagance.

Frontier folk sweeten their food with honey or molasses. If any sugar is to be had, it is by teaspoons.

"Yup, white sugar." He lifted his elbows off the windowsill and scratched the back of his neck. "I had Snell bring it in special. Paid him cash on the barrelhead. Need some? You take as much as you like. Free of charge."

I had no more need of white sugar than I did of silk or silver, which were equally as rare and opulent. I shook my head. "Can't say that I do though it's kind of you."

I started to turn away, but he spoke again. "See, what I really need is help carrying fifty pounds of sugar. It was too much

272

trouble to bring the wagon in, but I forgot how heavy fifty pounds is. And I thought that if I gave you some, you'd feel obliged to help me out."

"I'm not sure I have time just now..."

Thumb grinned his best medicine-show smile. "Come on, Doc. Effie and I are brewing a potion up on the Alcovy. A walk will clear your head. It'll be a nice surprise."

Thumb was right, a constitutional would help clear my head. If I happened to run into Effie, why, it would be innocent and accidental. I had made a promise to Rebecca, but I was not breaking this promise by helping Thumb with his chores or by looking after Effie to make sure she was well. I was still true to the promises of my heart. "Well, Mr. Thumb, you've persuaded me," I said, but I had persuaded myself.

Thumb whistled the whole way to the creek, filling in any silence that might turn to conversation or thought. He never kept to a single tune for more than three measures. Whenever I caught the melody, he would change to another in a different key. Matching his tune or his pace was impossible, and his nervousness prevented mine from dispelling. Our anxieties fed into each other's.

His camp was spread out along the shore of the Alcovy River. The glade looked beautiful, covered by a patchwork of ochre and crimson. Silver water in the river flashed in the long afternoon sun. Effie bustled among a laboratory's worth of barrels, fires, worktables, and bottles near the river's edge.

"La-la-loo!" Thumb hollered in greeting.

I'd been told that all frontier lovers have their own hollers. I hadn't worked one out with Rebecca yet. Hollering was not in my nature.

"La-la-loo!" she hollered back. Effie swung her arms over her head in greeting. "Hello, Salmon! Hello, Aubrey!" Joy animated her face.

She accepted the bags of sugar from us. "This should be plenty."

She poured water from a washtub into the largest of the barrels. Next, she took spice pouches, fist-sized bags of cheesecloth stuffed with aromatics. I longed for a single sniff though my olfactory system was less sensitive than it should be. The scent of ether clung to my nostrils. One odor was unmistakable: ginger. I would have expected sassafras or ginseng or even turpentine, but those were Rebecca's remedies.

Next, Effie picked up a broom that had been lying across the top of a barrel. As far as I could tell, it was a well-used corn-husk broom with a hickory or poplar handle. She stirred one barrel counter-clockwise, but the next clockwise. When the stirring was finished, she put wooden lids over the barrels, tamping them into place with a mallet. Did successive blows impart greater powers to the concoction?

Effie looked at Thumb and me. Her arms were crossed, the mallet tucked under her left forearm. A pleased smile covered her face. "It is finished," she said.

I folded my hands in reverence before her. "Tell me, what is it?"

"Ginger beer," she said.

I pondered the meaning of this gnomic pronouncement for a full minute before I admitted defeat. "I'm sorry, ginger beer?"

Thumb stuck his thumbs into his armpits. "Effie makes a mighty good ginger beer. Good pep on a lonely winter evening."

"Can it refresh the thirsts of the hydrophobe?" I cleared my throat. "Can it quench the regrets of the dying? Does it burn away agues, douse the flames of fever, or spice up a dull—"

"It's only ginger beer," said Effie. "A recipe I learned from... I'm not sure. Everyone knows how to make it. Except you, Aubrey, I guess."

My fingers curled until my nails dug into my palms. A thread that ran between my brain and my bowels stretched and then snapped. "Is this a trick?" My words came out hot and fast. "Are you mocking me, you and your sweetie?"

Effie reddened, a rare color on her face.

"Because if this is a game to you, if you are having a good laugh at gullible Aubrey—"

"Nobody's playing a joke on anybody," said Thumb.

"What are you to gain from my suffering?" The words came out with flecks of spittle. Pigeons decamped from their high perches and fluttered away. "I might have expected it from Sarah. Not from you, Effie." The strength seeped away from my legs.

"Aubrey, sit down," she said. "You look as if you're about to faint." She helped me to an empty wooden crate.

"What do you need, Doc?" said Thumb. "A little whiskey? Grove's Tasteless Chill Tonic?"

"I don't know."

Effie brought a dipperful of water drawn from the washtub. I wanted to drink. I was thirsty, so thirsty and exhausted and brain-addled. I put the dipper to my lips but could not tilt it back. The muscles of my arm resisted me. Nausea flooded up from my dyspeptic bowels. I shook my head, shivered down my spine, and tried again. Again, I could not drink.

Then my mind cast back to the bite I'd gotten from Ouida Bell. It seemed such a superficial wound, only in the soft part of my hand and not deep, and I'd bled it. What else explains such a symptom as fear of water, though? My mind was flooded with sudden terror. Panic shook my every nerve, and I could not think straight. No, it could not be rabies. It must be something else. Call it exhaustion, brain fever, gravel, quinsy, catarrh: anything but rabies.

"It's all right, Doc," said Thumb. "You're all nerves. Let it out. Let it down."

He clapped his hand down on my shoulder two times as though trying to expel my distress with back blows. The sudden shocks sent my eyes pressing into my eyelids, and curiously enough, that settled out the heavier particles of my dyspepsia. I started to feel a little better.

I wiped a fleck of frothy choler from the corner of my mouth. "I'm sorry. A fit came over me. Too much brainwork. Bad vapors in the office. Choler stirred up by the walk." I still grasped for another answer.

Effie studied me. I was a puzzle to her as much as she was a puzzle to me.

Thumb took off his hat and twisted the brim distractedly. "Doc, are your eyes working fine? Your ears? If you need another minute..."

"No, I'll manage," I said. "Why?"

"Well, you see, Doc," said Thumb. He was watching his heel dig a hollow into the soggy earth. "I need a witness."

"For what?" I asked though an ulcerous blemish on my stomach already knew.

The white sugar was meant to impress Effie. Though he was an itinerant peddler, he could provide her every luxury. I understood why he'd been nervous in his whistling. The question on his mind was momentous, and he was so fixated on it, he was ignoring the colossally bad timing.

"Effie..." he started, then his voice failed him. His eyes were wide and shimmering.

"Not yet, Salmon." Effie brushed her graying hair behind both ears. Her face was kindly, her cheeks tinted rosy.

"But I would—" started Thumb.

"Yes... but not yet, Salmon." She picked up his hands in her own. "Not yet."

They embraced, heedless of me. Thumb's face hid in Effie's neck, and Effie's sharp shoulders stuck out like wings as she reached over and around him.

My dyspeptic bowels rumbled. They were seized by a nervous flatus, but I squelched it, the bad airs bubbling back into other parts of my body.

Thumb intended to spirit Effie away.

20

FOR DEVILS AND ANGELS

I consumed the bulk of my ether in three days. I could not sleep a wink without it. I wondered about Effie, about Rebecca, about how I'd been unable to drink even though I'd since been able to take a little water. My headaches struck again and again. My brain, unless a draught of ether quieted it, buzzed with anxiety.

I did not relish the dull task of making more ether, but the matter was unavoidable. I couldn't go on without it.

I poured my ingredients—ethanol and sulfuric acid—into the glasses for distillation. I applied heat, setting the tubes and retorts at the proper height. Bubbles rose, each pop sending tiny droplets of liquid against the upper reaches of the glass. I smelled the ether more than usual. It gnawed at my raw nostrils. I looked over my connections to see if anything was leaking, but the lids were fastened and the seals tight. The odor was seeping out of the walls. I'd permeated my world with ether. A tickle started at the back of my throat, occasioned by the vapors, and I coughed full of phlegm.

I walked outside for clean air and allowed myself to dwell on Effie. If I could not find out how—or if—she cured, I myself would be incurable. How could I live in untreated, pathological, chronic ignorance?

In the hog yard were fewer inhabitants than usual. The animals had fattened up from the new crop, and before the lean times of winter caused that sweet fat to waste away, they were killed. The piquant fragrance of hickory smoke perfumed the air. I wondered who was barbecuing—P, Buck, Pendleton, or Pa Everett.

No, it was me. The smoke was pouring from my office.

I dashed back. My equipment had overflowed, and bottles had fallen over. Ether and unreacted ethanol had soaked into the wood and the corn sacks. The distilling fire greedily jumped into the fuel-dampened materials. The laboratory table was aflame in blue and pink and white—the colors of a chemical fire. Rolling blue vapors rose up the walls, leaving trails of sparks. I opened my mouth to cry out, but a retort, filled with half-made ether, exploded from the heat and sent showers of sparks across the room. Bags of corn exploded like gunshots.

"Waycross!"

"Oh, hell," I said unthinkingly. "Oh, hell, hell, hell."

"Waycross!" Snell's face appeared across the roil of fire. "Waycross, get out of there!"

"Water, man! Water, water! Oh, hell! Bring water!"

I had to act. I ran to the hog scalder and pried the metal basin from its rock surroundings. My desperation gave me strength. I ran to the spring, my feet slipping as alarms rang all around me— the church bell, the graveyard bell, dinner bells, clanging pots and pans. I filled the basin from the spring, but I knew it wasn't enough. Half the contents sloshed away as I ran back to the office. The fire had gotten into the roof. Purple fingers reached out from collapsing beams, a demon struggling to escape.

I approached the shimmering inferno. The hairs on my arms ignited, incinerated. I felt my eyebrows vanish. I heaved the contents of my basin, and the water evaporated before the flames. The sibilant hissing was the laughter of defeat.

The door gaped wide, the fire breathing in to stoke itself. I had no hope of rescuing anything. My lancets and chemicals—gone. Rebecca's herbs, Sarah's candles—cinders. My beautiful, beautiful bottles—the precious medicines inside turned to vapor.

Anonymous hands drew me back and into the crowd that had assembled to watch the destruction.

"Aubrey, Aubrey!" Rebecca was calling.

Behind her, Effie spirited through the crowd. Her gray hair was like steam, the pools of her eyes moist and deep and clear.

"Everything is gone, Rebecca. The books, the purgatives, the clysters. Your mortar and pestle. The hay in my hayloft. Those hams. No one got to eat those hams. Poor hogs, chopped up for nothing. Their whole lives, up in smoke." I could not hold myself back.

"Aubrey, shhh. What matters is that you're alive. Herbs grow back, but people do not."

The flames reached the facade of Snell's store. He and his wife stood at the head of the crowd. He wasn't trying to fight the fire though he had more livelihood to lose than I did. It was Lawrenceville's immense good fortune that the wind was calm. The crowd was free to watch someone else's catastrophe with jubilant horror. The timbers gave their final, mortal cry, and the building slumped, staggered, and died. A concussion of hot air blasted forth, and we all turned our faces away. When we dared to look again, only phantasms of flame and cooling ash remained. I looked over my shoulder to find Effie, but she'd gone.

"I told Waycross that this town would burn." Pastor Boatwright was clambering atop a rain barrel. The crowd convulsed as he swung his wide hat in victory. "He perverted his healing arts. He brought witches into our midst. And he has made this town to burn."

Everyone began jabbering. Lizbeth Samples and Mrs. Maltbie added amens to the hazy air.

"We suffer heretics in our midst!" roared Boatwright. "What have they done to us? Driven our most faithful friends to strange violence. Enchanted worms from our dumplings. Taken leeches and moldy bread and lobelia and other baleful things to the tenderest parts of our person. Crushed human skulls. Unnatural, unwise, unholy cures."

"Tell them, Boatwright!"

"Do they sound like cures a person of science would allow? Or like devil's work?"

"Scourge them! Scourge their souls!"

A wind from the west drew a line of smoke across familiar faces. The whites of eyes showed in the gathering darkness. Boatwright, on the rain barrel, rose above the smoke. "What have these witches done? They have brought a woman back from the dead."

There were gasps of shock.

"Ouida Bell was plagued with rabies. Rabies is certain death. It was wielded by their familiar, that panther. But the Winters resurrected her. Resurrection is not a power given to mortals. It is for devils and angels."

Eyes sought Ouida Bell in the crowd.

"And the Winters are no angels," said Boatwright.

Mrs. Snell shouted back, "But Ouida Bell's alive! You can't say that's an evil."

"Panther's almost dead!" shouted someone else.

"Waycross and the Winters set Eudoxia's leg right!" came another cry.

"By evil they have done this!" shouted Boatwright.

The smoke, the noise, and the vitriol were overwhelming. People were yelling at me, for me. I pressed closer to Rebecca. I did not know where my safety was, except beside her. The air felt hot with smoldering embers. Tempers rose. The atmosphere was rich with flame.

"And what have you profited by these witches and their cures?" continued Boatwright. He punched the air with his fist. "What have you gained or preserved? Your health? What matters your health if you lose your soul? The Winters will take your soul, friends, and they will take your mind, and when doubt and confusion seep into your heart, friends, evil will come, too."

"YOU SHUT YOUR GODDAMN MOUTH, BOATWRIGHT!" The storm of Rebecca's voice was so great that the angry bodies nearest to us fell away as though scattered by a thunderclap. "You shut your goddamn lying mouth."

"Listen to the devil's talk!" said Boatwright. "Blasphemy and heresy! Ride them out of town on a rail. Tie their hands, tie their feet. Pour them over with tar and with feathers. We will not suffer witches in our midst. The pyre is burning still."

Rebecca grabbed me, and we crashed through the crowd, knocking neighbors aside as she aimed for the demagogue on the pedestal.

"Waycross has brought you spells and potations and heresies. The fire has come to purge the enemy from our midst. Purge with fire!" Boatwright's voice cracked from the strain on the last syllable.

A riot was collecting at the corners of the crowd. Tremors of violence rippled through its muscles. Anger and mindlessness seized its sinews.

Rebecca slammed her shoulder against the rain barrel, and Boatwright fell backward. The close-pressed crowd caught him. "It was you, you son of a bitch! You burned it down."

"No, Rebecca—" I dragged at her sleeve.

She tried to shake me away. "You threatened Aubrey, you bastard." Rebecca was trying to get on top of the rain barrel, but I was holding her back. "You told Aubrey the town would burn, and you made your own prophecy come true."

"No, that's not what happened—" My grip on her sleeve was slipping.

"You could have killed me, Pastor!" said Snell. "Have you gone mad?"

"If a man of God sets a fire, it's God's will!" cried a defender of the faith.

"Friends, please! Please!" I said. Though Rebecca held her arms out for me, I elbowed her to one side as I climbed the rain barrel, opening my own arms in supplication. "It was an accident. No plot by your pastor, no supernatural agency. Just human failure. I was mixing up ether, and the flames—got loose."

"But you said ether was harmless," said someone.

"Harmless but not inflammable," I said, my voice falling. "And that's caused a great deal of harm, I'm afraid. I'm so sorry, everyone. Whomever you punish, whoever is to be tarred and feathered or run out of town on a rail, let it be me and no one else. Punish me for my incompetence and ignorance, which need no supernatural explanation."

I descended from the rain barrel. I approached Boatwright, whose anger had fused into indistinct syllables. He couldn't catch enough breath to rile up the crowd again. His faction was disappointed that the fire was not the cleansing wrath of heaven. Those in the crowd who sided with us also felt their righteous indignation cooling.

"Here I am, Boatwright," I said. "What will you do?"

Boatwright locked eyes on me. He reared back with his left hand, but the blow came from his right. The fist caught my jawbone. My body spun clockwise, and I fell to my knees. I tensed up against another punch, but none came.

I righted myself to a sitting position, then I stood. "What will you do, sir?" I asked again. Blood filled the space around my teeth.

Boatwright fell toward me. Perhaps he was trying to land another punch, but he was spent, exhausted, defeated, diffused. He fell toward me limp, and I gathered him in my arms. My shoulder grew damp with perspiration and tears.

"It's no hard feelings, sir," I said as his chest shuddered against mine. "No hard feelings." A little bloodletting does a body good.

Sarah had fetched her rifle at the first whiff of smoke. She'd climbed to the top of the courthouse roof and watched the whole farce from there. She could have gotten off several good shots if she'd needed to. But she never even drew a bead on Boatwright. Rebecca had done what needed doing. For the first time in a great long while, Sarah was proud of her oldest sister.

With the office in ashes, Waycross and the sisters had no place to practice their medicine. Mrs. Snell wouldn't abide them seeing patients in their little upstairs room. That was borrowed, anyway. Richardson might have let them have a corner of the courthouse, but that wasn't a home. Hope Hollow was the only place that made sense. That's where Rebecca would go, and she'd want to take Waycross with her if only he'd have the courage to ask.

That would leave Sarah... where? Homeless.

She wouldn't wallow in pity for herself. She had always had a home at Hope Hollow. She'd always had a place squarely between her sisters. Now, though, she had freedom—terrible, cruel freedom. She could go farther away, as far away as she pleased... if she broke her promise, if she let the bonds be sundered.

Rain started falling—just a little and far too late, but the rain served to cool even the most ardent spirits in the crowd.

Sarah watched from a distance as the crowd dispersed. Waycross and Rebecca walked away together, and so did Snell and Mrs. Snell, arm in arm. Boatwright turned to his constituents, but he did not find them there: punching a doctor in the face was a greater sin than drawing up a mob to cast three supposed witches out of town. Boatwright had lost the trust of even his most faithful. He could not turn the crowd into a mob, rain or no rain.

When no one was left around Snell's store but the hogs, Sarah came down and went to the ruin. Sarah kicked through in the ashes of Snell's store and the office. The cinders were still warm under the soles of her boots, which spurred her to keep moving, keep looking. She was looking for an answer or a sign, like some haruspex rooting around in the remnants of a burnt sacrifice. She knew looking for a meaning was foolish. The fire there and the fire at Tribble's mill were accidents of inattention. No one had caused them, neither mortal nor supernatural force.

A glint of metal in the dirt caught her eye. She rooted it up with a toe, curious, but even when she picked it up, she had no idea what she'd found. It was melted and mangled. No telling what it had been before, and it was no use now.

She had no reason to stay there. She had left Rebecca to load up their remaining possessions in the mule cart. Her sister had plenty of help from Mr. and Mrs. Snell, who seemed eager to reclaim their upstairs room. They would need the space. Maybe Snell could keep a little store there. The people of Lawrenceville still needed their soap and ink and fabric. Effie's few things were already gone. She or Thumb had fetched them.

Sarah wondered if the two of them were already on the road or if they were going to stay in Lawrenceville another night. They should just go and not dawdle for sentimentality. She wasn't going to waste any effort on finding them to say goodbye. They had each other.

What do I have? My mind and my wits. A gun. My freedom.

She realized she could go as far as she liked from those hypocrite townsfolk. She never needed to see to their croups and diarrheas again. She could go into the woods for the freedom and silence of the open world. She could find a regiment of soldiers and kill a man rather than cure him. She could go to the Cherokees or the Creeks and pretend she was one of them. She could walk west to Utah, to California.

When she had been a child, her life had been circumscribed. She'd been drawn into a circle of charcoal with her sisters, with lavender and sage and dove feathers woven into their hair. Long before, the three of them had poured molten wax into a bowl of moonlight to scry for their future. Rebecca had found a knife— a scalpel. Waycross. Effie had found a banjo. Thumb. She hadn't chosen a piece of wax.

"Hell, no. Waste of time."

Sarah kicked over heaps of broken ends, blackened pieces, twisted metal, and melted glass—just fragments: formless, meaningless, and void. The circle was gone. Her promises were fulfilled. She owed nothing more to the living or the dead.

Rebecca and I met in the grand lobby of the Rhodes Hotel, sitting in two carved armchairs beneath a heavy red tapestry. "I'm sorry I can't see you upstairs," I said. "Mrs. Rhodes doesn't let mixed company into the bachelor quarters."

"Well, you needn't have taken the bachelor's quarters," said Rebecca. The sentence hung in the air for several seconds before Rebecca spoke again. "How's your jaw? Did you bleed it?"

A large bruise reached from my ear to my mouth. "No, that would only aggravate it. The bones are fine. The skin isn't broken. The blood will go away on its own."

Rebecca nodded. "You could pack raw meat onto it. But that's more trouble than it's worth, I suppose. You'd stink like bacon."

I smiled, which made my swollen jaw ache.

"We're leaving, Aubrey," said Rebecca quietly. "I'm leaving. Back to Hope Hollow."

I felt like I'd taken another blow, this time to the stomach.

"The wagon's loaded up. Not that there's much—just the few things I had in the Snells' upstairs room. I'm setting out this noon."

I pressed a hand against my stomach to steady it. "I don't understand."

"Mrs. Snell has too much to worry about now, without having to see to house guests. And we don't have a place to see patients anymore—"

"Why not here, in this lobby? There's plenty of space. I'll ask Mrs. Rhodes. She's sure to say yes. And if she doesn't, Richardson will set us up in the courthouse. Or in the tannery. Or we'll make house calls."

Rebecca looked across the lobby. She leaned forward, and her voice dropped. "Boatwright—"

"Boatwright is broken. Even I saw that. He'll be on the first mail wagon out of town."

"This isn't my home, Aubrey. Hope Hollow is. I've left my garden fallow, and it demands tending. The nightshade is growing wild and angry."

I leaned forward, putting my elbows on my knees. "I don't want you to go, Rebecca."

She fiddled with her palms. "I'd be happy for you to come to Hope Hollow. It's a fine place. Much nicer than the bachelor's quarters here."

I felt an uneasy spasm. "Do you think that would work? Would patients come to see us, now that they're accustomed to the convenience of having a doctor in town?"

Rebecca's hands were in her lap, the fingers intertwined. She studied her thumbs as if the words she needed were engraved there. The half-moons at the bases of her thumbnails were intensely white, but the skin around the left nail was imperfect. She'd bruised or smashed it once, and it had never healed. "Aubrey," she said in a quavering voice, "sometimes, you are so stupid. Why can't you understand what I am asking you to ask me? You can be certain of my answer... if only you will ask."

I felt a rush of pulse through my hand, but I could not tell if it was her heart or mine that was beating faster. I was a sorry specimen, inferior even to medicine showmen: I had no money, no prospects. Also, my person was divided. My heart was given to Rebecca, but my mind was still tangled with the mystery of Effie. Rebecca deserved all of me, but that kernel of my mind, the dark core of fascination in my mind, still sought for Effie.

"And... and your sisters?"

"Damn my sisters! Am I not enough?" Rebecca daubed her hand at the corner of her mouth, settling herself. "Sarah does what she wants. She'll be lighting out for the territories. She's not following us. And Effie—Effie isn't going to Hope Hollow."

Green bile churned within me, and a hiccup brought it to my throat. I tasted acid and failure. "So, she's accepted Thumb's proposal."

"They're leaving tomorrow or the day after, bound for who knows where."

"But she can't leave—"

The muscles in Rebecca's cheek twitched. "She will, and she will be happy. I have never seen her happier." Rebecca stood up, brushed herself off, and fluffed out her skirts. "But why can't you be happy for yourself? Why can't you be happy with me?"

"Only, it's that, I—Rebecca, of course, but—"

"But nothing!" Rebecca's face was fixed in a snarl, but then, it softened. "Oh, Aubrey, I'm sorry. I should not press you. There's time enough. But think of me, too. I thought I'd lost you... in a fire..."

"Rebecca—"

"No. I want you to think, Aubrey," she said. "Don't ask out of pity or emotion because you are homeless or hopeless. I do not want a mindless reply. I want you to be certain of your life. And when you are, come see me. A day will make no difference."

She was wrong, though. Everything would be different the next day. Effie would take with her the answer to the question that consumed me, my last chance to answer the question that fascinated me.

Rebecca spun on her heels, and her skirts circled around her. My head pounded. I fumbled for my flask of ether, but my fingers didn't obey my demands. The cushions behind my head and below my buttocks prickled at me. Every minute spent dithering was a minute I would never regain.

I would not give myself to Rebecca as half a soul, riven with uncertainty. Either I would give my whole self to her, in sound body and mind, with no fascinations to distract me from my devotion, or I would not be worthy of life.

Only one proof of Effie's powers would suffice: to feel them work in myself. Only rabies would do. I would infect myself, then Effie would cure me. Or I would infect myself, and she would fail to cure me, and that would be its own answer. I'd find the rabid panther and have it bite me, then I would seek out Effie for my cure. That seemed to make perfect sense, the culmination of my personal and professional history.

It was the most extreme form of heroic medicine, more than a bleeding or a blistering, but science is greater than life, and knowledge is greater than death. Had not great scientists before, believing fully in the rightness of their discoveries, made themselves the first patient? Here, the medicine took the form of a person: Effie Winter.

A smile broke over my face. If anyone had happened into the lobby, he would have marveled over a grinning idiot in an over-stuffed red chair, his eyebrows singed off, ash streaked down his face, his clothes stained with soot and cinders, his future entrusted to a panther, hydrophobia, and the gray, unsolvable eyes of Effie Winter.

The weather was not ideal for finding a rabid panther or any sort of baleful creature in the piney woods. The crisp, coming winter tinged the wind with freshness. The crimsons and ochres in the trees were vibrant, bold against the blue sky, cleared of the lingering smoke from the fire. The songs of the towhee and the cardinal and the blue jay ornamented rustling leaves. Brilliant-green pines forbade sadness and promised that spring would return, that not all hope was dead.

I set off for the easy buffet at the grove of a million pigeons. That was the last place I'd seen the panther, but the beast was not among the clouds of guano the wingbeats stirred. The creature would avoid water. The hill behind Simonton's farm was the highest point around, dry and windy. I turned my footsteps in that direction.

The path grew harder with every mile. My collar grew damp, my armpits soaked through with my own stink. A moist swath covered my entire back. But the farther I wandered, the more weariness filled my blood and the more convinced I became of my mission's essential correctness. Curiosity was a pernicious disease. It possessed me, turning me into a thrall to its own satisfaction.

The creature caught the scent of sweat. I did not see the panther but heard its cry, high and ragged. I turned off the path and clambered through underbrush, crushing ferns and disturbing rocks grown over with a hundred years of moss. The panther's keening urged me on.

I followed the sound to a rocky bulge. In the ancient past, the rock had split, leaving a ten-foot cliff riven with crevices and fragmentary stones. I leaned against the cold granite wall. Beneath my back was the entire mass of the Earth, running in an unbroken block through all the continents, below all the oceans, and to the center of the globe. Anyone else leaning against a mountain was sharing my seat. Anyone else walking upon the earth was treading on my back.

Warm breath, sour and sickly, tickled my neck.

Slowly, slowly, so as not to spook the creature, I turned to face my quarry.

A vertical split, two or three feet wide, had been covered by fallen stones, making a shallow, accidental cave. The source of the breath stirred in its den. It put its snout into the light, and I could see that its white foreclaws were behind its ears as if it were holding its skull against a headache. The creature's mouth was filled with foam, yet it made no move more menacing than a yawn. The fur around its face was patchy. Raw skin showed in the bald spots. The creature could barely hold its head up. The hydrophobic rage, so visceral and violent, had passed and left a body too ravaged and exhausted to attack. The animal looked at me, suffering in its eyes, intelligence, sadness. In compassion for my fellow mortal, I stretched out my hand to scruff it behind its ears. Then I pulled back my sleeve, exposing the white flesh of my arm.

Then I realized the foolishness of my action—not only that I was seeking to infect myself with rabies but because I already had it. Ouida Bell's bite had given it to me. The inability to drink, the headaches, the exhaustion and nausea, salivation—all marked my symptoms. The madness of what I'd considered, to give my whole life over to the fascination of Effie, struck me. I did not need the creature to infect me. I needed a cure for my fascination, but I could begin it there.

The panther laid its head against my arms as though asleep. Its teeth were hidden. Its face was tranquil, beatific.

"Thank you, friend," I said. I ruffled the patchy hair behind its neck. "Thank you for sparing me."

Then the beast's head jerked, and an instant later, I heard the crack of a shot.

"Whoo-whee! I got him!" Pearson leapt up from behind the bushes. He held his rifle and shook it over his head, a savage rattling a spear. "Finally got that panther! Whoo-whee!"

"Damn near killed the doctor, too," said Hodgson, emerging beside him.

Pearson thumbed his nose. "Yeah, so what else is new?"

21

THE ONLY LIE SHE TOLD ME

My hands were covered in gore from the fatal shot. I wiped them on a mossy rock, leaving it stained red. I still needed to find Effie and beg her for a cure—not for the hydrophobia, but for the fascination. And poor Rebecca—how would she bear the loss of another suitor? It was for her that I needed the cure, so that if I were to die, it would be with all my heart and mind dedicated to her. Small consolation, perhaps, but a full love is better than a partial one, and I meant to love Rebecca fully.

I walked toward the descending sun, and my eyes became exhausted from squinting. Twilight, when it settled, was a relief. I welcomed the faint flashes of fireflies in the crepuscular shadows. The gloaming paths held no worry for me. I had no possessions anywhere to concern me, and I already had the worst of all diseases in my blood. What is left to fear?

The cheerful roll of a bonfire illuminated Thumb's wagon. It was as distinct from ether's blue flames as the day was from the night. The bonfire divided the dark and cold from the warm and welcome. It was a fire of life, promising my cure.

As I came closer, my head thrummed with a low, shuddering noise. I put my hands over my ears, but the disturbance grew stronger, spreading from my head and into the trees, their roots, and the vast surface of the earth. The entire world was trembling in B-flat. I wondered if it was a sign of Effie's power.

It stopped.

"Who's that out there?" called Thumb.

I hurried behind the wagon.

"Aubrey!" Thumb slapped his knee with one hand and waved a violin bow in the other. "Come see. Look at what I rigged up."

A metal wire, like a guyline, was stretched taut from the edge of his wagon to a large chestnut. The line was above Thumb's head, within reach but high enough that no one would be decapitated in the darkness.

"I rosin up the bow, and here we go!" said Thumb. He dragged the violin bow across the line. The wagon, the chestnut, the earth, and the sky resonated in the same B-flat.

"I thought—" I began. "What do you mean, torturing a fellow like that?"

Thumb eyed me. "I'm sorry, Doc. It's a new way to get folks' attention. Bells are fine, and the banjo, but it's all tired. A fellow's got to be new. Daring. Dazzling. I can still set up in three seconds and take down in a hurry, and it doesn't claim room in the wagon." Thumb pointed the bow at me. "Hey, want to give it a try?"

"Hell, yes."

I drew the bow back and forth as Thumb dashed up and down the line. He'd grab the string at intervals, trying to get real notes off it. Landing on pitch was hard. He remained an inch sharp or flat. But we stumbled through a reasonable rendition of "The Hayhover's Fork."

"To what do I owe the pleasure of your company, Doc?" said Thumb when I surrendered the bow to him, feeling quite clever in spite of my infection. "You didn't come all this way in the dark to play the world fiddle, did you?"

"I need to see Effie." I was startled to realize that I'd forgotten her for several moments. "To give my congratulations. To her. And to you. Both."

The firelight projected a circle of protection around us. At its periphery, oblong shadows gathered, faceless and void.

"Well, she's gone for a walk," said Thumb. "But I'll drink a toast with you, Doc." He filled two immense copper steins from a barrel and gave one to me. A great raft of foam sloshed off as we crashed mugs. "Hey, here's a nice one I stole from a rye drinker." Thumb locked eyes with me.

"Here's to us!
Who's like us?
Damn few,

And they're all dead."

"I don't pretend to understand your toast, sir, but I'll drink." I quaffed my potation. Ginger beer. The second sip was less refreshing than the first. My hydrophobic tongue expressed displeasure. "Effie's a fine lady," I said. "When do you think she'll be back?"

"Don't worry." Thumb took my stein and replenished them both. "We won't pull up stakes until you've seen her."

I refreshed my cup with the last of my ether. I would keep none of it for the next day or beyond. "She went to Mrs. Snell's, then?"

"Nope," said Thumb. "Said she was going to the old mill, Tribble Mill."

"What business could she have at those burned-out ruins?"

"Not my never mind," said Thumb.

"It'll be full night soon."

"Nothing's killed her so far. I figure she can fend for herself."

"You mean," I ventured, "whatever trouble befalls her, she can cure."

"Runs in the family, I gather."

"But Effie is... more."

Thumb's mule wandered over and scratched its flank against me. I petted the animal behind its ears. I loved that mule, whose name I could not recall, because it was furry and solid and alive. I ran my hand along the flank until it shook me away.

"Ouida Bell," I said. "The hydrophobia. How do you explain that, sir?"

"Effie's good for a lot of folks." He leaned back against the wagon. "Like my tonics are. As long as it works, let's not wonder why."

"And that's it? You haven't been the least curious?" He, more than anyone, should wonder at the powers of his companion.

Thumb pondered his ginger beer, looking into it like a mirror. "This happened to me when I was a small fry. We needed an onion because the baby was sick and Momma was going to make a poultice to get the bold hives out. And when I get to the onion patch, there's a woman sitting right there. I'd never seen her before. She was white as a sheet, and her hair was black and dirty and stringy, and she was in nightclothes not decent for being outside. Sitting right on the cold dirt. She was crying, just blubbering. Her face was wet all the way down her cheeks and down her neck and even her clothes. I say, 'Lady, is everything all right?' The crying woman starts screaming. I've never heard such angry, hateful sounds. The woman is trying to say something, but I don't understand the words. The screaming is so twisted with the crying that I can't tell what she's yelling. I'm backing away, but the crying woman stands up. She's getting closer, tears and spit and foam getting in my eyes. I put out my hand—not to hurt her, just to stop her. And my hand goes right through."

"A ghost story?" I said. The oblong shadows beyond the firelight became darker. They whispered to each other in their crepuscular tongue, all whistles and clicks and chirps and croaks.

"Doc, I didn't know what it was. But all that racket made Momma come out on the porch with the baby. 'You quiet down! Don't wake up this baby, or I'll fix up some peach limb tea!' By which she means give me a whipping with a peach-tree limb. And then she sees the woman, too. I run back, hiding behind her legs. The woman doesn't go away. We all see her. She comes right up on the porch, screaming, howling, mad out of her wits. I grab Momma and pull her inside, and I run for Pa. He's sleeping on the bed. The sound hadn't woken him up. I tell him, 'You've gotta come. Hurry!' And he gets out on the porch, takes one look at that woman, and goes right back inside. He flops on the bed, puts the pillow over his head, and just lies there. The woman's still outside. She's stomping and thrashing on the porch. 'Get up, Pa!' I say. But he's asleep, or he is playing at it. She's slamming into the walls. She rattles the shutters. And Pa never once takes his head from under the pillow. Momma and I are under the table. I've got the fire poker, but I know that's not going to do any good. I'm so scared that, maybe, I faint. Because next thing I know, it's supper. Momma's rolling dough. The baby's got his onion poultice on his chest. I go outside to the onion patch, and there's nothing. I never see her again. Never."

Thumb fell silent. He kicked at a pebble next to his right foot. "So, that's what I think," he said. Then, his expression brightened. "I just don't think about it."

He clapped me on the back, which dislodged an eructation I had been suppressing. A brassy belch rang out, my entire person vibrating with the sound. The wagon resonated, too, and the enormous fiddle continued it, and the trees and limbs and leaves. I made the world to ring with my mighty burp in B-flat. A breeze carried it up and up to dissolve amid the endless frolicking stupidity of the stars.

The garden at Hope Hollow was sick with abundance. The nightshades had profited the most from the absence of the gardener. Tomatoes, red as blisters even in the fading fall, choked out the corn stalks. Eggplants, fit to burst from their overstretched skins, grew where sweet potatoes should have been. The rows of herbs—celandine and snakeroot and angelica—grasped for light among the thickets of belladonna, far too much belladonna.

When Sarah came upon her sister working in the garden, day was already passed, and the evening had vanished by the time she'd sorted away her possessions. Anyone else would have left the gardening until the morning, but Rebecca could not abide the disorder, couldn't sleep until she'd settled the worst of the weeds.

Under the silver moon, Rebecca worked with a silver spade. She'd pushed up her sleeves. Her arms were filthy past her elbows. Sap, thorns, and thistles scratched her forearms. The last of the fireflies wished each other farewell in their arcane language of light.

"There is something so unwholesome," said Sarah, "about gardening at night."

Rebecca pushed her hair out of her face as she looked up at her sister. "I thought you might have been Aubrey," said Rebecca. "I hoped you were."

Sarah shook her head. "No decent lady should be weeding her rose beds after midnight."

"Then I suppose I'm not a decent lady. But you already knew that, didn't you?"

Sarah nodded. "I'm not staying. I'm only here to get a few things, and then I'll be gone."

"You don't have to leave in the middle of the night," said Rebecca. "You can stay until morning."

"What if Aubrey comes?" said Sarah.

Rebecca sighed. "He will blather and dither, waver on indecisiveness. Perhaps he'll come tonight, but I doubt it. Maybe tomorrow, maybe never."

"And would you be happy with that?"

"I tend my own garden," said Rebecca.

"But with no sisters, no Everett, no Waycross—what will you do?"

"What I always have, Sister, but alone."

"Do you want me to stay?" said Sarah.

Rebecca wondered at that. "No. I don't think Hope Hollow is your home anymore, nor Effie's. I'm the one to stay behind, alone or not."

Sarah knelt by the pile of waste that Rebecca's garden tending had created: broken branches, twisted vines, and sticky fruit. She picked out a twig of belladonna on which clusters of black berries clung in a heavy harvest. "Effie says that nightshades are full of hate." She turned over the branch in her palms, considering each berry. "Not when they're cut, I think."

"Because they're dead," said Rebecca.

"Maybe nightshades are happier when they are let wild. Maybe their hate comes from being planted in rows." Sarah dropped the belladonna twig back on the bracken.

"We tried to plant Effie in a row," said Rebecca, "but she never thrived, did she?"

"That's your way to put it," said Sarah. "I think I'm most to blame. I started to believe, you see. In the bond, like it was magic.

It wasn't ever real magic. No such thing. A person's just a person unless everybody else thinks otherwise."

"I shouldn't have blamed Effie," said Rebecca. "I shouldn't have let her have that power. It would have been better to let Everett be the victim of powerlessness rather than cruelty."

"I was worse. I believed that she would always need me to take care of her. That she would always need someone to look after her. That was the promise that Mother made me give. And that was a damn-fool promise. Mother didn't ever think we would grow up. She didn't ever think that we'd need to be apart."

"Let her be happy if she can," said Rebecca. "Her happiness isn't here. Let me be happy, so long as I can."

Sarah looked up into the sky. "And where does that leave me?"

I awoke when a pigeon alighted on my head.

It had a clump of my hair in its beak and was trying to remove it for its nest. The hairs somehow connected to raw nerves in the center of my brain, and my headache was excruciating. I batted at the vile winged beast, and it squawked and took to the sky. A hundred of its brethren ascended with it, the air shaken into a tempest. I covered my head until the world settled again.

I was on the dirt between Thumb's wagon and the extinguished ashes of the fire. A blanket was tangled around my legs. Thumb must have thrown it over me when I fell asleep.

I unwound myself from the blanket. My legs held my weight, but they were displeased by it. I could not mistake the hydrophobia then. It had come on swiftly. I felt ragged and panicked. I needed Effie. I made my way to Thumb's wagon.

"Morning, sunshine." Thumb opened the little door.

I was standing too close, and it hit me in the nose. I stepped back, pinching the injured part with my right hand.

"I thought you would've slept till noon, Aubrey."

He thought I was suffering a hangover. Whiskey had never caused a man to foam at the mouth.

"Effie, please," I croaked, my voice unused to speech.

"She's not back yet," said Thumb.

"What? It can't be."

Thumb threw up his hands. I could see the whole interior of the wagon, with nowhere to hide.

"What if something terrible has happened?" I said.

"I'm sure she's fine."

"I have to find her. You don't need to come with me, sir," I told him. "This is a task I must complete on my own."

"Who said anything about coming with you?" He retreated a half step from the door and fell back into a hummock of pillows. He placed his hat over his face and waved blindly to me. "Go make your peace, Doc. But have a little water before you go, or that headache is going to get worse."

My body shivered in revulsion. The animal particles or vaporous spirits or malignant miasmas pulsed inside my temples.

Yet again, I followed the forest paths. It occurred to me that I had done more walking in Lawrenceville than curing.

Overnight, winter had settled in for a long spell. I dragged my feet through the leaves, mashing them into dirt beneath my heels. Nuts and acorns cracked as I passed over them, making the same sound as my creaking bones. When I was near the ruins of Tribble Mill, I saw that rain or snow higher in the Appalachians had swelled the river to a torrent. It crashed over the old dam, leaping and splattering. The water ran so fast and frightful that the millrace roared again. The ruins themselves were invisible beneath the swollen current. Great trees rose around me, and the sky was slate colored and smooth. The trilling laughter of pigeons sounded overhead.

Effie was kneeling at the riverside.

Again and again, she put her hands into the water and drew them out. She was performing a ceremonial ablution in the frenetic water. Washing one's hands can be harmful. The blood, chilled in the extremities, brings the chill back to the heart. Perhaps Effie owed her cold complexion and melancholy moods to her compulsion for handwashing.

I searched for footing among the slick stones.

I came closer. Effie still hadn't noticed me—or hadn't deigned to notice me. She rubbed her fingers and scraped under her nails. Her clothing was a simple white dress. The fabric was too light for the chilliness of the day, the cold splash of the water, the wind that curled through the forest. Her hair was pulled back through a silver band.

I stopped breathing, and the silence drew her attention.

"Hello, Aubrey." Her expression was inscrutable. "How's everything?"

"Fine," I said as a reflex and then, "I'm dying of rabies."

"I'm sorry," she said, standing up. Her voice was light, out of character with the sober surroundings. "And this dying of rabies— you would prefer not to?"

"I would prefer not to," I said.

She held her arms against herself. The fingers of her right hand scratched her left elbow, leaving red marks in her pale skin. "What do you think will happen, Aubrey?"

"I am not worthy of a cure. I nearly let fascination consume me. I would have let the panther bite me and then come to you to test you, to see if you would cure me and if I, in the curing, would learn your secrets. If I'd risked everything like I'd planned, I would have been in your total fascination and not worthy of your cure."

"But you're still sick, aren't you? Ouida Bell bit you."

"Yes. But I'm not here for my own sake. I'm here for Rebecca."

"For Rebecca?"

"My sickness is fascination, and I wish for a cure for it. I think that is a cure that only you can work." My hands ached at my side. They begged to be fretting, supplicating, praying, and not hanging idly.

Effie closed her eyes. "Go see Rebecca. She'll do more good for you than I can."

"If you cure me, I can go to Rebecca as a whole person, not one half crazed with fascination."

"You need a doctor, Aubrey, not me. Rebecca is a doctor."

Effie's false humility rang hollow. I fought it with truth. "You are the greatest physician who has ever lived. I'd smash all busts of Hippocrates and Galen and put yours in their place."

"That would be a waste of plaster."

I could not tell if that was a joke.

I shifted my weight from my right leg to my left and back again. I couldn't remember which one I'd hurt when I slipped into the Alcovy on my first journey to Hope Hollow. I'd credited my own body for its repair that night. She'd healed me then, without my knowing, and I knew she would heal me again since my need was so much greater.

The pigeons, emboldened by the continuing silence, crept from concealment and peered down at us. Some started a song, a melody of food and sex and other animal concerns.

My headache pulsed anew. I was thirsty. The last water I'd had was hours, days before. Then my hydrophobic brain spat back, and the thirst turned into a sour taste. A bit of spittle collected beside my teeth, but I couldn't swallow it. The rolling crash of the river matched the pulsation of my head and the ragged fear in my breathing.

"What if I do nothing?" The breeze stirred a susurration of leaves to blend with her voice.

"Effie, I know you are kind and good." I willed myself to move closer. "You'll cure me."

"I am kind and good if I heal all the sick of the world. I'm wicked and cruel if I do not?"

"No, I mean—"

"All mortals die. They die of old age or misadventure. They die in war or excitement. They die of foolishness and curiosity. The universe condemns them to oblivion, sooner or later. So what's the use of doing anything?"

"I'd rather die in my old age, resting on my bed of good works, than in my prime, before my useful years have begun."

"But you almost chose to risk that old age for... a secret."

A rush of blood traced the artery that ran over my ear. Despite the pain, I did not risk breathing, blinking.

"If you knew this secret," she said, "would you work these cures yourself? Not for fame or fortune, but for the sake of others, so that they may frolic and feast?"

"Yes," I whispered.

"When a child's face bears the scars of smallpox, you'll make them disappear."

"Yes."

"When a maiden froths at the mouth from rabies, you'll cool her mind."

"Yes."

"And whenever a soul stands at the edge of eternal bliss, ready to shuck its tired body and step into the light of heaven, you will take that person's shoulder and say, 'Sir, not yet?'"

A white pigeon—a dove—landed precisely above my head. The naked hickory branch bobbled under its weight. I looked up and found myself staring into its tail feathers, directly in harm's way, but I dared not move, lest the rapture of the moment change.

"Everyone wants to go to heaven, but no one wants to die," I said.

"But they must die, Aubrey."

She said my name, but she was not talking to me. Behind me were the empty woods, the dead branches, the leaden sky, and behind the sky, the void. She addressed the infinite.

"And when they do, you bear the stain of their deaths because you could have cured them this one time, this one more time. Choosing who lives, who dies, and when, and how—Aubrey, I will not give you this disease."

"But why must anyone die?" My voice rose louder than I wished. "Teach the secret to me, and then I will teach it to the next, and she the next, and he the next. Then no one need bear

301

these stains of death. Why must mortals be mortal? And do not give me a mystical answer. Do not say that immortality is a crime against nature and the soul or that the gods will not abide new rivals. That is all hoodoo and superstition. What natural reason condemns us to die?"

The slate sky filled her eyes. "I don't know," she said.

"Unacceptable!"

My cry shook the air. The dove above my head let loose its bowels. Shit trickled down my temple. My eyebrows might have stopped it from oozing down further, but they'd been singed off in the fire. The bird crap dribbled into the outside crease of my eye and down my cheek, but I did not move. I bore the shame of being shat upon.

Effie's laugh began as a lonely sound, yet it was infectious like a yawn.

"Oh, Aubrey," Effie said, and I smiled, too. "Here, let me help you." She knelt to the river, leaning far over so that her arms disappeared into the current. The toes of one bare foot curled on the slick, mossy surface of a stone. Her other foot rested on sand.

When she arose, she held her palms in front of her. Water drained from between her fingers, and the wind flung droplets back into the river. Then with her wet, clean hands, she wiped bird shit from my forehead. Her fingers ran through my hair. She cleaned the corner of my eye with her thumb, the skin so thin that her blood looked an iridescent purple. I did not move under these ministrations. My humors stood still in my veins. The orbits of my skull resonated with her tenderness and humility.

Then using the sleeves of her own plain dress, she daubed at my dirtied clothes so that, when she had finished, I looked no worse for my sufferings, and she... she was dirty and wet. Her hands were stained. Effie brushed her palms against the sides of her dress, but that did not make them clean. She smiled at me, and that smile was the only lie she told me. Her eyes betrayed her.

"Don't worry, Aubrey," she said. "I won't tell."

I had only been to Hope Hollow in the summer, when the green leaves and jewel-like fruits had attracted no special notice. In the wan winter sunlight, though, those things glimmered. It was well past fall, yet the orange trees there were heavy with fat, round spheres, swollen with juice. The lemon trees, too, were gilded with perfect specimens. One must be exceedingly clever to grow oranges and lemons in Lawrenceville, Georgia. It's too far north, too susceptible to frost. A hard-luck farmer or struggling goodwife would see that rich grove and mutter, "Witchcraft, sorcery," but I saw only a mortal's cleverness.

Sassafras and yellow lady's slipper and nightshade and foxglove bloomed in neat rows. The tomatoes were ripe—the corn, high and ready. Pole beans, cabbage, lettuce, and turnips had all peaked though they should have come of age in different seasons.

I reached up to pluck an orange from a low branch. It came away in my hand without resistance. The skin peeled away eagerly, and the sweet juice trickled down my palms. The fruit was warm and tasted of afternoon sunlight.

A firefly lighted on my nose. I'd thought they had all died for the year. I blew it away with a short breath, and a willow tree laughed at me.

My heart skipped three beats. Rebecca was leaning against the willow's trunk, her curves melding with the tree's own, like a caryatid. She approached me with a callipygian sway.

"I'm sorry, Aubrey," she said. "You looked happy. Silly, but happy."

"I am indeed happy," I said. "I am enjoying a little summertime. How do you do it?"

"Pigeon guano," she said. "You can scoop it by the shovelful in the groves around here."

Bees flitted between branches, visiting flowers that, against nature, were still blooming. "I'm sick, Rebecca," I confessed. "Diseased."

"Exhaustion. Nausea. Paleness of the face. Irregular breathing." She put her hands on my neck. "Low pulse. Cold skin." She lifted my chin so that she could look into my face. "Salivation. Copious salivation. Headache?"

I nodded, the movement of my chin rubbing against her palm.

"I know, Aubrey. I should have intervened sooner."

"I wouldn't have listened," I confessed to her. "I had to come this far by myself, or I never would have understood." Tears welled in my eyes.

"Aubrey, dear, we'll have you feeling better soon from the acute symptoms. I'm sure I can help with the chronic ones, too." She sighed. "I've known for weeks."

"But how can you cure a case of hydro—"

"Ether poisoning? Simple. Just like the hell-roarin' trots."

"But it's not ether poisoning..." Then I realized that it was. I'd fooled myself.

My mouth must have hung open because Rebecca closed it with a gentle lift of her hand. She wiped away the drool from my lips.

I had ether poisoning: the exhaustion, the headaches, even the aversion to drink. All of it fit. I was so inveigled by my own fear than I could not see the obvious answer.

No, I had rabies. No competent physician could be so mistaken about his own health. What about when Ouida Bell had bitten me?

"Clay, charcoal, and lots of water," said Rebecca. "A few days, and the headaches will go away." She sounded as bright and fragrant as her garden.

No, Effie did nothing. I was never sick.

My addled brain was shaking. My face still felt the memory of Effie's cold touch. What if I still carried the seeds of rabies inside me, or whatever I'd caught from Ouida Bell's bite? Effie knew. She'd sent me to get the cure from Rebecca.

"Do you still have the madstone?" I asked, swatting at a winged creature that flew close to my ear.

"Why?"

"You said it was for poisoning."

She gave me a skewed glance, but for love or convenience, she humored me. She went inside to get what she needed, and I laid myself back on the earth and let the garden rise above me. If I needed to be buried, I could sleep soundly there. Ah, what maudlin foolishness. The dead don't care where they are buried.

Rebecca returned with a pottery bowl brimming with milk. She took out the madstone—hard, irregular, and unpromising. It looked like dried excrement.

"Undo your buttons," she said.

I undid my jacket and waistcoat and lifted my shirttails to expose my navel. Rebecca pressed the madstone hard into my stomach, pressing my breath out, too. As she held it, I was asphyxiating. When she relaxed, I drank in the air with gladness.

Rebecca took the madstone, dangled it over the milk, and dropped it. It submerged with a plop and bobbed back up. A yellow-and-green sheen formed on the surface of the liquid.

"Is that poison coming out?" I asked, not feeling an instant relief.

"No, only oils running off the stone."

I realized I was thirsty, and the thought of a drink did not frighten me. "How... how will I know that the cure worked?" I asked, but I did not mean only the madstone.

"Every day that you are still alive, the cure has worked." Rebecca put a kiss upon my nose. "I prefer you alive."

I thought those were the kindest words ever spoken.

Richardson was accepting handshakes high and low, from fine farmers to the lankiest of shopkeeper's sons. The word had come down from Milledgeville in a letter. The first legislative session of the new year had approved Lawrenceville as the county seat. The town would get a splendid brick courthouse and a smart gallows and straighter roads. Lawyers and land agents and tax assessors would arrive by the carriageload, and with them would come more boarding houses and taverns and wives and children, another school, a proper church. Prices on crops and land would improve. Regular transit would be available for goods to town, as well as a market for surplus produce. A great many more sick folk would arrive, too, enough to keep Rebecca and me hopping in our new practice at Hope Hollow.

All the revelers had bundled up in their warmest against the chilly day. No room in Lawrenceville was truly big enough for the festivities, so the party was taking place on the courthouse lawn despite the weather. Coffee, whiskey, hot molasses, and square dances would keep the revelers too happy to notice the cold. "Cracking job," they said. "Splendid." With each compliment, Richardson's spirit grew. I could see it in his shoulders, in his heels. He'd made himself worthy of his position.

Rebecca and I sat near the bonfire. We had neither coffee nor hot molasses. We needed our senses, should anyone require treatment for a misstep in a boot or labor brought on by vigorous dancing. I shivered and moved closer to the bonfire, and Rebecca moved closer to me. Ah, this is enough.

When Sarah appeared, she was glum. She'd been gone for weeks, ever since the day the office had burned down. Only at our invitation had she returned for the festivity. "I thought I'd get Ouida Bell to dance with the mayor," she said, "for a lark. But he's not up for it."

"Hmm," I said.

"I suppose Richardson thinks he'll wait for one to move to town who's even prettier." She snorted, as if the thought was ludicrous. "Though I suppose I would do a better turn under the sheets."

Rebecca said, "Hush that talk."

"What, like Mr. and Mrs. Waycross haven't been squaring the circle? I know all about the white liver, the wild cherry tonics, the yarrow, and the yellow sarsaparilla." Sarah exhaled loudly. "Effie ran off with hers," she said to me. "And you've got yours." She blew some hair out of her face. "I don't know why I'm the one left out." She looked over at Ouida Bell.

"Maybe it's your filthy mouth?" I suggested.

"My filthy mouth is my strongest feature," Sarah countered.

Rebecca put her hand on mine, which was resting on my knee. After a time, I felt her fingers tapping out the rhythm to the dance.

"Go," I said. "Go dance."

She put a kiss on my lips. We tilted our heads in our practiced way, so that our noses did not collide, and then, she was caught in the whirl of the dance.

With Boatwright gone—run out of town on a rail for punching the doctor in the face—and the new pastor not yet arrived, no one was there to shame the dancers. The exchanges and intertwining looked quite complex. It seemed to be chaos, yet everyone stayed to the beat, and at the crescendo, every foot was in its destined place.

Pa Everett was arm in arm with P and Snell. Pendleton was on the end of a row, his pinned-up sleeve not distracting him from his part in the steps. Ouida Bell and Rebecca and Old Elizabeth, holding hands, skipped sideways among them, following the intricacies of the dance. Mrs. Maltbie and Lizbeth Samples stood at the edge of the firelight and ate sweet-potato biscuits, but even they smiled when a scampering Eudoxia Everett brought them cups of hot coffee and molasses. They watched, as did I, the little girl join her elders around the fire. She careened from partner to partner, Rebecca to her father to P to Pendleton, without care or curiosity, with only happiness. Green wood cracked in the bonfire, and the wind lifted the frolicking sparks—lifted them higher and higher into the welcoming night.

I summoned my tenderest smile, and Rebecca reflected it back to me. I was loved and loved in return. Also, I was happy. Not ethereally happy—that is, not as happy as the pure hilarity of ether—but I'd paid a high price for the genuine article. I wouldn't buy any more happiness on ether's discount.

22

EFFIE WINTER'S WIZARD GINGER ALE

That's right, Effie Winter's Wizard Ginger Ale!"
I would have preferred if he hadn't used my name, but
Salmon said folks would rather buy it from a pretty lady. That
wasn't flattery. He believed it, and it made me happy to think he
did, whether or not I agreed, whether or not it was true. The face
on the lithographed label was my own, nothing like a real advertising beauty's. I told him he ought to put some glad and charming
girl on the label, but Salmon said, "Just you look at that smile.
That'll sell better than any dreamed-up theater girl. Besides, it's
your recipe for the ginger ale. Oughtn't your face be the one on
the label?"

"Why 'Wizard'?" I asked.

"'Cause I'm not going to say 'witch'!"

He grinned with all his perfect teeth and threw his arms
around me, and I laughed because that word had lost all its power.

Salmon said he never cared for his name, either. It was ridiculous, and it had set him on a path to act ridiculous. He only liked
the sound of his name when I said it, so I called him "Salmon,"
and only I called him that.

With five thousand bottles of Effie Winter's Wizard Ginger
Ale, we'd followed the path of the western frontier. Coming up the
Federal Road out of Georgia, we'd seen only little logging towns
and hunters' camps. In Cherokee Territory were tiny pockets of
Indians, most without even a nickel to spare. Tennessee was even
less populated. We'd go days between even the smallest farms.
Sometimes, Salmon gave a show for the trees because he wanted
to practice a new tune.

We could have gone east, where the people were, but we didn't.
The frontier was Salmon's fascination. He said he wouldn't turn
the wagon east until Holtzclaw the mule had put his feet into the

Pacific, and I didn't mind. All the nation was pressing west, pursuing life and liberty and happiness. To follow seemed only right.

Thus, we continued west until we met the Mississippi, the great river so wide and slow and brown it didn't seem like a river at all, just a field of mud slowly sliding toward the ocean. But human life teemed at its shores: farmers bringing in their crops to merchants, crews of pole boats tying up for the night, roustabouts loading up corn and cotton, and passengers bound for New Orleans. Everyone was thirsty because the river wasn't fit to drink unless you wanted a bellyful of mud. We weren't even at a town, just a nameless bend of the Mississippi, but it held the biggest crowd we'd ever had for Effie Winter's Wizard Ginger Ale.

Salmon kept up his speech. He'd seen crowds, and I borrowed from his courage to stay at my task. I focused on his words because I liked the sound of his voice. Even when he was speechifying loudly, it was the same voice that whispered quietly to me.

"Effie Winter's Wizard Ginger Ale, from her own secret recipe!" he said. "Not another soul on this long, long road will sell you anything like the same."

Salmon lit into a banjo lick. The first string had broken, and we hadn't been near enough a proper town to get another. Poor Thumb had to sing all the higher to make up for the missing notes.

"All the church folks on their knees
Askin', beggin', sayin', 'Please!'
They're all cookin' in the wrong pot.
They don't know what I've got!"

The hint of scandal caught the men's ears.

"That's right: Effie Winter's Wizard Ginger Ale! I can't tell you all the recipe because this fine lady here..." He held up his hand to point at me where I stood, to one side of the stage, waiting for my turn. "This fine lady knows where I sleep, and if I gave away her secret recipe, I think she wouldn't let me sleep there anymore!"

The crowd chuckled, and Thumb sang again to the accompaniment of the crippled banjo:

> *"If you're dyin' of powerful thirst,*
> *Effie's Ale will quench it first.*
> *Glass of water makes you queasy?*
> *Effie's Ale is nice and easy."*

He hadn't found the right song yet. Every night, once we'd set up our camp beside the wagon and made beans and coffee over an open fire, he'd tinker on his rhymes while I brewed up more ginger ale. He would say, "Effie, what do you think about this?" and try to rhyme "water" with "quarter," and I'd laugh.

"And how much? Just a nickel. A nickel of whiskey will leave you even thirstier and, what's more, a nickel poorer. That's not Effie Winter's Wizard Ginger Ale. It's good for what ails you, if what ails you is a thirst. And we'll buy the empty bottle back for a penny, so it's not but four cents for the best ginger ale you've ever had, and you'll feel the zing in your step all day."

Thumb started to applaud, and applause, since it is infectious, spread to the crowd. "Let's have her on out here. Effie, dear, where are you and your Wizard Ginger Ale?"

Then I stepped out into the crowd, carrying a great gunnysack filled with tinkling glass. Salmon wondered how I could manage such a huge weight, a hundred bottles hefted over my shoulder, but I hardly noticed. Most of the weight was water, and my shoulders knew the weight of water very well.

So many sick, suffering, and sorrowing people... I couldn't help but see the crippled hands of an old farmer and the paralyzed leg of a mule-driving woman and the clouded eyes of the fur trappers and the rictuses of past and future apoplexies in a hundred men and women. So many were there. I hadn't thought the world could hold so many in one place. All the sicknesses blurred into a single vision of human frailty, and no one wanted anything except a drink. Even the dying—they were all dying, all mortals—did not demand that I save them.

Every hand that reached out to trade a nickel for a bottle of Effie Winter's Ginger Ale was dirty. Their hands told their lives—dirt, manure, oil, grease, wisps of cotton, dry dust of milled grains. I must be clean, and whenever I was near water, I washed my hands. Putting them in the Mississippi wouldn't have done a bit of good, though. They would have come out dirtier than they'd gone in. I couldn't stand even the smallest smudge.

Thumb sometimes poked gentle fun at my silly habit. "You're gonna wash away all your skin, Effie, and then you'll just have bare bones for fingers."

I thought that was the only way I could feel for the edges of life—with clean hands. So much dirt got under Rebecca's fingernails, and so much blood splashed onto Aubrey's skin—if they'd only wash their hands, perhaps they would work more healing and less hurt.

Also, if I was clean, only so long as I was clean and blameless and selfless and good, then there was some power inside me. It did not exist in the same world as alembics and balances, so I couldn't prove it except by its strange consequences nor describe it except by feckless and feeble words. The sick and suffering could draw on my cleanliness as though drinking from a well, and the well was deep, but it did not go on forever.

Rebecca believed that either I could have cured Everett and did not, which meant I was evil, or that I could not have cured Everett, which meant I was powerless, a charlatan and huckster, a medicine woman selling alcohol and empty promises to a deluded people. Therefore, since, in truth, I could have cured Everett but preferred not to, then she must have judged me evil. Even if I'd cured Ouida Bell, I was still evil. The life of one did not atone for the life of another. They were not coins that could be traded. For even one failure, everyone must judge me guilty.

The multitudes along the Mississippi did not know my failing. They knew me only as the girl with her face on the bottle.

Salmon quit the melody he'd been playing and called out, "And why does Effie Winter's Wizard Ginger Ale cost just a nickel? Every other medicine man comes through and wants a dollar from you, and what do you get for your dollar? No medicine. Just a long list of lies."

He'd made the same speech in Hog Mountain and Johnson Ferry, Vann's Tavern and Rock Spring and Rossville, Bell Buckle, Indian Mound and Indian Forks. I never thought it sounded much good, and the bottles never sold any faster, but when he wound into the speech, there was no stopping him. It was a confession.

"Friends, I used to sell patent medicines." Salmon set down his banjo. His voice was not the medicine man's peptic shout. He was thinking. "I had one called Grove's Tasteless Chill Tonic. Doesn't that sound fine? And one called Elixir Salutis: the Choice Drink of Health, or Health-Bringing Drink, Being a Famous Cordial Drink. Can you believe that? I remember the whole name."

Hands reached toward me. I took their nickels and pressed bottles back into their palms.

"Not a dollar worth of good in those patent medicines," said Salmon. "Not even a nickel's worth. A superstition was all they were. They worked 'cause folks believed in them, not because they were real medicine. The only real medicine—"

He looked at me, but I lowered my eyes because I did not want him to say.

"The only real medicine is time, friends. You keep on living as long as you have time, and when you run out of time, then you're not living anymore. And that's all there is, no matter how many promises you make on your label, no matter how many nickels or dollars you pay because you believe in those promises."

Though Salmon Thumb talked bad about them, his elixirs had done some good. The alcohol and the empty promises were the sweetness that made a bitter medicine easier to take. Aubrey and Rebecca did not cure all their patients. Did that make them evil or powerless? They were different, so they did not understand.

No one, who was not born to this same burden, can understand. They are new creatures, who can be both good and happy. Their pleasure in life does not diminish their capacity to love and to heal. But I think I was an older creation—not greater than Aubrey or Rebecca, but different, with a strange power that is ill-fitting in this world. If I was given a capacity for miracles, then I could not be good and keep that power. Miracles cannot be worked by the selfish. The good show favor to none, and first, above all, they do no harm. The good sacrifice and suffer. That purifies their goodness, so that they can be good for others.

Waycross couldn't understand, nor should he. If I was real, then his world was incomplete, and I did not want it to be so. I wished only happiness for him and for Rebecca and for every living creature. I wanted them to discover, one day, that I did not exist anymore, so every capability for redemption and healing and joy could belong to them without my intercession. I was a remnant, left from a time before understanding.

"Do you know what I think about medicines?" said Salmon. "I think that, one day, a physician or an apothecary—or, hell, a pastor—will turn up with the best medicine there ever was or ever will be. Better than whiskey, better than ether. Better than sassafras and better than turpentine. And he'll get up on the stage and say that his medicine is a sure and certain specific for every ailment under the sun. And it won't be a lie. He'll be right. He'll call it the Brain Salt of Universal Delight, and it'll be worth a dollar, ten dollars, all the money that ever in this world was ever made."

The customers who'd drunk to the end of their ginger ales were content to keep listening, but I was worried. He'd never gone on so long without picking up the banjo and going back into a cheerful tune.

"And that Brain Salt of Universal Delight, what a marvel it will be. When the mocking hand of death reaches out its fingers, as it must for all us mortals, we'll go into the abyss with a grin."

A gunshot rattled the crowd. The mule, used to quieter places, bucked. Salmon fell. A thousand hands were between him and me. A thousand hands wanted Effie Winter's Wizard Ginger Ale.

Perhaps I was not good. Perhaps I was not powerful, either. Others before me might have been powerful, but I, born too late, was only a poor imitation. I'd mixed up a marvelous illusion for myself, thinking that, through water, miracles could be made, and others had believed, which cast the illusion wider and wider. How could I ever know?

I'd thought I wanted to be happy. I had never tried it. I preferred not to, and I was afraid. If that meant I would never work another miracle, then I had to accept it. If I wanted happiness—and I was willing to give away all honor and power and goodness—then I never deserved to be good or powerful, and I must have been neither.

The age of miracles is passed. I do not need to live for the world to thrive.

Epilogue

1848

"The same man cannot make both a beginning and an end."
—Galen, *On the Natural Faculties*

Aknock woke me from my nap in the sunlight. The door at Hope Hollow was smooth from all the knocks that had sounded on it over many years—ten thousand knocks of bleeding men, suffering women, children with fevers, babies broken out in bold hives. No one went to the doctor when everything was well. No one went to Hope Hollow without hope for a cure.

Rebecca came in from the annex, where she'd been mixing up a tonic for Judge Richardson. Liza Jane, our youngest, descended from the loft to see who'd come.

The three people at the door, two men and a woman, were strangers. They were covered in a dust foreign to Georgia. A hotter, dirtier, and harder place stained their shoes.

"Are you Miss Winter?" asked the woman. "The herb doctor, Rebecca Winter?"

Rebecca nodded. "But I've been Rebecca Waycross for a long time."

The woman exchanged glances with her companions. "We... we've come to ask you about your sister," she said.

We invited the strangers inside, let them wash their hands and faces, and sat around the table. Liza Jane brought in coffee, and our unexpected guests drank as if they'd gone without any refreshment for days. Rebecca hadn't touched any form of coffee in years. It brought on her dyspepsia. We let the strangers finish bread and cheese and a little wine before we put any questions to them.

"So, how's Sarah?" said Rebecca, folding her hands on the table.

My wife was testing them. We'd seen Sarah a week before. She was following an expedition from Milledgeville's 17th Army, which had passed through Lawrenceville on the road up to Rabun Gap. An Indian unpleasantness there threatened to inflame an already incendiary miners' strike. Sarah had no official post in the army. As a woman, she could not have one. But no soldier, when mortally wounded, concerns himself with the sex of the healer caring for him, and no soldier turns up his nose when a crack shot armed with a ten-foot rifle lays low his enemies.

No news about Sarah could have come from a trio of wide-eyed fanatics from the far frontier. Rebecca asked about Sarah only because she dared not ask about the other.

The female stranger—Annie was her name—said, "Your sister, Effie."

"Oh?" I said mildly though my blood was coursing at double speed. Liza Jane, who'd never heard a whisper about an Aunt Effie, quivered in her chair.

"It is strange to call her by her birth name," said Annie. "We called her the Great Sister though she never liked it."

Then Annie told us about Great Sister Effie's life. She did not have the full history because Great Sister Effie had spoken so little about her past. As near as we could figure, the medicine show had ended at the Mississippi. Rebecca hazarded that Thumb had thrown Effie over, leaving her for a younger and fleshier specimen. Annie disagreed. She believed the Great Sister's husband was killed in an accident. Effie had a visceral dislike of mules, she said. Perhaps a mule had thrown him.

Whatever the truth, Effie had drifted west, always by foot, moving as the frontier moved. In the villages she passed through and on the farms where she bedded down for a day, there were happenings. Fevers cooled and poxes healed. Paralytics lifted their hands in greeting when Effie glanced at them. The deaf turned at the sound of her voice. The blind smiled when she bent her head. A girl in the grip of hydrophobia shook off her madness, hugged her brothers, and took a bath in the river.

She began to attract notice. The faithful came to see what prayers she offered to what god or goddess, but they never heard a prayer. The stink-eyed came to see what sorceries and incantations the witch invoked, but they never saw any spells or charms. The physicians came, a few of them, to see her surgeries, but they saw nothing they could adopt in their practices. The people who came seeking an explanation always left without one. Wherever Effie went, a parade of followers came too, filling town squares with little tents and shelters. Word spread faster than the wind, and those ailing within a hundred miles brought their blisters and bone spurs and brokenness to her.

Effie tried to elude her followers. She would wake early, wrap herself in straw, and creep away from whatever town she had spent the night in with the herd animals. Or she would cling to the bottom of a wagon bound for a far market. Or she would run, run away into the forest or the prairie and vanish for days. Her followers would scatter in every direction to search for her. They always found her again. Rumors would surface of children delivered from yellow fever or catarrh or blood poisoning, and the followers would come. Effie never seemed distressed when she was found. Then, a week later, she would slip away again.

Her reluctance and humility were essential to her following, said Annie. One who demands a following never deserves it. Effie never claimed any special powers or skills or connections to divine mysteries, and that, too, magnified her fame. Thus, by running away, Effie found more followers, and by doing nothing, she healed multitudes, and by claiming nothing, all power and honor were ascribed to her.

Then she and her camp arrived in a town where silver was in the hills and guns were in the streets. Effie and her followers arrived when one mine was proven rich and three others proven false, and fortunes turned out to be phantoms, and the streets turned into a riot.

The authorities blamed the uprisings on the new strangers and their prophetess. Armed men arrested Effie in the night and confined her in an old powder storehouse.

The followers of Great Sister Winter could not stand idle. They found guns of their own and marched on the powder storehouse, and shots were fired. The jail doors were opened, and reinforcements came on all sides. The air was a cloud of sulfur smoke, and when there were no more bullets to fire, Effie—and only Effie—was dead.

Liza Jane clapped a hand over her mouth. Rebecca and I had already guessed the end.

"We don't know who fired at the Great Sister," said Annie. "We don't know if it was on purpose or if the Great Sister was a victim of the confusion and crossfire. I had a gun. I was fighting for her, but I might have... It might have been me..."

Annie shuddered under the weight of her confession and her doubt.

Rebecca picked up a cup of cold coffee and looked into its depths for secrets that were not there. "So, why are you here?" she asked. "We can't bring the dead back to life."

Annie shifted in her seat. She looked to her companions, but they shrank away. "We thought that Great Sister Winter might have run away again. She might have come back east, back home?"

"Is Effie dead," demanded Rebecca, "or isn't she?"

"I saw her dead." Annie bowed her head. "But I have also seen her wonders, which are greater than death."

Liza Jane, my daughter, took the stranger's hands. They communed in silence, grieving a loss they did not presume to understand.

O Physician! Do not leave us so unsatisfied. Promise that not even death should be our end.

Author's Note

In 1846, a Boston dentist demonstrated the world's first painless surgery. Before a fascinated public of eminent medical men, William Morton removed a tumor from the neck of a patient made unconscious by inhaled ether. The press was rhapsodic with the news of a successful surgical anesthetic. Ether freed the patient and doctor from the strictures of pain. The surgeon could take care with his work, for the patient would not struggle against the scalpel. New surgeries were possible: the opening of the abdominal cavity, explorations into the skull, and the removal of tumors in the most delicate of places. With that one marvelous invention, the possibilities of medicine had enlarged tenfold.

But Morton was not the first man to operate painlessly on a patient using ether. In 1842, four years prior to Morton's demonstration, a Georgia country doctor named Crawford Long had removed a neck tumor from his own patient.

Crawford Long, young and unmarried, was known to indulge in the custom of ether frolics in little Jefferson, Georgia. Following a particularly rambunctious and hilarious party, the doctor found himself covered in bruises. He couldn't recall how he had acquired them. While he was pondering, a patient arrived in trepidation over the scheduled excision of the neck tumor. Dr. Long offered him a rag soaked in ether, a remnant from the last evening, and the patient awoke an hour later, reporting no memory of the procedure. Long continued to use ether in other surgeries and for amputations and childbirth. He shared the discovery with his colleagues, but the practice did not spread. To some, Dr. Long's discovery was too much like witchcraft. Others objected on religious grounds. God had ordained that women were to suffer the pain of childbirth as penance for Eve's transgression, and it was not for mortals to contradict that.

Morton's later but more public demonstrations complicated the issue of who should receive credit for the discovery. Dr. Long did not publish his findings until 1849, but numerous credible witnesses proved he had been the first to use surgical ether. No one before Dr. Long had seen how ether could be turned from entertainment to usefulness. Because it was such a fine toy, no one thought of ether as a tool.

A statue of Crawford Long, donated by the state of Georgia, is part of the special National Statuary Collection housed throughout the United States Capitol. Dr. Long stands vigil in the capitol's crypt. Atlanta's Crawford W. Long Hospital was renamed Emory University Hospital Midtown in 2009.

ABOUT THE AUTHOR

Tim Westover, a graduate of Davidson College and the University of Georgia, lives in suburban Atlanta.

Born in the north, educated in England, and frequent visitor to Russia, he found his home in the North Georgia mountains. In addition to writing, Westover busies himself with programming, playing the clawhammer banjo, and raising his daughter to be a modern American eccentric.

Learn more about this book at:

www.QWPublishers.com

Connect with the author at:

www.TimWestover.com

Made in the
USA
Columbia, SC